CW00809021

SOPHIA'S SECRET
Volume Two

SOPHIA'S SECRET
Volume Two

By

Don Treader

UCF Publishing
Ireland

Copyright © 2021 Don Treader
All rights reserved.

ISBN: 9798746671912

Contact The Author
don@upliftfm.com

Dedication

Dedicated To My Granddaughter
Sophia Joy McFarlane

…and my longsuffering wife Sheila

"All things are possible, only believe!"

Table Of Contents

Preface

Being born in the 1950's, I seem to have arrived in the world just at the right time to experience the post-war optimism that characterised the late '50s and '60s. Indeed, it appeared to my young mind, that the sky literally was the limit! Many stimulating and fascinating ideas influenced me, in a time that is now generally considered to have been a period of great scientific and philosophical expansion. As a result, many of these innovations and concepts went into bringing about my world view.

As a committed Christian, teacher and broadcaster, I have spent many years developing the kind of communication style which I hope will interest and captivate my audience, bringing to them some of the more 'unusual' phenomena that have affected our world. It's my desire to take conventional thinking and make it realistic for a new, perhaps more sceptical, generation.

'Sophia's Secret' was my first venture into print, taking an ancient story and making it alive in a new and carefully meaningful way. As my reader, you were invited to sample the events of a bygone age as if you were living them yourself, and in the process come away with a greater realisation and appreciation of the conditions and characters portrayed there. In Volume Two the plot continues. Sophia is called upon again to image with Judith to face horrific challenges and devastating anomalies. Familiar characters are seen in a new light, emotions are constantly running high and the supernatural is never very far away. A story . . . yes, it may be. But the realism might just encourage you to think again! Isn't that really what storytelling is all about?

Acknowledgements

Throughout this volume, quotations are primarily taken from The New Living Translation of the Bible, and acknowledgement is due to Tyndale House Publishing for their marvelous supportive resource.

I am indebted to Alicia Silvester who has most professionally produced a cover page which reflects the ambiance of *Sophia's Secret Volume One*. She has made it a labour of love and the results are truly and spectacularly authentic.

Michelle Marie, my narrator of the Audible version, most definitely deserves my grateful thanks for her painstaking efforts to make the text come alive successfully for the reader. Collaboration with her has been of great value.

Sophia's Secret

Volume Two

Part One - Relocation

Chapter One

"Ireland! You must be joking!"

Aunty Jane looked at her sister disbelievingly. "Most people move nearer their families when they get older, but not this...Ireland!"

Sophia's grandma looked uncomfortable. "It's not that far away. We'll still be able to see everybody."

Sophia's grandpa joined in, "No. We're not abandoning everyone. We'll see them as often as we see them just now. We'll be back over regularly – three or four times a year."

Aunty Jane rolled her eyes. Uncle Eric said nothing.

Sophia decided to get involved at that point. "I've only just found out myself – and I'm quite excited about it. I'll be sad to leave here, but it'll be something new."

"Something new all right!" Aunty Jane appeared unconvinced. "What induced you to go there?" She said this with an air of resignation, as if having now made her surprise and objections clear, she was ready to hear the details.

"We just feel we should," Sophia's grandma replied. "We've been here a long time, and we're getting on a bit. If we don't move now, we never will."

"Were you thinking of moving? You never said." Aunty Jane looked rather sad.

"No, we weren't," Grandpa smiled. "We'd have lived out our days here until we dropped. It hadn't crossed our minds to move, but sometimes the unexpected happens to change your thinking."

"It certainly does," Aunty Jane responded. "This is extremely unexpected."

Grandma and Grandpa set about the task of trying to soothe this fractious situation with their relatives, by going over the details and giving their reasons for their bombshell news. Sophia decided it was best to keep out of the discussion and so she moved into the open area of the living room separated from the others

3

by a glass partition. She would play at classes and set out her pupils' name tags she had written earlier placing them on their imaginary seats. She had wanted to be a teacher for as long as she could remember, and somehow going through the motions of this would help her de-stress from the fractious situation being played out on the other side of the partition. She gained immense satisfaction from ruling and bossing about her class. On her laptop was a programme that registered each pupil's name and logged their 'dojos' – the points she awarded them for doing something good. She was in full command of her class, even when speaking to each pupil, managing to emulate the voice, tone, and mannerisms of her teacher which she had down to a 't'. Soon she was ensconced in 'school world', able to escape the tension elsewhere.

The conversation continued at the other end of the room. The adults were now settled, sipping refreshments, and speaking now in a more congenial manner.

"You remember we went round Ireland this summer?" Grandma was talking.

"Yes, just after you visited us," Her sister replied.

"That's right. It was to be the journey of a lifetime. We'd never been there before and had often talked of going."

"Is that what made you go mad and do this?" her sister was smiling now.

"Yes," Grandpa spoke up. "Of course, we don't think we're mad, just a bit unusual."

"You can't deny it's a big move," Uncle Eric decided to join the conversation too. "Two blind people, a little girl and two dogs upping sticks and relocating to a different country. You didn't even consider going to a part of the UK. Northern Ireland would have been an easier move. You're thinking of going to the south."

"Nothing wrong with that. We like it there." Sophia's grandpa was now laughing. "We like it there - and it's not too far away."

"I really can't understand why you want to do all this," Aunty Jane said seriously. "Why?"

Sophia's Grandma and Grandpa paused for a moment, wondering which one of them would speak first. Grandpa did.

"Well, we travelled around the country, disembarking from the ferry at Larne. Billy our driver – we told you about him before…"

Sophia's aunt and uncle looked blankly at him, "No," they said in unison.

"Ok then. It's a bit of a long story, but I'll go over it quickly. When my sister was ill three or four years ago, I had to go down country quickly. She wasn't expected to live, you see. I hired a taxi and had to pay almost £500 for the pleasure and quickness of it. Miraculously my sister recovered, against all expectations – we're thankful our prayers were answered – and again and again over the last few years, when she went downhill and then came back up again. She was written off many a time, but she always seemed to come through."

Aunty Jane interrupted, "Billy…?"

"Oh yes," Grandpa got back into his stride. "Well on the way back home the first time she was ill, I hired a local taxi driver – Billy – and struck up a friendship with him on the journey. We even went for a meal at a wonderful service station on the way up the road. You should have seen the massive plate of macaroni cheese and strawberry crumble they gave us..."

"Billy!" Aunty Jane interrupted again. Grandpa had digressed because of food, not an uncommon occurrence.

"Oh yes," he said, suitably corrected. "I had hired Billy a number of times to take us places for the day when we were down visiting my sister on various occasions after that. On Millport, Sophia got her hands stuck in the display of crabs in the Maritime Museum and started dancing about. And on another occasion, we went round all my old haunts in Glasgow where I had lived as a boy. You'll never believe it, we went to the west end, to Kersland Street, to the very tobacconist shop my gran had owned in the late fifties. I used to play in front of it on the pavement with my marbles. We pulled up outside it and were shocked to see it was no longer a tobacconist. It was called 'The Naked Soup'! My gran would have turned in her grave. We went in, however, and sampled some of their exotic soups. They were delicious..." Grandpa smacked his lips, "and the inside of the shop wasn't that different from how I remembered it fifty years ago...but the soup..."

He was interrupted by a shrill chorus of three voices, "Billy!"

Grandpa continued unabashed. "I was just filling in the background for you." He grinned, "I like soup!"

"Do you want me to tell the story?" Sophia's grandma asked with a hint of impatience.

"No, no. I'll tell it," her husband said. "Well, last Christmas when we were down at my sister's again, I asked Billy if he fancied going to Ireland and doing a tour with us. We'd pay him of course. He said yes, and so we started to plan our trip. We'd do an all-round trip, from Larne in the north down through Belfast, Dublin and Bray, to Cork in the south, then back up via Galway and Donegal, finally arriving in Larne for the crossing back to Scotland. We did it not long after we left you, and it was brilliant. We saw all the sights and sampled all the foods. You should have seen the Irish Stew..."

This time he was interrupted by Sophia who had re-joined the adults having dismissed her class. "And Grandpa kissed the Blarney Stone."

"So that's the reason," Uncle Eric said smiling.

Everyone looked at him quizzically.

"He's hardly stopped talking since we've got here!" They all laughed, including Grandpa, who quite liked being the centre of attention, even if people joked about him.

"Yes, indeed, we climbed up the rough steps of Blarney Castle – but you wouldn't kiss it Sophia?"

"No way!" said Sophia emphatically. "You had to lie down under this great boulder, your head almost hanging over a huge drop, and yuck…you had to kiss the place where millions of people had kissed it before. There was a man wiping away people's spit!"

"Maybe it's as well I couldn't see all that," Grandpa grinned. "It didn't however stop Billy or me though. We both lay under the stone and gave it a big kiss. There was another man there, and he made his money well that day. Because after kissing the stone, I had to get up again, something I had great difficulty in doing." He patted his large tummy, indicating his heavy weight. "Indeed, both men earned their money that day - getting me back onto my feet again."

"Tell them about our next stop, Grandpa," Sophia said. "I was nearly sick."

Sophia's grandma took up the story, "Oh, you mean our trip to the Aran Isles?"

"Yes."

"Well, we spent the next night in Galway. Saw Galway bay. And the following morning we got the boat over to the Aran Isles. It was very rough…the crossing."

"I went outside the cabin while everyone else was sheltering, to get some pictures. The boat was going up and down something terrible," Sophia said. "I was nearly sick."

"We had a good time on the island though," her Grandma reminded her. "We went shopping…remember Sophia…while Billy and Grandpa climbed up to the fort on the cliffs."

Sophia smiled at the thought of the memorabilia she had purchased.

Grandpa cut in, "The fort was amazing, but it was a steep climb. On the way back down at one point Billy and I were dancing – at times holding onto each other when one or the other of us slipped on the rocks."

His listeners smiled as they tried to picture the sight.

Grandpa continued, "But the best thing was when we got back down to the bottom. Something wonderful happened just before we caught the boat to the mainland again."

The others waited expectantly.

"Near the harbour was a wonderful Coffee Shop…and you should have seen the marvellous slab of coffee and walnut cake I ate there. The butter cream icing was to die for." Grandpa smacked his lips for the second time that conversation.

"Stop it dear," Grandma decided to interrupt him before he went any further. "You'll be making our guests hungry."

They all smiled again.

Grandpa, suitably admonished, continued. "Well, our next stop that day was Donegal. I had, when I was researching the holiday, discovered the Daniel O'Donnell hotel." (Daniel O'Donnell is a singer who in the early days of his career also owned a hotel near a small village called Kincasslagh in Ireland. His fans used to congregate at his house where his mother was reputed to have refreshed them with tea on the lawn, then came the hotel.) "Daniel no longer owns the hotel, but it seemed a good quiet place to end our holiday before coming back home. Instead of sightseeing, we would just take it easy for the last day or so before getting the ferry."

"I quite like Daniel O'Donnell," Aunty Jane said enthusiastically. "He sings good songs, ones that appeal to the older generation."

"That's true," said Grandpa. "Apparently in the early days in the summer, they pitched a marquee behind the hotel and thousands would come to hear him sing. Sometimes they would surprise him by bringing in a mystery guest – one year it was Cliff Richard, another Loretta Lynn."

"That must have been something special," said Aunty Jane.

The not so keen country music lovers of the group were grinning.

"But I like Daniel O'Donnell," Aunty Jane protested.

Grandpa went on, "We had thought it would take four hours, thanks to the Satnav, to get from the Aran Isles to the Viking House hotel in Kincasslagh, but we hadn't bargained on the roads."

"They got narrower, hillier and bendier – and Billy was unfamiliar with them," Grandma added.

"It was getting later and later, and we just weren't getting there. However, one good thing did happen," Grandpa said. "When we got to Sligo we stopped at a McDonald's – Billy went to the KFC next door – both of them were almost empty, and the staff treated us like kings. Oh, the burger, and the lovely milk shake!"

"Get on with it!" everyone shouted.

Grandpa laughed and continued. "What should have been a four hour journey or so was turning into a six hour one. We were phoning the hotel to make sure they remained open for us. Finally, at half past eleven, we got there…and what a welcome. The hotel owner ushered us in. The welcome was fantastic. And when we got into the bar, it was packed. Everyone was extremely friendly and, making a sandwich for us was no trouble at all – even at that time of night. I sampled their Guinness. You'll never believe it, but their Guinness there tasted so much better than anywhere else!"

"Dear…" his wife tried to move him on.

Uncle Eric chipped in, "Yes, they say it tastes better in Ireland. It apparently doesn't travel well."

"It was good…and so was the welcome," Grandpa said. "The next day we decided to have a lazy day. Billy took us into Dungloe where we shopped. It's only a small town but has everything you would need. Sophia played in a soft play area and loved it."

Sophia smiled, looking a little embarrassed that a girl of nine years old would enjoy soft play. She thought to herself, it had been good though.

Don Treader

"It was then that the bombshell came about. We had been amazed at how quiet and tranquil the streets had been. After walking down the main street we turned into a road where there was a children's play park. The sun was shining, it was warm, quiet, and restful…and then an older couple strolled by. We all got into conversation, and it turned out they had just moved there from Manchester. 'It's wonderful here,' they said. 'We love it. The pace of life is great…and you can get a doctor's appointment when you need one.' It was clear that Manchester didn't afford that luxury." Grandpa paused for a moment. "It was then that it happened. As they said, 'We've just moved here' I felt a nudge inside, I suppose a nudge on my spirit saying 'This is something you could do.' It was something that popped into my head out of the blue. We hadn't been thinking of moving at all. We've lived here for forty years or so. We assumed we'd be here all our days, but this nudge was beginning to imprint itself on my mind. I put it aside at that moment, and later that afternoon once we got back to the hotel, Billy, Sophia, and I took the dogs down to the beach which wasn't far away, and while the dogs were splashing about in the pools left in the warm sand, left by a tide that seemed to go extremely far out, the tranquillity, the peacefulness the solitude of the area just got to us. There was even a lovely little bridge going over to a small island offshore. It was clear that a lasting impression was being forged. The nudge about moving, although worrying at first, was now beginning to appeal to me. I said nothing about it till after our meal that evening. I don't think any of you took it seriously," he looked at his wife.

"Probably not," she agreed. "It was so outrageous, so out of the ordinary, we just concentrated on enjoying ourselves, getting home and back to normal after having had such a wonderful holiday."

"When we got back, I couldn't let the thought go," Grandpa said. "I felt as if I needed to do something with it. When looking at things rationally, it made no sense. The remoteness, the lack of transport, the dangerous narrow roads. It didn't make sense for a blind person to go there."

"Don't put it down totally, dear," his wife said. "You did do a lot of research – checking up on buses – only two a day – talking to the school about Sophia. You even went to the length of speaking to the local priest. Being Christians, we would need a spiritual home."

"True, dear," Grandpa said. "More and more it looked as if it might be a possibility." He smiled, "Taxis were available, and for Sophia…" his eyes twinkled, "if we were to live there, she would be in a school of about forty kids, and she would be in a class of four pupils."

Uncle Eric whistled.

Grandpa looked at his wife, "But you weren't keen though."

"Not true," she said, aware that her sister was listening carefully for any sign of dissention. "It was something unusual, and a bit of a challenge. But over the weeks you were doing all that research, I felt myself warming to going. There

8

were just so many insurmountable problems though it seemed. We'd been here so long. There were our friends and families to consider. And of course, we'd have to get our house on the market and sell it. It seemed just too much."

"There was one Sunday," Grandpa said. "I was walking up the field while you were at church. I had got to the point of wondering where all this was going. Things seemed to be favourable, but you hadn't indicated too much interest. I remember praying I needed you to change if we were to go on. At the end of that walk, I felt a strange confidence…but I said nothing for a couple of days."

"What happened then?" asked Aunty Jane.

"On the Tuesday I mentioned something about Ireland, and you could have knocked me over with a feather when your sister said she thought it might be the right thing for us after all. This was the answer I needed, and so I sped on with my investigations.".

"Yes, I said I was warming to it. I just didn't tell you till I was sure." His wife said mischievously.

Sophia chimed in now. "This was all going on and you didn't say anything to me."

"We didn't want to worry you dear or unsettle you…at least until we knew for sure. We knew you'd have difficulty in dealing with the change. Your mum, your school friends."

"Yes, but you could have said," Sophia sounded hurt. "I didn't know about it till Grandpa disappeared!"

Chapter Two

"Disappeared?" Uncle Eric asked. "How did you manage that?" He was laughing.

Sophia had captured all their interest and so they waited for Grandpa's response. Sophia realising that she might have been just a little dramatic, sought to clear the confusion and justify herself. "I had been away for the weekend staying with friends, When I went there, they usually took me to school on the Monday morning. It was only when I got back home after school, that I discovered Grandpa had vanished."

Their relatives looked on with concern. Their bafflement was added to by Grandpa grinning and laughing.

"It wasn't nice of you," Sophia said accusingly. "You went without telling me you were going." She looked at her grandma. "Both of you knew, and you didn't tell me. I cried my eyes out when I got home. I wasn't used to Grandpa not being there!"

A smile was playing on Grandma's lips, but Uncle Eric and Aunty Jane were not so amused. They weren't in on the joke.

Aunty Jane broke the silence, "Go on. Tell us what happened."

Grandpa decided to come clean, "An unfortunate choice of phrase, Sophia," he said. "and actually, Grandma and I didn't tell you in case it worried you, that's all. We didn't want to spoil your weekend away."

"It did when I got back," Sophia retorted, "but I understand now."

"Well, we don't!" Uncle Eric and Aunty Jane said in unison. Aunty Jane continued, "Will someone tell us what happened and put us out of our misery."

"He didn't actually disappear, Jane," her sister said, "he just went to Ireland for a couple of days."

"On his own? Without help?" Aunty Jane looked perplexed.

"Of course," Grandpa said. "It was a thought to do so – there were so many challenges – but if we were to consider moving to Ireland, I had to take the next step. I had already researched many of the possibilities as I've already said. Now I had to be there on the ground to see if it was viable."

They looked at him in wonderment. This was so much out of the ordinary. They waited for him to continue.

"I hope I'm not boring you," Grandpa was smiling.

"Not at all," said Uncle Eric. "Just go on with your story."

"Well, it was early September. We'd been back from Ireland about three weeks when I decided to go. One of the attractions of going there, and living there, was that there was a direct bus from Glasgow to Dungloe, which was six miles from Kincasslagh."

"Wouldn't you have to get the ferry?" Uncle Eric quizzed.

"That was all included in the journey. The coach from Glasgow to Cairnryan, the ferry over the Irish Sea, and then the coach from Larne to Dungloe – or more precisely Kincasslagh. The company take you right to the hotel."

"Wow," said Aunty Jane.

"Yes, I was amazed too. No Billy's taxi this time as before. The good thing however was that it was virtually door to door. There were however some drawbacks."

"What were these?" Aunty Jane asked.

"The bus left Glasgow at seven in the morning. It was going to be just under a ten-hour journey."

"I think I see where you're going with this," Uncle Eric said. "You wouldn't be able to get to Glasgow in time for the bus."

"Exactly," Grandpa said. "I would have to stay in Glasgow overnight. And a blind person with a guide dog finding the hotel and making my way about it, and then having to find the bus station – it was all quite a thought."

"You did it though," said his wife.

"I did. I was amazed myself at how well it went. I found the hotel in Glasgow with someone's help – I had met them on the train. You should have seen the hotel though. I had to go up to the second floor in a lift to get to reception. They then stuck me on the seventeenth floor. It was however a beautiful room." He began to wax lyrical. "It was so comfortable. It was easy to settle in. In the morning I got up, got myself and Raffles ready, made myself a cup of coffee – this was at six o'clock – then I went down to reception where a friendly porter pointed out the way to the bus station. He actually went with me. It was all so easy. Raffles and I were beginning a great adventure together!"

"You sound like you were lucky," Uncle Eric said.

"No, not lucky, but very fortunate. It was amazing, there were only two of us on the big bus, and the driver of course. We chatted for miles – I probably talked his ears off. And then there was the boat. I was met by the same Purser I had met only weeks before when we had gone there on holiday. She gave me my breakfast free. It was so big, and so good!"

They hurried him on in case he got stuck in his food fantasy again. "What did you do when you got there? Did you stay in the same hotel?"

"I most certainly did!" Grandpa said emphatically. "I was surprised at the welcome I got. Marie, one of the hotel staff, came running out when I arrived. She obviously remembered me."

"It was probably the dog she remembered, Grandpa," Sophia said softly.

"Of course, Sophia," said her Grandpa, smiling.

"But why were you there?" Aunty Jane asked.

"To look at houses. To see if we could actually live there."

"Wow," she said again.

"I only had one day there. The two surrounding days were taken up with travelling. I had to pack a lot into that one day. Before leaving, I had contacted two auctioneer estate agents after looking at houses on their websites. I had identified two houses that might be appropriate."

"How did you do that?" Uncle Eric asked wonderingly.

"Well, now that we're getting on a bit," Grandpa's eyes twinkled, "as older people we were thinking of downsizing."

Grandma cut in, "Yes, if I was to move, I would have liked a bungalow."

"Good choice," agreed Aunty Jane, "kind of like our ground floor little flat."

"Well, actually, after looking at the websites, I couldn't find any bungalows. But I was very taken with two particular houses."

"Yes," said Grandma dryly, "so much for downsizing. We've got three bedrooms and two bathrooms here. You were looking at four bedrooms and in the case of the house we've settled on, three bathrooms!"

"I know, I know," he said laughing. "but you liked the sound of them too."
She smiled.

"To continue," Grandpa went on, "and to cut a long story short, I went with the two auctioneers, one in the morning and one in the afternoon, and videoed my way around both houses. I had my iPhone with me."

His relatives looked at him for the second time that hour in bafflement. "Why?" said Aunty Jane.

"Simple," said Grandpa waving his hand by way of explanation. "To send the videos back to Scotland, for these two to look at them and make a choice."

"That must have been some sight," smiled Uncle Eric, "a blind man and a guide dog being shown round a house by a stranger, while at the same time filming the event."

"Yes, but it worked. That evening Sophia and Grandma were able to see what I had seen that day. They were involved."

"A good idea," Uncle Eric admitted. "Did you do anything else?"

"Yes, a couple more things. The first was to make a visit to the Primary school to which Sophia would have to go if we moved there. It was about a third of a mile from the hotel, and with directions, I made my own way there, Raffles guiding. You should have seen the road. The main road only has room for two cars' width. There were no pavements. And to add to the fun, there were often ditches on either side. Raffles was excellent however, and I found the school without too much trouble, after having had to stop and move in, to allow many a car to pass."

"What was the school like?" queried Aunty Jane.

"It was quaint, but charming." Grandpa said. "I love the simple way things seem to happen in the country like that. I overshot the school when turning down a lane but was met by two of the pupils apparently coming back from the chapel. It was Confirmation time, and they were practicing. They were lovely, and they very politely showed me the entrance."

"Was it a big school? Lots of kids?" asked Uncle Eric.

"Well, I told you that Kincasslagh was a small rural village – Wikipedia has it down as having forty-nine residents…"

"Yes," said Aunty Jane.

"Well, the school has the exorbitant number of just under forty pupils. Sophia will be in a class of four – and that includes her!"

Aunty Jane and Uncle Eric gasped. Sophia said, "I'm in a class of thirty just now."

"Are you sure about going?" Aunty Jane looked at her questioningly.

"I wasn't at first – I'll be sorry to leave all my friends – but now I'm beginning to get a bit excited about it."

"There's two teachers. She'll get an expert education." Grandpa had been a teacher for thirty-three years. He said this knowingly and with quite a bit of enthusiasm.

"That'll be some change," said Uncle Eric. "But you said there was something else you had to do?"

"Funnily enough, I didn't realise it till I was there. I'd had my meal in the hotel one of the nights, and it struck me. If I was going to live there, I'd have to be able to get about. Everyone was telling me that the roads were bad – too dangerous for me to negotiate, especially with a guide dog." He thought for a moment, "It's Raffles that made it work though. It was all to his credit. We probably wouldn't even be considering going to Ireland if it wasn't for him! Pauline the hotel owner warned me against walking to the village, about a mile away, but I had the sense that I had to do it. Apart from the road being narrow, risky, and fairly busy, I had only been to the village once, and that was when we passed through it on our holiday. I knew roughly the distance but couldn't be sure I wouldn't turn down a country lane or go up a driveway by accident and get lost. I remember setting out and wondering if I'd know when I reached the village. It seemed that as I progressed, the road became quieter and after a while it occurred to me that I might have passed through the village, it being so small. I knew it had a shop and a pub and had hoped that some noise might help me get orientated. After some time, I found myself going down a steep hill and stumbled onto a semi pavement. I reckoned I was nearing Kincasslagh. But there was no sound. I really hadn't a clue where I was. I was determined to make it to the pub, however, to say I had been there. Suddenly my hand touched a metal sort of grill – the kind that can act as a shutter for a shop front. I assumed therefore there were buildings near by although there were no cars on the road and there was absolutely no noise at all. Eventually, I heard a tiny sound just ahead of me, and found my way to a door. A man appeared when I knocked on it – the place was deathly quiet. He very kindly showed me across the road to where the pub was. The road might have been quiet, but the pub certainly wasn't. It was a tiny room, but about a dozen people were squeezed in there watching football on the TV. Raffles and I were made very welcome, and I spent about an hour just chatting with the locals who were amazingly friendly. Everyone's friendly there! When I left, I found my way back onto the main road and started up the hill. After a few minutes a car stopped beside me and the occupant asked me, 'Do you want a lift back to the hotel? Pauline was worried about you and sent out a search party.' I laughed, and said I was managing fine. 'I've just been to Iggy's,' I said. 'I'd like to make my way back to the hotel on my own if you don't mind so that I can prove to myself that Raffles and I can do it.' He drove on, and after about half an hour I assumed I must be nearing the hotel, but I didn't know when to turn in – there were a few openings off the road. Suddenly a great thought struck me. I could use the satnav on my phone to find the hotel. I took it out, and surely enough I found the entrance no bother, and Raffles and I went in. Everyone seemed glad to see us and I'd proved to myself that the road was possible. Raffles had indeed won the day – he had been absolutely brilliant, doing his job perfectly! I spent the rest of the night, until about two in the morning, talking to the locals. We had a great time." Grandpa looked at Aunty Jane. "You'll never believe this, two of them asked where we came from in Scotland. When I said your sister came from Broomhouse in Edinburgh, an almighty roar went up in the bar. They too had lived there in their early lives. It just seemed we had so much in common There was a rapport."

Aunty Jane raised an eyebrow. "We lived there in the fifties and sixties. Did you catch their names?"

"He did," said her sister, "I'm not sure we knew them, but I think there might have been people they knew that we knew."

"Amazing, it's such a small world."

"You fairly packed a lot into that one day," Uncle Eric said. "When did you get back?"

"So many things seemed to go well. I'm sure it wasn't just coincidence – and everyone was so friendly. I felt welcomed. But something else was to happen which convinced me we were on the right track."

Uncle Eric raised an eyebrow.

"On the bus back to Glasgow, a lady got on in another remote village near Dungloe. We got talking and it appeared that she ran a horse farm. I told her about my thinking of moving to Kincasslagh and she said that as a businesswoman, she had had challenges, but she was up for them. She looked for, and took, opportunities when they came along. We continued our conversation in the restaurant on the boat, when suddenly she saw her brother-in-law. She talked to him for some time then introduced me to him. When he had gone, she said, 'If you're serious about moving, he can help you. He has a haulage business – actually, he's on the boat now with his lorry – Perhaps he could give you a quote for taking your furniture over when you're ready to go.' This seemed a good idea to me, as I'd already investigated removal firms and found they could charge as much as £4000. 'It couldn't do any harm to ask him anyway,' so she called him back, and we had a lovely chat. He seemed a decent individual and I warmed to him. He was more than willing to divert a lorry to take our furniture over. He could have knocked me over with a feather when he quoted me £1300. It felt as if another piece of the jigsaw was falling into place, without me even having had to try and find it. I said I'd be in touch with him when and if a decision was made, then we went our ways. quite amazingly. I got home that night at ten o'clock, tired but greatly encouraged."

"And I didn't see you till the morning," said Sophia softly. "but you did bring me a present off the boat, and grandma too."

They all smiled.

"Let's break for a bite to eat," said Grandpa. "I've droned on long enough. I'm sure you'll all be quite hungry by now. I know I am."

Chapter Three

The Brig 'o Don pub and restaurant was the usual eating house to which Grandpa and Grandma took their guests. Aunty Jane and Uncle Eric were a long way from home visiting the various members of their families before the winter set in, thus their presence at Sophia's house that day, and now their eating of a meal with them. It was October and the nights were beginning to draw in. Light streamed from the big building, fully illuminating the car park. The interior was spaciously furnished with tables and seats set in booths. Sophia liked this arrangement as each booth had a miniature television. Strangely enough, Grandpa liked the arrangement too as they served very large platefuls of food. After eating a fairly capacious meal each of them settled in their chairs to continue the conversation they had begun earlier.

"You've certainly stunned us with your bombshell news," Uncle Eric said. "What stage are you at now?"

Sophia's Grandma took up the story, "We had some serious thinking to do when he returned from Ireland. We had to either let the idea go or make up our minds to go. I can tell you we prayed much about it and after a little time we both agreed we should continue to go down that road. We kind of thought if it wasn't the right thing for us, things would close up on us. I remember…we spent the next weekend agonising over which of the two houses to take. Eventually it seemed right to go for the one that was in-between the village and the school."

"It also seemed a more spacious house. Big rooms – and a big garden," Grandpa added. "Not only did it have three large areas of grass, at the front and sides, but at the back there was a massive hill going up about thirty or forty metres covered in bushes and trees. At the top it was bounded by a drystone wall pretty well obscured by brambles and other foliage. The amazing thing that fascinated me was that although the wall may have bounded our property there was more hill beyond it – more trees, more vegetation and bare rock. It eventually went up to the main road, or so we were told, but it was a lovely natural feature. I could see the dogs having a great time in the entire area."

"It does sound rather amazing," said Aunty Jane.

"And it extended the total width of the property, Grandpa added. "We felt we were really in the country."

"But what about neighbours?" asked Uncle Eric.

"Imagine a little estate in the middle of nowhere. Five houses well spaced out with good grounds, a mountain track leading from the main road to it, and a lake nearby."

"Sounds idyllic," Uncle Eric nodded.

"The next step though was to put our house on the market.," Grandma said. "We'd put in an offer on the Irish house and had had it accepted, but we couldn't buy it if we didn't get ours sold first. We saw this as a test – if it was snapped up, this would be a further indication we were on the right track."

"And what happened?" asked Aunty Jane.

"Well," Grandpa took over the narrative again, "we went with an estate agent most of our friends said would make it difficult to get a sale. Within a week though we had an offer!"

Aunty Jane and Uncle Eric looked impressed.

"Yes," said Grandma. "A nice young couple viewed it and were so enthusiastic about buying it. They asked us to hold off and not to give it to anyone else. They seemed assured that their house would sell quickly."

Sophia chipped in, "They had twin one year old babies too! They were lovely."

"Yes, they were a lovely young couple," Grandma agreed. "Our hearts warmed to them, and so we agreed to their request, assuming that we had made a quick sale."

"But you hadn't?" surmised Uncle Eric, picking up on the last statement.

"No, we're still waiting," Grandpa said. "They've still not sold their house. We're kind of stuck at present until they can sell theirs."

"That can be a problem," said Uncle Eric knowingly.

"It's been a little while now, but we're still hopeful," Grandma said quietly.

"And what about the family?" Aunty Jane asked. "What did they say when you told them?

"That's another matter," said Grandpa seriously. "Just as it did for you, it came as a bombshell to them too. Our son was surprised but tried to be supportive. Our daughter took it badly, however. She felt as if she was losing the link with her childhood home – and I understand that."

"But what about Sophia's mother?" Aunty Jane asked. "What did she say – about her daughter being whisked off to Ireland?"

Readers might remember from the first volume, that Sophia had been awarded by the courts to her grandparents, due to her mum not being able to look after her. Contact since then had been sporadic and legally limited. In the early days Sophia had hankered after her mum, but as she had grown older, although she still loved her, the distance between the two of them had become great relationship-wise, and inevitably emotional drift had set in. Efforts had been made to meet with her, but those had often ended in an awkward silence.

"We saw mummy in the street recently," Sophia volunteered. "I'd broken my iPhone screen and Grandpa and I were getting a new one in town, when we bumped into her."

Aunty Jane and Uncle Eric looked expectantly at her, but Grandpa took over.

"It was difficult. I hadn't intended telling her until we could meet up for a meal or coffee indoors somewhere. But when we bumped into her," he looked over at Sophia, "you put me in the position of having to break the news in the street."

"I only asked if you were going to say anything to mummy."

"That's true, but it must have looked strange to those round about us, the three of us crying in the street."

"It was perhaps the wrong time and the wrong place," Uncle Eric said gently.

"She was upset that she might never see us, and we were upset because we were upsetting her," Grandpa said. "But I sought to reassure her that we'd be back regularly, and that she would see us no less than she had done over previous years."

"Did that help?" asked Aunty Jane.

"A little, although it had been a big shock for her." Grandpa had a tear in his eye. "We didn't want to hurt her. After all, she is our daughter. But as the likelihood of things not being too much different from normal is the case, we don't think it will affect her that much."

"It sounds like you're ready to go," said Uncle Eric. "You're just waiting for a sale then."

Grandma and Grandpa nodded. Sophia was dosing, still trying to keep her eyes open as she watched the television.

Grandma leaned forward, as if to impart a special piece of information. She spoke quietly, "Actually, we're going over in a couple of weeks, the two of us without Sophia."

"You've got it bad," Aunty Jane said smiling. "You can't leave Ireland alone, can you!"

"Too right," laughed Grandpa. "But remember, I've seen the house, she hasn't, except on video."

"Yes, we're going over for a couple of days with our son, to let me see the house and get used to the area. I'm quite excited about it. Sophia will have a good time staying with her friends. Of course, the dogs will come with us"

"That makes good sense," said Uncle Eric. "You can't buy a house without having seen it properly."

The conversation from then on drifted onto other topics, related and unrelated, and by the time they left the Brig o' Don, the little party were talked out and tired

It was always good when Aunty Jane and Uncle Eric visited. They had been looking forward to seeing them and telling them their news, but it would be an understatement to say that they had been not a little surprised at their reaction to it. Before the evening was ended though and they had left, their relatives seemed to have slipped into acceptance mode, and promised that if and when the family moved to Donegal, they would certainly pay them a visit. Everything had ended well, and Sophia felt glad. She wasn't however looking forward so much to the next few weeks when she would have to start preparing to leave her school, her friends, and her activities. She would have to tell them she was going and found herself dreading the worst. Although she was a resilient girl, and much as though the goal might be an exciting one, she had first to get over the hurdle of facing, then making, this major change in her life. That night, as she thought about it in her bed, she found herself mulling over her earlier experiences, especially those as Judith, and tried to draw from them a strength that could lift her spirit. How had Judith coped with changes especially the ones which involved traumas and deaths in her close family? Could she rely on Josh to help her? He had always come through for her ultimately. How she wished she had that glowing little pendant; and yes, the picture she had been given by Josh and Abbas. She would have given much to see that comforting smile again which always made her feel good and lifted her spirit. With these thoughts pervading her mind, she drifted off to sleep fairly quickly, leaving these questions to be faced on another day.

Chapter Four

Sophia sat in the big car, her heart racing. She was experiencing conflicting emotions, and for the next few minutes or so she moved between abject sadness and utter excitement. Outside her window she saw her friend Eve and her mum waving, Chris and Julie her neighbours smiling, along with others who knew them - all of them wishing them the best. Her window was up but she shouted her own goodbyes to them and waved vigorously. It was a sunny Tuesday morning in May about eight thirty. The air was already warm. Why did she have to feel so conflicted, she wondered? She didn't have much time however to consider this as the driver was putting the big car into gear, and it slowly started to move off. She wondered if she'd ever be back. Or ever see these people again. Desperately she wound down her window and had to take one last lingering look, wave one last frantic wave, before it all disappeared. She was leaving her house, the house in which she had spent the last five and a half years with her grandma and grandpa. So many good memories! She could see into the living room from where she sat. It was empty - bereft of furniture - and she felt sad, so sad. It wasn't as she knew it any more. Suddenly her attention was taken by a burly man who was shouting at her driver. "I'll follow you down to the ferry. I'll catch up with you there." He grinned in the window at her, "It's your big day!" and with that, he climbed into the driving seat of the massive lorry parked in their driveway and started the engine. It really was their last moment in Aberdeen, she realised. She was panicking now, and so she stuck her hand well out the window and waved even more furiously as the car began to glide off. The cries of goodbye seemed to echo down the street after them. She looked out the back window at the fast-disappearing house, noted that the lorry full of their furniture was pulling out of their driveway and was about to block her last view of it. As they turned the corner out of her street, the lorry trundling behind, she caught one last glimpse of the house and the people who had come to say goodbye to them outside it on the street, and she cried. Then it was all gone, and the journey was truly begun.

21

Sophia was sitting in the back of the Mercedes beside her grandma. Grandpa and Morris the driver were in the front, and Raffles in the boot. While no-one was watching she allowed herself to shed a silent tear. She wanted to be brave. Looking sideways however, she noticed her grandma's tear-stained face. She was quite upset. Sophia didn't feel so embarrassed now, and so she let out a few more sobs herself. It was to be one of the most exciting days of her life, but why didn't she feel so good? She held her grandma's hand and the two of them shared an unhappy moment. Grandpa was talking to Morris in the front, seemingly oblivious of their sadness. He was so caught up with the business of moving.

Grandma spoke first. She sounded sad but was trying to be cheerful, to encourage her granddaughter. "We've been a long time there. Almost forty years. You've only been there a short while. But we've all got lots of memories - good, and not so good ones. I came to that house when my babies were young. I watched as they grew up there, then left when they were older. Almost my whole life has been tied up in that house – in this city. Yours too, but not for so long." She wiped her eyes, "But we have to move on now. Life doesn't stand still for us. We're going on to new pastures and we feel it's right. It'll be good, just you wait and see." Neither of them was feeling good at that moment, but Sophia knew that her grandma was right. The sadness at leaving something she loved was only natural. But it would pass and give way to the excitement of a new start. She was already beginning to feel that tinge of excitement. She hoped her Grandma was too. Both of them settled down to their thoughts as the car sped through the familiar, then the not so familiar, streets and roads. They were well on the way now to the ferry, and their new life in Ireland.

Sophia had quickly realised that she was going to be bored. Scenery can only interest a nine-year-old girl for so long, and so she set to busying herself with her iPhone. It would help to pass the time till it ran out of power. She had the charger with her which usually accompanied her almost everywhere; and she knew she would be able to cajole Grandpa for his iPhone hot spot if she ran out of data. The journey might be long, but she was going to make the most of it.

Like scenery, iPhones can only interest one for so long when you're feeling sad. The battery waned then cut out when they were an hour or so into their journey. She couldn't be bothered setting up the charger. She didn't feel like more games at that moment. She looked sideways at Grandma instead who was now dosing. Indeed, she was slightly leaning against Sophia who was quite crushed up against the door.

"Are you all right, dear?" Grandma mumbled sleepily and changed her position. There were still a couple more hours to go till they reached the ferry terminal.

Sophia stretched, then sank down into the plush seating, deciding to follow her Grandma's example and fall asleep., however the movement of the car, rather than sending her to sleep, kept her awake. In the background too, she could hear Grandpa and Morris talking quite loudly about this, that and everything. As she settled down, she found herself going over the events in her mind that had led to her being in that car. It had all started quite slowly, but then, in recent weeks, things had moved on at a whirlwind pace. Somehow by going over them in her mind she felt better. Could she feel the excitement rising?

After Aunty Jane and Uncle Eric's visit last October, things had become quite boring. The initial excitement about a move to Ireland was dampened by the fact that Grandma and Grandpa couldn't get their house sold – and without selling the house, there would be no Ireland. Actually, as nothing seemed to be happening, she had stopped telling people that she was moving at all and found herself secretly hoping it might all go away. She liked her school, her teacher, her church and other activities, her friends too – she was quite comfortable and happy as she was.

Two things had happened in that slack period, one good and one bad. She remembered the excitement Grandma and Grandpa had exhibited when they returned from their trip to Ireland at the end of October. They were literally buzzing about it. The talk was of nothing else. Sophia would have loved to have had the opportunity of going with them, but she had had a superb time with her friends. She would get a chance to see it all later if they were to move. She reasoned, there was no point in getting excited and building up her hopes, if they didn't eventually manage to go.

The second event was not so pleasant. Grandma's dog had died unexpectedly at the beginning of December. According to Grandma she'd had a great time in Ireland. She had worked perfectly on the unusual roads. However, she had been developing a limp, and when they returned, an x-ray indicated she had cancer at the top of her front left leg. An operation was planned to remove the leg and therefore the cancer. Many dogs could survive with only three legs and lead a very happy life. Ireland was still a good possibility for her. However, the operation didn't go well, and Sophia had returned home from Brownies on that fateful Tuesday night to find her Grandma and Grandpa crying. Their little faithful friend had bled during the operation, and after a number of phone calls from the vet to say that she had stopped breathing but had been put on a ventilator, and then that her heart had stopped beating and the vets were pumping it manually, they had had to make the decision to let her go. Sophia was devastated. She had skipped gaily to school that morning fully expecting to see Grandma's doggie again soon. She just wasn't ready for that and felt guilty she hadn't taken her operation more seriously. Grandma took it all very badly too, blaming herself often for not having been there with her lovely little friend at the end. "She must have been very scared," she said over and over, "and very alone!"

Sophia found this painful to think about, so she moved on quickly. Their little furry friend wouldn't be going to Ireland with them after all, she thought sadly!

Christmas that year had been spent in the hotel they frequented traditionally at Windermere, and while they were there, they had met up again with Uncle Eric and Aunty Jane.

"Nothing to report then? No sign of a move yet?" both of them looked quite happy at this thought.

"No, the house hasn't gone as yet, but we're still really keen to go," Grandpa said.

"I absolutely loved it when we went over and saw over the house and the area," Grandma said enthusiastically. "It'll be a good move." She paused reflectively, "The only sad thing is my dog. She was so good over there…and now she is gone. She seemed to love it there. I'm really going to miss her." She wiped a tear from her eye.

"That was so sad," Aunty Jane sympathised. "Do you think it still good to go then? Would it not just be better and easier to stay in the UK?"

Grandma and Grandpa shook their heads, looking decidedly anxious and uncomfortable at the thought, then they changed the subject and said no more about it.

Sophia found herself wondering if Aunty Jane was right, and that perhaps it might all be going away. It's Christmas now and we've still not sold the house. Things are just not looking good for Ireland, she thought.

Spring came, and with it another Easter. Sophia was fully involved in her church and enjoyed attending there. However, at the back of her mind, there was always the thought that she might be leaving it soon. At gymnastics too each week Grandpa used to have a cup of hot chocolate with Eve's mum while both of them waited for their little athletes to perform, she often heard Alison ask what progress there had been with the move. Grandpa always sounded hopeful and enthusiastic about every new happening, but she noted that his enthusiasm had begun to wane as absolutely nothing tangible seemed actually to be transpiring. Perhaps they might just stay in Aberdeen after all!

It was on April fourteenth that year, that everything seemed to spurt into life. It was Grandpa and Grandma's anniversary that day, and Sophia had gone to dancing in the morning. For a day or so before this, Grandpa and Grandpa had seemed quite worried. She learned that the agreement arranged over their new house in Ireland was about to be broken. "They can't keep it for us for ever," Grandpa had announced. "It's taking too long for our house to sell, and so they're going to put the Irish house back on the market."

By the end of a day spent in soul searching and deliberation, they had decided to put their own house back on the market too – that was the only thing to be done if they were to have any hope of keeping the Irish house. The UK agent they had dealt with before had agreed she would put their house back on the market and website the following morning, Grandma and Grandpa's anniversary. She arrived back home from the dancing that morning to an atmosphere of hope, almost exuberance. Grandpa never tired of telling the story, and although it appeared to be slightly unbelievable, it did seem to hold a promise of change.

"I was reading the story in the bible – the one about Joshua being reprimanded by God for doing a deal with some local people. They had pretended to have come from a distant land in order to deceive him. God had told him not to make agreements with the people of the land He was going to give them – they would only be a thorn in the Israelites' flesh when they eventually occupied it. This audacious deception was in order to save their own skins as they knew Joshua was intent on blotting them out. When Joshua discovered the ruse, it was too late – the deal was done. The Israelite leaders hadn't consulted the Lord first and had therefore put themselves in a place of disobedience with Him. I felt strongly there was a message in that story for us. Perhaps we hadn't consulted the Lord. I got to thinking about the young couple to whom we'd so quickly agreed to hold back our house for. We'd been enthused by the quickness of their response to our initial venture onto the market. To have taken it off it again, in the enthusiasm of assuming it was a done deal, was just too premature., and maybe even wrong. I was sitting there that Saturday morning with my headphones on having listened to the story. Both grandma and I considered it a possibility we had done something wrong. We did what Joshua did therefore, and confessed. Instantly, and I mean instantly, in my headphones I heard the sound of an email coming into my inbox. It was amazing. Our house must have just gone onto the market again, and instantly someone was wanting a viewing. It was so exciting."

Sophia, when she had heard this, had begun to feel excited too, and the following morning when the people arrived to see the house, they had definitely seemed quite interested in it. When she came home from school on the Monday, she discovered they had made an offer for the house, and by the Tuesday the deal was pretty well done. All that was left to do was the paperwork, which Grandpa threw himself into with great gusto. The leaving date was set for the end of May, just six weeks away - there was so much to do. Sophia reflected as she sat looking blandly out of the window at the countryside whizzing by, that possibly if she'd been dragged away to Ireland six months earlier, she might not have been so happy. But now with all the rush of leaving, and yes the sadness of parting too, she also could feel a tremendous excitement. Perhaps she was more ready to go now than she would have been then. She seemed to feel an inner strength about what she was doing.

There was a day too, the previous week, when she had come home from school and found Grandma and Grandpa bubbling with excitement. By now most of the arrangements had been made – they were just waiting for the lawyers to finish off things, for the packers to come, and the removal people to finalise details.

Grandpa was exuberant, "You remember John, the man I met on the boat last September?"

Sophia had no idea what he was talking about. "Yes, you remember the man who gave me a good quote to take our furniture over to Ireland when we were ready?"

She had some vague recollection of that from what seemed the dim and distant past.

"Well, I've been in touch with him in the past couple of weeks, and it's all been arranged, as you know. He's the one doing the removal. But I was speaking to him today, and you could have knocked me over with a feather."

Sophia looked at her Grandpa curiously. He seldom seemed this excited.

"Well, he told me this morning, he'd thought about it and that he was going to put his Mercedes on the lorry."

"What's a Mercedes, Grandpa?"

"It's a car, a luxury car."

"Why's he going to do that?"

"He says he'll put it on the back of the lorry and when he gets near to us, he'll find a forklift which will take it off. He's coming with another driver you see, to help put our furniture on the van."

Sophia looked at him blankly.

He continued, "They'll get all our furniture onto the van and then he'll put us in his car and take us all the way to Kincasslagh himself!"

This was totally unexpected as the family had determined to travel by train, bus, and boat to get there on the designated day.

"Wow!" said Sophia.

"It's so amazing" He's such a kind person!" Grandpa enthused. "It was totally unexpected, but it convinces me, if I need any more convincing by now, that we're definitely on the right road." He thought again, "There might be a delay when we get over there. The house isn't fixed there until we get the money for it into the lawyer's office. It might take a couple of weeks before everything's totally sorted. There is also a possibility they might sell the house to someone else, but that's unlikely given the time it's been on the market. It's going to be an act of faith. Anyhow I told John it might be a couple of weeks before we could get the furniture into the house. He said that would be no problem whatsoever. He'd just keep it on the lorry till he could bring it to us. What a guy!"

Sophia couldn't help feeling some of the excitement and exuberance her Grandpa felt. The whole business of moving was appealing more and more to her.

Their last week there in Aberdeen was something she would never forget. Saying goodbye to her class, her teacher, her school friends had been difficult. Not only was she losing them, but they too would miss her. Gymnastics, Brownies, choir, dancing, and drama workshop – they all had to be left behind. She loved them, but she was buoyed a little by Grandma and Grandpa's promise of getting her involved in similar activities when she arrived in Ireland. The church and her friends were going to be a big miss too. People there were happy for them, but she couldn't help noticing there was also a sense of sadness in the individuals she met there on their last Sunday. There was given to her a beautiful Bible and some other items she would treasure for ever. Having lunch at Brian and Janet's after the service was also a sad affair – they had been such close good friends over the years. She even remembered seeing a video of them holding her as a baby when she was just weeks old. Inevitably therefore, that last week had been difficult for them all but with the prospect of starting a new life, the pain was somewhat ameliorated.

Sophia's mind now focused itself on the previous night. it had been something special. They had awaited the arrival of the removal men, and true to their word John and Morris had arrived late Monday afternoon. The plan was that they would load all the furniture onto the van that evening for an early morning getaway. Grandpa, Grandma and Sophia would sleep in the house on mattresses laid out on the floor. She smiled when she remembered that Grandpa's dog Raffles, had seemed quite perplexed that they were now on the same level as him. He seemed also to be sensing the excitement that was building up. John and Morris would spend the night in the lorry with the furniture. At last, when everything had been loaded, they had all been invited into the neighbours' house for fish and chips. Chris and Julie had gone out of their way to be so helpful. They were good neighbours whom they would surely miss, she thought. And after the meal, she had gone out to the lorry and had had some fun playing with its trolley and lift until it was almost dark. The adults themselves were having a good time in the house, eating, and talking. John discovered that Chris their host had an interest in electric cars. He had even done the Mongolian Rally in one go, quite a challenge. He was a strong ambassador for these cars! John had been considering buying one too, and so the conversation flowed. But all too soon, the evening had come to an end, and the little moving family had finally trooped into their house for the last time. Fortunately, tiredness kicked in quickly and everyone had slept. Regrets would be something for another time.

Sophia had needed no encouragement to get up that morning. Excitement had taken hold of her and they were all now keen to get moving. She had helped take out to the van some last things that had been required the night before and that morning. Grandma and Grandpa looked around the house for the last time. It was empty and sombre. Fortunately, the pressure to get going was strong enough to diminish and curtail any last minute regrets. ON his way out the door, as he looked back into the hall, Grandpa prayed that the new owners would take care of the house and experience good times in it, just as they had done. Sophia had thought his mood seemed heavy as he made his way to the car, but once he had placed Raffles in the boot and settled himself in the front seat, he seemed to perk up again. After all, they were about to start a new chapter in their lives, one they believed would be good for them!

Chapter Five

Due to a last-minute change of plan the lorry and the car had to take separate routes to the ferry, Morris driving the car and John at the wheel of the lorry. The car was making for Belfast while the lorry had been booked in for Larne. The journey however was uneventful and given the spaciousness and comfort of the Mercedes, the family settled back, refreshed themselves and looked forward to arriving in Kincasslagh. It had been determined that they would spend a couple of weeks in the Viking House hotel until the legalities of buying the house were completed and the house was made ready for habitation. Surveys and inspections had thrown up a number of issues, and a wonderful longsuffering local contractor called Joe was hired to tackle the long list of repairs and renovations that were required. Nothing was any trouble to him, and he was always ready with suggestions for improvements when asked for his opinion. By the end of two and a half weeks he had completed the vast majority of the work, and the house was ready to be cleaned, carpeted, and furnished. John, true to his word, had kept the furniture on his lorry and delivered it as the carpets were going in. The day after they had arrived in Kincasslagh, Grandpa and Sophia had walked down to see the house. Until that point, Sophia had only seen pictures of it on the video. Having no keys at that point, they were content to walk around it. Sophia was impressed at the garden, the size of the house and the rugged hill that stretched above it. It was just perfect.

She was, however, disappointed that the school could not enrol her till the following week. Naturally, she felt slightly apprehensive that she might not get on well there. She knew no-one in the area at all, and that scared her. Would she be able to make friends? She didn't have long to wait to find out. A day or so after their arrival the weather was blisteringly hot and some parents and their children came into the hotel. Within seconds Sophia was talking to the children, and the parents invited her to join them as they went down to the little bridge that led onto Cruet Island. Here they could jump off it and swim and splash in the pool below.

Sophia did not need to be asked twice, and immediately started the process of making firm friends with those she would spend time with in school. In the days that followed, some of these girls visited Sophia in the hotel too, and she got to know them well. It was very heartening for Grandpa the day he took Sophia to school for the first time. As they were walking down the road and nearing the building, a chorus of friendly voices floated out of the playground, "Sophia! Sophia!". She would have no trouble in fitting in, he thought. She had already become known to most of them before she had even started.

The morning after the furniture went into the house, the little family left the hotel and moved in too. Many of the items had been allocated to rooms, but the living room was jam packed with things that still needed to be placed. They got there to find that Joe had already set much of the living room furniture out. Grandpa was slightly underwhelmed by this. He had had in his mind a different layout plan. Sophia remembered that he had asked Joe to rearrange things to his specifications, and Joe had willingly complied. Nothing seemed quite right however, and when Joe had been asked for his opinion on the matter, the words 'car crash' were used. From then on, Joe's opinion was sought first, then acted upon seldom with any further changes being necessary. The man was invaluable!

Settling in happened fairly easily. They had met so many of the locals in the hotel in their two and a half weeks stay, and they would meet many of them again on their frequent future visits there. On their first Sunday they went to Mass and although it was not what they were used to, they found it a pleasant experience; and once they had got to know the local priest they felt very settled there indeed. A pattern began to emerge; Sunday service followed by a trip to the Viking House for breakfast and then sometimes staying on for lunch. It was an ideal opportunity to get to know the community. Wherever they went they felt welcomed. One of the things they discovered was that Irish schools have ten weeks summer holidays. As a result, Sophia was only there for about ten days before the term broke up. This did not please her, as she liked school, and would have much preferred to have worked through the summer unlike the other pupils. Ten weeks seemed a long time, but it would soon be over, she thought. They had decided not to return to Scotland till October. They would take their summer holidays where they lived, just getting used to the place. Occasional trips on the local buses, of which there were two a day - to Dungloe and Letterkenny - were undertaken. McDonald's and the cinema were particular favourites of Sophia's when she made the hour and a half long trip to Letterkenny. Because of the extensive holidays Summer Clubs were run for kids and Sophia found herself doing weeklong camps for HipHop, Football, swimming and a two-day course on cookery. She loved all of it. Also, Grandma and Grandpa had set aside one of the bedrooms for guests, and over the summer, two or three visitors stayed with them for a few days at a time, including Aunty Jane and Uncle Eric who kept their word. Having visitors was a good excuse to explore the area – Glenveigh Castle, Mount ERigo, Dunfanaghy, Bloody Foreland andGlenties to name but a few of the hotspots. Aunty Jane and Uncle Eric had been especially impressed with a trip on a local boat around the islands – Uncle Eric had been a sea captain in his time.

Soon the summer was gone, and school started up again. Sophia threw herself into her work and seemed in general to be acclimatising to her new situation. Indeed, it became noticeable that her accent was beginning to change into a light Irish brogue.

But in all this, I hear you ask, what happened to 'the secret'? What did Sophia do with it, and what happened next? It was, however, necessary, and important for you to first understand the background as to why she was in Ireland and how she was able to deal with this amazing alteration to her circumstances. She was a resilient girl but coping with such a major change needed much more than resilience. Her strength of character came directly from what she had experienced in another lifetime – Judith's.

So far, we've talked of the physical change and some of the emotional changes experienced by our heroine, but we've said little of how her life was impacted by the knowledge she had lived in another time with Judith and Josh. We left her, having surrendered the picture and trinket to Abbas, in exchange for being made aware of her link with them. She had determined under Abbas's guidance, to tell her story to those who would listen. If truth be told however, she had had very few chances to say anything, and she felt wary of telling anyone in case they thought she was mad. Her understanding, however, was growing in leaps and bounds, especially where spiritual things were concerned, and when the option of moving to Ireland came along, she found an inner peace and strength which saw her through the transition. After arriving in Ireland, Grandma and Grandpa had encouraged her to get involved in the church. She wanted to do so anyway, and at her first school mass she was one of those who showed enthusiasm to become an altar server. Within the next year she had studied for her First Communion and had had a great day when the ceremony eventually came along. She was learning all the time and adding to her faith. She still however did not find it easy to communicate what she had understood from Abbas that she should. The opportunities just weren't there. She had a wealth of understanding inside but couldn't communicate it. Inevitably, as time went on, she began to drift. The influence of friends – those at school and those on the internet -was dulling off her keenness to communicate her experiences and beginning to have an effect on her memory. She was sinking into complacency and inaction, so much so that she pushed it all to the back of her mind while she got on with the business of living. Sophia's first year in Ireland took up all of her time and effort – what with all her activities and her schoolwork. There seemed little room for anything else.

31

Don Treader

It was the summer after her First Communion and the family had gone to Bray, just south of Dublin, and back to Scotland again to visit family and friends. They had returned from this major holiday, and for the first time in a long time, Sophia was beginning to feel bored. There was a month to go before going back to school and Sophia found these days hanging heavy even with the clubs she still attended. She liked her karate, but there was only so much you could do. As she hung about the house, her friends being unavailable or otherwise engaged, she found time hanging terribly on her hands. As the saying goes, the devil finds work for idle hands to do, and Sophia was in grave danger of finding this out for herself.

It was Tuesday, about three weeks before school was due to start, and Sophia was really bored. None of her friends seemed to be about. People on social media also seemed sparse that day. After lunch she had gone upstairs to lie on her bed and listen to some music. A cool breeze was coming in the window providing some welcome refreshment. Her window faced the side of the house and was out of the full glare of the sun which was shining at the front. She was in a semi dose, feeling fairly full after her lunch. She found her mind playing over some of the things that had happened to her a few years earlier. Although the opportunity to do anything about them hadn't been there, the clarity of the images had not diminished much. Abbas, Josh, Judith's daughter Tabitha, Mikha, Little Faithie – dear Little Faithie – scenes from her past, or more appropriately, Judith's past were filling her thinking. She found herself wondering what had happened to Judith, Mikha and Tabitha after her last time with them. She had often wondered how Mikha and Tabitha had responded when Judith returned home without Little Faithie. Would they believe she had met Josh? Indeed, she had heard about their last meeting in a very unexpected place. Not long after arriving in Ireland one Sunday when the Bible was being read in chapel, the story had been about Jesus meeting with his disciples at the Sea of Galilee after his resurrection. They had been out fishing all night and had caught nothing. Jesus had called to them from the shore asking if they'd caught anything, and when they replied negatively, he had told them to put their nets out again, and this time they caught a large number of fish. She had been totally astounded that the actual number of fish was mentioned – one hundred and fifty-three – just as she had heard his disciples tell him from the other side of the outcrop while she had been sitting with Little Faithie's head on her lap. She hadn't realised that this story which she had lived out, had been included in the Bible texts. Before he dealt with Peter and re-commissioned his disciples, he had invited them to breakfast. They had brought some of their fish, but she couldn't help giving a secret smile, knowing how Jesus had come about the fish he had already been frying.

She was thinking over these things when she felt something going over her. It was like a wave of cold air. Simultaneously she felt scared and energised. What should she do? She got up quickly and closed the window. Was the weather changing? It didn't seem as if it was. The sun was still shining brightly at the front. She lay down again and turned her music up. Perhaps she might go to sleep. But…there it came again. A cold wave rolled over her making her shiver. What was happening to her? Whatever it was, had her attention. She sat up and whispered a prayer. "I don't know what's happening, Lord, but please keep me safe." She was shaking now, not only because of the cold draught, but because she was scared. What is happening to me, she wondered again? Something was now affecting her music. It just wasn't right. The song seemed out of tune. Then she realised that another sound was superimposing itself over it. She turned the player off quickly and heard a wispy but insistent sound coming apparently from outside. She went back to the window and opened it wide. No, she could still barely make out the sound. It wasn't coming from that side of the house. Moving back towards her bed she realised that the sound was coming from the back of the building. Quickly she opened the skylight that faced the back garden. This was the right direction – the sound, although still quiet, was clearer now. She thought it seemed familiar, and when it strengthened, she knew exactly what it was - a solitary girl singing a beautiful refrain - it was her lifesong. She had heard it on occasions before when she had been with Josh and Abbas, and had learned what it was when she was talking with her dead brother and daughter in a vision she had had of heaven. The fear inside her was turning to excitement. She rushed down the stairs and out the back door. She was in time to hear the end of the song - it went just as quickly as it had come. She had been drawn to it, but it had stopped. Indeed, she couldn't be sure she had actually heard it at all. Was it a figment of her imagination, a ghost from the past that had taken advantage of her sleepiness? She didn't think so – for the moment or two that she had heard it; it had seemed so real. She stood at the back door wondering what to do, wondering if she would hear it again. The air was still now. Nothing stirred. And then she heard it, coming straight into her mind. Not a song this time, but a voice, "Come!"

Her body stiffened. Had she heard right? Was she imagining it? She was about to turn back into the house when she heard it again. "Come!" She had to obey it. There was no time to tell anyone. She felt a strong desire to "come". She felt as if she was to go into the back garden and climb the steep hill. She baulked at this, as since she had lived there, she had seldom ventured up the hill except for going a few feet to retrieve a dog toy. There were too many nettles and brambles for her liking; she hated the thought of getting scratched. There had therefore never been any inclination in her to go up the hill but now she felt an insistent demand to do so. She had often wondered what might be beyond the bounding wall but had never had the courage to go and see. It now looked as if the voice she had heard was calling her to do so. She could either obey it or ignore it. Tempted to ignore it she allowed many excuses to fill her mind. She might fall, she might get scratched, she might get hurt – but none of these resonated with her. She had to do something about the voice. She just couldn't put it aside. She went indoors again and found her strongest shoes. She knew she would have to climb that steep hill, possibly getting torn to bits all the way. She also pulled on a light jumper. This might help protect her from the nettles and brambles. It was clear she had set her mind to going up the hill.

She opened the gate into the garden and began to climb. It was as bad as she'd thought, if not worse. The bushes at the top were thick and difficult to get through. She moved one particularly bad bramble aside and found herself staring at the bounding wall. The other side was no better than she had imagined. More bushes, even thicker ones. She looked back down the hill. She was almost on a level with the roof of the house. She could see through her skylight window a room that looked very inviting at that moment. Grandpa and Grandma were somewhere at the front of the house. Should she go back and tell them what she was doing just in case anything happened to her? It was so far down again, and she had struggled so much to get this far. She would wait to tell them all about it later. Turning back to the bushes beyond the wall she thought she saw a slight gap in them just a little further along to the left. As she moved towards the gap, she had an overwhelming sense now that she was doing the right thing. She didn't know what to expect, but she was sure there was something to be discovered. Reaching the gap, she noticed it extended quite some way into the bushes, forming something of a small passage. She nimbly clambered over the wall, and started down the passage, her heart beating quite quickly. Walking between the bushes reminded Sophia of a large Maze bounded by high hedges. She didn't feel scared but did wonder what she eventually might come across. She had been told that beyond the wall and the foliage behind it, was the main road, but she could hear nothing, not one motor car. All she could see was a wall, and a thick wall at that, of trees and bushes much higher than her. Pushing her way down the passage, it very quickly came in on her till it was scratching at her arms and legs. If it hadn't been for the insistence she felt inside, she would have turned back. She didn't know how much longer she would be able to move forward. If it became any tighter, she would have to stop. Suddenly she broke out of the bushes into a clearing. It was flat and sun drenched, no longer in the shadow of the trees and foliage. She had been growing cold as she pushed her way through the bushes, so now the sun was a welcome friend. All that paled into insignificance however, with the sight that met her eyes. She was in a fairly large clearing, and on the other side of it was…she screwed up her eyes, closed them and opened them up again to make sure she wasn't seeing things…a tall, well pitched large blue tent. She recognised it instantly as the one Judith had seen on numerous occasions, the one that belonged to Abbas. She had to pinch herself to see if she was dreaming. What was it doing here – in Ireland? Maybe she'd got it wrong. Maybe it was just holiday makers who had found a secluded spot to pitch their tent. But inside, she knew it wasn't that. She knew very well it was Abbas's. In an instant her apprehension had turned to excitement, and she quickly made her way over the ground to the front of the tent. The nearer she got to it, the more light-headed she felt. Her eyes too seemed to be bothering her. Was it her imagination or was the tent shimmering? She remembered before, that as Judith, she had never entered the tent through the front flaps. She stopped, realising she couldn't just barge in. Her excitement was high now. She was desperate to go inside – it had been such a long time since she had been there as Judith. But she felt so lightheaded, so faint. And what was that? There was that singing again. It was loud now and filling her ears. It was overwhelming yet invigorating. How was she going to get inside, she wondered? She knew she had to do that, but in her current state she couldn't see how. She had the desire but couldn't marshal her thoughts clearly. It didn't matter anyhow. She felt exhilarated, peaceful, and unbelievably happy. She just let herself go and as the singing filled her ears, she dropped to the ground in a deep sleep.

Chapter Six

"Good, Sophia. You've arrived. I've been waiting for you." The gentle voice seemed to penetrate her thinking, and her lifesong which was slowly ebbing away. The voice seemed to be calling her out of a lovely dream. It seemed vaguely familiar. She recognised the voice. She had heard it before somewhere. She was aware it was gentle, soothing, encouraging. She didn't feel worried, only sad that she was having to leave her dream behind. She had no idea what she had been dreaming – she only knew it was good, a beautiful feeling. She was in no hurry to revive, or to open her eyes – but the voice, apart from being gentle and coaxing, was also insistent.

Sophia was now aware of a soft glow with a bluish tinge filtering through her eyelids. She decided to open them and reconnoitre her surroundings. She saw a glowy kind of mist and the shape of a face quite close to hers. It was indistinct because of the mist, but slowly her perception began to clear and with it her vision. Things didn't seem quite normal though. Her perception seemed heightened, her senses sharpened, to the point of being fully enriched and enhanced. She felt a strange exhilaration, a vividness of spirit she had never felt before. Flashing into her mind came the awareness of a scene from Judith's memories. Her senses had been invigorated in a dream. Perhaps it wasn't a dream, but it had seemed like heaven to her. As the image flashed away, suddenly her vision corrected itself, or adjusted to the refined atmosphere. She saw the face more clearly and gasped, "Josh!"

"Sophia. I have been waiting for you. I have loved you with an everlasting love, and I have much to tell you." He was smiling at her and the sight of him lifted her spirit. Judith's memories came flooding into her brain – Josh as an eight-year-old boy stroking his lips with a blade of grass as he listened to her tell him about holding her dead brother in her arms, Josh going through his Obligation ceremony with her, Josh turning to speak to her as he healed her dead daughter, and Josh hanging on the cross in absolute pain and dereliction. The one image

37

that held her attention was of her last meeting with him at the Sea of Galilee. He was smiling at her as she stroked Faithie for the last time. It was the same Josh, and she knew she loved him.

"Where am I? What am I doing here?" A thought struck her, "Am I in heaven?"

"No, you are not. You are in my Father's dwelling. You've been here before, you remember?" He gave her time to think. Suddenly flooding into her brain came her journey up the hill behind her house, the pressing through the bushes and the sense of amazement and joy she had felt when she came upon the blue tent in the clearing. This must account for the bluish tinge in the soft glow she was seeing. She must be inside the tent, she thought.

"Yes, you are," he said, seeming to know what she was thinking. "My Father and I need you to be here, and so we have come to you."

"In Ireland?" she murmured.

"Yes, anywhere. We are where you need us to be, and so here you are."

Sophia very naturally seemed to be tuning into Judith's thoughts, after all, she had lived out much of her life with her. She remembered being in the tent twice before as a little girl, the first time when she had met Abbas, Josh's Father, and he had given her the strange beautiful yellow trinket; the second time when Josh and she had managed to get left behind in Jerusalem, and Abbas had warned her that her smile would leave her in the future but that it would return again. She had also been in it as a woman, on the day before Josh's death when he had told her he was going away and that it was part of his Father's plan. His smile was broad, open, and warm, and it invigorated her spirit now.

"Why do you need me?" Sophia ventured to ask.

"My Father and I told you that you had a purpose. We have come to share more of it with you. You've already given us your heart, and more. It's now time for you to receive. You are in 'Heart's Desire' and once again we have something to give you. My Father is preparing it for you now, and when you and I have finished our time together, He will come to you."

Sophia sat up, "You seem very real." She stumbled over her words in a haze of guilt, "I've not been...I was beginning to forget, to allow everything to slip."

"I know, dear one, I know. You've allowed the cares of the world and the pride of life to suck away your lifesong...but I can restore it. It is my Father's good pleasure to give you the kingdom."

"I'm sorry," Sophia murmured. "I didn't mean..."

"We know. We are here to strengthen you, and in doing so, you will strengthen others, indeed your image." He drew back from her, "But more of that later. I told you I have much to show you, and time is pressing. Judith is coming...indeed will soon be here!"

This drew Sophia up short. "Judith is coming? Will I meet her?"

"Wait dear one. Do not fret. When two become one all is clear. First come with me. You have times to experience, times to learn." Josh touched her arm, and it was as if a charge of soft electricity went through her body, and she was no longer in the tent. She was on a wooded hillside in the near darkness. A group of rough dishevelled bearded men were moving around a small campfire on which a pot was boiling. One of the men was sharpening a knife on a stone to the side of it. She could see he had already sharpened two others. A smaller man was cutting wood for the fire, while another seemed to be shredding leaves into the pot. Suddenly, emerging from the trees, came two other ruffians, dragging what appeared to be two children behind them. They gave a shout as they entered the camp and deposited the children near the fire. They made them sit down and stood menacingly over them, brandishing their knives. Sophia drew back into the shadows just behind a big tree. She didn't know if she could be seen or not, but she wasn't taking any chances.

"Look what I found," one of the ruffians shouted gruffly at those in the camp.

"Where did you get them?" the man sharpening the knives looked up and spoke.

"We found them skulking about just down the hill a bit, Barabbas."

Barabbas grinned menacingly, "Well, we'll take care of them! No trouble." Sophia could see that the prey the two bandits had captured were indeed two little boys who appeared to be quite cowed in the presence of the men.

"What's your names, boys," said Barabbas, drawing himself up to his full height. He was dressed in a rough robe with a leather belt around his waist.

"Simon, sir," said the one who looked the most scared.

"And your name, son," growled Barabbas, glaring at the other boy.

"Josh, sir."

Suddenly it dawned on Sophia that she was looking at a young Josh. She tried to see a bit better past the tree by going around to its other side, attempting at the same time to avoid being seen by any of the men. That wasn't likely to happen anyway as their full attention was focused on the boys.

Suddenly flashing into her mind came another familiar picture. Judith's memories were throwing up a scene from her childhood. On the day Joe, her brother, had been killed, she had seen a 'knife man' skulking around the houses in her village. He had silenced her by glaring at her and pointing to his knife. It was that same horrible cruel menacing face she was looking at now – the face of Barabbas. She had been convinced then that he surely would have killed her if she had made a noise. Seconds later he and those who were with him had vanished, and within the next minute, the Romans who were chasing them had galloped through the village and had left a very sad little bloodied bundle on the path, which she had been left to cuddle into heaven.

Don Treader

Sophia felt sick as Judith's memories were so real to her. She shivered and moved further back into the shadows.

"Are you scared boys?" Barabbas growled at them.

For some seconds the boys said nothing - one of the boy's teeth seemed to be chattering. Eventually, he spoke through the malaise, "No sir. I want to be a Zealot freedom fighter when I grow up, just like you."

Barabbas looked interested. "It's a hard life boy. We're chased from town to town, village to village. And…we kill Romans!"

"I know," the boy said.

"What's your name again?" Barabbas asked him.

"Simon, sir. My father was like you until he was wounded."

"His name?" the man shredding leaves into the pot, barked.

"Judas ben Jonas, sir," Simon said.

"I know him, or I knew of him," Barabbas grunted. "He was a good man."

He looked at the other boy, "And what about you son…Josh was it?"

"The boy nodded, "I stay in Nazareth with the carpenter."

"Who's your father? Where is he?"

"He's everywhere and anywhere. I meet him sometimes in these hills. He owns land."

"Really?" said Barabbas with interest. "Are you worth anything to him? Might there be a ransom in this?" He turned to the other men and laughed. "We make our living by killing and stealing. I wonder if he can help us? He might give us something for you. We've no hope of getting anything out of the carpenter – he'll be too poor!"

"No sir, that won't happen. My Father has told me that those who live by the sword shall die by the sword. Zealots are not part of his plan."

Barabbas's face hardened. "Really? If that's so, then we might gain his attention and recruit him to our cause, if we kill his son. A bit of intimidation, a bit of murder, can work wonders"

"You can't sir. My time is not yet, and my Father looks out for me."

Barabbas moved around the campfire and went up to Josh. He took his blade and held it to his throat. Josh didn't flinch.

"Scared? How would your father react if we were to spill your blood?"

"I've already said, my time is not yet. When my blood is spilled you will be free."

"What on earth are you talking about, son?" Barabbas was angry that he seemed to be making no impression on the boy. He suddenly threw his blade and it stuck into a tree.

Josh's face remained calm, and Barabbas thrust his own face into his. "I kill people. Aren't you scared?"

"No sir. I told you, my Father looks after me. Not one hair of my head will be harmed without him knowing it or allowing it."

"I could kill you. I like killing people. Death follows me."

"I know," Josh said calmly. "You killed a Roman soldier recently down at Capernaum and were the cause of a little Jewish baby to die in what resulted."

Barabbas started back in surprise. "How do you know that?"

"My Father told me, and their blood is on your hands. You will not escape judgment unless you repent."

Barabbas was enraged and pulled his knife out of the tree. "We are fighting for freedom. You know nothing."

Josh said calmly, "Freedom will not come from the blood of Romans or little babies. Yours is a lost cause."

Barabbas thrust his knife at Simon, "You want to be a real knife man?"

"Yes, sir," said the boy shaking.

"Well, take this, and stick it in him."

"No, sir...please..." Simon stuttered. "He's...he's my friend."

"Boy, zealots will kill friend or foe if the cause is right. Go on, stick it in him!" His voice and attitude were menacing. It appeared he might kill Simon if he didn't obey.

Sophia's tongue was stuck to the roof of her mouth. Her heart was beating fast. What was going to happen to Josh. She couldn't bear to look, but she couldn't draw her eyes away either.

An eternity seemed to pass while Barabbas was intimidating Simon, and then suddenly without warning Josh stood up and walked quietly and confidently out of the camp.

The atmosphere was so charged, and their amazement so strong, that nobody tried to stop him. The silence that stunned the camp seemed to go on for a minute or so, then Barabbas cursed. "Get out of here boy, before I kill you myself."

Simon's shaking form stood up and ran for the cover of the trees, keen to surround himself with the thick branches. It was dark now, but he pushed his way through the undergrowth in roughly the same direction as Josh.

Sophia's breath seemed to be rasping in her throat. She had been terrified. She now breathed a sigh of relief and was beginning to wonder what might happen to her now that she was left alone with the men, when suddenly the scene dimmed and she was back in the tent, surrounded by that calming bluish glow. Josh was beside her. "That's one of the things you need, something you need to know for survival. All will become clear." His eyes looked concerned for a moment. "But Judith is coming...she'll be with us very soon." He touched her arm again and once more the tent vanished.

Chapter Seven

It was hot and Sophia felt the sun burning her head. Her hair wasn't enough to protect her. It was so bright after the bluish glow in the tent, it took her eyes some time to adjust. Where was she, she wondered? Am I alive? Why am I so hot? She was aware of her feet burning and hot air all around her. Sitting directly in front of Grandma's tumbler dryer was just how it felt, but more so, much more so, than this. The heat of the atmosphere around her enveloped her, smothered her, made her feel faint. She had to get out of this furnace. Her eyes were now becoming adjusted, and appearing out of the shimmering heat she found herself in what appeared to be a sandy desert landscape. She was leaning on the edge of a structure that reminded her of an old well. A few yards away was a roughly built shelter comprising of three wooden walls and a roof. She could make out large water pots inside it. She needed to get under that shelter to avoid getting burned. Suddenly she heard the sound of voices, quite distant at first, but coming closer. She had an irresistible urge to hide. She didn't want to be seen. She quickly darted into the shelter and pushed one of the pots out from the wall and squeezed in behind it. She was able to see round it to the well structure and beyond. Being now in the shade her eyes were now able to see a few hundred yards to the right, a small group of old-fashioned wooden shacks she supposed to be a village, and on the left, a group of men in the distance approaching the well from the other direction. They looked tired, hot, and bothered, the sun obviously getting to them too. She felt safe where she was, glad she couldn't be seen. She felt she was exactly where she was meant to be, and wondered what Josh had in store for her.

"We'll go to the village and get some food," one of the men said. He looked at a man in the centre of the group, "You look exhausted. You'll have to eat something."

"I have food you don't know about, Andrew," the other man said. Sophia thought his voice sounded vaguely familiar.

43

"You'll have to eat, Master."

Suddenly Sophia realised that the man in the middle was Josh. He looked tired and weary.

"Sit down under the canopy," Andrew motioned to the well with its overarching cover. "You'll at least get some shade there."

Josh looked glad of the opportunity to rest and be alone. As his men made their way towards the village , he sat down gratefully on the well's parapet sheltered from the burning heat of the sun by the canopy.

All of a sudden, Sophia's attention was drawn to something happening a few yards away from her further along the shelter. She had rushed into it and squeezed herself behind a large waterpot without taking notice of anything else. She had thought she was alone, but evidently not. One of the other pots moved and out from behind it came a small wiry woman in her late twenties or early thirties. Sophia was sure she must have seen her enter the shelter moments earlier, so she waved a greeting to the woman and put her finger to her lips to warn her to remain silent. The woman looked in her direction before reaching for a small jar beside her. She had looked at her with blank eyes as if she hadn't seen her. Am I invisible, wondered Sophia?

The woman was standing up now, and grasping her pot, she started to walk Towards the well. Sophia wondered if like her she had spotted the men coming and had decided to avoid being seen by them. It seemed, however, that she didn't feel that the solitary Josh was as much of a threat.

She approached the well and made for the side opposite him. He seemed pre-occupied and she looked curiously at him as she placed her pot on the parapet and prepared to let down the bucket.

"Please give me a drink." Josh had suddenly raised his head and was now looking straight at her.

The woman started back, looking surprised so much so that she almost knocked her pot off the parapet.

"But you're a Jew, sir. I'm a Samaritan woman. Jews have nothing to do with us."

Josh ignored this. "If only you knew...that Yahweh has a gift for you...and whom you are speaking to..."

She looked askance at him, not sure what to make of him.

Josh continued, "You'd be asking me, and I would give you living water."

Sophia saw the woman roll her eyes. She said in a sceptical voice not without a hint of impatience, "Sir, you don't have a rope or a bucket. This well is very deep. Anyhow, living water? Where would you get it?"

Josh looked at her kindly as she continued, "Do you think you're greater than our ancestor Jacob who gave us this well? He, his sons, and his animals, they all drank this water. How could your water be any better than theirs?

44

Josh said quietly, but definitely, "Anyone who drinks this water will become thirsty again, but those who drink the water I give them will never thirst again. My water becomes a fresh living spring inside them and will give them eternal life!"

The woman looked smitten; her sceptic attitude gone. Something about his words had broken through it, and her defences were gone. Sophia had seen this so often before. Josh always seemed to have the right word for every situation.

"I'd like some of this water, sir; then I won't be thirsty again. Please give me some, and I won't have to come here every day."

Josh looked directly into her face. He said quietly, but firmly, "Go, get your husband."

She looked at him startled for a moment, then looked down, unable to meet his gaze. She said eventually, "I don't have one, sir."

"You're right," Josh agreed. "You don't have a husband. You've had five...and you're not even married to the man you're living with now. You've certainly spoken the truth."

The woman's jaw dropped, and she hung her head. There was a silence for a few moments before she spoke again. "Sir...you must be a prophet." She paused again. "Please tell me, why is it that you Jews insist that the only place to worship is Jerusalem? We believe it is here at Mount Gerizim, where our ancestors worshipped." It seems that she had thought the best way to get the focus off her was to change the subject and try a different tack, a religious one. She had gone for the age-old issue that perplexed the Samaritans.

Josh pushed past her ploy, and spoke with conviction, "It doesn't matter!" he said. "Believe me, my dear woman, the time will come when where you worship won't be important – either here or there." He smiled at her. "You Samaritans know little about the one you worship, while we Jews know all about Him. Deliverance and eternal life come through the Jews." She was staring at him now, transfixed. He continued, "Believe me indeed, the time is here now, when true worshippers will worship the Father in spirit and in truth. These are the kind of people He's looking for." A smile was beginning to play on her lips as he continued, "Yahweh is Spirit; therefore it follows that those who worship Him must worship Him in spirit and in truth. There's no need for limitations any more. He's there for everyone, everywhere!"

It was as if he was speaking manna to her soul and pouring living water into her spirit. She was smiling now. "I know the Messiah is coming, the Christ, the Deliverer." Her face took on a slightly apprehensive air, as if she was thinking ahead, "I believe when He comes, He will explain everything to us." Sophia could see light was beginning to dawn on her face, and Josh cemented it with the words he spoke next.

"I am the Messiah!"

The scene dimmed, and Sophia felt herself drifting in consciousness and thought, until she found herself back inside the tent again, gazing into Josh's face. Both were bathed in that soft bluish glow. "You have seen...and have understood," he told her. "It's now time for you to leave."

Sophia wanted to ask for clarification, but felt a request would be inappropriate, being thought of as unnecessary. She had all she needed to know. She contented herself with, "Am I going back now?"

He smiled at her, "No, not yet. You remember I told Judith I would always be with her?"

Sophia easily remembered Judith's experience when she was in the self-same tent. Her smile would go, but Josh and Abbas would be with her, and her smile would return. She nodded.

Josh continued, "Judith needs me now, and I need you – but I can tell you no more. My Father wants you, to give you something to enhance and strengthen your image." He held out his hand and helped her to her feet. She felt invigorated, as if her body was being filled with a supernatural strength. He pointed, "Go! Remember I am with you both." She started to walk in the direction he was pointing. Both...what did he mean, she wondered. There was only one of her.

Josh did not go with her. A few steps further on and she found herself confronted by a heavy hanging which divided the tent. She hadn't noticed it before but as she walked, it seemed to emerge out of the dim bluish glow. She pushed her way through a slit in the middle of it, and as she did so a bell rang beside her and she gasped. What was she seeing? She stopped to take in the scene. Right in front of her was the "Heart's Desire" antique shop., perfect in every detail to the one she had visited twice before. Old clothes in racks, shelves laden with knickknacks, a broad counter, and a window area crammed with quaint old-fashioned objects. She knew exactly what she should do. She walked up to the old wooden counter and waited for Abbas to appear. She was not disappointed because he was sitting as she had seen him before, in the corner. He rose to greet her.

"You have arrived, my dear, and you have seen my Son." This was more of a statement than a question. "You are here for a purpose. My Son needs you, and I need you. Your image has to be informed and strengthened so that renewal might come. If you are strong, then Judith will be strong. She needs you, and the strength of your image. You have been given insights which both of you will need."

Jus as before, Sophia did not understand all that Abbas said, but she supposed that she would when she had need to. At present she was content just to listen.

"Your image needs strengthening. Josh started it and I completed it for your first journey. I want you to know I have added more for your help, and I will again add more before you come to me at End's Door."

"I don't have the image you gave me. You took it back."

46

"But Judith has it and needs it for her survival. Your presence will enhance and strengthen it. Point out the change!"

"But I don't know the change, what it is!" Sophia looked worried.

"You will, when you see it," Abbas said cryptically. She had grown used to this way of speaking and so decided not to say any more.

"Your image is with you and will lead you," Abbas continued, "but yet, there is something you lack. You are not complete."

She waited for an explanation, but none was forthcoming.

"Go, receive and strengthen!" He was now pointing at the door. "Remember Judith needs your insight and strengthening. You will say nothing, but your spirit and image will encourage her in her great time of need."

She wanted to ask more but realised he would only tell her what he wanted her to know. She moved towards the door.

"You will need this too," he said., and she saw something green sparkling and glowing in his hand as he stretched it out towards her.

"You returned your heart's desire and more which I asked of you the last time we met. I promised you would have what you needed when you needed it again. This is 'the more' you need now. You have your heart's desire, but the 'more' I am giving you will keep you and encourage you, will dispel the darkness that will envelop. Do not be afraid but take this and survive."

She took it from his hand and he quickly retreated to his corner and sat down, the interview apparently over. She reached for the door handle and the bell rang again as she opened it. Why was she not surprised that she found herself back in the dim bluish glow of the tent and not out in a cobbled street? She was however totally on her own now, and so she decided to take a moment to look at what it was that Abbas had given her. Yes, it wasn't unlike the yellow sparkling trinket she had received before. But this time it was green and in the shape of a cross. The slender gold chain was attached to one arm of the cross. Just like the original trinket, it glowed unnaturally, even in that dim bluish light. On closer inspection it looked like a holographic image, and the longer she stared at it, it seemed to project an image that encompassed the whole object from top to bottom and side to side. As it formed, bit by bit the face of Josh appeared, and seemed to be speaking to her. Was his mouth really moving, she wondered? The cross began to pulse and shimmer, which gave his face the appearance of talking. Now, there it came again! She could hear a clear voice singing, almost imperceptibly at first and then increasing in loudness to fill the tent. She recognised it immediately as her lifesong. What did all this mean? What was she to do? Where was she to go? What had Abbas meant? Why did she need 'the more'?

She looked down again at the trinket in her hand, the singing now ringing in her ears. Josh's face was now formed and seemed to be speaking to her. Over the singing came his gentle strong voice, "I need you; my Father needs you, Judith needs you. And remember I am with you through the darkness and beyond."

As she felt that familiar overwhelming exhilarating feeling sweeping over her, and as she began to sink to her knees, she tightened her grip on the throbbing glowing object in her hand to keep it safe and close. She could now give way to that familiar beautiful unconsciousness that would envelop her, caress her, and usher her into a paradise far beyond her imagining.

Sophia's Secret

Volume Two

Part Two – Pursuit

Chapter Eight

Judith roused herself. She was wet, and for a moment she didn't know where she was. It was dark, or to be more accurate, almost dark. Around her were many shadows as the twilight was merging into stygian blackness. The shadows seemed menacing – some above her, and some at her level. Again, she wondered where she was, and deduced that she was lying down, and quite cold. Her eyes took in the fact that the shadows were caused by branches all around her. She had come round in a small patch of grass surrounded by trees, bushes, and foliage. Oh, how cold she felt…and wet. Why was she lying outside, in the dark, and why was she so wet?

Suddenly into her mind came the memory of what had happened, the reason why she was there…and in such an exposed state. The horror of it filled her mind, so much so that she trembled and almost vomited. It took all her strength to stop herself disposing of the contents of her stomach as she lay there. She felt so sick, so horrified, that she very nearly sank into unconsciousness again. She had to force herself to hold onto every vestige of sanity to avoid blacking out. A strange sound was filling her ears – what on earth was it? She realised with horror she was listening to her own voice, or at least, the sounds made by her mouth. A howling, a wailing, a crying out – first a low moan which developed into a full-blown shrieking. Now her body, which had wanted to wretch with sickness, was wracked with uncontrollable sobbing. It was involuntary – she just couldn't help herself. The grim realisation of what had happened was taking hold of her, and she couldn't escape from it. It was so horrible, so unbelievably bad, she found herself thinking or was it hoping, for a split second that perhaps it actually hadn't happened at all. But she knew it had, and the abject misery and dreadful horror she felt took hold of her emotions and dominated her body, dictating its reactions for the next few minutes. She struggled with herself, trying to gain control of the desperate state of affairs she was experiencing. To go on like this for much longer would stress her heart, cause damage to her brain, or perhaps bring about a state of mental instability from which she would be unable to recover. She had to gain control, and so she endeavoured to slow down her breathing and quell her loud wails. This began to work and helped steady her emotions. What was she going to do, she wondered? She was in such agony of mind and spirit. The horror which had swept over her had concentrated her mind fully upon it. It was a very narrow focus and seemed unable to tolerate any other considerations. However, as control was gradually being re-established, she could sense something else. A level of calm was beginning to infuse her soul. Not much at first, but as her body steadied itself, the calmness seemed to be more tangible. She felt desperate but knew her survival depended on her having a cool head. The sobs stopped, the wailing dwindled, and her heart started beating more regularly again. A last ditch feeling of panic overwhelmed her – how was she going to cope – but she quelled it before it could cause her further distress. She had to remain calm.

Judith now took more note of her surroundings. She knew where she was. She had indeed come there for sanctuary, for help. She turned her head and looked behind her, knowing what she expected to see …and she was right. She could just make out in the ever-increasing darkness, the shape of a tent. She was lying in front of it. Why was it dark? It should be blue, she thought, then realised that the gathering darkness around her had robbed it of its colour. She moaned again as yet another wave of grief and panic struck her. Where was Josh? Where was Abbas? She had come to the Garden of Gethsemane to find them. She needed them more than she had ever needed them before … and she felt a deep sense of despair. She hadn't met them. They hadn't come to meet with her. She felt so alone, so helpless, so let down. The tent was there- but where were they now she needed them? She had collapsed in the clearing that she and Josh had spent time in on occasions years before … and now she was awake, she knew she was still on her own. Nothing had changed. What was she going to do?

She was about to rise to her feet, and possibly try to locate the entrance of the tent. Desperate times needed desperate measures. She would never have countenanced doing such a thing before, but she needed help now. Surely, they wouldn't deny her it because she barged in? Josh had told her before, that he was with her and would protect her. He would look out for her. But what had gone wrong this time? Where was he, and his father Abbas? Had they forgotten about her?

She tried to get to her feet but couldn't. Her legs wouldn't let her. She then tried to push herself up by using her hands but was unable to exert enough pressure. She did however manage to roll onto her side, and eventually rested on one elbow facing the shadowy image of the tent. She could do no more than this. This done, she became aware of a supernatural stillness all around her, then slowly, and unmistakably, she heard the sound of a girl singing, the sound of it floating towards her from just beyond the tent. She recognised it as her own lifesong, and she found it calming. Was Josh going to come to her rescue now?

She longed to bury her head in his chest and sob her anguish away. But there was no Josh!

Up until that point she had been fully aware of the darkness which surrounded her. It was becoming quite thick. It hemmed her in and was making her feel quite claustrophobic. She realised she could not stay there much longer. It would soon be too dark to leave. However, the stillness and her lifesong – both seemed to be telling her to rest. There was something to rest for? She was torn. She needed to get away, but she also wanted to see Josh … if he was there. Her legs and arms being unable to help her move, somewhat sorted out her problem for her. She would have to remain there, at least until they worked properly again.

Now what was happening? She felt a heightened awareness stealing over her spirit. It was somehow added to by the stillness of the scene. There was an air of expectancy about it. It didn't feel as if it was just her imagination. It seemed real. Was Josh going to come to her?

What were her eyes doing now? Was the darkness becoming lighter? It was so obviously night. How could it seem to be getting lighter? Her ears now pricked up. Was that a sound she heard, a rustling or even just a shifting of air. It was barely perceptible over the singing, but she was convinced that she had heard something. Her eyes were drawn in the direction that she had believed it to have come from, and as the darkness still continued to appear to lighten, she found herself looking directly at the flaps of the tent. They didn't move, but something was forming or appearing in front of them. She closed her eyes, then opened them again, to make sure she wasn't seeing things. She was right. There was something there! It was almost like a ghost, a pale translucent figure that might well have materialised through the flaps. The flaps most definitely hadn't opened though. Its luminous presence added to the sense that the darkness was being dispelled in the clearing. There were more now, at least a dozen of them. They were appearing just in front of the flaps, and the glow from them seemed to fill the whole area. Indeed, Judith felt as if their light was penetrating her mind and bringing peace to it.

They began to move toward her. They looked like angels, girl angels, and as they approached, she was surprised to realise that each of them bore an uncanny resemblance to herself. They seemed to bear the mark and likeness of the image Josh and Abbas had given her so long ago. How could this be, and why were they there? What were they going to do?

They continued to move towards her, or rather glide. Their motion seemed effortless, and before she realised it, they had gathered around her. Their presence encircling her seemed to be acting as a shield or buffer, protecting her from the waves of grief and darkness that might assail her and expunging the feelings of horror and grief she felt, giving her the strength she so badly needed. Into her mind flashed a memory – had it been said at one time, that the night Josh had been in this very garden in agony praying that his Father's will would be done – it was the night before he had died – that when he had finished praying, he was strengthened by angels? Was this what was happening to her now? She submitted. "Your will be done, Father," she found herself saying. "You give and you take away. Your will be done." The reality of what she was saying hit her, and she said, "But I need your help to go on." The angelic beings stretched out their hands and touched her. A strength seemed to fill her. She had come to the garden weak and in horror of spirit, but somehow these beings were removing all that from her. She closed her eyes and allowed the soothing, calming feeling to waft over her. It felt as if their combined arms were enfolding her. It was helping her gain perspective, and a sense of Josh's and his Father's presence. She would drink it in, allow the balm of it to overwhelm her and uphold her. The horror, and all the ramifications of it, could be dealt with later. For now, she just needed the comfort and peace that was being given her.

She wasn't sure how long she had been in that state, but when she opened her eyes, she saw in front of her only one being, the others around her seeming to have disappeared. This being was smiling at her. Again, she wondered at the similarity of the being to the image given her by Josh ... and her smile. It was so natural, so lifelike, so much like hers. She didn't feel the need to fret.

"Who are you?" Judith asked her.

"Sophia," came the response. Her mouth didn't move, it didn't even lose its smile. The word just seemed to form in Judith's brain.

The words came again. "I have something to give you. Josh is with you. He hasn't abandoned you. He knows of your sadness. He knows you are here. Abbas needs two to become one again for you to overcome and survive." The angelic being held out her hand, and Judith could see something that glowed green hanging from it.

"Judith, I'm glad to be with you. Your image needs strengthening and renewing. A new age is coming and is already here. As long as we are one, this will guide you. You have not been left alone." And with that the angel moved towards her and suddenly it was dark. Where had the being gone, Judith wondered? It was as if it had walked into her. She looked behind her to see if it had gone past her, but no. She was now on her own. The clearing had returned to its near dark state. She could barely make out the tent now. She felt a compulsion to leave. It seemed the right thing to do. Where would she go, she wondered. That wouldn't matter. She felt sure it would be shown her as she went. She knew she just had to leave.

Chapter Nine

Judith pushed her way through the bushes and thick foliage to make her way out of the garden. In the process she was torn by thorns and clung to by bushes with barbs. She had never been there in darkness, and so she put up with it as a consequence of her inability to se what was ahead of her. Indeed, she became disorientated by the darkness, and for a moment let go of the peace that had pervaded her spirit, to allow herself a moment of panic. How would she find her way out of the garden, back onto the main thoroughfare? Just then she heard the rumble of a cart on hard ground. She thanked her luck – or was it luck – she now had her bearings. She could find her way out. One or two bushes more and she was standing at the entrance. She was aware of a rising tide of anxiety beginning to engulf her. It felt as if the nearer she got to the road, the more   the amazing serenity and peace she had been given was evaporating. She was afraid to go any further in case she lost it altogether and became overwhelmed with the horror and fear she had entered it with. Inside the garden she had felt an impulse to leave. She had to carry this out now, regardless of the negatives she might face. She had been strengthened supernaturally. Would the Father not protect her now? She turned into the road that led downhill to the bridge over the Kidron, and into Jerusalem itself. Her mind was in a whirl. Where should she go? Should she go home? No, she couldn't face that. It would be too much for her. The horror was too real there. She had to go somewhere though. Where?

It wasn't until she had crossed the Kidron that she knew what she should do. She could have gone to Esther's but that would mean she would have to go into the lower city. Some parts could be rough at night. At present the road seemed quiet. There was hardly anyone on it. Darkness having fallen, most people were eating their evening meals at home. Only an occasional cart passed, and she slipped into the shadows between houses when that happened. Her experience that day had made her wary, scared of everyone and anyone. Everyone was an enemy in her mind, and anyone might hurt her - and so she didn't want to be seen.

She determined that the quieter route to take was the one to the Upper City where the rich lived, and of course her Aunt Mary and Uncle Joel. Could she go there? Might she bring trouble and danger upon them? She knew they would support her however, so she followed the road past the southern end of the Temple Mount then started to climb the Western hill known as Mount Zion, to reach their house. It was the only logical choice, and on her spirit, she sensed she was doing the right thing. When she got there they would know what to do and how to help her. As she walked, she did feel guilty, however. Shouldn't she go home? That's where she was needed or needed to be. But she was scared. She couldn't bear to see what she knew was there. It would finish her. She had to put some distance, at least for the moment, between her and it. She comforted herself with the belief that Joel would know what to do. These thoughts brought tears to her eyes. She needed to grieve, she wanted to cry. Soon she wouldn't be able to keep it all in!

In her efforts to avoid being seen by a cart trundling up the hill, she squeezed herself into a doorway and suddenly felt very cold

And wet. The front of her robe had been pressed against her skin as she had hugged into the side wall of the entrance. What was wrong with her? It had felt wet in the garden, but as she'd been walking she hadn't noticed it. It hadn't been raining, she thought, and so after the cart had passed without incident she came out of the shadows again and took advantage of light filtering from the window of the house whose doorway she had sheltered in. She stopped short in horror and disbelief. What met her eyes almost made her scream. From the top of her robe to three quarters of the way down it, she was drenched in blood. Some had congealed, but much was still wet and for the second time that night she almost vomited. She sank to her knees and then sat down, her arms hugging her knees. She couldn't cope. It was just too much for her. She didn't care about the blood on her, or if anyone saw her. She just wanted to curl up and die. She must have sobbed for about ten minutes until weariness took over. Any motivation she might have felt from her earlier experience in the garden was now gone. She would happily have rolled under a cart's wheels if it had passed at that moment. However, once again after that wave of horror was gone, awareness of where she was began to take hold of her. It wasn't good for a woman to be wandering the streets on her own in the dark. She would be prey for anyone intending mischief, even if at that moment she didn't care what happened to her. Amidst the coldness and wetness of the blood, and the misery of her condition, she felt something stir in the lower portion of her robe. IN fact, she became aware that it seemed warmer than the rest of her. Instinctively she put her hand down to feel for the cause. There was a lump in the centre of that area. Was she bleeding, and was that why she felt so warm there? Again, another wave of panic. Could she afford to lose any more blood? She was already feeling weak from the events of the day. She heard footsteps coming towards her and tried without success to hug closer to the wall just under the window. A man passed her, staring at her sorry state in the light it gave. He cursed her, saying that women like her gave Jerusalem a bad name. She was a slut. She deserved to be stoned. "I'm glad another man has done to you what I would have done. You don't deserve to live!" He kicked her with his boot and went on his way swearing. He seemed to find it easier to abuse her rather than to ask what might be wrong with her and offer some help. She cowered away and cried again sorely. She felt so low, and the world seemed to be conspiring to keep her there. Again, there was a stirring in her lower robe and her hand went to that hot spot again. What was it? It wasn't a wound. She put her hand through the slit in the side of her robe into her pouch. What would she find there, she worried? More hot blood? Was she dying? Had she been wounded somehow? What exactly was in her pouch? She was touching a warm hard object which seemed to vibrate at intervals. It had a thin strand of metal wound around it. What was it?

Could it be … she wondered? For years she had had a yellow trinket she had kept there, except for the year or so she had attached it to her wedding headband. Abbas had given it to her so long ago, and it had served her as a talisman in her hard and dark times over many years, until Josh had asked for it at her last meeting with him at the Sea of Galilee. Indeed, he had taken both Faithie and her trinket at that time, and if truth be told, she had missed both of them for the five years or so that had passed since then. Could she dare to believe that it might be there again? After all she had been through that day. After the tragedy that had befallen her? Was it too much to believe that somehow Josh may have returned it to her to help her? It felt similar … but it wasn't the same. It had a different feel about it. Her fumbling fingers grasped hold of it and pulled it out of her pouch. She gasped. It was green and glowed.

"Sophia!" she said out loud, as she remembered the angel image holding it out towards her in the garden. "Sophia!" she said again.

Instantly inside her, she felt a sense of satisfaction as if she had made the correct connection and given pleasure to the giver. It was just a feeling, there were no words this time.

She took the object up to her face to examine it more closely in the darkness. It certainly had a distinctive glow. She separated the strands of the chain from it and let them dangle. Now they were no longer wound round it she could see it better. Unlike her yellow trinket, there were no distinctive markings on it. It was plain. But it wasn't round as her trinket had been. It was in the shape of a cross. However, just like her original trinket, it was warm and comforting. The thought impressed itself on her mind, it's been given to me by Abbas. The sense of satisfaction again inside her told her that she was on the right track. She thought again, Sophia brought it to me from the tent. Why did she look like me? Was it me? Where did she go? She must have given it to me somehow. She said something about it being necessary for two to become one again. There was that satisfied feeling again. Judith shook her head. It was too much for her to understand. It's enough for the moment just to have it, she thought. She was feeling better.

As she was about to slip it back into her pouch it started to throb, glow and pulse. She looked at it more carefully and saw something forming on it, reaching to the extremities of the four arms of the cross. Was it a face?

For the second time in moments, she gasped. It was absolutely, and utterly, the spitting image of Josh. How was this so? Was it some kind of magic? The throbbing glow seemed to animate his face, making his mouth appear to open and close. He was looking at her with those piercing, but kind eyes. He seemed to be bypassing all the grief, fear, horror and misery she had felt that day. What was he saying? Was he saying anything? Was it just a trick?

Suddenly into her mind came the words, "Go … leave … Mikha … The Way." AS quickly as his image had appeared, it disappeared again, and the cross became a cross once more in her hand.

She had been startled and unnerved. What did it mean? What did he mean? Was it really Josh talking to her? She rehearsed the words in her mind, determining to hold onto them. "Go … leave … Mikha … The Way" She was baffled but grateful for them. A sense of pleasure came again when she thought of Sophia and so she gave thanks for her bringing the gift to her. So much tragedy that day, and so much blessing and comfort! She was struggling to keep it all together. Deep down however she felt a safety, a security, that somehow Josh was with her and looking after her. She had to get up. She could no longer sit there. She must get to Joel and Mary's and tell them. Perhaps they might be in mortal danger too!

She rose to her feet and walked briskly up the remainder of the hill, then turned into Joel and Mary's road. It was flat and so she quickened her pace. With every step however her anguish grew. She seemed to be alternating between peace and terror. The more she thought about the reason for her horror, the worse it got. She was very much in danger of being overwhelmed again by it. She felt faint… and extremely conscious of a sickness rising in her stomach. What was she going to say to Joel and Mary, she wondered? How would she pass on her news without causing herself major trauma…and them too? The more she thought about it she wondered if she was doing the right thing by going there. But she had to go somewhere, she reasoned. Where else would be as safe? Now she felt lightheaded and wanted to vomit. Her fear, her trauma, her sense of horror was affecting her wellbeing. Suddenly she couldn't hold on any more. Her mind filled with grief, her body about to close up on her, she grasped hold of the big bell at the side of Joel and Mary's gates. And clung to it for grim death as she sank to the ground. Sickness came up in her throat and everything began to go black. The bell rang loudly as she thudded to the ground.

Chapter Ten

Judith struggled out of the blackness into semi consciousness. Where was she, she wondered? It can't have been the ground, she surmised. She felt softness underneath her. With a strong effort of will, she forced herself to relinquish unconsciousness and re-enter living. Where was she, she thought again? So far, her eyes had been closed, so she determined to open them. She saw above her a marked ceiling. Her ears were now perceiving sounds around her, and as her eyes adjusted and focused, some familiar faces swam into view. They were looking down at her, with concern in their eyes.

"Joel! Mary!" she whispered. As consciousness took hold of her, she realised that her body was feeling weak and painful, and most certainly her voice was cracking and feeble. "What…"

"Don't speak, Judith dear," said Mary. "Gather your strength first."

Judith struggled to make herself heard, "Where am I? What happened?"

Joel said, "You're in our atrium, Judith. We found you lying at the gate."

What!" Judith didn't seem to be taking this in. It was difficult. Her mind was such a jumble of thoughts, feelings and emotions.

"You didn't half give Esther a shock, dear," Mary asserted. "The bell started to ring frantically while we were all praying. She went to answer it and stumbled across you lying on the ground. You must have pulled the bell with all your might before collapsing."

Slowly now, Judith's memory was beginning to return, and she didn't like it. Pain, misery, sickness, horror – they all invaded her brain simultaneously, and she flagged. She had to struggle to avoid becoming unconscious again. She wept.

"What's wrong, my dear?" said Mary continuing to look really concerned. "What's happened?"

Judith couldn't control everything now. She remembered she had had to focus to get herself through the streets to Joel's and Mary's, but now that her memories were returning with a vengeance, she was utterly overwhelmed by them.

Joel, Mary, and Esther looked on, saying nothing. They could see Judith's agony of spirit and waited patiently for her to come through it and regain some vestige of composure. For her Part Judith allowed the searing emotions to wash over her. She felt as if she was falling into a quagmire and could do nothing about it. She was scared, but allowed herself to go with it, knowing of no other way to surface again. The images that now filled her brain were crippling, destructive, heart wrenching – she couldn't protect herself from them. She was losing her sanity.

Suddenly she heard a sound at her ear. A voice was praying. "Dear Lord, whatever our sister has being going through, whatever she's going through – please give her your peace. You died to give her life. Let that life and strength flood into her now. Don't let her sink and become prey to our enemy. You love her Lord. Didn't you say, 'I will be with you and never leave you comfortless'? Comfort and strengthen our sister now."

She began to feel a stabilisation coming into her spirit. Joel's prayer was having its effect. Her spirit was being massaged and revived. Josh was coming to her.

Once Judith had stopped sobbing and shaking, and her obvious distress was abating, Mary said again, "What's happened, Judith?"

Judith sat up on the couch she had been lying on, a pathetic waif of a figure. She looked around her. She was indeed in Joel and Mary's atrium. She wanted to speak, but her mind was so grieved, she couldn't form the words; couldn't give voice to her feelings. It was as if to do so, would plunge her back into her abyss of horror.

She shook her head. "I can't..." she whispered. "I can't..." The rest in the room waited, giving her space to grapple with her thoughts and words.

Eventually, Judith marshalled her emotions and said flatly, all emotion gone, "Mikha's dead. They killed him."

There was a stunned silence. No-one moved. Surprise and disbelief showed on their faces. Suddenly there was a scream from Judith's left side, then it was followed by a thud. Involuntarily Judith looked toward the sound and froze. Her daughter Tabitha had been standing in the doorway leading to the guest quarters. On hearing her mother's words, she had gone into a dead faint and was now lying sprawled on the floor.

Instinctively, Joel went to her, calling to his son Jonas who had been following Tabitha through the door, "Come on Jonas, give me a hand to get her onto a couch." The two men carried Tabitha to the nearest one and laid her on it carefully. Esther who had been soothing Judith's forehead with water before she revived, now did the same for Tabitha. She began to come round.

Judith rose unsteadily to her feet, and went to her daughter, "Tabitha, Tabitha," she moaned. "I'm sorry, I'm sorry."

62

Tabitha may have been seventeen, but she was not too old to be held close by her mother, who did so as if she was holding a dying baby.

"Father, father…" Tabitha moaned. She looked into her mother's eyes, "Is he…"

Judith held her even more tightly. "Tabitha…Tabitha…he's gone…" The two women broke down, sobbing pitifully. The others could do nothing but look on helplessly. No-one knew what to say to alleviate their grief. No-one knew what had happened but each was equally stunned by the news. If it was true, they needed answers. But now wasn't the time to barrage Judith with questions. Instead, the allowed the women space to comfort each other, and waited for the moment to pass.

Joel prayed again, "Father, we don't know what has happened and we're concerned for our sisters. Please come into this room and make your presence and healing felt. We need you now, more so now than ever. We saw your servant Stephen stoned today in this very city. Our enemies seem to be gaining the upper hand. And now…if…" he broke off, becoming overwhelmed himself. After a long minute's silence, he continued, "If it's true, Father, and if our brother has fallen foul of them too…" he paused again, "then we need your help right now. We cannot do without you. We need your comfort. Send your Holy Spirit again and fill us. We need you now! Help us all."

In the silence that followed, Judith and Tabitha pulled apart and both of them sat on Tabitha's couch. Joel, Mary, Jonas, and Esther gathered round them to offer any support they could.

Joel looked into Judith's tired tearstained eyes, and said gently, "Take your time. Tell us what happened. Where's Mikha?"

Judith sobbed again, "I told you…he's dead. I saw his body…his bruised and broken body." She shuddered and wailed loudly. Tabitha moaned agonisingly again.

"How?" said Joel gently. He motioned to his wife to get closer to Judith, to comfort her.

"They came for him…after Stephen," she couldn't speak, being wracked by emotion. "I saw it…I saw it!"

"What, Stephen?"

"Yes, yes. I was there…with Mikha." She paused, then continued, "We just couldn't do anything. We saw him go to be with Josh!"

"We heard," said Joel grimly. His face was deadly serious. "It's terrible! He was such a good man. A few of us had gathered together and were praying when you arrived."

"Father…what happened?" said Tabitha haltingly.

Judith looked pained and agitated, "I told him…I told him…but he had to have the last word. He had to have his own say."

"Who…Mikha?" asked Joel, not sure what Judith meant.

"Yes, we saw Stephen die. His face was glowing. He said Josh was coming for him. But Mikha was incensed by the injustice of it all. He had grown quite close to Stephen in the last year. The two of them shared so many things…" she began to cry again. "He couldn't stand by and let his friend die. He shouted out, 'You're killing an innocent man! Leave him alone. He doesn't deserve this Yahweh will hold you accountable for your actions today!" It was clear they heard him, even over the sound of the falling stones. One or two of them looked around at him, savagery showing on their faces for having been criticised by him. I took him by the arm and tried to get him away, but he was having none of it. Stephen had sunk to his knees, and we could all hear him saying, 'Father, don't hold this against them,' This was too much for Mikha, who wrenched his arm out of mine and tried to place himself between the throwers and Stephen. A stone hit him on the head, and he fell to the ground. His head was bleeding. I tried to get to him and help him to his feet. They stopped throwing for a moment surprised at the presence of a woman. They allowed me to pull him aside quickly before they went on with their murderous task. They weren't going to stop till a pile of stones were on top of Stephen. Mikha limped away from the scene, leaning heavily on my arm - he'd obviously hurt himself when he hit the ground. We had to pass a man who seemed to have the job of guarding the coats of the throwers. He had some in his arms, and some round his feet. They'd obviously been left in a hurry as the murderers were keen to execute their grim task. He looked at us menacingly as we passed, "You're next!" he growled. I don't know when I've ever been so scared, not for myself, but for Mikha. He was a small man but seemed as if he meant every word."

"A new breed of religious zealot, I'll bet," Joel commented. "Some of the high priest's recent recruits from far and wide are gaining a terrible reputation for brutality. My friend saw him there holding the coats. It wouldn't surprise me if he organised it all, then stood by to watch."

Judith broke in, in despair, "Mikha didn't let it go though. He told him, 'You're just as responsible as they are. You're holding murderers' coats!'"

The man spat at him and cursed. "Remember what I said!" He looked closely at both of us, then said menacingly, "I won't forget you, either of you!"

I pulled Mikha away and got him back to the house. He had been hurt, but his anger affected him more. My sweet sweet Mikha – I don't think I've ever seen him so worked up!"

"By all accounts it was an awful scene," Joel said. "Such a tragedy."

"When I got him home, I bathed his wound. He was shaking," Judith continued. She looked at her daughter, "I'm so glad you weren't there, Tabitha I'm glad you were visiting with Jonas. Your father was struggling, and then…"

It was clear she was coming to the point she was dreading. How would, how could, she tell it?

"Do you wish some water, dear," Mary asked with concern for her niece's state of mind.

"Yes, aunt," said Judith gratefully. She sank back on the couch to gather her resources for the next ordeal. Esther brought her a bowl of water from which she drank gratefully. It seemed to revive her spirit and she continued.

"We were at home, and I was bathing the gash on Mikha's head, when it happened." She stopped. The others waited for her to go on when she was ready. Judith pursed her lips and resumed.

"There was a commotion in the street, and an extremely loud banging on the door, enough to wake the dead. We could hear angry voices outside, and I heard one say, "This is the house of the traitor!" Mikha struggled to his feet. He was visibly angry that they should have followed us home and appeared to be threatening and intimidating us, especially with him being a man who worked in the Temple. "I'll deal with this," he said, and stumbled to the door, still experiencing pain from his injuries. I tried to hold him back, but he wouldn't listen. 'I'll diffuse this Judith. They shouldn't be putting us under this pressure! Just in case they become violent or difficult, get into the back room and hide behind the hanging.' I didn't want to, but he looked at me as if he expected me to obey, so I did. Once I had closed the door, I heard him go to the front door amidst a fury of banging. I thought they would break the door down. Mikha went out and the shouting stopped for some moments. I thought he had calmed them down and heaved a sigh of relief. I was about to come out of the back room when the shouting began again. "He's dead and buried," I heard someone say. 'You're a traitor to Israel. Jesus was a liar, a heretic. He deserved all he got.' It was clear Mikha had been speaking to them about Josh, trying to reason with them, to convince them just like Stephen, that He really was the Messiah. It's clear the crowd was in no mood to listen. The word 'Traitor' was chanted again and again, and then..." she paused to gather her strength. This was going to be difficult. "They rushed him as he stood with his back to the door. There was a pounding sound. Stones were hitting the door and crushing your dear father." Judith looked at Tabitha. "I heard him say 'Jesus, forgive them. They don't know what they're doing. Please don't hold it against them. Have mercy...' and then his voice trailed off. The chant of 'traitor' had increased to fever pitch, and then stopped. I wanted to rush out, but I was transfixed. I just couldn't move. Then I heard the door opening, and there was a dragging sound. A rough voice said, 'We'll leave him here till the morning. He's going nowhere anyway. He won't curse Israel again with his lies. We'll send the guards for him then and they'll take care of him.' Someone else said, 'But what about the woman that was with him? If she's in the house, she'll be a witness.' The original man said, 'Who'd believe these Jesus lovers anyway? All they do is lie. Just in case though, look in that room.' I felt panic fill me. I couldn't be found there. They might kill me too. I rushed to the other side of the room and got in behind the hanging just as I heard the door opening. I prayed that the hanging wasn't still moving after I'd slid behind it. The man obviously wasn't in the mood to do a thorough search. It sounded like he just stood in the doorway, took a cursory look around, cursed, checked out the other rooms and then went back to his friends. My heart was racing, but for the moment it appeared I was safe. I thanked the Lord for that. I heard the original man say, 'Good, I'm glad she's not here. She might have witnessed against us. However, I know what she looks like. If I ever come across her again, that'll be another Jesus lover that will be removed from the face of the earth. This man was a 'religious'. If that was his wife, then they of all people should be eradicated. They're the biggest and greatest danger to our faith.' With that he slammed the door shut, and the crowd seemed to move on. Suddenly any strength I had in me left me, and I panicked. I just couldn't cope. What had they done to Mikha? I rushed into the other room. There he was lying in a corner, absolutely still, still bleeding profusely. There was a trail of blood from the door to where he lay. His head, his lovely head, was bruised and battered, pulverised almost beyond recognition. I went over to him and held him hoping against hope that he would revive, but no…there was so much blood… He was lifeless…it was so grotesque, so horrible. I think I screamed in horror and then utter panic swept over me. I had to get help. I had to get away." She stopped and looked guilty. "I should have stayed, but I just couldn't look on my poor precious Mikha. It was just so awful. And suppose someone came back to check on the body and found me there. I had to escape. I had to get out and go somewhere else. Anywhere. Fear took a hold of me and I rushed into the street and just ran and ran. I'd no idea where I was going. I just had to get away from it all. Fortunately it was getting dark and I didn't attract that much attention given the state I was in. When I stopped for breath, I realised I was at the southern end of the Temple Mount, just at the bridge over the Kidron. It seemed to me that the best place, the only place, I should go, was to the Garden of Gethsemane. I could be alone there and calm down. Josh and I had been there before, usually in or before moments of crisis. The sun was going down as I rushed in between the houses that led to the garden and tried to find the clearing Josh and I had often frequented before. It seemed to me that the bushes around it were more obstinate, thornier than before, but I couldn't care. I just had to get away. I pushed through them, and collapsed, my fear induced strength gone. I cried and poured out my heart to Yahweh, asking 'Why? Why take Mikha?' I just said it over and over again, until absolutely exhausted, I fell asleep."

By now, everyone in the room, including Tabitha, were gathered around her trying to console her. Their grim faces were lined with concern for their ailing sister.

"That's awful, Judith," Joel said quietly. "You've been through too much. You must rest. We'll look after you."

"No," Judith said, getting to her feet. "I can't rest. I have to go back. I can't leave Mikha there. I shouldn't have left him!"

"Stay here. We'll go and see," Joel said.

"No, you don't understand. I had an experience in the garden. I was strengthened by heavenly beings. They gave me the strength to go on. I have to go back to Mikha!"

"What happened in the garden?" asked Mary suspiciously, believing her niece might be delusional.

"Abbas's tent was there, and angels came out of it and gathered around me to strengthen me. One was called Sophia."

The others now all looked at her disbelievingly. Her ordeal must have turned her mind.

"I know what you're thinking," Judith said, "But if our Lord rose from the dead, and those who saw him weren't believed, why couldn't angels strengthen me? Can't you believe? You've been through so much over the last five years. Why couldn't Josh strengthen me in this way?"

Jonas spoke sympathetically. "You'll all remember that the night before Josh died, I followed him into the garden, an while his men were sleeping, I was the only one who heard him praying?"

They all nodded.

"Well, do you remember I told you that after he had prayed for the third time in agony, I saw what seemed like angels coming to him to comfort or strengthen him, I don't know. They seemed real though."

Judith looked at him gratefully for backing her up. "Now do you believe me? I felt strengthened somehow. I don't know how I could feel that way, especially after…" She nearly broke down again, but then pulled herself together. "I felt I had to come here to let you know…as well as to warn you. These people are looking for us. Something new is happening. We're not safe! There's a new mood in Jerusalem."

"Stephen's turned the tide," said Joel agreeing with her, "and now, Mikha too. There's a purge coming. The leaders are up for it now, I believe. We'll have to be very careful!"

"I'm going back," Judith said fiercely. "I should be with Mikha."

"No," Joel said firmly. "Jonas and I will go to your house and see if there's anything we can do."

Judith shook her head. "I'm going whether you like it or not. He's my husband, and I must say goodbye properly. Josh would want me to do this, I know it."

Joel refrained from arguing further. He could see she was determined to do what she said, and he wanted to spare her any unnecessary agony caused by disagreeing with her. "Well then, we'll get ready and leave in a few minutes."

Don Treader

"If you're going Judith, you'll have to change," Mary said. "You're absolutely covered in blood. You'll stand out a mile if anyone comes across you."

"It's dark now, and we'll probably slip through the streets unnoticed," Joel said. "Apart from the watchmen patrols we probably won't meet anyone. Only some misguided people in the lower city will be celebrating the death of Stephen. We can avoid them. Your house isn't as far down in that direction anyway."

Mary took Judith into the living quarters and offered her the chance to wash and change. Minutes later she was back in the atrium, ready to set off on her gruesome journey.

"We'll need torches," Jonas said.

"No," his father replied, "the flames will only attract attention to us. We don't want to be seen!"

"Quite right," agreed Jonas. "We'll just stick close together. There'll probably be enough light coming from houses on the way."

"Let's pray," Joel said, and all of them bowed their heads. "It's been a terrible day, Father, but we know all things are in your hands. Nothing happens without you knowing and comforting. We're sorry about Mikha, our brother...and Stephen. They were servants of yours who didn't deserve what happened to them. Please forgive those who violated their spirits. We know however that they are now with you...and theirs is the better place. Thank you for them, and now as we go to Judith's house, please help us with what we see, and give us wisdom to deal with whatever happens. We place ourselves in your hands...and keep us safe. If persecution is beginning in Jerusalem, then please keep all people of 'The Way' safe tonight! Amen."

With that, the three of them went out into the night.

Chapter Eleven

The night was dark, a black dark, so intense it seemed to swallow them up. It was difficult to see and so the three of them linked arms as they made their way along Joel and Mary's road to the junction with the road that wound up the Western Hill known as Mount Zion. It was only there that a little light filtered from windows that bordered the road on both sides – Joel and Mary's road being populated by rich people's houses with big walls and no windows.

Mikha and Judith's house was plain and functional. When they had relocated to Jerusalem, Mikha had been employed on the Temple staff but had joined it in a much more inferior role than that of Joel. The little family had accepted this gracefully as they were only too glad to be given employment there at all. Many posts in Jerusalem were highly sought after, and so Mikha was grateful for the strings Joel had managed to pull for him. Consequently, their house was situated near the bottom of Mount Zion, just out of the Lower City where the ordinary citizens lived, and further down the hill from the villas of the more affluent priests. There was little traffic on the road at that time of night and so they made their way downhill to the turning off to the right to Judith and Mikha's dwelling. AS they turned into the road, Joel stopped abruptly and pushed them all backwards into the main thoroughfare. He put his finger over his lips to warn them to be quiet, and not to complain loudly at his rough action.

"What's wrong?" asked Jonas in a hoarse whisper.

"" Look, just down there…" Joel pointed down the road and Jonas popped his head round the corner. "I see it," he said.

Judith asked, "What?"

"Just down there," Joel whispered, "there's a light outside your house."

"Oh," said Judith, feeling a sense of annoyance at a possible delay. She just wanted to get it all over with. She was scared as to what she would find in the house and was dreading seeing Mikha again. He had been so awfully treated and the thought of seeing his poor battered body filled her with a horrible sickness.

She knew she had to face it, but at that moment she felt like running. She also felt guilty that she had been unable to help him or tend to him when he had been left for dead in the living room. The men had said he was dead, and she could tell just by looking at him that they were correct, but she had allowed her panic and horror to overwhelm her and so she had run to the garden. Now she was steeled to deal with what she might find. This hold up was more than she needed, and as a result she felt her resolve weakening.

Joel was whispering again, "There's another way into your house?" he asked.

"Yes, there's the back path. It goes behind our row of houses. Why?"

"There's someone down there holding a torch, or perhaps it's a fire in a brazier. It's difficult to tell."

"What do you think it is?"

"I'm guessing, but I wouldn't be surprised if those Temple villains that murdered Mikha, had a guard posted on your house until any evidence could be removed tomorrow."

"Evidence?"

"Yes, Mikha's body…and anything else that might lead any investigation to them."

Judith felt a shiver running down her spine. "Should we just go back to your own house again?"

"No," whispered Joel. "We need to get in there to see exactly what's happened and do anything we can for Mikha if doing anything's possible. Maybe just even to say goodbye…" he hesitated, about to say "for the last time" but thought better of it. He turned round and led the other two back to the path a few metres further up the road. It was not obvious that it led behind the houses, but rather it looked as if it just led into the garden of one of the houses facing onto the main road, which pleased Judith's neighbours as it gave them a sense of security and privacy.

"It's down here," Judith said, and led the way between the two houses, then down behind the row in which she lived. The path was deserted. The guards being unaware of its existence had posted no watch there. Although it was inky black, Judith knew that path like the back of her hand having walked down it many a time, and soon she was leading them into the small walled garden that lay behind her house.

"No noise now," Joel whispered. "It's as quiet as the grave here, any noise from us will be heard by the guard out front. Take off your sandals."

The others complied and Judith pushed the back door open.

"Just leave them behind the door. We can get them on the way out. We can't afford for them to be heard on your tiled floors, Judith. Now, how to we get to the room Mikha's in?"

Judith motioned, then led the way past Mikha's and her bedroom, Tabitha's bedroom, then into the spacious dining room. She whispered, her heart beating fast, "The living room's through that door." She pointed. "That's where they left him." Her voice caught, about to give way to a sob.

Joel's finger went to his lips again. The others could barely make it out.

Judith pushed the door open silently. She gasped. There was light in the room. She drew back quickly, but Joel who had been standing behind her pushed her forward, whispering, "It's all right. There's no-one here. The light's coming from the window."

He crept forward and hiding behind the closed portion of the shutter he surveyed the street outside through the tiny gap through which the light was streaming.

"We're safe for the moment. The light's coming from a torch the guards have set up outside.

I can only see one of them, and he seems to be dosing – he's sitting just beside it, warming himself. He looked around, and suddenly caught his breath. "Oh no!" he exclaimed. "Don't look, Judith."

He was too late. Judith had already seen. Mikha's bloodied and battered body lay crumpled in a corner of the room, the one furthest from the window, the light shining fully on him. She gasped and let out a cry. Joel quickly put his hand over her mouth and looked toward the window. Her cry seemed to have gone unnoticed by the half dozing guard. Judith's tears coursed down her cheeks and wet his fingers. He took his hand away when he was sure she was able to control her sadness.

"All right?" he asked. "I know, it's awful. But we can't afford to be found here. They'll take us too!"

Judith nodded. Joel went over to Mikha and inspected his limp body quickly but thoroughly. "He's dead, I'm afraid. There's no way he could have survived his ordeal. You were right not to hang around. You might have suffered the same fate and been lying beside him now."

Judith shivered. The thought horrified her, and though she would willingly have given up her life for her faith or for Mikha, she wondered if she would have been able to endure the onslaught he had suffered. She was grateful that for the moment she had been spared.

Joel looked at her. "Do you want time with him?" He looked kindly at her, sympathy oozing out of him.

She knew what he meant. It would be her last chance to see or be with Mikha. She desperately did want to be alone with him for one last time, to hold him and kiss his horribly violated body. She knew it would be her last chance and so she grasped at his suggestion gratefully.

"We'll wait in the next room. Just don't make a noise. There's no guarantee the guard won't wake up, or that another will join him and they'll want to make a check on Mikha."

Don Treader

She nodded, and Jonas and he left diplomatically, Joel looking back over his shoulder to check she was all right. She waved him away, while silently praying for strength to cope with what she knew would be a harrowing few minutes.

Suddenly all vestige of strength left her, and she felt her stomach coming up to meet her. She had held up for the past hour or so, but now…all that was gone. She was now alone with Mikha, her wonderful husband…and now facing the ending of their relationship. It would be true to say that it had been a rocky one for so many years, but also…it had been wonderful too. From their courtship in the beginning to the time after Josh's intervention when Tabitha had been raised from the dead – she had lived with a wonderful man, one who had loved her, cherished her, even in the bad times. She was feeling a great sense of loss now. As she looked at his bruised and battered body, lying in a pool of congealing blood, she felt sorry…sorry for the way she had treated him for such a long time, sorry for her blaming him for the death of her baby, sorry for her moods, for her humiliation of him for so long in front of his synagogue flock and their daughter – her sorrow seemed endless, and she felt wracked with guilt. How awful she had been to him when he had only offered her love. He had been a good man, and she was petrified about going on…going on without him, without his strength, his love, his care for her. What was she going to do without him? The tears came, and although she made no noise, her chest heaved with the sorrow she felt. She had cried many times in her life – at the death of her brother, her father, her mother, and of her little baby – but never like this. Tears coursed down her cheeks and fell on Mikha's still face and onto the floor, mingling with his blood. She didn't care any more. She couldn't contain her grief. It took all her energy not to wail and mourn aloud – she didn't care for herself and her own safety, but for those who were with her. At that moment she could have died happily with Mikha, but she had to make sure the others with her were not compromised.

She tried to compose herself, afraid she might alert the guard only a few feet away beyond the shutters. She stroked Mikha's lifeless face for the last time, running her fingers down his cheeks wet with her tears. She kissed his bruised and cut forehead, ignoring the congealed blood. "I'm sorry my love, my sweet, sweet love!" she wept. "I shouldn't have left you earlier. I was just so scared, I panicked. I shouldn't have left you alone! I'm so sorry!" When she had run out of the house earlier, she had believed him to be dead according to his murderer's assertion. It struck her now that perhaps she should have waited with him just in case he had still been alive. She might have been able to help him. At her lowest ebb now, with the guilt flooding in. Not for the first time during this crisis, was she beginning to feel overwhelmed by her emotions. Then into that forest of self-condemnation came a ray of light, just like a beam of sunlight filtering through a dense canopy of leaves and branches. Mikha had told her to hide, to leave him, to protect herself. Yes, panic had overwhelmed her at the time, but if she hadn't left, she wouldn't have had that experience in the garden, in which Josh seemed to

72

help her. And what about Tabitha? If she had died with him there, what would have become of Tabitha. She was Mikha's pride and joy. If both her parents were killed in such a violent way, how would she have coped, how would she ever have recovered. Logically it was right that she was still alive, to take care of their daughter. That's what Mikha would have wanted. She felt comfort in this thought, as if it had been intended that she should live. Was Josh helping her, she wondered?

"I'll always love you Mikha," she breathed into his ear. "Even when I treated you so badly, deep down I loved you and respected you. You didn't have to keep loving me...but you did. And you've brought out the best in me. I'm so thankful for you, for your love and care all these years. Please forgive me for how I treated you. I did love you...and I do love you..." Her tears came again, and she buried her head in his chest, her long blond hair falling around them into the pools of blood and tears. She didn't care. He had been the love of her life – the only love of her life – and she was going to have to go on without him. She remembered earlier that day, how he had stood up to those who murdered Stephen. She was proud of this man who had exemplified courage, loyalty, support and love throughout his life. She had been privileged to know him, to love him, to bear his children – but now all that was gone. She felt alone again. It was all just so awful! She heard Joel whisper from the doorway, "Judith..." She knew he was concerned about the time. They would need to be leaving. But at that moment, she just couldn't. Her heart was breaking. How could she leave this sweet kind amazing man? She would never see his smiling encouraging face again. She placed her finger on his half open eyes and closed them. "It's all I can do for you my love," she whispered. "I don't want to leave you or let you down ever again. I'm just so...so sorry!'" She wept again, and her heart sank to the lowest depths it had ever been. Once more her head buried in his chest and she put her arms around his body to hug him to her, regardless of the blood and mess. She was having to leave him, and her heart was breaking. As she lifted herself up from this embrace, she felt something hot at her side. She put her hand down to where the heat was coming from wondering if somehow it was warm blood. But it couldn't be. Mikha had been dead for hours and his blood was cold. Was she bleeding? It felt hot like blood, but she wasn't wet. Her hand felt a lump in her robe. That's where the heat was coming from, she surmised. And it was vibrating, ever so gently. Before even she put her hand into her pouch, she knew exactly what it was. It was the cross trinket she had been given by Sophia in the garden. She drew it out quickly and looked at it. It was pulsating in such a way that the green light from the cross was morphing into something bigger than its shape...and once again, as she looked, she saw the face of Josh beginning to form on it. There was a stillness in the room, even more so than there had been. Gone were the crippling emotions of despair and guilt. Somehow her senses felt focused and invigorated, her awareness heightened. She now felt as if someone was behind her. There was a presence in the room with her. She felt a sense of peace, a sense of intense love. It was as if the person was absolutely focusing on her and massaging, lifting her out of how she felt.

"Josh!" she whispered. She didn't look behind her. She just knew it was him. His image may have been in front of her in the glowing object, but she knew without a doubt he was there with her. From the depths of despair, his presence had lifted her to virtually heaven. She daren't look round in case he would disappear, and it would all go away. It was just as she had felt when he had personally lifted Tabitha from death and had given her back to Mikha and herself. In a matter of moments, she was now feeling soothed, comforted, renewed, loved, and exhilarated, all in one. Should she cling to her guilt and fear? She knew this would be wrong. She knew that she shouldn't. Josh was trying to reach her. She threw herself into what he was giving her...wholeheartedly. She couldn't afford to go back. That wasn't what Josh wanted. Into her mind flashed Josh's words from so long ago, "You will smile again. I will not leave you." She looked at the image throbbing in front of her. Was Josh's image smiling at her? Suddenly she had the uncontrollable urge to place it upon Mikha's forehead. She did so, and her heart leaped. Had Mikha jerked under her? She dismissed the thought. The image glowed on his forehead. She heard a rasping sound. Was Mikha trying to breathe? She held him close and tried to feel if his heart was beating. She could feel nothing. She was about to put it down to her imagination, when the rasping sound came again, and Mikha's body appeared to jerk and try to cough. She said excitedly, "Mikha! Mikha!" into his ear. His eyes flickered open and he looked up at her with recognition. "Judith!" he breathed, as if his breath was coming from deep within him. "Judith!" he breathed again.

"I'm here, my love," she whispered excitedly. "I'm right here beside you."

Did she fancy his lips moved into a smile?

"Judith, I love you."

"And I love you too," she said. Once again, her tears washed his face.

"You mustn't cry, Judith," he said. "I'll always love you...and Tabitha!"

For a moment with Josh's presence so real in the room, she had wondered if he was going to raise Mikha into life, just as he had done for Tabitha before.

She wanted more than anything for this to happen. She believed without the shadow of a doubt that Josh could have done it. He had proved his power over death. But this time wasn't like that time in Capernaum. She sensed that this wasn't going to be the outcome. This wasn't his purpose. After experiencing this height of exhilaration and expectation, she could feel a hint of sadness beginning to creep into her being.

Mikha struggled to speak again, "No, Judith. Not now. I'll see you and Tabitha again. I must rest now, but you both have work to do." Judith wanted to cry and held on to him tightly again while kissing his forehead and his lips.

"I love you," she said again and again.

"I know," he said. "Josh wishes me to go…but he will go with you…and Tabitha." He closed his eyes, and once again his body was lifeless. There was no sound of breath at all.

The sense of Josh's presence began to fade too. It seemed to Judith that while all this had been happening, the room had been filled with light, although physically it had remained the same. The light had been in her spirit. The cross had stopped throbbing now, Josh's image was no longer evident upon it. She was about to replace it in her pouch, when something stopped her. It was as if she wasn't finished there yet. The object was still hot, and she held onto it. Suddenly she heard a sound from outside the window. A shadow flitted over the room. Something was at the window! She heard voices, and she froze.

"Aare you sleeping Joseph?"

"Not at all, Tobias. I was just resting my eyes. There's nothing happening here. We're wasting our time."

Tobias laughed. "You're probably right, Joseph. I'll just take a look." The shadow flitted over the wall again, and Judith knew he was looking through the slit in the shutters, his body blocking out some of the light from the torch. She prayed, "Don't let him see me Lord. Make me invisible." She held her breath, hardly daring to move or believe.

"That's odd," she heard Tobias say. "I could swear I saw two bodies in there at first. It's too dark inside. My eyes must be playing tricks on me though. I've had too much for supper."

"Hold the torch up," said Joseph laughing. "I'll take a look. I'd have heard something if someone else was there. And anyway, who'd leave another body there? They'd have had to be mad!" His shadow now flitted over the wall as he approached the shutter, then it vanished suddenly.

"You fool!" she heard him shout, and then he cursed.

"What's wrong?" Tobias asked. "Do you see another body?"

"No, you fool I was just about to look in when you allowed some ash from the torch to drop on my head. You almost set my hair on fire."

"What hair!" Tobias joked.

Joseph laughed grudgingly, "There's nothing there," he said. "What could there be? I'd have had to be asleep not to notice."

It was Tobias's turn to laugh now. "You probably were. At least the ash has wakened you up!"

Joseph snorted. He wasn't amused but gave way to his friend's banter. "We're wasting our time, looking after a dead body. It's to be collected in the morning, according to Saul."

"Oh, I know. He's got the bit between his teeth. He's all out to get the people of 'The Way'. The man inside there is one of the Temple Religious. Saul really wants to smoke them out."

"They're the worst kind. They're diluting our religion with their rubbish. How could the Messiah have been already? We'd all have known about it."

"Too true. But what about that weirdo who got killed today? He seemed to know what he was talking about. I was there when he made his defence. He knew our history like the back of his hand."

"Yes, but he went too far with this stuff about Jesus. He claimed that he came back from the dead. Never!"

"Dangerous talk indeed! He was convincing though."

"How do you mean?"

"Just before they took him to stone him, his face was glowing. I thought he looked like an angel."

"You're mad yourself."

"No, he did look different. And there's something else…"

"What's that?" said Joseph dryly.

"People who are about to die don't usually ask for their accusers or killers to be released from any blame."

"Did he say that?"

"Yes, I heard him. It was as if he was forgiving us for stoning him. The religious in there said the same thing."

"These people are weird! If they had their way, they'd corrupt our faith."

"That's why Saul's got it in for them. He's like a madman. You can see the fire in his eyes when he talks about them. He's a man driven!"

"And that's why we're guarding a dead body. Do you think he thinks it might rise again?" Joseph laughed.

"Who knows. But I think it's more because of the wife."

"The wife?"

"Yes, apparently he had words with the man who's dead in there. He was egging on the stoning party, looking after their cloaks, when the man passed him and gave him abuse for helping them."

"I can see why that might annoy him. And that's why he brought the stoners here?"

"Yes, but the man's wife was with him and helped him away. Saul was convinced they were people of 'The Way' He wants her too. "

Judith stiffened. They meant her.

Tobias continued, "He's determined to get her. I don't know why he's got it so bad. He says he would recognise her anywhere. She's one of them. What her husband said to him seems to have got to him and he's out for vengeance on anyone linked with him."

"Did you not say she helped her husband away? Wouldn't they have come back here then? After all, that's where the stoning party found him - inside."

"After they threw his body inside, they did have a look to see if anyone else was there. They didn't find anyone, so they left. But Saul's not happy. He wants to find the woman. He's convinced there's a network of religious involved in 'The Way' and he's determined to find them all and stamp them out."

"So, she's gone to one of their cells?"

"That's what he believes, and he's convinced that if he finds her, he'll be able to destroy them, cell by cell."

"That Saul's ambitious!"

"You're right, and while he's rising up in the eyes of the High Priest, he's got us spending the night looking after a corpse!"

The two of them laughed bitterly, with a hint of sarcasm, then after a few moments silence, Joseph said, "I'll leave you to it then, Tobias. Don't let your charge get away!"

Again, they laughed at the ludicrousness of it. "I don't think the wife will come back."

"I think you're right. These people are gutless. They may talk religious, but at the first sign of trouble, they run."

"The man inside didn't."

"Well then, their either timid or mad!"

"Maybe so," said Joseph, and left whistling as he went, happy to have discharged his grim task.

"Remember, don't let him get away now," he shouted back to his friend, and they both guffawed.

Judith looked over to the door leading to the dining room and saw Joel framed in it. He must have been there much of the time the men had been talking. She hadn't seen him as she had been preoccupied with what they were saying and with her own preservation. Inwardly she thanked Josh for making her invisible when it had seemed so real that she might have been seen. She slipped the cross back into her pouch then leaned over Mikha again. She kissed him lovingly and lingeringly on the forehead, and knew it was time for her to go. She hated leaving him there, but she knew in her heart that he was no longer there. Like Joe, like her mother and father, her little baby and Faithie before him, they were all now safe with Josh. His body might be lying there, but it would soon be disposed of by cruel men. She shuddered at the thought but allowed her belief to push that thought away, and she stood to her feet. Joel motioned her to come to him, and she quickly crossed the room.

"Are you all right?" he whispered, sympathy in his voice. In the darkness she could barely see his face.

"Yes," she said.

He squeezed her arm. "He's with the Lord now," he reassured her.

"Oh, I know. Without the shadow of a doubt. Josh has told me."

"Is there anything you need. I heard what those men said. You won't be able to come back here again."

Judith shook her head, only too glad to get away. Then a thought struck her, and she darted into her bedroom. Joel stood at the door and heard the sound of a drawer opening followed by frantic rustling and it closing again. Then something scraped across a wooden surface, followed by a bang as it fell over.

"Sorry," Judith breathed. She was standing beside him again. "I had to get this, but it fell over. I couldn't see in the dark." She was clutching a small squarish object in her hands. Joel couldn't make out what it was, but he wasn't in the mood to linger. Judith quickly tucked it into the folds of her robe.

"Come on, let's get out of here," he said, "and don't forget your sandals." These were retrieved at the back door then all three of them left the house and made their way through the garden onto the back path. Soon they were once again hurrying along the pitch-dark empty roads that led to Joel's house, and safety.

This had been one of the worst days of Judith's life…and yet…once again Josh had so clearly met with her and been with her. In deep distress she might have been. In terrifying despair, she might have wallowed. But she wasn't defeated. She would press through…yes, without the love of her life, but not without her Lord.

Chapter Twelve

The mood in Joel and Mary's house was subdued when they entered. It was clear to Judith that Tabitha had been crying. She had had the unenviable task of having to wait for news of her father without being able to do anything. Mary and Esther her part-time maid as well as a childhood friend of Judith's when she had first visited her aunt, had done their best to comfort her, to occupy her, but without much success. Tabitha was the light of her father's life, and she adored him. He had been there for her in the early days, being her supporter and encourager when her mother had been depressed and unpleasant. She had come to love her mother in more recent times, understanding why it was she had been so difficult during her childhood, but also appreciating now the love she poured into the family. Nevertheless, she was her father's girl, and now felt his apparent death terribly. Should she hope that perhaps Josh could bring him back as he had done her? Was this too much to ask? She prayed and prayed again, but somehow didn't feel as if her prayers cut through. She felt despair and abject fear. She would just have to wait till her mother and the others returned to find out the worst. Maybe they would find he had not died, but just been unconscious. She could only hope; but realistically, this possibility seemed futile. Where was her mother? She really needed her now!

When they returned, it was clear to Tabitha that they were not bearers of good news. Their faces showed their sadness and their resignation to Mikha's death. She ran to her mother and embraced her. "He's dead, isn't he…really dead?"

"Yes," said Judith sadly, unable to look her daughter in the eye. "He really is." She wished she could have given her daughter the news she was hoping for. "He really is. But…"

Tabitha drew back and looked at her mother. What did this 'but' mean? Was she about to tell her of a miracle? For a moment, her heart raced, but she all at once realised that if her father had been alive, they'd have brought him with them. She sank down in a couch and cried sore heart wrenching tears.

Judith sat down beside her and comforted her. Joel looked on grimly then said, "It's been difficult…we need something to drink. Esther…?"

Esther looking sombre too, knew what to do, and left the room. She returned with a brimming jug and some bowls which she proceeded to fill. This done she went around the group giving each person their bowl. When she came to Tabitha, she held it out to her, but Tabitha shook her head. She was still weeping, although now silently to herself. Her mother took the bowl from Esther and held it to Tabitha's lips. "Come on, dear. It'll help. Sometimes doing normal things helps."

Tabitha allowed her mother to place the bowl against her lips and sipped.

She then looked at her mother and said, "What did you mean by the 'but'…?"

Everyone in the room looked at Judith as she started to speak quietly. "I spoke to Mikha."

"You spoke to him, mother," repeated Tabitha incredulously. "Was he alive then?"

All eyes were fixed on Judith now, and she said, "Yes…and, no."

"What do you mean?" asked Tabitha. "Please tell me…I need to know."

Joel looked over at her and spoke sympathetically, "We got into the room where your father had been left. A guard had been placed outside the house. I saw your father. I'm sorry, Tabitha, but he was very much dead. He could never have survived what they did to him." Tabitha looked crushed after having placed all her hopes on what her mother might say. All eyes remained on Judith, however, waiting for her explanation.

"Yes, your father was dead when we got there." Her hand went to her eyes to wipe away the tears that were forming there. "They'd treated him so badly. I can't begin to, or want to, tell you how he looked or how they had treated him. It was awful. He was so bruised, so disfigured. They'd left him in an awful mess. His blood was everywhere!" She now wept.

"But what did you mean by 'but'?" Tabitha asked. "How could there be any 'but' in that situation?"

Judith pulled herself together and stopped crying. She said quietly, but definitely, "With Josh, and with Yahweh, all things are possible."

The others looked on in rapt silence while she told her story. At the point where she mentioned that Mikha had spoken to her, their jaws dropped open. There was no hint of disbelief – they all knew Josh too well to doubt. When she told them Mikha's words for Tabitha, Tabitha physically wilted, dropping back into her couch and weeping copiously. Judith put her arm around her daughter and held her close. "He loved you very much. He had your name on his lips with his dying breath." The two of them rocked back and forwards in grief for some moments. The comfort Judith had brought her daughter by relaying Mikha's words, and her experience, began to have an effect, and both women slowly ceased crying and re-joined the others.

"That's some story, Judith," said Joel. "Jonas and I were on the other side of the door and heard nothing." Jonas nodded in assent.

"We had to be quiet," Judith said, "but it's all true. It didn't take long – it was over in seconds – but it was all very real. I felt as if Josh were there with me, making it all happen. He's given us a message."

"Message?" asked Mary.

"Yes, we've work to do for him. It's not the end for Tabitha and myself."

"Of course not," said Mary, trying to grapple with what Judith meant.

Judith looked at Tabitha, "He said he would go with us."

"What did he mean, mother?"

"I don't know, dear, but when a message like that is given, I know that Josh will keep his word. Time will tell."

In telling her story, Judith had omitted to mention the glowing green cross with Josh's image. She felt it was enough to tell of Josh's presence in the room with her. The cross had been given to her as something special, and just as in the case of her earlier trinket, knowledge of it was not for public consumption. It would only be shown to those who needed to know about it.

She hadn't as yet got to the conversation between the two guards. She had only focused on Mikha.

"It's clear that Josh is doing something new," Joel said. "Things are changing here in Jerusalem, and not for the better. However, just as Judith says, whatever happens he will be with us. Did he not say before he left for heaven, 'I will never leave you or forsake you'? He's proved that today – what with Stephen's death, and now Mikha's."

Esther chipped in. "That's right. I heard that Stephen claimed to see Josh coming for him as they stoned him."

"And now your story, Judith," Joel said. "Your experience earlier today in the garden, and then in the room with Mikha. It's clear that Josh will be right beside us, no matter what happens to us."

Judith nodded, and Tabitha allowed herself a slight smile.

"But these are changed days, and I sense there's a real change coming." Joel said. "I believe Josh is preparing us. We may be headed in a direction we wouldn't choose to go, but he's showing us we're not alone. He'll be with us." He went on to narrate the conversation between the two men outside Judith's house. He'd heard everything, and as he spoke his face became even more lined with concern.

"We've had things fairly easy so far. We've been allowed a good bit of freedom. The authorities haven't really clamped down upon us. They've been waiting to see how things go. As you know, Gamaliel urged the Council some time back to make sure they weren't fighting Yahweh by fighting the people of 'The Way'. But that's all changing. Who'd ever have thought that one, or two, of our number would be killed. Today will go down in history as the day 'The Way' received its first martyrs!"

Everyone looked solemn.

Joel continued. "We're all in danger now. They'll turn over every stone to flush out our people. None of us will be safe, or exempt. I may work for the Sanhedrin and command a position of respect, but if they knew we had been holding meetings in our upper room for the past few years, my position would count for nothing." Mary looked alarmed.

"And you, Judith. You're in grave danger too. They know you. You've been seen. You've been identified. They'll be all out looking for you. Once they get things together and find out exactly Mikha's position as a religious in the Temple, you'll be even more valuable to them. They'll want to know what you know…and who you know."

Judith looked troubled. "They seemed to know about Mikha already. One of the men mentioned that he was a religious" She trembled, "Where should I go, what will I do?"

"Nothing," said Joel, "…at least for the moment. We'll look after you and hide you here. Tabitha too. Because of my position, they won't think to look here." He looked concerned as a thought struck him. "We'll all have to be careful though. We're vulnerable. If persecution takes hold of Jerusalem, many people have been at our gatherings and in our house. Under pressure, someone might give us away."

Mary began to tremble now, joining Judith.

Joel looked directly at Esther, "I'm glad it was you working for us tonight and not Martha and Jeremiah. It was maybe providential that it was their night off. But your working for us might put you, or us, in danger. You've seen everything and know about Judith and today's events. Are you sure you wish to be involved with us? It might be dangerous for you?"

Esther looked him back in the eye, "I'm with you, sir. I've served this house for years, even if at present it's only when Jeremiah and Martha have days off or holidays. I'm Judith's friend…and yours too. I'm a follower of Josh's. I'll never betray you, or him. I want to continue with you and the mistress whenever it's possible."

Joel looked glad and gave her a hug. Mary joined them. "We love you, and appreciate you, Esther. You are much more than a servant to us. You are indeed our friend, our sister." They all hugged again.

"We'll have to develop a plan of campaign," said Joel. "If Judith and Tabitha are to stay here from now on, they'll have to disappear off the streets totally." He looked at Judith. "Who's going to miss you? Who knows anything about you and your movements?"

"Well, Mikha will be missed from work, but they'll know about the circumstances. After all, they killed him, and are now hounding me."

"What about your maid?" Joel asked. "Won't she miss you?"

"Elisa? Yes, of course. She didn't work full time and only stayed with us on the very few occasions necessity dictated – for a bit of cleaning and cooking whenever we had guests. We did most things ourselves. She's one of us, of course."

Joel's brow furrowed in thought, then he said, "She'll have to disappear too. You say she's one of us?"

"Yes, she was recommended to us by a fellow believer, actually one of your friends. We'd just arrived in Jerusalem and he suggested her as a good worker and good sister."

"Who was that?"

"Nicodemus."

"Good old Nicodemus," Joel smiled. "Good, I'll get a message to him in the morning to warn her family to help her make herself scarce. Did she know anything about your link with us?"

"No, I don't think so," said Judith. "We tended to be here quite a lot, and due to the increasing tension we didn't give out our locations when we went out. She was quite friendly with you, Tabitha. Did you tell her anything?"

"No, Mother. She was a good friend, and we shared much about Josh. But that was all. I don't think I ever spoke about Aunt Mary and Uncle Joel." Then as an afterthought, she added, "I did mention Jonas, however. She knew I was seeing him and liked him a lot." Jonas flushed.

Joel's smile broadened. "We all knew that, Tabitha. You're almost an item. Would she know where he stayed?"

"No, sir. It was just girl talk."

"Good. Well, that's settled. There are thousands of Jonas's in Jerusalem. They'd never track him down if they ever interview her." He breathed a sigh of relief, "It looks like we're safe for now. However, we must be vigilant. Over the past few years our people have multiplied in the city. Most of them know the houses where we meet, although they tend to stick to their own fellowship groups. I'm going to do two things. With today's martyrdoms and a possible surge of persecution about to happen, I'll warn other leaders not to make public where our houses are and try to keep their members from moving between them. It's very unlikely that no-one will ever mention us. We've been here since the beginning, although it doesn't appear the authorities suspect anything. Since Josh's resurrection, I've tried to keep a low profile, especially because I didn't want to bring attention to Josh's men who often stay here. However, that may have to stop for a while. They can't move about openly. I'll get some of my believer friends to warn me if they're coming to us and we can prepare for them if they wish to stay here. If we're reported to the authorities, we'll have to be ready. The second thing I'll do is devise a plan as to what we should do if the Temple police come to raid us." He turned to Judith and Tabitha, "Are you sure you want to stay here? You might be at risk."

Judith replied, "I'd feel safe here, Joel." Tabitha nodded. She smiled wryly, "I'll get to see more of Jonas." Jonas smiled.

Judith went on, "My only fear is that we put you at risk. You've managed to avoid detection up till now, and I wouldn't want either of you to be in trouble."

"With a good Yahweh-given plan, we'll ride things out, I think," Joel replied. "Persecution may go on for a while, but it can't go on for ever. The authorities will get tired, and there are now so many people of 'The Way', if they clamp down too much, there'll be precious few people left in Jerusalem." He smiled, "They'll all be in jail, or have left the city…and that won't help economically. No, Judith and Tabitha, you're welcome to be our guests as long as we're here."

They looked at him gratefully, and Judith said, "We won't compromise you though, and at a good opportunity perhaps we ourselves might leave the city. We'd be anonymous in Galilee if we settled there."

"Not in Capernaum," Mary said.

"No, certainly not in Capernaum," Judith agreed. "Our history is tarnished there. But there are other places."

Joel said, "Let's leave that for Yahweh to work out. You don't have to leave just now. Just rest and recover from your horrible ordeal. Yahweh will move things on when He wishes. Look at how He's kept us and been with us so far. And all your experiences today – in the face of such horrors – I know you'll be hurting, and are devastated, but I also know that He's with you. It's funny how in the face of such trauma and danger, He makes Himself real and so near. His hand is upon you!"

Mary spoke, "Joel, I think we've said enough tonight. Judith and Tabitha will be tired." She looked at them, "Do you wish me to spend the night with you? Might it help either of you feel better?"

Tabitha shook her head. Judith replied for them both, "No, thank you all the same, Aunt Mary. It's been an awful day in many ways, but Josh has also been close. I need to sleep and to cleanse my mind of everything. I just want to pray and go to sleep…if I can sleep."

Tabitha nodded, "Me too. My father's dead and I don't know how I'll go on without him. I just kissed him goodbye this morning…" A tear rolled down her cheek.

Judith hugged her. "I know Tabitha. It's just how I feel too. But he was incredibly brave, and although it might not help much now, remember when he spoke his last words to us, he told us he loved us." Both women were crying now. "Josh is with us, and Yahweh will strengthen us. He's given us His Spirit."

"Do you wish a room each?" Mary asked, a bit sceptical that either of them would manage on their own on their first night after Mikha's death.

They looked at each other and agreed, "Perhaps not tonight. We want to be there for each other. But maybe later…"

Mary nodded in understanding. "Esther, would you please make up the mats and prepare a room for them both?"

"Gladly mistress. Would it help if I stayed the night to help with things in the morning?"

"Most certainly, if your family won't need you. It is late for getting home.

"The boys are at friends, and Rhoda's with my sister. They knew I was working here today, and anyway, they're getting old enough to look after themselves."

"Well, we'd be glad to have you," said Joel smiling.

Esther bustled off to do her duties, and the others sat down again, and finished their drinks.

It was as if everything that needed to be said, had been said, and all that remained was silence. Each drank it in gladly, trying to come to terms with their new circumstances. Eventually Joel said, "I'd like to pray, if you'd like?"

The three women and Jonas nodded, and each bowed their heads.

"Father," Joel intoned, "we're here today after probably the biggest trauma each of us has ever faced. In the city there was the death of your servant Stephen, and in our hearts and lives, the tragic death of our friend and brother, Mikha. I can't begin to imagine what Judith and Tabitha are feeling, but I know you know. You've already met with, and comforted Judith. But both the grief and loss that she and Tabitha share is raw, is real. They need your continuing comfort and presence. You promised us Lord when you were alive, that you would send us the Comforter, and that you did on Pentecost so many years ago. Now Father, now Lord, send Him now into our hearts, into Tabitha and Judith's hearts, and work a healing miracle. While on earth you did many miracles. Now we're asking you for a special one. We know you love us, and we thank you for that. But we're going to need your help and strength, your guidance, and your comfort, for the days that are coming. Pour out your Spirit on your church and keep us all safe. I ask these things in Josh's name, your Son Jesus."

A stillness settled on the room, and they kept their heads bowed as they savoured it. The silence was broken by Esther who came in, stopped, and whispered, "My Lord!" They opened their eyes and looked at her. "I saw it again," she whispered.

"What?" Joel asked her.

"Something like a fire, flickering for a split second over each of your heads as they were bowed. I wouldn't have interrupted if I'd known you were praying, but I'm glad I did. It was like a smaller version of that first Pentecost."

Each knew what she meant. They had all been there in the upper room when the Spirit arrived.

Don Treader

Joel closed his eyes again and spoke, "Thank you Lord, for giving us that sign of your love and peace. We thank you!"

Each of them concurred.

Esther said, "The room's ready ma'am."

"Thank you, Esther," Mary said, and she led Judith and Tabitha to their room.

Joel said to Esther, "Thank you Esther for helping us out tonight. I don't know where we'd have been without you."

"We all go back a long way sir, and we all have the same Lord, and the same Father. I believe He places us in the right place at the right time."

"You're absolutely right, Esther. And you've indeed been a blessing to us tonight."

"Thank you, sir."

At that point Mary returned. "That's them settled, poor dears. What an experience for them to have gone through today. It's awful!"

"Indeed," Joel agreed. "But in everything Yahweh knows what He's doing It's His plan. Remember five years ago, we sat here and debated what He was doing with Josh. We couldn't see how His death fitted in. Well, now we know. It's difficult to see how Yahweh will work out Stephen's and Mikha's deaths, but He will. Nothing happens without Him knowing about it or sanctioning it. We may not see it now, but He'll have a way of bringing good out of this evil."

The others looked at him, not sure what to believe. Jonas said, "I'm tired, sir. I need to go to bed too. I've seen my first dead body ever today."

"Sorry Jonas," Joel said. "I hadn't thought of that. Are you all right?"

"Yes, but I feel desperately sorry for Tabitha. She had to wait here while we were away, and she needs much comforting."

"You know something, Jonas. The scriptures say, 'Yahweh places the solitary in families'. You know what that means?"

"Yes, sir. I think so." Jonas seemed a little unsure what his father was getting at.

"Well let me tell you, son. Tabitha feels on her own now. Her father's gone. Yahweh has placed her here, in our family, for us to comfort her…for you to comfort her."

"I see, sir. I'll do my best." He confessed, "I'm developing feelings for her."

"I know, son. I've seen it happening over the past five years since she first entered our house. You were both so shy then, but now…Yahweh has given her to you to comfort, to encourage and to perhaps love."

Jonas looked gratefully at his father for his understanding and for the lack of condemnation he had half expected.

"Thank you, sir," He said, and turned away. "But now, I must go to bed. I'm tired."

When they were alone, Joel and Mary sat on separate couches facing each other. Both said nothing for a while, each lost in their own thoughts. Mary had a strained look on her face, something Joel was not unaware of.

"What's wrong, Mary?" he eventually asked softly and kindly.

"We're in a bad position, aren't we Joel?"

"No, I don't think so." He paused, "You mean with the Sanhedrin and the leaders?"

"Yes, and any hotheads that wish to persecute us."

"Anything's possible, dear. I can't deny it. Yahweh didn't spare Josh, and He didn't spare Stephen or Mikha today. We've no reason to believe He'll spare us."

"You're not making me feel better, Joel."

"I know, I know," he said with a concerned look on his face. "But we have something going for us that people who are not believers haven't. We know whom we believe in and we know He loves us and is close to us. Whatever happens, He won't let us go."

Mary nodded, but stayed silent.

Joel continued, "The reports of Stephen's death today were amazing. Before Judith arrived on our doorstep, I heard from a man who had been there, that Stephen had spoken before the Council and put up a wonderful case for Josh, and a superb history of Yahweh's dealings with us. He was inspired. What annoyed them all was the fact that as he spoke his face glowed like an angel's and he claimed he could see Josh sitting at the right hand of the Father. It was like He was coming for him. It was then that they grabbed him and decided to stone him. And again, as the stones were hitting him, he seemed transfixed. He knelt and said, 'Father please don't hold this against them.'

My witness said, it was just as though he fell asleep before them."

"That's terrible," whispered Mary, beginning to shake.

"Yes…and no. Just look. He wasn't on his own when he died. Josh was with him. It was like he was being welcomed into heaven!" Joel continued, "And Mikha. We don't know what he felt when he was being killed outside his house. He certainly knew what he was doing when he stood up for Stephen at his stoning. I believe Josh was with him, helping him. But whatever he suffered as he was being stoned himself, we know Josh was with him, because of what Judith said…and I don't believe she imagined it. Josh was there in the room with her at that very personal moment…and Mikha, yes dead Mikha, spoke to her and told her Josh was with her. He would see her and Tabitha again. What more proof do we believers need that he will see us through our tribulations, our testings, and even our deaths?"

"I believe you," Mary said. "He's kept us so far. He can take care of us with all that might happen next." She was trembling though. Joel went over to her and cuddled her.

Don Treader

"It's been a hard day," he said. "I didn't know Stephen well…apart from his reputation for being filled with Yahweh's Spirit; but Mikha…we've lost a dear friend today. We knew him as a young man. We encouraged him to continue his studies in the village synagogue where your relatives brought you up. We saw him happily married to Judith, and later when he arrived with his family for Passover - remember Tabitha had been not long dead, then raised?"

Mary nodded.

Joel went on, "We saw him next when he lost his job and came to us for help. He was full of high praise for Josh. It was he, and Judith, that helped us come to faith ourselves – I even watched Josh die with him. The two of them, and Tabitha, struggled a bit when they came to Jerusalem. We helped them as he settled into his new job. It was good we could share so much time with him and his family as 'The Way' was growing. He was a man of faith and integrity. He didn't want to compromise his beliefs about Josh. That's what lost him the synagogue in Capernaum, and at times put him on the wrong foot with his bosses here in Jerusalem. He was a good man. He certainly didn't deserve all this. Neither did Judith or Tabitha. It's our duty to look after them now."

Mary nodded again. "Yes, Yahweh's speciality is with the widows and orphans, dear."

"You're right, as always, Mary. You've given us the right words for the right time. It'll take time, but we'll all come through this."

"Bed!" said Mary. "You're exhausted, as am I."

They walked out of the room, holding hands.

"I hope Judith and Tabitha will be all right tonight!" Mary said.

In their room, Judith and Tabitha hugged each other before going to their mats. Both felt a strong sense of loss and were not a little tearful. Judith said to her daughter, "You were very brave today. I'm sorry I had to leave you to cope while I went back to the house. Perhaps you'd rather have been there too?"

"No Mother. I don't think I could have stood to see father that way."

Judith thought back to when she was seventeen and had had to deal with the emaciated body of her father. "You'd have coped, dear. But I'm glad for your sake you didn't see him. It was awful."

"It's amazing he spoke, mother."

"It was Josh's doing. He allowed it to happen. He was there."

"What did father say? Please tell me again."

"He said he loved you. He had to go but he would see us again. And…that Josh had work for the two of us to do."

"Is that all?"

"Yes, but that was enough. I wanted him to go on. I had hoped Josh might bring him fully back to life, just as He did with you…but he didn't." Judith began to cry, and Tabitha hugged her.

"Both father and I have something in common, mother. Both of us were brought back from the dead, even if father was, only for a brief moment."

"I've been so privileged," said Judith.

Both women smiled through their tears. Tabitha continued, "I believe we're more privileged than many families!"

Her mother agreed with her. They pulled apart and got ready for bed. Tabitha was ready first, and snuggled down under the covers on her mat, and soon was snoring gently, totally exhausted from her trauma-filled day.

Judith on the other hand took her time, sitting on her mat deep in thought, trying to make sense of all the day's events. It had started as a normal day with Mikha going to work, Tabitha leaving at lunchtime to go and see Jonas, and her meeting Mikha in town when he left his work. They had become caught up in that awful crowd that had stoned Stephen, and had somehow or other annoyed that little man holding the coats. As far as she understood, it was he that had sent the murderers to her house, the ones that had killed Mikha. He had perhaps even been with them. In a few short moments her life had been ruined, changed for ever. And what about Mikha's, she thought? Then there had been the amazing events in the garden...and Sophia's cross! She didn't know how she had had the strength to get to Joel and Mary's, or for that matter, the courage to go back to her own house to face Mikha's dead body. She sensed inside her a deep sadness, and a strong awareness of despair. Things were never going to be the same again. Her memory took her back to how she had felt when her brother, then her father and mother had died. The despair, the loneliness, the sadness. And then there was her first baby. The bottom had fallen out of her world...her smile was gone... She was brought up short in the midst of these thoughts. Her smile, where had that thought come from? She knew very well from where. It was Josh. Away back, he and Abbas had told her that her smile would be lost but would return again. She clutched at her robe, putting her hand into its inner fold, and drew out a familiar object. It had been with her since she had been given it by Josh when she was seven. It had seen her through the dark days, of her teens, her marriage and Josh's demise. It was the main thing she treasured in life, and the only thing she had wanted to take with her when she had left her house for the last time earlier that day. She looked at it lovingly, and yes, there was the smile of that seven-year-old girl. It reassured her, it calmed her, it soothed her. Josh and Abbas had created it for her, for that very purpose. She got up to put it in the top dresser drawer, as she had once done on her first visit to Jerusalem with Mikha and Tabitha five years earlier. It's funny, she thought, it was the self-same room too.

Something caught her eye, as she placed it face upward. She took it out again to have a good look at it. What was it that was round her neck? She knew what to expect – she had seen it so often. Of course, it was her beautiful yellow patterned trinket she had surrendered to Josh when he had met her after his resurrection early that morning in the cove at the Sea of Galilee. But that wasn't it! She looked more closely. IN the light of the flickering candle she held in front of it, she saw something different. Something green. Something cross shaped. Surely not! It must be a trick of her eyes. Pictures don't change like that. No-one could possibly have changed it in the course of a day. Was she imagining it? She put her hand into the pouch in her robe and drew out the cross and its golden chain. Yes, it was exactly the same as the one in the picture. What did it all mean? Josh and Abbas had given her the picture. She was in no doubt of that. Then, if they had wanted to change it, it was totally their right to do so. Her old yellow trinket had given her such happiness, comfort, and joy through the difficult and dark times – and then Josh had taken it from her. She had missed it over the past five years. In this day of all days, this terrible day of trauma, was this their way of encouraging her, of restoring to her something that would help her through her current dark times? She didn't know. She was tired. But she felt glad, and somehow, reassured, if indeed she needed any reassurance, that they were with her. They had already demonstrated it to her that day. She found herself saying, "Thank you Josh, thank you Abbas," and as an afterthought following a brief pause, in which she had undressed and slipped under her covers, "Thank you Sophia!"

Chapter Thirteen

The days that followed were heavy and hard for Judith and Tabitha. Both woke the following morning with emptiness gnawing at them, causing them to feel nauseous, sick to the pits of their stomachs. Neither wanted to get up. The thought of food was the last thing on their minds. When they had first wakened, both of them had turned over and had tried to stave off the day by going back to sleep. Tabitha had managed it, but Judith was not so lucky. Into her mind flooded the events of the previous day, and she knew that any hope of sleep was gone. Instead, she decided to go with these thoughts and the emotions they engendered, while listening to Tabitha's gentle breathing on the other side of the room. How was she going to cope, she wondered? The future stretched ahead without Mikha. There was nowhere to go, no-one to go to, and although she appreciated their hospitality and care, she was to be locked down for the foreseeable future at Joel and Mary's. At that thought, her heart sank. She found herself saying, "Why, Yahweh? Why Mikha? Why me? Did it have to happen this way?" She stopped. She was feeling guilty for thinking these things. All her life she had been taught not to question Yahweh or His ways, but she hadn't felt as low as this since her brother Joe's death...or was it since the death of her first baby? She had asked similar things then too, but her experience had taught her she was asking the wrong question. Josh! He was the one that had taught her. She went back to the day she had been lying in the little clearing amongst the bushes in the hill above her village in Galilee. She had been giving vent to her grief about Joe's death, when Josh had come along and reassured her that Joe was safe with Yahweh. Then there was Tabitha. She hadn't so much questioned Yahweh at that point, why He had allowed her to die. She accepted the blame for the situation. Her intense guilt forced her to believe that she had deserved what had happened; that it had been a punishment. However, yet again, amazingly, Josh had come into the situation and restored her faith in Yahweh and his love for her. A cloud flitted over her mind, why could He not have rescued Mikha yesterday? A pang of guilt stabbed at her and took away any sense of stability she had been experiencing. She felt nausea rising up inside her now. She knew she was treading the wrong path and was being shown that she was disturbing her own equilibrium. She was being ungrateful and painting Yahweh in an uncaring light. She knew she was wrong to do so. Hadn't Yahweh met with her in the garden…or at least sent his angels to her. Hadn't Josh been with her in her house and allowed Mikha to revive enough to talk with her? She felt utterly guilty now, and deeply ungrateful. She wanted to vomit. It was as if the spirit had gone out of her and she was drained, left to face everything as an unbeliever might. She retreated quickly, the thought of being

sick and being punished for her disobedient thoughts frightening her. She repented. I'm sorry Lord, she said in her heart of hearts, every word meant. I'm not being fair. You've done more for me than I could ever have expected. Millions would have given everything for what you've given to me. Help me not to think this way. Help me to overcome.

The sickness subsided and a relative calm was restored. She knew she had to get up and get on with her day. Wallowing would only lead to depression, doubt, and disobedience again. She couldn't afford to allow this to happen. As she got washed and dressed, the thought struck her. It wasn't easy for Josh, or His Father either. The Father had to allow his Son to die. And although Josh was Yahweh's Son and the Messiah, that didn't enable Him to avoid the suffering. He had died for her, and for the world. He was the only one who had ever lived who was innocent and didn't deserve to die, but yet…He had embraced His Father's plan and gone willingly to the cross, to die in her place…in their place. He had come to her on two occasions now since His resurrection. She was so privileged. She determined to put a brave face on things, and trust that He would help her through these dark and difficult times. She opened the drawer to look at her picture. The smiling image spoke strongly of Josh and his comfort toward her. She felt her spirit lifting instantly. She thought, why's it in the drawer? It's doing me no good there. She placed it on the top of the set of drawers, right in the centre of it, and smiled. She said to herself, thank you Josh, and left for breakfast.

Mary and Joel were already up and just finishing their breakfast. They called to Esther and asked her to make sure Judith had what she wanted.

"I'm not feeling like much this morning," she said. "I felt quite sick when I woke up. I'm having trouble believing what happened yesterday actually happened."

They looked at her sympathetically and said nothing. It was difficult to say anything meaningful. A moment or two later Joel broke the silence.

"How's Tabitha this morning?"

"She's still sleeping. It's probably the best thing for her. There'll be enough time for grief later on." Judith felt a twinge of guilt because of what she had said.

Her earlier experience in her room should have been enough to avoid being over negative and expecting the worst, she thought.

"It'll take time," said Mary. "You've both got as much as you need living with us."

Judith looked at her gratefully. "We don't want to be a burden though," she said. "We can't live with you forever."

"You're welcome for as long as you need," Joel said, a reassuring smile on his face. "We're your brother and sister as well as your uncle and aunt. If we can't help in your time of need, it doesn't say very much good about us!"

Judith smiled at him, "Thank you…but we still don't want to be a burden."

"You aren't, and you won't. I have however something to say, and I hope I'm not speaking out of turn just after Mikha's passing."

Judith looked at him expectantly. Mary did too.

"I've been thinking," he said. "Things can't go on as they were. With Stephen's, and Mikha's, killings we're in a whole new situation. I've detected a change in Jerusalem recently and it culminated in yesterday's events. After Josh's resurrection, we all, the believers, and disciples, went into hiding. There was a real sense that the authorities would come after us too. With the coming of the Holy Spirit, however, and the subsequent teaching and miracles carried out by the apostles, 'The Way' began to grow, and the people accepted us. The authorities backed off hoping we would go away or eventually that the people would get fed up with us. With only a couple of exceptions in which they tried to get tough with us, we pretty well had free reign in Jerusalem. Believers met in houses, even your house and ours, with the apostles moving around teaching the scriptures and doing miracles. It was a great time. However, we didn't go away, and the people still flock to us; and as we've seen there's been antagonism in the ranks of the leaders. Some of them have become impatient, and no doubt worried, that we'll upset things and bring down the wrath of the Romans upon our nation. The rumour is however that the High Priest and Governor Pilate think alike. It's a relationship viewed with great suspicion by many. To avoid the possibility of the Romans striking first and locking everything down, Caiaphas wants to show that the authorities are in control of what's happening in Jerusalem, and so that's why they're clamping down. Stephen and Mikha fell foul of them and have been useful victims to display to the Romans. I believe they'll try to eradicate us. They want rid of us. I think we can expect a wave of persecution."

Both Mary and Judith looked troubled. At that moment, Jonas entered the room and sat down for breakfast, "What's wrong – apart from yesterday of course," he asked, noticing his mother's and cousin's worried faces.

"I'm explaining, Jonas, that I believe we're in for a time of trial, probably quite a fierce persecution. Attitudes are hardening, and some of the authorities are becoming quite fierce and antagonistic."

"I've noticed that too," commented Jonas.

"There was that small man that Mikha angered by standing up for Stephen," Judith commented. "I won't forget his face. It was so utterly full of hatred."

"A point in hand," Joel said. "It was clear from what the two guards said last night that he got a good look at you and claims he won't forget your face either. He may try to hunt you down. It seems he wants to finish the job."

Judith shuddered. "It was only for a few seconds, but his loathing of us was obvious on his face. He was furious."

"Well then, that's the reason you must stay here...and for the foreseeable future avoid going out. Hopefully in time things will settle down, and he will stop looking for you."

"That's going to be difficult," said Judith. "I just can't sit in my room all the time. For the last five years I've been involved in the groups, as was Mikha."

"We'll all have to lay low for a while," Joel said. "After yesterday's martyrdoms, 'The Way' must keep out of the way. I'm sure the house leaders will want to be more careful in their actions, and more vigilant about whom they trust. I don't think the apostles will want to stop though. They're more likely to find a secret place to continue their work from. They'll spend most of their time praying, reading the scriptures and teaching in various safe houses. It won't last forever though."

"I hope you're right," said Mary.

Joel continued, "I've made up my mind about two things. First, I'm hoping to meet with other leaders today to devise a strategy to preserve what has been gained. We want to lose no-one else to the persecution."

"And the second thing, father?" Jonas asked.

"We have to agree on a strategy for our own safety. The Father wouldn't want us to go blindly on. Faith's important but we must take reasonable steps to make sure we, and Judith, are safe."

"What have you in mind, father?"

"Well, it's good that I'm a known quantity with the Council and the High Priest. I've kept my head down since Josh's resurrection, and since then, as far as I'm aware, no-one has suspected my involvement with 'The Way'. However, at any moment, all that might change. It wouldn't take much for one of our friends, perhaps under torture or threat of excommunication, to mention my name, and it would be all up for us. I propose first, while Judith and Tabitha are here, to avoid any chatter, that we scale down our meetings to those we can really trust. I know we've filled our upper room in the past with believers, but now we have to be more careful. We can still go on teaching and praying, but only with a trusted few."

"That sounds fair," said Jonas.

"I'm also proposing that we plan for being found out."

They all looked at him with concern.

"Not that I'm expecting that," Joel reassured them. "But we must be prepared for all eventualities. I believe the Spirit has helped me with this. In the possibility that we are raided, Judith must vanish, and vanish quickly."

Eyebrows were raised.

"You know the cistern up on the roof?"

"You're not proposing that Judith jump in there?" asked Mary , half smiling.

"No, not at all," said Joel seriously. But the bricked area around it could be altered."

"How do you mean, sir," asked Jonas, looking interested.

"Well, the high walled room around it is to protect it from being affected by sandstorms. Yes, there's no roof of course to allow rainwater to fill it, but the walls stop other things getting in. I think we could line these walls with wooden panels and leave a small gap at one side, behind one of the panels for someone to hide in."

"Isn't that going a bit far? Do you really think they'll come for Judith?" Mary asked, looking sceptical.

"I hope not, but I have the sense that we must be prepared, and that's what's come to me. We can easily line that room to make sure that the loose panel blends in, and that everything looks natural."

"But how would I get there?" asked Judith.

"You'd have to get onto the roof at the first sign of trouble. Two sets of stairs from inside the house, and one from outside, can get you past the upper room onto the roof. From there you would go to the cistern shelter and get behind the panel then slide it back into place, so that no-one would know you were there."

"Isn't that a bit extreme?" asked Judith.

"Well sometimes we need extreme measures for extreme situations," Joel grinned.

"What about Tabitha?" asked Judith. "How would you explain her away?"

"We could pass her off as a maid, a helper for Esther. She's not as much of a known quantity as you are."

Judith nodded. "I see the need for vigilance, and I certainly don't wish to get Mary, Jonas and you into trouble by being discovered here. It sounds a fair plan. I just hope it never needs to be executed."

"Neither do I," said Joel smiling, glad that his proposed plan seemed to have been accepted. "I'll start work on this soon. We can't afford to be too long. We can't be sure when any backlash will start, or for how long it will go on. It's best to be ready."

Tabitha appeared in the doorway leading from the atrium.

"Good morning," she said sleepily. She looked strained.

"Come in dear, and have some breakfast," Mary said. "Esther will attend to you."

"I'd like to go to my room, if you don't mind," said Judith feeling a sudden need to be on her own.

"Yes, I must get on too," said Mary.

"And I'll go into Jerusalem and look out the wood we'll need," said Joel.

Tabitha looked worried at this sudden exodus.

"Don't worry, Tabitha," said Jonas. "I'll stay with you and keep you company till you've had your breakfast."

She smiled at him gratefully. It was clear that there was a fondness, which was fast becoming a bond between them. The others smiled knowingly and went about their business, allowing the two young people to share some precious moments, one of them unburdening herself to the other who was concerned for her and willing to be a ready listener.

Chapter Fourteen

It was difficult for Judith to go back to her room. Although she wanted space to think, she was also aware she would be opening herself up to the dark thoughts which encircled her. Of course, she appreciated Josh's and His Father's efforts to comfort her, but she had a mind of her own too, and this seemed to slip quite often into negativity. After all, she'd just lost her husband of eighteen years or so. She was on her own now. How was she going to cope? She had also seen him in his bloodied state and couldn't easily get these images out of her mind. The images seemed to supplant the eighteen or so years of good images. How was she going to leave them behind? She also felt a bit guilty about wanting to do so. They may have been awful, but to forget them made her feel that she might be forgetting Mikha, or at least doing him an injustice. Every so often into her mind came the counteractive comfort but she found that her mood wasn't always ready to fully go along that way, and so she mourned.

She was glad to be in Mary and Joel's house. In some ways she felt like a little girl again, being looked after by them. Her mind went back to happier, if not equally apprehensive days, when she and Josh had been left behind in Jerusalem, and she had awaited the return of their parents. She longed for these days. Why did being an adult come with so many responsibilities, so many hassles, so many disappointments? She had had her fair share of them, and for many years she had sunk into a bitterness and depression which seemed to have no end. At this moment she felt as if she was falling back into that misery. It was so tempting to wallow. Life was treating her badly again. Why was this happening to her? As she lay on her mat contemplating all this, she had to resist the desire to give way and to indulge in self pity. What right had she to feel sorry for herself. It was Mikha that had suffered and died. So many dark emotions, now added to by self-pity and self-reproach. She felt as if she was being swallowed up into a black pit. Her tears flowed freely, and her groans and wailing could be heard by anyone who passed her room. It became a topic of conversation for the others, but they

97

felt it best for Judith to be on her own for a while and to work through it until she was ready to meet up with them again. They felt inadequate to deal with the horrible thing that had happened to her, and rather prayed that Yahweh would help her.

Mary and Joel instead spent much time with Tabitha who seemed more willing to be about the house. She was subdued and prone to burst into tears at a moment's notice. She had been her father's girl and the thought of his vile death, and him no longer being with her every day, was breaking her spirit. She was glad, however, she hadn't gone to the house with her mother the night before. She just couldn't have faced seeing him in such a terrible state. But part of her wished she had been there. She had missed out on experiencing Josh's presence and her father's momentary revival. The others surrounded her with love and prayer, and she found their support something she was able to rest in. She also found comfort in Jonas's company. Since she had come to Jerusalem five or six years earlier, she had always felt a bond with him, and recently had sensed that for both of them this bond was becoming stronger. Did she love him? She wasn't sure, but certainly in the midst of this tragedy, she felt supported by his obvious consideration and presence. She was also concerned for her mother, whom she had heard crying piteously in her room. She wanted to help her, but like the rest of them, she didn't know how to. She had known her mother in the dark days in Capernaum. Things had been so different since Josh had come into their lives again, reviving her from the dead, and restoring her mother to her husband and daughter. They had been a close and happy family since then. Were things destined to go back to how they had been? She hoped not. But in dealing with her own misery, she had to leave her mother to Yahweh. Josh had helped them before, and if her mother's words the night before were to be believed, he was doing and going to do so again.

In the days that followed, this was to be the pattern of things. Judith spent much time on her own, only coming out of her room for meals, and sometimes to pray with the others. For privacy's sake, Tabitha had been allocated another room, the one next to her mother. She too was sad, but tried to draw strength from the comfort of the rest. The days passed, and slowly but surely, the rawness of the experience diminished, and their faith began to rise again. Tabitha resorted to filling her life with the things that made her feel better, and much of this came from spending more and more time with Jonas. The others looked on and silently encouraged it. They could see it was helping Tabitha to regain something of what she had lost. Judith, on the other hand, took longer to recover. Day after day, she found herself plagued by fearsome images, deep dread, and confusion. Sometimes the pit seemed so real. She was scared that she might enter it again, as she once had done after the death of her baby. And then at other times, she almost felt enraptured when she thought of Josh's presence with her when Mikha had spoken to her. His words had been so definite, so energising. And her experience in the garden…It was clear that Josh did not want her to give way. Once again, he had been with her and strengthened her at her lowest ebb. She found herself wondering why she couldn't just believe what he had said and throw herself into the future with him. It was all so difficult! Why had Abbas and he met with her so definitely…in the garden, and at her house? She felt privileged to have had these experiences but couldn't somehow hold onto the peace and encouragement they were designed to give her. Her emotions were conflicted and erratic. She didn't always feel in control of them. She knew that Josh's presence was meant to help her through the dark days – had he not said he would be with her on many occasions before. She knew he was with her, but she somehow couldn't grasp and hold on to him. The negatives were just so bad.

One day, some weeks later, she was in her room just after breakfast and preparing herself to face that now commonplace raft of feelings, when she sensed something was different. She felt scared. She felt as if she had done something wrong and that she was going to have to face the music. It was so unsettling. She felt as if she had displeased Yahweh, and she was awaiting his word of condemnation. She felt sick to her stomach. Drained, weak and helpless. What was going to happen? In her fear, she did something she hadn't done for some time. She reached into her pocket and felt for the green cross. Just as the yellow trinket had done, it seemed to offer her some comfort when in time of trouble. She drew it out and held it in her hand. As she did so her feeling of fear and anguish intensified. She tried to rise to her feet, but immediately collapsed on the floor. Her strength was gone. She was terrified but didn't lose consciousness. Into her mind came the word, 'decision'. What did this mean? As she thought about it, the terror seemed to lessen. "What decision, Lord? I'll make it, I'll do anything," she promised, fearing she was going to die. Was she being punished for something? Was she about to lose her life for it? Then it was clear, as clear as day. She wondered why she hadn't seen it before. She was being brought to a point of decision. It was now time to make up her mind. She knew exactly what was wanted of her. She had been playing about with her feelings. She had indeed been disobedient and was about to suffer judgment for it. "I'll go your way, Lord. Not my will, but what you want – let it be done." She had been disobedient by allowing herself to wallow, to think about, to consider the negatives. Josh and his father had done their utmost to speak to her, to comfort her, to draw her away from self-indulgent feelings in order to overcome what had happened. She had not walked the walk of faith by trusting them. She had allowed herself to be tormented by the negatives, and so had become disobedient. Faith was required of her in order to overcome. She was in danger of being given up to her doubts and fears. Her confusion and doubt were the direct result of her lack of faith. Was she going to be punished? Was she going to be let go of? Had she gone too far in not going their way? She should have known better. Suddenly her apprehension was replaced by peace. She sensed she was now going in the right direction, and relaxed, the extreme tension gone. It was as if for a moment she had lost the Holy Spirit's presence, she thought. She had felt abandoned and didn't like the look of what she might have been abandoned to. She breathed a sigh of relief and lay prostrate on the floor. The green cross at the side of her head began to pulsate. She kept her eyes fixed on it, and slowly the image of Josh began to assemble itself on it. "Arise!" She heard or saw nothing, but the word seemed to form in her mind. "Go."

Inside her head, she said, "Where Lord?"

"Be ready. Go, nothing doubting." The pulsating ceased.

She knew in her heart, this was the end. There was no more to be said. She had been commanded to do something and she must obey. No doubting, no dallying. She had to embrace the path she had chosen and hadn't to hold back.

Relieved that the terror and sense of disobedience had gone, she lifted herself off the floor and made a mental decision not to give way to the negatives again. She sensed inside her a burst of satisfaction, as if she had pleased the Spirit. As she straightened up, her eye caught sight of her smiling picture on top of the set of drawers. She found a smile coming to her lips at the joy of seeing it. Once again Josh had come to the rescue, she thought. And yes, he's giving me back my smile!

From that moment on, she was restored to her family. No more did she adjourn to her room to be with her thoughts. She fully engaged with the people she was staying with.

"I'm sorry, Tabitha," she said. "I should have been there for you."

"I understand, mother. It wasn't your fault. You couldn't help it. You were struggling too."

"I was, but I was being selfish. Of course, losing your father was horrible, but he lost his life standing up for Josh. I should have been proud of him – and I am. He was a good, a great, man!" A tear came to her eye. "But I miss him. We both miss him…but we'll meet him again."

Tabitha and her mother hugged. From then on, Judith played a full part in family life. She had no wish or desire to reap the proceeds of her disobedience. And for that matter, she knew that Mikha would have wanted her to engage again. She was now ready to do so with a vengeance, nothing doubting.

The days very quickly turned into weeks, and Judith took comfort and gained strength from being in Joel and Mary's house with all its comings and goings. It was a refuge for her in her avoidance of the authorities. And it most certainly was a time for avoidance. Since Stephen's very public martyrdom, the authorities had come down hard on the people of 'The Way'. They were no longer ignored or tolerated – they were public enemy number one. Believers were rounded up, either if they presented themselves at Solomon's Colonnade in the Temple or while they shared their faith in each other's houses. It became fashionable to carry out raids in the evenings, while the believers were together in one place. Many had been imprisoned by overzealous Temple police, some beaten and some excommunicated from the synagogue. Raids were commonplace and so the believers had to be careful as to where they went and as to whom they trusted. Judith felt herself cocooned from all this.

Joel and Mary's house offered her the sanctuary she needed. Now in her spare moments which she spent on her mat in her room, she chose to put aside the negative thoughts, and rehearsed over and over again the good times she and Mikha had experienced together. She found they made her feel better and helped push away the past. Mikha and she may have had their difficult years, but after Josh's intervention, life had been sweet. The two of them had come together and provided a happy home for Tabitha. There had been a close bond between the three of them that none of them would ever let go of. She thought back over these days and their friendship with Josh, a friendship which had led to their being drummed out of Capernaum. According to the main synagogue leaders, they were encouraging their flock to defect from true Jewish ways and to run after a heretic. They had not, however, allowed themselves to be intimidated. They were both beginning to believe that Josh was the awaited for Messiah, and so they had made sure everyone knew it. Mikha had cheerfully decided to go to Jerusalem and ask his old friend Joel to help him secure a new job in the Temple, which he duly was offered and accepted. Apart from the unexpected horrific crucifixion of Josh which had taken place during the visit, things seemed to be looking up for their little family and it had appeared that their future might just have been secured in Jerusalem.

Her mind went back to the day she had met Josh at dawn at the Sea of Galilee. She had brought fish and bread for him…and of course, Little Faithie. Who could forget Little Faith, she thought? The loveliest furriest dog in the world! It had been a sad day as well as a glorious one. Josh had been there to meet with his disciples, to commission them for the way ahead. In a funny way, he had also commissioned her. The sad part was that she had had to give up Little Faith, who had been injured and was limping badly. Josh had said he wanted to take her to make her better. Judith had at first resisted. She loved Little Faithie. She didn't want to let her go. But as Josh had given her to her in the first place, and he was now offering to help her, how could she be so selfish as to hold back? He had also asked her to relinquish her yellow trinket, something she had treasured over the years since the time Abbas had given it to her in his tent. She had been stroking Faithie for the last time as she had fallen asleep, and then when she had wakened up, she had found herself in the living room of her Capernaum home. Tabitha and Mikha were just getting up. Dawn had broken. Mikha was extremely unhappy to find out that his wife had been wandering the streets and coastal areas of Capernaum during the night. Both he and Tabitha were even more distressed that she had returned without Faithie. They had grown so used to her being around and they loved her. Tabitha had cried for days after that. She and Faithie had been great friends. Then there had been the leaving of Capernaum itself and their friends including Marius the Centurion, which was quickly followed by their arrival in Jerusalem and all the excitement of starting afresh there. They had found a house in the lower environs of Mount Zion, not quite up to the standard of Joel and Mary's mansion further up the hill, but not quite in the lower city too where poor and ordinary citizens lived. Tabitha and she had had great fun in setting it up. It had just been right for them and not long after arriving the employed the services of a maid to help with everyday chores. Tabitha had been sad at first that Chloe, their maid in Capernaum had refused to leave her family to go with them – she had been through so much with them - but very soon she had befriended Elisa and the two of them had become firm friends. Elisa was just a few years older than Tabitha and a believer too. They had shared much together as Tabitha grew up. There was a tinge of sadness in Judith's mind. She had loved Elisa too and had regretted having to dismiss her so suddenly after Mikha's death, without even saying goodbye to her. She hoped that the authorities might not have put too much pressure on her to find out Judith's whereabouts.

These had been heady days, their first weeks and months in Jerusalem. She remembered the excitement she had seen in Mikha a few days after he had started his new job. He had come home absolutely full of it.

"What's happened?" she asked him.

"Well, after work today, Joel met with me and told me about last night's events. He learned of them from the disciples who are lodging with them."

Judith was interested.

Mikha continued, "Apparently Josh appeared to them in the upper room, and somehow opened their minds to understand the scriptures. He said to them 'When I was with you before, I told you that everything written about me in the Law of Moses, the Prophets and the Psalms must be fulfilled. Yes, it was written long ago that the Messiah would suffer and die and rise from the dead on the third day. It was also written that this message would be proclaimed in the authority of His name to all the nations beginning in Jerusalem. There is forgiveness of sins for all who repent. You are witnesses of all these things. Now I will send the Holy Spirit, the gift My Father promised.' Then he led them out towards Bethany, up the Mount of Olives. After they had gone about half a mile, he stopped and said, 'Stay here in the city until the Holy Spirit comes and fills you with power from Heaven. Jonas baptised with water, but in just a few days you will be baptised with the Holy Spirit.' They had asked him, 'Lord, has the time come for you to free Israel and restore our Kingdom?' He replied, 'The Father alone has the authority to set those dates and times. They are not for you to know. But you will receive power when the Holy Spirit comes upon you, and you will be my witnesses, telling people about me everywhere, in Jerusalem, throughout Judea, in Samaria, and to the ends of the earth.' And with that, he raised his hands to heaven and blessed them. While he was blessing them, he left them and was taken up to Heaven. They were dumbstruck, amazed. Suddenly beside them were two men in white robes, 'Men of Galilee,' they said. 'Why are you standing here staring into Heaven? Jesus has been taken from you into Heaven, but someday he will return from Heaven in the same way you saw him go.' They were exhilarated, joyful. They came back to the upper room hardly able to contain themselves.

"Wow, so Josh has gone?" Judith said.

"Yes, but it's wonderful. He's given us a mission...and we'll see him again."

"How do you know it's a mission for us? It might be just for his men."

"No, that's not what they believe, I think. It's work for all his followers."

"Women too?"

"Why not. You've got a story, haven't you? You knew Josh better than many. Why shouldn't you be involved?"

She looked at him gratefully. He seemed bereft of the standard male prejudices of many Jewish men.

"What's the Holy Spirit?" she asked.

"I'm not sure. He's to come from the Father. It seems He couldn't come till Josh left."

"What does it mean that He'll fill us? Isn't that a bit strange?"

"According to Joel, Josh's men don't think so. They see Him as the energy, the power, the Spirit that Josh had. He's going to be given to those who believe so they can have the same power Josh had to carry out his work."

"Women too?" she asked again.

"Why not?" Mikha surmised. "You won't be able to work otherwise. Remember, in the scriptures the Spirit sometimes came upon people so they could understand Yahweh more, or undertake great tasks. I think it's the same Spirit who won't just come upon us. According to what Josh said to his men last night, He's not only going to come upon us, but will fill us, just as He did Josh."

"Isn't He here already...among us?"

"No. We've to wait in Jerusalem for Him to come. I imagine we'll know it when He arrives."

From that day on, all three of them had spent much time in Joel and Mary's upper room with other believers and Josh's men, praying, searching the scriptures, and sharing their experiences. They were joined by Miriam, Josh's mother, and some other women who had followed Josh from Galilee. Not long after her son's resurrection, Miriam had spent a little time with her cousin Elizabeth in Bethany, but had returned to Joel and Mary's to be with her sons and the other disciples. Indeed, she had been allocated a room there for as long as she needed it. Judith was glad of her company, not only because of her close link with Josh but also because of her depth of wisdom and faith. There was an ardency about her which seemed to rub itself off on Judith. Very quickly, she, Mikha and Tabitha became fully involved in the group, and were often to be found at Joel and Mary's house, whose upper room was regularly used by Josh's men as a base and also by the steadily growing number of believers as a meeting place for prayer. They were able to be frequent visitors. Their house not being far down the hill made it easy for them to attend meetings early morning and at other times of the day. Initially, the believers had been scared that they might have been discovered. Some indeed were extremely timid, trembling at the hint of any sound that might mean a raid was in progress. However, a common bond was developing between them, and a growing excitement that Yahweh was going to do something…and do it soon. Josh's men seemed to believe so anyway and their enthusiasm was contagious. Judith had been there when Peter had stood up and declared that they should fill Judas's place. The company had been subdued one day when they had learned of his apparent suicide. Rumours were rife. One said that he had tried to give back to the priests the money he had been given for betraying Josh. They had refused to take it, so he had thrown it at them, realising how wrong he had been; and then he had gone out and hung himself. Another said he had purchased a field with the money and had somehow burst open in it, his blood soaking into the ground there. The group had decided upon the traditional way of drawing lots and Mathias had been chosen to be the twelfth apostle.

"Why 'apostle'?" Judith had asked Mikha.

"Josh's men believe that as his closest disciples, they have been given the job of overseeing things. They were with him for three years and were taught by him. They lived with him and saw him close at hand. They experienced his miracles. They believe that because of Josh's last words they have been sent to tell the world, or at least to equip ordinary believers like you and me to do so. An apostle is someone with authority who has been sent."

The Day of Pentecost was now very near, and Jerusalem was filling up with pilgrims from all over the empire. The believers thought this would be a good thing, as it would distract the authorities from looking for them. The festival was fifty days after Passover and was celebrated in late spring. Josh had returned to Heaven about forty days after his Resurrection, and the ten days or so between this and Pentecost were spent in ardent joyful prayer. Those gathering in the upper room numbered about one hundred and twenty, and there was a fervency about them accompanied by an incredible sense of unity.

On Pentecost morning Judith, Mikha and Tabitha had risen early, before dawn, breakfasted quickly, and then left for Joel and Mary's. Although it was still dark, the pre-dawn grey just beginning to lighten the sky, the streets were already filling with pilgrims intent on going to the Temple to be ready for the beginning of festivities. As they walked in the opposite direction, up Mount Zion, Tabitha remarked on this fact.

"We're going the other way," she said.

"We'll get there later, after the meeting," Mikha replied. "Do either of you feel an excitement?"

Both nodded. Since leaving home, each of them had felt a strong sense of purpose almost verging on excitement. The nearer they got to the villa, the stronger it got. They went through the gates as the sun was coming up. Judith thought, the birds seemed to be singing excessively loudly this morning. They climbed the stairs to the Upper Room and were surprised to find that it was full. Almost every believer they knew was there. Each had an excited look and talked of a sense of having been driven there.

"Do you think something's going to happen?" Tabitha asked Jonas.

"I've no idea," he responded, "but this is the biggest early morning prayer meeting I've seen!"

They both agreed it was unusual, then found somewhere to sit. The head table was occupied by Peter and the eleven. They had apparently been up all night praying but showed no sign of a lack of sleep. Everyone else sat on the low couches or on the floor. Judith was pleased to see Miriam and Josh's brothers sitting near to the apostles. She waved to them. Then her eye caught Esther, her childhood friend and aunt's maid. She was there with a girl Judith didn't recognise, most probably her daughter she surmised. Esther waved over to her, then she and the girl came across and sat down beside them.

"This is my daughter, Rhoda," said Esther. "She wanted to come. She's only recently come to faith."

The introductions were made, and then the gathering settled down to await what the apostles might say.

Peter spoke, "We're here today not only to celebrate Pentecost, but to remember the Lord Jesus. I believe the Father has drawn us all together for a purpose. Every one of us has sensed we've been led here today. I myself also have a sense of great excitement. I believe Jesus and the Father are among us and want to do something special at this festival time. All of us are fully aware of Jesus's horrible death and his marvellous resurrection. Some of you will know that he met with us only ten days ago and took us up the Mount of Olives where we saw Him rise into heaven. We've been told to wait for Yahweh's power, the Holy Spirit, to come, and that's just what we're doing. And we'll do that till as long as it takes. I want us all now to pray to the Father, to thank Him for Jesus, and to ask Him for His will to be done among us. There's a quickening in the air – I'm sure you all feel it." With that, he started to pray. Others joined him, and very soon there was a cacophony of sound filling the room. Everyone was praying out loud, no-one waiting for anyone else. It just happened, and the sound was harmonious, strong, and focused. As each one prayed, they became aware of a oneness, a holiness, a cleanness, a beauty – it seemed to be enveloping them They more they felt it, the more they reached out, further into it. Judith was aware of Josh's presence beside her. Her eyes were closed, but she knew He was there. She heard his name on the lips of others and realised that they were experiencing what she was. This was such a special moment and she wanted more of it.

Gradually the cacophony of sound diminished so much so that the only whispered sound that could be heard was 'Josh'. Peace, joy and an immense sense of love filled them all, and the air was charged with a pregnant expectation. The whispering ceased and everyone seemed to be holding their breath. It was then that Judith heard it. Above the house,

in the distance, seeming to come from the mountains surrounding Jerusalem – was it thunder, or wind. It seemed to be getting closer and much louder. It was rushing, surging and powerful – a wind that seemed to be heading toward them at high speed. Suddenly it was in the room. Not a window or door had opened. It was just there, a roaring, thundering wind filling their ears with sound. Judith didn't feel it was something to be scared of – the previous experience had prepared her for it. However in the midst of the noise she made out a crackling. Her head too was beginning to get very hot. Curiosity got the better of her and she opened her eyes. An amazing sight met them. Over the heads of each person in the room was a tongue of flame. The crackling – that was the cause of it, she realised. She must have had one too. Still no fear. Just an amazing infusion of love and peace, a sense of patience and waiting. Then came the eruption of joy. It just seemed to burst into their minds. First from where the apostles were sitting came the sound of babbling voices, quiet at first then rising to a crescendo. Very quickly the room was filled with many voices speaking in languages Judith didn't recognise. Suddenly the joy she was experiencing felt as if it needed expression and she found herself babbling too. She didn't know where the words came from, but she gave herself to them. She had never felt so energised, so full, so complete. She felt a burning desire to share what she was feeling and found herself moving towards the stairs. Others were doing the same. Seconds later they were bursting out into the street, making their way onto Mount Zion, laughing, singing, and praising Yahweh. They were met by a crowd of pilgrims who had heard the sound of the rushing wind and had come to investigate. Some of the apostles continued past them and made their way downhill to the Temple where their progress was stopped by an even larger band of pilgrims. They were still laughing and singing and babbling in unknown words.

"What is the meaning of this?" the pilgrims looked confused. "We're from all over the empire; we've come here for the festival. Something strange is happening!" Many of them interrogated their neighbour, "Where are you from?", then, "What are you hearing? These men are saying wonderful things about Yahweh and I'm hearing it in my own language. They're only from Galilee!"

"Me too," their neighbour said. "It's either a miracle, or they're drunk!"

"But how can they know my language, and how are each of us hearing what they're saying in our own languages?"

Peter and the eleven gathered themselves together and addressed the crowd, "Fellow Jews and residents of Jerusalem. These men are not drunk. It's only early in the morning. What you see was predicted long ago by the prophet Joel when he said, 'In the last days Yahweh says, "I will pour out my Spirit on all people. Your sons and daughters will prophesy, your young men shall see visions and your old men will dream dreams. In those days I will pour out my Spirit even on my servants, men, and women alike, and they will prophesy, and I will cause wonders in the heavens above and signs on the earth below. Blood and fire and clouds of smoke. The sun will become dark. and the moon will turn blood red before that great and glorious day of the Lord arrives.

But everyone who calls on the name of the Lord will be saved." People of Israel, listen. Yahweh publicly endorsed Jesus the Nazarene by doing powerful miracles, wonders and signs through him, as you well know. But Yahweh knew what would happen, and his prearranged plan was carried out when Jesus was betrayed. With the help of lawless Gentiles, you nailed him to a cross and killed him." Peter emphasised the 'you'. "But Yahweh released him from the horrors of death and raised him back to life. For death could not keep him. King David said of him, 'My body rests in hope, for you will not leave my soul among the dead or allow your holy one to rot in the grave.' Brothers," Peter stopped again, "think about this. David wasn't speaking about himself because he died and was buried, and his tomb is just up the hill there." He pointed. "He was a prophet however and knew that Yahweh had promised that one of his descendants would sit upon his throne. David was looking into the future and speaking of the Messiah's resurrection. Yahweh raised Jesus from the dead, and we're all witnesses of this. Now he's at the place of highest honour in heaven at Yahweh's right hand, and the Father as he had promised gave him the Holy Spirit to pour out upon us, just as you see and hear today." He went on, "So let everyone in Israel know for certain that Yahweh has made this Jesus whom you crucified to be both Lord and Messiah!"

Peter seemed to be getting through to them, his words piercing their hearts. They said, "Brothers, what should we do?"

"Each of you must repent of your sins and turn to Yahweh and be baptised in the name of Jesus the Messiah for the forgiveness of your sins. Then you will receive the gift of the Holy Spirit. This promise is to you, your children and to the Gentiles, all who have been called by the Lord our God. Save yourselves from this crooked generation."

About three thousand people in all were added to the church (or 'The Way' as it soon became known) that day.

Don Treader

"You should have seen what Yahweh did!" said Mikha enthusiastically when he caught up with Judith, Tabitha, Joel, Mary, Jonas, Miriam and Esther later in the atrium. He was bubbling with it.

"We did, we were there," said Judith smiling.

"No, you only got as far as Mount Zion..."

"And that was great!" laughed Judith.

"Yes, but some of us followed the apostles and got down to the Temple." He enthused. "The pilgrims could all hear about Yahweh and Josh in their own languages. We'd no idea what we were saying but they understood!"

"It was the same with us," Mary said.

"Peter spoke so wonderfully well. He was a man inspired. He told them, the authorities...they...had crucified Josh, their Messiah, but that Yahweh had raised him as promised. They had to repent and save themselves...and they did!"

"That must have been something," Judith said. "How many...ten, twenty? Will they meet with us?"

"Try about three thousand!"

Judith's jaw dropped. Miriam beamed. "It's happening!" she said. "The Spirit has come!"

When she could take this in, Judith said, "But how will we cope with them? Where will they go?"

"That's for Yahweh to work out, my dear," Miriam said. The others grinned.

"Indeed," said Joel. "They can't all get in our upper room."

Everyone laughed.

"But what will we do?" Mary asked.

Joel spoke again, "The Holy Spirit's in control now. You should have seen the wonderful way He spoke through the apostles to reach three thousand people. If that's what he wants then he'll have a plan as to how to deal with them. All we've got to do is speak about Josh – He'll do the rest."

"That wasn't all," said Mikha excitedly. "Once Peter had finished speaking, the apostles involved some of us in baptising the new believers."

Again, Judith's jaw dropped. "How?"

Well, we found a pool in Bethesda. It's a place with five porches. One of the believers who were with us this morning pointed it out. He said Josh had healed him there."

"Really?" asked Miriam smiling. "Everything seems to fit together."

"Yes, that would have been Hosea," Joel said. "He has a wonderful story to tell. You'll no doubt hear it from him sometime."

"What a day it's been!" Jonas said. Everyone laughed.

"We could never have imagined it," Tabitha said. "I'm just glad Yahweh's involved me."

"Me too," said Esther. "It's something I won't forget!"

"None of us will," said Joel. "And just think. This is only the beginning!"

"He promised…and it's happened," Miriam said. "Yahweh always keeps his promises."

"And He's included us women," Judith said. "It really is a new age!"

Everyone was smiling as they thought about it all.

"What about some food?" asked Jonas. "Is anyone else hungry? I haven't eaten since breakfast." There was a general murmur of agreement.

"How about a prayer first?" suggested Joel. He started, "Josh, we were so sad when you were crucified," he paused, "then we were glad when we heard you'd risen. Some of us saw you. But now, you've kept your word and sent the Holy Spirit, to fill us to work with us, to make us just like you. You've included us. Make us worthy of your purposes. Help us to tell others about you. Help us to extend Yahweh's kingdom. We don't deserve any of this, but we thank you for your love towards us. Help us always to be aware of your presence."

As Judith thought over these early days, she felt a buoyancy in her spirit. She realised that she always did so now when she thought about Josh. His death had floored her, but now she was coping…no, much more than coping. She felt alive and vibrant. Was this what she might eventually experience with Mikha? She had indeed been floored by his murder, but might she in the future feel equally alive and vibrant? These were matters of faith, and time would tell!

Chapter Fifteen

In one of her quiet times, when she felt the need to have some space alone in her room, Judith allowed herself to think beyond the pain of losing Mikha to those early days when she and Mikha had embraced the amazing and enthralling events of the beginning of 'The Way'. After the Holy Spirit had arrived in such a dynamic and dramatic fashion sending the timid believers out into the streets to boldly proclaim the good news about Jesus, and usher into the Kingdom an unbelievably large group of new believers, it had become painfully obvious to all that something would have to be done to take stock of them, and bring them into the fold. It was to be a massive feat of organisation, a task which was possibly going to be too much for the apostles alone to countenance, after all they were just simple fishermen and ordinary working people. At the next gathering in the upper room, it was patently clear that it was beginning to become too small for the growing number of believers, some of whom had gathered there just by word of mouth. There was a great joy in the gathering after what the Holy Spirit had done – enthusiasm abounded. People were clamouring to speak to the apostles, and their words were seriously devoured, especially by new believers who were hungering for stories about Josh. After a while, the apostles called for silence and Peter stood up.

"If the Holy Spirit's going to do this regularly, and our numbers increase amazingly, we'll have to do things differently. We can't all squeeze in here...and if and when the authorities decide to regroup and come after us, it'll be too dangerous for Joel and his family."

Someone shouted from the floor, "Do you think it'll come to that? Just look at the way everyone's accepted us. The people of Jerusalem are excited. Yahweh is doing a new thing!"

"Don't be too sure, my friend," Said an imposing man from the other side of the room. Judith had to look twice before she recognised the distinguished figure of Nicodemus. "Yahweh is indeed doing a new thing, but the authorities won't recognise it. Danger will come."

"It will," Peter looked sombre, "but we must be ready, and prepared. It's not long since they crucified Josh, and what did Josh tell us before he left? 'The servant is not greater than his master. If they treat me badly, they'll also come for you!' The authorities won't be happy if we begin to multiply. Yes, there's great joy because Yahweh is working, but that joy isn't shared by all."

People looked serious and a heavy silence ensued.

"What will we do then?" someone else asked.

"This is Yahweh's work," Peter said. "We had no hand in the Holy Spirit's coming, and He's the one in control. We'll have to take our lead from Him. It'll work out the way Yahweh wants. If He is increasing our number in such a way, He'll work out how to deal with us."

There was a general nodding of assent. He continued, "There are some things we can do however to help. We mustn't compromise our brothers and sisters by leading the authorities to them. I believe the easiest thing is for us to gather with our friends in each other's houses. We apostles can circulate and encourage these small groups. Invite new believers into your groups and help them to find out more about Josh. In the meantime, we apostles will use this place as a base, with Joel and Mary's permission, so we can study the scriptures and pray. We will then move between all the meeting places and teach what Josh taught. Every afternoon, it's also our intention to meet in Solomon's Colonnade where we'll preach the good news about Josh our Messiah. If you gather there with us it will lend us support, and of course show to the world just what wonders the Holy Spirit is working. The authorities won't touch us there if we gather in large numbers, but make no mistake, they'll be looking for ways to deal with us, so once again, be careful not to betray a brother or sister, or a meeting place. Josh said in our dealings with the world we should be 'as wise as serpents, and as harmless as doves'. To be forewarned is to be forearmed."

Once again there was a general nodding of assent, and after a lively time of prayer, the gathering broke up. Judith remembered that she and Mikha had felt enlivened that night. Just praying seemed to fill them with joy and a deep sense of love. As they had walked home with Tabitha, they had agreed that they wanted their house to be one of the meeting places of 'The Way'.

"Won't it put us at risk with your employers, dear?" Judith had asked.

"Undoubtedly, if they find out," Mikha had grinned. "But I don't want to miss out on what Yahweh's doing. He'll take care of us if we honour Him!"

"I believe you're right," Judith said, putting her arm through his. "We must be careful all the same. Yahweh wouldn't want us to be reckless."

Tabitha had looked a bit offended. "What about me?" she had asked and linked her arm with her father's other arm. "I want to be involved too. I knew Josh as well."

Her father and mother laughed, "Of course you will. Your story will amaze all who meet with us!"

And from that very night, all three of them threw themselves fully into spreading the good news and encouraging believers in their home.

Judith smiled when she thought of these exciting heady days, and how Mikha especially had been so energised. The family divided much of their time between Joel and Mary's and their own house, attending meetings, going to the Temple, and talking to anyone who would listen about Josh. They could hardly go anywhere in Jerusalem without bumping into someone who had become a believer under Peter's preaching on the Day of Pentecost. Her smile broadened at the next thought that entered her mind. Just a few days after Pentecost, the little family had gone up to Joel and Mary's for an early morning time of prayer. Joel and Mary were rushing about in quite a flap.

"What's wrong?" asked Judith. "Aren't you coming up to the meeting?"

"No, not just now," said Mary, appearing quite flustered.

By way of explanation, Joel said, "We've just heard that my nephew is coming."

"Your nephew?" asked Mikha. "I didn't realise you had other family. You've never mentioned him."

"No, I haven't seen him, or my brother for that matter, for a long time. My brother was the black sheep of the family. He's been abroad for more years than I can remember. I think he ended up in Cyprus."

"That's a long way away," commented Judith. "What did he do to deserve being sent there?" she smiled.

"No, it's not like that," Joel said. "He didn't fit in with the family's Levite background. I was the eldest son and so my inheritance and calling were clear. He seemed to resent this, and being a bit of a tearaway, with a liking for travel, he flew the nest when he got the chance, the last I heard he had settled in Cyprus where many diaspora Jews live, and owned a bit of land there. The opinion of some of our acquaintances who visited them, was that they were fairly well established but were still very much the 'unorthodox' side of our family."

"How so?" asked Mikha.

"Wheelings, dealings and lifestyle. They may have been of the tribe of Levi, but they were well integrated into Gentile culture." Joel wore a look that Judith had seldom ever seen - a disapproving one.

"Not so good," agreed Mikha.

"Why's your nephew coming here?" asked Tabitha.

"Well quite by chance he found out where we lived. My brother left home just before Mary and I moved here, so he wouldn't have known where we stayed. Apparently, my nephew seems to have been in Jerusalem for the festival – I don't know, perhaps he's been here for longer. He would have known that I worked in the Temple, and so I suppose he must have made some enquiries, and having found out about us, had a message sent to us last night to say he'd be with us in the morning."

"So, he'll be here soon," said Judith. "Aren't you worried he'll interrupt the meeting and find out what's been happening?"

"We'll be careful, but Joseph – that's his name by the way – if he's anything like his father, that won't bother him. He always relished something new, especially if it was anti authority."

"Will we meet him?" asked Tabitha.

"Yes. You all go up to the meeting. Mary and I will stay here to get things ready for him. I expect he might want to stay here. You can all meet him after the meeting. The apostles are up and ready."

Judith, Mikha and Tabitha climbed the stairs to the upper room and found it quite full, even at that very early hour. The men who were present, at least those who weren't retired, would stay for one hour before going to their work. Mikha had agreed to meet with Joel after the gathering and assuming Joseph had arrived, they would spend a few minutes with him before leaving for the Temple.

Judith really enjoyed these early morning times of prayer. There was a buzz about them. Everyone would pray together saying what was on their heart and somehow all the prayers seemed to join together in one harmonious sound. No-one bothered about their neighbour. Each was caught up in their own world, and somehow Yahweh seemed to be speaking into their hearts by His Holy Spirit. It was beautiful and thrilling, enlivening and powerful. Sometimes one voice would rise above the others and often it seemed that a different language was being spoken. There were moments too when Judith felt such an overwhelming spiritual joy that she just gave vent to the words coming into her mind. She had no idea what she was saying, but she knew she felt energised when she did so. She sensed she was pleasing Yahweh, and yes, even for a few moments, she felt as if Josh were close. After a while the voices settled, and Peter began to speak.

"You all know that Josh did many miracles which were pointers to us that He was the Messiah. We didn't all see it at first, or believe it, but now it's so clear. We were with him one day when what you're going to hear about happened. I've asked Hosea to share his story with you." He beckoned to a thin small wrinkled man in his forties whose face was beaming. There was no doubting he had a story to tell and he was bursting to tell it.

"Friends, brothers and sisters," he said, "It gives me such great joy to share with you what Jesus did for me. I was a wretch, a bitter man before my time. I didn't deserve anything out of life and I've absolutely no idea why Jesus came to me, but he did. It was one of the first times he came to Jerusalem. I was some thirty-eight years a cripple. I couldn't get off my mat. I'd got a bit fed up with life, and I suppose, a bit cynical too. I'd got into the position of cajoling the few friends I had - mainly acquaintances rather than friends, people who felt sorry for me - I'd managed to get them to take me to the pool of Bethesda most days. I don't know why I went there really. It was full of the blind, the lame and other poor wretches who had nothing going for them. I don't know whether we were superstitious or not – our religion seemed to allow this – but we were all there because we believed that an angel made the pool ripple every so often, and when it did, the first person into the water would be healed. Oh, you should have been there! All day long, moaning, complaining – and when the ripple came, the cursing from those who weren't fast enough to get into the water. I don't remember ever seeing anyone getting healed, but somehow, we all came there every day, hoping. That's what superstition does for you!

Anyhow I was lying there on my mat one day, and I saw this man approaching me. He was surrounded by those..." he looked around and smiled at Peter and the other apostles, "He seemed to make straight for me. I didn't know him from Adam, and so I suppose I was a bit hostile at first. I didn't need his pity, or anything else. I didn't want to get distracted from watching the pool in case the ripple came.

"Hosea," he said. "That drew me up a bit. How did he know my name? There was something about the way he spoke that made me want to listen rather than to be rude to him and brush him off. He looked into my eyes – he seemed to look deeper than anyone else I'd ever known. "Would you like to get well?" What kind of question was that, I wondered? I wouldn't have been there if I didn't. I'd been there for years just waiting for the pool to ripple. At that very moment it seemed hopeless. I suppose I might have given up really expecting to be healed. Time and disappointment can do that to you. I'd become used to lying there and moaning a bit like the rest. It was also a good place to be, to gain the pity of those who passed through. Most days I went home with some money which allowed me to buy the little food I needed. It was as if Jesus knew what was going on in my soul. Maybe I didn't expect to get healed. Maybe I didn't want to get healed. Maybe I'd given up expecting to be healed. Suddenly it seemed very important to listen to this man. "I want to get healed," I said, "but I've no-one to put me into the pool when the water bubbles. Someone else always gets in before me!" It hit me at that moment that I was stupid. Why on earth had I spent years there when I'd no way of getting help. I was holding onto a stupid myth. I realised I was moaning. I must have sounded full of self-pity. Jesus however saw beyond this. His face was close to mine now and he gazed into my eyes. "Stand up. Pick up your mat and walk!" He said it softly, but it was a command. I would have laughed in his face. The impossibility of it all. I would indeed have laughed, if I hadn't felt something strange happening inside me. First of all, I felt a warmth. It seemed to start in my heart and work over the rest of my body. I began to shake. There was something compulsive about these words of his. They were doing inside me what I could never have done for myself. My senses seemed to become alive, and about to burst. Could the impossible become possible? I actually felt I could be healed...and I didn't need any angel or any pool! It was so powerful and yet so gentle. I might have wanted to laugh at him moments before, but now I really wanted to obey his words. I wanted to get up. First of all, I felt I couldn't. It would be stupid to even consider trying to rise up off my mat. But then slowly and steadily, I began to believe it might be possible. Tentatively I tried to move my paralysed legs. I saw them move. I kind of tried to reach out further. I tried to get them under me and lever myself up with my arms. Something was happening, I felt I could. These..." Hosea looked behind him again, "got around me and helped me. I didn't need much now – the more I believed I was able, the more it happened. I seemed to have the strength to get up! It was so good. I felt such a gratitude. My senses were bursting now. I felt such a love, a warmth, towards this man. I suppose I was shouting now. Others around me began to as well when they saw me leaping about and giving vent to my exhilaration. I felt compelled to obey the rest of his words. I bent down, rolled up the very mat I'd had to lie on for years and I put it under my arm. I was dancing now" I was ready to go with them wherever they went."

People in the group gathered in that upper room began to clap. All were smiling.

Hosea continued, "The mat's a funny thing. all these years it had carried me, I had relied on it. It was the symbol of my disability, my crutch. It had supported me and my infirmity. I'd grown so used to it. Now that Jesus had come to me, and radically changed me, healed me, I no longer had to be dependent on it, to be carried by it. I now carried it! It need no longer rule my life. My circumstances were no longer in control of me, but with Jesus's help I was now in control of them. I carried that mat so proudly. I was now able to. And to make it go where I wanted to go!"

The clapping came again, and Hosea began to cry. "Jesus knew I'd never get healed there. The angel, the pool – they were all just superstition. He offered me something better, something real, something he knew his Father wanted to give me. I don't know why he chose me. I was nothing special, and those other poor wretches...why not them? I just don't know, but I do know that I was thankful to him, so indebted to him. I just wanted to be with him wherever he went. Oh, the joy I felt!"

Judith looked around her and saw that everyone's faces were glowing. She felt her own burning, sharing in Hosea's happiness and joy.

"But that's not all folks," he continued. "The crowd around me was large, and there were religious leaders there now beside me. I'd lost sight of Jesus and his men. The leaders had been attracted by the commotion. They however didn't look quite as happy as those I'd spent years with at the pool. They looked positively annoyed. It was the Sabbath, you see. Jesus had healed me on the Sabbath. They said to me, positively spitting, 'You can't work on the Sabbath. The Law doesn't permit you to carry that sleeping mat.' I told them, 'The man who healed me told me to pick it up and walk.' I suppose I expected them to recognise that a miracle had taken place and make allowances, but no. They weren't interested in the fact I was healed. They would have preferred I'd remained disabled, rather than break the sabbath laws. 'Who told you that?' they shouted at me, as if I was a criminal for being healed, and Jesus an even bigger one for doing such a miracle. At that point I didn't know whom it was that had healed me, and I couldn't see him in the crowd. Eventually they left me alone, and I went into the Temple to give thanks. Later, in a quiet spot there, Jesus found me again. I thanked him profusely. He said to me, kindly but earnestly, 'Now you are well, so stop sinning or something even worse may happen to you.' He wasn't being unkind or threatening. It was clear from the way he looked at me, he was just concerned for me and wanted me to continue enjoying what he had done for me. I've come to realise since that Jesus wants to break barriers, traditions, superstitions. He's not happy with the old order. His...our...Father's bringing about change. I felt loved that day. I felt the Father was real and loved me, stupid insignificant me. The Law, our leaders and no amount of tradition, could ever have done that. I decided to go back to the leaders and declare to them who it was that had healed me, now I d found out who it was. They needed to know, and know that perhaps the Messiah was among us."

Again, a clap, this time accompanied by a roar, went around the room.

Peter stood up and raised his hand for silence. "That's the Jesus we know, and we love. Our Father is real and is certainly doing something new. Our Messiah Jesus has indeed come, and now we've received the Holy Spirit. A new thing is indeed happening, and we're involved. The same Spirit that was in Jesus is now in us, So Jerusalem watch out!" He smiled, and added, "...and the world too!"

The meeting disbanded with everyone buoyed up. Many of the men left for work but some of the women hung around to talk. Judith went downstairs with Mikha to seek out Joel and to see if his expected guest had arrived

When they entered the atrium, they had found themselves looking at a near middle-aged greying man. Judith had felt drawn to him right away. There was a warmth about his smile and a kindness about his eyes. Could this be the same man whom Joel had described as one of the black sheep of his family. He wasn't unlike Joel – perhaps a younger version of him. Lines around his eyes, mouth and forehead along with his greying temples, gave him the appearance of being older than he was, but Judith, on closer inspection, estimated he was probably in his early to mid-thirties, about thirty years Joel's younger. Unlike Joel, however, he was tall, and of slimmer build, almost too thin, for his own good. His leanness seemed to add height to him, making him seem deceptively tall. He came over to them immediately, and before Joel could introduce him, he said, "I'm Joseph, Joel's long-lost nephew, the good looking one of the family!" His face was wreathed with smiles now as he made to hug each of them in turn. Judith did not fail to notice Joel rolling his eyes at his nephew's joke at his expense. Both were smiling though, and it looked as if they were getting on well.

Mary, who had been standing in the background, said, "You'll all have some food now? Come and sit in the dining room. We can chat there while we eat."

"Great," said Joseph. "I'm famished. With all these pilgrims in Jerusalem and my Levite quarters serving small portions, I'm ready to eat anything!"

Judith thought, his build didn't suggest a man with a big appetite.

Mikha said, "I can't stay long, I'm due at work soon."

"Me too," said Joel. "With all these pilgrims in town I've got to be on duty. I'll sit down for a moment and have something to drink, but I must be off soon."

They all sat down and exchanged pleasantries, then after a swift drink, both Joel and Mikha left, making their farewells. "I'll come back with Mikha later and we'll have dinner. The women can stay here, and we'll all spend the evening together, getting to know each other."

"I'm afraid I'll have to leave soon too. I have studies and other jobs to attend to. And I have to be in the Temple at Evening Sacrifice," Joseph looked suddenly quite serious. "I'll be back for the evening meal though," he looked at Mary, "if I'm invited?"

"Of course you are. You're more than welcome."

"Then that's fixed then," and Joseph went back to doing what he did best, Judith thought - smiling.

The small talk continued for some minutes, then first Joel and Mikha took their leave, and again a half hour after that, Joseph left too. Judith welcomed this chance to talk to Mary as she hadn't seen much of her since returning to Jerusalem. They were joined later in the day by Miriam who had for a while after the morning gathering been in great demand with some of her son's newest believers. Martha and Jeremiah were clearing away the dishes when Mary spied through the open shutters Esther, Judith's childhood friend and her part-time maid. She was leaving the courtyard and about to go through the gates. Mary called to her and asked her to join them, which she did. It was just like old times again, thought Judith. They were just all a bit older, a good bit older.

Tabitha and Jonas hung around for a little while, but felt out of place in the reunion atmosphere that prevailed, so after some time, Jonas asked his mother if they could adjourn to the garden in the centre of the villa, and she gave them her permission.

"Joseph seems quite nice," Judith said to Mary when the conversation came round to him. "He's older than I was expecting though…to be Joel's nephew, I mean. And Jonas's cousin."

"You're right," said Mary, "but remember, his father left home before Joel and I got married, and we had to wait almost twenty years to have Jonas. He probably settled down fairly quickly and had Joseph." She paused for a moment, "It's only first impressions, but I've a feeling we've got things a bit wrong about him."

"How do you mean?" asked Judith.

"Well, we've always seen that side of the family as the bad ones, the rebels, the unorthodox of the clan, but certainly, he doesn't seem anything like that."

"No," agreed Judith. "I had quite a warm, strong feeling about him."

"So did I," confessed Mary.

"Do you think it was the Holy Spirit?"

"How do you mean?"

"Giving us that feeling, I mean. There seemed a genuineness about him. He seemed trustable."

"I felt that way about him too," said Mary. "You might be right. Perhaps by giving us the Holy Spirit, Josh has given us a way to know things we wouldn't have known otherwise."

Judith nodded. "It's like an extra sense."

"You two aren't alone there," Miriam joined in, "I've been sensing things too." Esther also was nodding.

"It's almost like we have a link with other believers," Judith said, trying to make sense of what they were talking about. "The Holy Spirit is in all of us and we feel a common bond."

"Yes," Mary agreed, looking slightly troubled too, "but Joseph isn't a believer," she added, "as far as I know."

"True," Judith paused, "Actually we don't know that. but maybe we'll find out more about him later. Didn't I hear him say he was a Levite, or involved in Levitical studies?"

"You're right," Mary agreed. "That would be a turn up for the books, especially for that side of the family. We'll have to be very careful what we say to him though...in case he's working for 'the other side'. He'll soon get suspicious if he sees our upper room full of people most days."

"When the men get back later, we'd better warn them to be careful."

"Indeed," said Mary, and the conversation drifted on.

Later that day just before darkness fell, the men returned home, and Joseph was with them. They were deep in conversation but much of what they were saying was punctuated by serious bouts of laughter and merriment. Judith and Mary tried to communicate with their husbands at first with meaningful looks, suggesting they should be careful, but the men seemed oblivious to them. When Joseph went to freshen up before the meal, the wives took their chance to instruct their husbands, but they just laughed and played it down. It was clear they knew something their wives didn't, and they weren't quite ready to tell them.

"What's got into them?" Judith said to Mary.

"I don't know, but no doubt we'll find out in good time."

The dinner was served, and they all took their seats, with Joseph being seated in the place of honour, reserved for special guests.

Joel gave thanks, "Blessed are You, Lord our God, Ruler of the universe, who brings forth bread from the earth, and blessed are You, Lord our God, Ruler of the universe, who creates the fruit of the vine. And thank you for bringing Joseph to us and letting us share together this fine evening, and for your Son...the Messiah."

Joel's departure from the traditional blessing threw Judith and Mary into a quandary. They looked accusingly at Joel, implying he had gone too far, but he only laughed. Indeed, the men were all laughing now.

"It's all right, Mary, Joseph is one of us. We bumped into him today at Solomon's Colonnade. You'll get a chance to hear his story later, after we've eaten."

The women looked relieved, and the meal continued with a fair degree of merriment, something which even Jonas and Tabitha were able to enter into.

After the dishes were cleared away, and everyone had had enough, they adjourned to the atrium and relaxed with some light refreshments in front of them.

"You've done us well, uncle," Joseph smiled. "This is far better than I'd have had at my lodgings."

"All right then, I think it's time for you to tell your story. I know the women are keen to hear it...and the young ones too."

Joseph seemed glad of the opportunity to speak, and so he cleared his throat, "Well, I'm the black sheep of the family, you know." He looked round them all, his eyes twinkling. Joel looked at him, urging him on.

", I was a bit of a problem when I was young, not unlike my father, or so I'm led to believe. Our family ended up in Cyprus because Joel here was the successful one, taking up religious orders. He was going to get married. My father couldn't stand it. Everything seemed to be going Joel's way. My father wasn't like that. He didn't want to get involved in the system. Our religion was too stuffy for him. He couldn't envisage a lifetime caught up in it, so he left home and travelled. He actually settled down after a while in Cyprus and became rich from making cloth and selling it. Because of his success, within a very short time, he was able to buy a bit of land there and do a little farming. He married my mother, and that's when I came on the scene. I grew up in a secular Jewish culture, and when I was old enough I began to get involved in my father's business - the goods and the bads of it. I enjoyed life, but there seemed always to be something missing. I couldn't put my finger on it. Was this what I really was cut out for, I often wondered. It wasn't as satisfying as I had hoped. Eventually I gave up trying to convince myself it was what I wanted, and I decided to give in to a desire to go home. I suppose the old family ties were drawing me back." He paused, then continued, "I knew I wouldn't be welcome though. Our side of the family had burned their boats. Our grandparents were gone, and I knew there was no love lost between Joel's side of the family and ours. So, when I returned, I decided to avoid him and get on with my own life. I could make my own way, and perhaps…one day…if things got better, our family might become reunited. But…" he paused again, "I didn't bargain on Josh."

Now Judith's ears pricked up.

"I was back in Jerusalem, and I was enjoying myself. I had enough money from Cyprus to do so without working. It was an easy lifestyle, and I didn't hold back. I made many friends, most of whom were friends only because I bought them. I took advantage of the night life and threw myself fully into it. I became involved with a married woman, although I didn't know she was married at the time. At first, we were just friends. She always seemed to be in the places I frequented. I wasn't mixing with the best. We talked a bit, and I'm afraid to say I was quite attracted to her. Her rough disrespectful way of speaking made me feel good, and I liked the way in which she seemed to flirt easily with men…and with me. It all became too much, and I found that I wanted her, and not just to talk to. She really dazzled me with her rebellious outrageous lifestyle and so I decided to take part of it for myself. On a particular night, we'd both been drinking, and she was especially provocative. She was throwing her body at me, leaving very little to the imagination. Every time she touched my arm or my face, I felt a tingle go right through me. I made the suggestion that we go somewhere quieter and she told me of a secluded place where we wouldn't be disturbed. I'm not proud of myself but I was so caught up I didn't care where we went." He looked apologetically at the women. "She took me down a dark alley and we climbed over a gate into a garden which had an outhouse. I heard her swear when she found the door was locked. By this time, I didn't care where we did it. I just wanted her, and the weeks of longing which had built up just spilled out. She wasn't unwilling, and as we pressed our mouths together, both of us became frantic with desire." He looked down, guilt and shame written on his face. Our robes became an impediment but that didn't stop us, and we were in the full act when we heard loud shouting just beyond the gate. We were in easy view of those on the other side of it who were holding torches. We hadn't heard them arrive as we'd been indulging our passion. The woman cursed, pulled her robe down and whispered, 'My husband!' It was obvious he must have been following us, and by the light of the torches I made out a man with him dressed in religious robes. It's clear he had brought a witness. Her husband leaped over the gate and took a flying kick at me, knocking me to the ground. I was winded and couldn't get up. He continued kicking me while I was down, and I began to see stars. However, he wasn't really interested in me. He grabbed his wife and dragged her by the hair to the gate, saying 'This is the very last time. We'll see what the elders do with you at the city gate in the morning!' She was screaming as I fell unconscious, lying there in a very undignified state with my robe up around my waste. When I came round again, I was cold and wet with dew. I struggled to my feet, feeling bruised and battered, aching all over. Although I was glad I had not been arrested, I felt a bit guilty for the woman. I hadn't exactly been blameless in it all, and so I wondered if there was anything I might be able to do to help. I knew exactly what her husband had meant by saying they would be at the city gate in the morning. There the elders gathered to meet out justice and settle property issues. The man would be looking for a divorce, and worse than that, if he could prove she had been caught in the act of adultery, he might even get the death penalty for her. As you know, adultery under the Law can be punishable by stoning. I certainly didn't want her to undergo that! But I had to be careful. I had to keep out of sight in case he recognised me and involved me. I wasn't sure what I would do if she was to be stoned, but I wanted to be there anyway just in case there was anything - anything at all - I could do."

Joseph settled into his story. He knew he had the others' undivided attention. "I went therefore to the gate where the elders were known to sit in the mornings. It wasn't long after dawn and I saw a crowd of people gathered there already looking for their services. I spied in the crowd the woman I'd been indiscreet with. I've got to say, she didn't seem so nice in the light of day. I'd only seen her in drinking places by candlelight. She looked exactly what she was, one of the brazen kind. She had a hard look on her face, her hair was unkempt and her robe dirty and dishevelled. She wasn't someone I would normally have associated with, but it's clear that my desires had got the better of me. I could see however she'd been crying, and I think I noticed a darkening bruise on her temple. Perhaps her husband had beaten her before dragging her in front of the elders. Beside the man I assumed to be her husband was a pharisee, probably the man who'd accompanied him the night before to be a witness. It was clear they were becoming impatient as the queue before them was quite large. I watched from a doorway slightly down an alley facing the place of judgment near the gate. The pharisee was joined by some of his colleagues and a good bit of whispering and consulting was done. Suddenly the pharisees gathered around the woman and her husband and they all left the scene. I wondered what was going on. Were they going to carry out their own religious stoning ceremony? It struck me that no-one would have bothered if she'd got what she deserved. But it wasn't fair, I was getting off with it. I decided to follow and observe. With fewer of them, perhaps I might be able to get her away from them. I didn't want her now. My only concern was to avoid her being killed. As I followed, it became clear that the woman didn't want to co-operate with them. She was screaming, tearing at their robes, gouging at them, trying to bite them as they restrained her. But they were too much for her, and she was dragged rather unceremoniously from the gate toward the Temple Mount. They took her screaming and kicking up the steps and into the outer courtyard where a small group of people were listening to a fairly tall man of medium build who was sitting in the midst of them. He had long brown hair and was in full flight. The atmosphere appeared intense, the crowd absolutely focussing on his every word, and some of them looked round rather angrily at the disturbance that was making its way toward them. Because of their respect for the Pharisees, however, they moved aside to let them through. They were obviously making for the man in the centre of the group. They deposited the screaming and cursing woman at his feet, then the crowd closed in behind them. I stood a little way off. They were all so preoccupied with the event, I was in no danger of being noticed.

'Teacher,' a pharisee said, 'this woman was caught in the act of adultery. The Law of Moses says to stone her.' The other pharisees looked ingratiatingly at him while the accuser smiled at him, 'What do you say?' It was clear that they were testing him, for some reason or another. They didn't want alternatives; they weren't interested in them. They just wanted her dead and seemed to be looking, for whatever reason, for his approval.

The man stooped down and wrote in the dust with his finger, saying nothing. He was quietly and deliberately ignoring them. I couldn't see what he was writing, or whether he was just drawing. They kept on accusing the woman their voices getting shriller, becoming more and more frustrated by his lack of response. With a quick action he stood up again. 'All right,' he said, a serious expression on his face, 'but whoever has never sinned throw the first stone.' Then he stooped down again and wrote in the dust. It was amazing to watch." Joseph said, his face deadly serious. "Starting with the oldest, the pharisees slowly left one by one. They seemed to feel convicted. Their plot, their rage, had been no match for his words. The woman looked stunned, having fully expected to be awarded the death penalty. She was whimpering. Her husband was standing over her, but when the last pharisee left, he cursed, glared at the man, and walked away muttering that there was no justice, and that he'd get even one day.

There was an astonished silence. No-one dared speak. They wanted to hear what the stooping man would say. He stood up slowly and looked at the woman. Her eyes were fixed upon him, with a mixture of gratitude and wariness. He spoke softly, his eyes boring into her...and Yet there was a kindness about his face. 'Where are your accusers? Didn't even one of them stay to condemn you?'

'No, Lord,' she whispered. She stopped whimpering, and the crowd craned to hear what he would say next. I had trouble hearing myself.

'Neither do I,' he said. 'Go and sin no more.'

The crowd gasped. I needn't tell you I was surprised too. One moment she was about to be stoned, and the next she was allowed to go free, with just a caution. Did he know what he was doing? If he'd known what she and I had done, would he have been so forgiving? He seemed to be pardoning her, and the crowd who would normally have been baying for vengeance, were in agreement with him.

Don Treader

He offered her his hand and helped her to her feet. Her eyes were fixed on him all the time. I saw a remarkable thing as I watched her. Her face softened and became quite lovely, no longer the hard callous soul she had appeared earlier. She smiled at him and nodded. It was all in the eyes. Something from inside him had wakened something inside her, and she looked as if she was a new woman. She let go of his hand and turned to go through the crowd. They opened a path for her and she walked through it, and made her way to the Temple exit. I was going to follow her, but my feet wouldn't move. Perhaps it was for the best, I thought. I'd caused her enough damage. At least I knew she was safe. Anyhow I had other things on my mind. Who was this man? What on earth had he done to totally change this desperate situation? Not only by forgiving her had he done something for her. He had done something for me too. I wanted to know more. I had a deep sense of gratitude in me too. I felt drawn to him. Who was this man who seemed to have the power to forgive and remove sins? I made my way into the crowd which was now dispersing. The man and his men were leaving too. 'Who is he?' I asked one of the men standing beside me. 'He's the Messiah, Yahweh's Son,' he said simply, as if it needed no explanation. 'He's Jesus from Nazareth, a mighty prophet and healer. Have you not heard of him?'

I confessed I hadn't, and he said, 'When he speaks our hearts burn. He has healed the blind, made the crippled walk and cast out demons, even in this past week. He's the Lord's Christ!' I didn't doubt him. I'd just seen him at work, and I knew, I just sensed, it was true. Somehow or other I'd been forgiven too by his words, and I wanted to thank him. As the man I had spoken to was walking away, I turned to find this Jesus. I jumped when I realised he was standing right beside me. He was looking at me with those eyes, those eyes which had granted forgiveness to the woman.

'Joseph,' he said, his eyes searching my soul.

'Yes Lord,' I said taking my eyes away from his. I couldn't look into that steady searching gaze. 'I am the good shepherd and my sheep - even the black ones - know and hear my voice.'

I looked up again, startled at his personal reference to me. How did he know my name and how did he know about me? He was smiling at me now. 'I want you to come into the sheepfold. My door is open for you. Today is the time for you. Your sins which are scarlet will now be as white as snow, as white as pure wool. I have come to give you life, abundant life. You will not search anywhere else for it any more. The door is open for you right now. Don't delay.'

'I will follow you Lord,' I stammered. 'I'll follow you,' and as he left the Temple with his men and some other followers, I joined them and rejoiced with them at the wonderful things I had seen and experienced that day. It didn't occur to me to do anything else. I'd found my goal in life and I wasn't going to let it go. I still had money to survive, and so I was free to follow him wherever he went. I had to find out more, I had to know more. I wanted to find out all I could about

124

Yahweh and help bring about the Kingdom of His Messiah. I heard Jesus, or Josh as we know him, speak later to a crowd. He talked about a man who had great wealth, but when he came across a pearl of great worth, he sold all he had in order to possess it. This was me. I'd found what I really wanted in life and was prepared to give up everything else to get it. The next few months were wonderful."

"Before you say any more, Joseph my brother, let's have a break for further refreshment," Joel said.

"I hope you don't all think any less of me for what I've told you," Joseph said. "I'm not proud of myself, but it led me to Josh, and I am proud of knowing him."

Heads were shaken. Mikha said, "None of us a particularly proud of our lives before Josh, but I can assure you, we're all like you, glad to have come to know Josh and want to tell the world about him."

Drinks were passed round and then Joseph continued with his story.

"I saw so much in the weeks that followed. There were times I was at a loose end. Josh took the twelve with him to teach them personally, and the rest of us were left to our own devices. I spent a bit of time with the seventy too that he had chosen near the beginning of his ministry. They had been sent out, two by two, to take the good news to every village. Some of their stories of miracles they'd been permitted to do were absolutely amazing. I learned so much from them and became desperate to work like them. I valued their friendship and the camaraderie between us. Then one day Josh took me aside. He looked at me with those brown eyes of his, searching me. I couldn't hide from their gaze, but neither did I want to. It was as if he was reaching right into me to find and bring out my best. 'You are not for here, Joseph,' he said. 'I have plans for you, beyond anything you can imagine. These will stay with me till the end,' he indicated his men who were sitting apart from us. 'You however are set for the world. You will reach places And teach people you can only dream of. I need you to teach others and for this you must prepare.' He paused, as his words were sinking in. Up till that point, I had assumed...I had wanted...to stay with him and his men, but he was sending me away. I suddenly felt unworthy. 'I know nothing. I cannot teach,' I stuttered. 'I've fallen away from our faith...'

'But not from me,' he said. 'You have discovered life and cling to it dearly. You must bring others, from your own nation...your own countrymen...and from beyond the seas.' Again he paused, then placed his hands upon my head. 'You must study. You must learn. I have called you to this. In doing so you will meet and encourage those who will walk with you on the way. You are to be a lifter of spirits, a light to men...my son of encouragement.' I wasn't expecting any of that! Those who had overheard Josh's words started calling me Barnabas, which apparently means 'son of encouragement'. Now I'm back in Jerusalem taking up my studies, the name Barnabas seems to have stuck."

"You're studying here in Jerusalem?" Mikha queried. "Are you going to take up Temple duties with us?"

"No, not at all. I don't believe that's what Josh meant. Unlike in my youth, I now have an insatiable longing to learn. Where it will take me, I know not yet...but it looks like I may be going over water." His eyes twinkled again. Judith thought, even the way his eyes twinkle, make me feel encouraged.

"Whom are you studying under?" asked Joel with interest.

"Gamaliel," Joseph replied.

"He's a good man," said Joel. "I think he could be sympathetic to our cause. He's steeped in the law and the prophets, and is a pharisee with faith. He goes beyond the letter of the law to its spirit. I've heard him speak often and he makes sense."

"He does. I find him refreshing too, but he's not so popular with all his students. They respect him, but they're not all prepared to be as flexible as he is."

"I can believe that" said Joel, "there are a few hotheads in his class, real zealots for the law."

"Yes, but they're sincere," Joseph defended them, "and I believe it's my task to 'encourage' them beyond the Law into faith."

"You've got your work cut out then...Barnabas," said Joel smiling. The others laughed at Joel's use of the name, and the conversation went on.

"I'm curious," said Joel. "Why didn't you make contact with us sooner?"

"Well, I'd been warned by my father to stay away from your side of the family, and when I first came over from Cyprus, I did that. I didn't know who you were anyway. Of course, I made subtle enquiries when I first took up my studies, and one day you were pointed out to me from a distance, but I thought you'd be opposed to me, being one of the high ups, and me with my faith in Josh."

Joel nodded.

"It was at Pentecost there, that I thought I saw you in the Temple precincts with Peter as he was preaching. I couldn't get to you– it was so busy. But I decided at that point to get a message to you – to let you know of my existence." He smiled. "We're on the same side. The family is well and truly united...and all because of Josh!"

Chapter Sixteen

Judith found herself smiling at these memories. These had been good days, ones full of excitement and expectation. Thinking about them helped alleviate the drastic loss of Mikha. He would never be forgotten but remembering him in the good times helped diminish the horrors of the recent past. She determined to keep doing this – if remembering the early days of 'The Way' and their involvement in it would act as a soothing balm. Wasn't it typical of Josh? Thinking about him and his work made the days seem lighter, and slowly but surely , she was beginning to see the way ahead.

It had been, in the main, a period of fresh advance and supreme consolidation. Every time the Spirit led them into something new, there needed to be a corresponding action to it, in order to bring the new believers into their ranks. Groups mushroomed over the city, followers found themselves conscripted into being leaders, with the apostles providing much needed structure and teaching. There was a fervour amongst the believers underpinned by an insatiable hunger for Josh and the Father. People felt liberated. Gone were the structures of old. They met in each other's houses, shared meals, told of their experiences, prayed much, and broke bread together as often as they ate and drank bread and wine. Their excitement and their generosity led many of them to share their possessions, or to sell them for money to distribute to the poor. Very soon, Jerusalem was buzzing with excitement about 'The Way'. People respected them and were open to hearing more.

Barnabas had been a big addition to their circle of friends. Their little house group had started almost immediately, and on a number of occasions Barnabas had joined with them. He and Mikha became close friends. Sometimes their group had been privileged to be visited by some of the apostles, usually in twos, and their stories of Josh and their teachings were lapped up by the new converts who met with them. They were also joined by Esther who lived not far away in the lower city and could leave her family to be with them for short spells. It seemed that almost every day something new and exciting happened. It was difficult to keep up with events.

Judith remembered a day not long into this period, when Jonas arrived at their house, out of breath and very excited. He had been on his way home to the villa but couldn't contain himself and had to stop off to tell them the news. He had been down at the Temple for the afternoon meeting at the ninth hour in Solomon's Colonnade. Indeed, he admitted to having followed Peter and Jonas there. He had taken to doing this regularly when they left the upper room just in case he might miss anything by staying at home - he had been so enthused by Peter's speech on the Day of Pentecost. So on that particular afternoon, therefore, he had been following behind them, not too closely in case they might have objected. He had watched as they had been about to go in through the Beautiful Gate when something unusual happened. A crippled man was half sitting half lying there. Indeed, Jonas had seen him there on numerous occasions over the past year or two when he had visited the Temple. The man was looking quite deliberately at Peter and Jonas. Jonas knew exactly what he wanted. He positioned himself there daily, or more precisely friends of his positioned him there, so that he could beg a little money for food to keep himself alive. Most people ignored him, and Jonas expected Peter and Jonas to do the same, after all they were in a hurry to get to Solomon's Colonnade. Indeed, he nearly bumped into them before he realised that they had stopped. He held back though and watched. The man must have thought he was in for some good fortune. His attention was fixed on them now that they were upon him. "Alms, sirs, alms, sirs," he called to them. Peter's eyes were now rivetted on him. There was a strange light in them as he spoke. Jonas was sure something special was about to happen. He wasn't wrong. Peter said, "Look at us! I haven't got any silver or gold...but what I do have I'll give to you. In the name of Jesus, the Christ from Nazareth, get up and walk!" Peter moved forward and took the man by the arm and helped him up. The man looked startled, but it was evident he was experiencing something inside him, because he co-operated with him. He seemed to be undergoing some kind of transformation. As he stood up, it seemed that his ankles strengthened. Very soon he was able to stand on his own feet. Indeed, it didn't end with him just standing. Jonas watched as this lifelong crippled man started to jump about, leaping, and praising Yahweh. "He was so loud," commented Jonas, "he was causing a commotion!" A large crowd gathered around him. Many of them had seen him lying there for years and had no doubt passed him without giving him a second thought...but now, he had their full attention, and it was clear he was attributing his good fortune to Yahweh. The party moved into Solomon's Colonnade, the man who had been crippled clinging tightly to Peter and Jonas. A sizeable miracle had taken place and people wanted to know more.

Peter took full advantage of this and preached. "People of Israel, what is surprising about this?

You're looking at us as if we healed him by our own power or spirituality.

It's Yahweh, the Yahweh of all our ancestors, the Yahweh of Abraham, Isaac and Jacob who has brought glory to his servant Jesus by doing this. This is the same Jesus whom you handed over and rejected before Pilate, despite Pilate wanting to release him. You rejected this holy righteous one and instead demanded the release of a murderer. You killed the author of life, but Yahweh raised him from the dead, and we are witnesses of this fact. This man was healed through faith in the name of Jesus, and you know how crippled he was before. Faith in Jesus's name has healed him before your very eyes.

Friends, I realise that what you and your leaders did to Jesus was done in ignorance, but Yahweh was fulfilling what all the prophets had foretold about the Messiah, that he must suffer these things. Now repent of your sins and turn to Yahweh so that your sins may be wiped away, then times of goodness will come from the Lord, and he will again send you Jesus your appointed Messiah. For he must remain in heaven until the time for the final restoration of all things, as Yahweh promised long ago through his holy prophets. Moses said 'Yahweh will raise up for you a prophet like me from among your own people. Listen carefully to everything he tells you.' Then Moses said, 'Anyone who will not listen to that will be completely cut off from Yahweh's people.' Starting with Samuel, every prophet spoke about what is happening today. You are the children of those prophets and you are included in the Agreement Yahweh promised to your ancestors. For Yahweh said to Abraham, 'Through your descendants all the families on earth will be blessed.' When Yahweh raised up his servant Jesus, he sent him first to you people of Israel to bless you by turning each of you back from your sinful ways."

Jonas's eyes were shining as he paused for breath.

"What happened next?" asked Judith, sharing his excitement.

"Well, the priests, the captain of the Temple Guard and some Sadducees came along, and what do you think? They were disturbed that Peter had been teaching about the resurrection of the dead. That's the Sadducees for you!"

"And..." said Judith looking concerned.

"They arrested Peter and Jonas and put them into prison. I think it's only for this evening though. The Council will meet tomorrow."

"Not so good!" exclaimed Judith, now looking alarmed.

"But it was good," insisted Jonas. "Literally thousands of men and women became believers!"

Don Treader

"Really?" said Judith, her face brightening. "But we'll need to call the groups together tonight to pray for Peter and Jonas. Surely our leaders will see that something wonderful has happened. Maybe they'll come to believe in Josh too."

No-one else appeared to share her optimism, however they got together to organise prayer meetings all over the city, to petition Yahweh for the safety of his servants.

The following morning the Council met. The rulers, elders and teachers of Religious Law were there, including Annas, Caiaphas, John, Alexander and other relatives of the High Priest. Joel had also been privileged to attend as he often worked closely with the High Priest.

"By what power, or in whose name, have you done this?" they asked them.

Peter filled with the Spirit answered, "Rulers and elders of our people, are we being questioned today because we've done a good deed for a crippled man? Do you want to know how he was healed? Let me clearly state to all of you, and to all the people of Israel, that he was healed by the powerful name of Jesus Christ the Nazarene, the man you crucified but whom Yahweh raised from the dead. For Jesus is the one referred to in the scriptures where it says, 'the stone that you builders rejected, has now become the cornerstone'. There is salvation in no-one else. Yahweh has given no other name under heaven by which we must be saved."

The Council were amazed at Peter's boldness. They could see that they were just ordinary men with no special training in the scriptures. They also recognised them as men who had been with Jesus. But with the healed man standing among them, there was nothing they could say. They ordered them out of the chamber so they could confer.

"What should we do with these men? We can't deny the sign. Everyone knows about it. To stop them spreading their propaganda we must forbid them from speaking in Jesus's name again."

When they brought in Peter and Jonas, they Commanded them never again to teach or speak in the name of Jesus.

Peter and Jonas replied, "Do you think Yahweh wants us to obey you rather than him? We cannot stop telling about everything we have seen and heard."

The Council threatened them, then let them go. They didn't punish them to avoid having a riot.

Everyone was praising Yahweh for this miraculous sign. The man had been lame for more than 40 years!

Peter and Jonas returned to a packed upper room that night. Almost every believer possible was there, keen to hear their story and to pray with them. The two apostles told them what had been said, and the Believers prayed, "Oh Sovereign Lord, creator of heaven and earth, the sea and everything in them, You spoke long ago by the Holy Spirit through our ancestor David, your servant,

130

saying 'Why were the nations so angry? Why did they waste their time with futile plans? The kings of the earth prepared for battle, The rulers gathered together against the Lord, and against his Messiah'. In Fact this has happened here in this very city, for Herod Antipas, Pontius Pilate the governor, the gentiles and the people of Israel, were all united against Jesus your holy servant whom You anointed, but everything they did was determined beforehand according to your will. And now, o Lord, hear their threats. and give us your servants great boldness in preaching your Word. Stretch out your hand with healing power. May miraculous signs and wonders be done through the name of your holy servant Jesus."

The Meeting place shook and everyone was filled with the Holy Spirit.

Judith and Mikha had been there that night with some of their fledgling group. As they were going down the stairs, they literally bumped into Barnabas. He was bouncing and bubbling with excitement. His face glowed, and his normally merry expression was radiant with joy.

"What's happened to you, brother?" Mikha asked him.

"It's happened, it's happened!" Barnabas enthused.

"What?" asked Judith.

"The Holy Spirit, that's what! A few days ago, I missed being in the Upper Room for the Spirit's coming. I heard all about it from you all, but I hadn't experienced it. Yes, I knew Josh, but that didn't give me the Spirit when I was with him, the disciples neither. You all seemed so lucky when I heard about it the other day. Since then, I've been pleading with Josh and the Father to give me the same blessing as yourselves. I can't help telling you I felt a bit second class. And then tonight…"

They knew exactly what he meant. The Holy Spirit had come in the thunder at the end of the meeting. He had been filled and was now on fire.

They clapped him on the shoulder and hugged him joyfully.

"Yahweh's doing a new thing," said Mikha, "and He's making us all one."

"I feel like bursting!" said Barnabas grinning. "I now know what it feels like. I have to tell others," and he bounced away shouting his good news to all who would listen.

The next time they saw him a few days later, he was much more sombre.

"The other night people, when I saw you, I was in the third heaven. Nothing could spoil my joy. However the following day, I received a message from home. My father has died, you know, Joel's brother?"

They nodded.

"We hadn't heard. We haven't' seen Joel since that night," Judith said sympathetically. "That's a real blow for you!"

"My father and I weren't that close, at least not in the past few years; but I respected him. He and my mother had made a good life for themselves...and us...since living in Cyprus.

"Will you go back to Cyprus then?" asked Mikha.

"Not at present," Barnabas replied. "I'm too late for the funeral, and anyway I've not long till I finish my studies. Perhaps after that. I know I'll go back some day."

"We're sorry for you, brother," sympathised Judith. "Is there anything we can do?"

"No, Judith," he said gratefully. "Actually, I've made up my mind about something."

Mikha and Judith looked at him quizzically.

"The messenger who brought me the news, I've instructed him to sell a portion of the land I've inherited when he gets back to Cyprus. I'm not likely to need it, and I think it could do much more good here. I want to benefit the poor, and so I'm going to give the money I make from it to the apostles. They can distribute it!"

"That's quite something," said Mikha.

"It's not any more than anyone else is doing here at present. I want to be involved, and this is something I can do for Josh."

"A great sentiment, brother," said Judith.

"Yes, well, it looks like you may have me for a good bit longer in your house group."

"We'll be proud to have you there. You have much to offer the new believers."

"I hope so...but I'm still learning too."

"We all are," said Mikha. "We've only known you a short time, but we're proud to have you as our friend!"

From that day on, Mikha, Judith and Barnabas, along with the group they belonged to, became a close-knit unit. As they spoke out with boldness and shared their possessions with the poor, it seemed that Yahweh's favour and blessing rested heavily upon them.

Chapter Seventeen

Over the next few months, the work had progressed in Jerusalem with Judith, Mikha and Tabitha fully involved in it. They continued to enjoy visits to their little group from Barnabas and some of the apostles; and there was always a constant stream of new believers arriving at their door. First of all, they had to limit numbers when there simply wasn't space for another body to sit down, and then eventually they held meetings on various evenings for different believers. This became the pattern for all the groups throughout the city. They also balanced their time between their own meetings and attendance at Joel and Mary's Upper Room. It was a busy and exciting time. Surprisingly, with such a 'revival' affecting so many people, the authorities didn't seem to want to take an interest in them. Perhaps the positive spiritual atmosphere pervading Jerusalem evidenced by the 'love' and sacrifices demonstrated daily by the believers for the poor and needy of the city was making its mark. Added to this, an inability to know what to do with these ardent believers, along with a growing number of miracles attributed to the apostles, caused them to delay any response, and to turn a blind eye to what was going on. Indeed, there was also a positive spin off for the Temple. People seemed to be more involved in their faith, attending services and donating money. The authorities were not unaware of this and decided to bask in the benefits rather than to cause dissension. Also the fairly close relationship between the High Priest and Pilate often took up much of the Council's time and energy. Pilate seemed intent on inflaming tensions between the people and Rome by promoting the Emperor's image throughout Jerusalem in different ways, and although the Sanhedrin usually collaborated with their overlords, they had their hands full dealing with the tensions that resulted from these actions.

So while things were spiritually buoyant in the city, politics in the province was descending into chaos, and the Council was fully taken up with this rather than a burgeoning faith.

The more Judith dwelt on these things, the more she longed for the past. Mikha had been in his element, and after doing a day's work at the Temple, he literally threw himself into 'The Way'. Tabitha seemed to be growing up quickly too and was taking an active part in the work. It did not escape her parents either, nor Joel and Mary, that this was not the only active interest she was taking. Although she was still young, it was clear that she had feelings for Jonas, and he for her.

Judith herself was fully involved at Mikha's side, welcoming guests to their group, speaking about her friendship with Josh and the wonderful ways he had intervened in her life. There was a hunger and thirst in the new believers which spurred them all on and made spreading the good news about Josh something special. The days flew by almost untrammelled by opposition, and there was a great joy throughout. From time to time in the meetings in Joel and Mary's, the Holy Spirit would speak through one of the apostles, and increasingly through one of the attendees, warning them of a time of persecution. The good times would not last. They must prepare for adversity. Often now, during the prayer time, people wouldn't just speak in an unknown language, they would give an inspired message, the thrust of which was to get ready to go out. The apostles encouraged everyone to be involved. It was their duty. Yes, they had to spread the word that the Messiah had come and that the Father was doing a new thing, but they also had to be aware of the Spirit leading them and follow his every impulse. The apostles told them that Josh himself had said believers would do greater things than he had done if they would only believe. Therefore inspired messages, prayer for the sick, and even miracles were to be expected…and actually happened at the hands of this dynamic band. Josh's presence was very real as they went about their business allowing the Spirit to lead them.

Fear also had had the power to motivate them, as they had all discovered to their cost.

Perhaps laxity and familiarity had crept in? Some weeks into the sharing programme, with people distributing and selling their goods to help out the poor, the Spirit taught them a powerful salutary lesson. The rule was that if you wanted to sell land or houses, you did so voluntarily, and then voluntarily you gave the amount of proceeds you wished to the apostles for them to distribute. This worked well as happened with Barnabas when he sold his land in Cyprus and gave the money to the apostles. However, some weeks later, Tabitha had come home quite shaken and pale one day. She had been at one of the meeting places with Jonas, and something dreadful had happened. The apostles were sitting receiving money and goods when a man named Ananias had come in and deposited a sum of money at Peter's feet. Peter had enquired as to the cost and the man had assured him that this was all the money he and his wife had received from the sale of their property. Peter suddenly stiffened, as if a thunderbolt had struck him. "You're lying," he said. "Did you think you could deceive the Spirit?" The man dropped down dead at Peter's feet, and terror filled the room. Tabitha was crying as she said, "Jonas helped wrap the man up in a sheet, and he, along with some of the young men, carried him out to bury him." Her mother tried to console her, while feeling the same fear gripping at her heart. "But that's not all, mother," Tabitha wailed. "Three hours later, the man's wife came in. I think you know her…Sapphira?" Her mother nodded. "Straight away Peter asked her if the sum her husband had declared was the full price they had gained from the sale of their property. She readily agreed with him. Then he said, 'Why have you both conspired against the Holy Spirit, trying to deceive Yahweh? The young men who carried out your husband will carry you out too.' And mother, she actually died there and then, and Jonas and his friends who were just returning from burying her husband, had the job of burying her too." Judith was horrified at this. Lying, she believed was bad - but this bad? She knew that Yahweh demanded holiness in his followers - but going to these lengths? She knew she couldn't quibble over Yahweh's justice. Only a fool would do that, and so she like many others accepted it, and allowed the fear of Yahweh to focus her ardour and actions, not only in a path of liberty but also in one of holiness.

As she thought over these things, she could feel that rising anxiety again. Was her hankering after the old days and regretting the loss of Mikha, disobedience which she might easily be punished for? The Holy Spirit knew her thoughts and would know whether she had been straying outwith her limits. Yahweh had done so much for her in comforting her. Was she being ungrateful for all this by longing for the past, and Mikha? She decided to pray, confess any unintended disobedience, and move away from that line of thought altogether. Her fears subsided, and she was about to leave the room when something else came to mind that brought her up to the recent past.

The months were passing, and 'The Way' was growing. It was strengthening and fast becoming established. There was an urgency, an energy, about how it communicated its message, and in the way it energised its members. Those who became believers quickly seemed inspired by the Holy Spirit, gripped by a, fervent desire to pass on what they had received, and a healthy holy fear to make sure they remained obedient to the call. During this time many found themselves doing things they would once have shrunk back from. The most unlikely people were prophesying in the meetings, speaking boldly in public even to people in authority, and following the example of the apostles and praying for, and healing, the sick. Regularly the apostles spoke boldly in the Temple and were renowned for doing miraculous acts including delivering people from demon possession. They gained such a reputation that the townspeople brought out their sick and laid them at the sides of the street, so that Peter's shadow might fall on them and heal them. Even large numbers from the surrounding villages brought their sick and possessed, and they too were healed. 'The Way' was enjoying popularity, but it was slowly growing evident from increasing skirmishes with the authorities that they were becoming jealous and more worried about its acceptance by the people. Daily now, Mikha Joel and Nicodemus confessed to their families their worries about becoming exposed to their colleagues. In their discussions and actions, they had always, and would always, try to ameliorate any bad feeling towards 'The Way', but increasingly they sensed that their positive spin on things was becoming suspect. Things came to a head when the apostles were arrested in the Temple while in the midst of healing the sick. A band of Temple Guards was summarily dispatched to stop their activities and put them in prison until they could be tried the following day in front of the full Council. Joel, Mikha and Nicodemus had attended the meeting in the upper room that night relaying what had happened to a horrified assembly. The boldness and audacity of the authorities' action had thrown them. It had been totally unexpected. Those in charge of the meeting reminded them of the apostles' words, and numerous prophecies too, telling them persecution would come and that they should be ready for it. The gathering with great solemnity got down to prayer and spent hours petitioning Josh and the Father for their friends. Eventually they left, encouraged by the Spirit to believe that Josh was in this, and that Yahweh would work on their behalf. The following morning Joel had gone into work with a heavy heart, to find the Temple authorities in confusion. The Council had gathered early to discuss the case and to deliberate on what they should do with the apostles. They had sent the guards to bring them from the prison. Consternation and bewilderment had broken out when the guards returned saying that the apostles weren't there. The prison gates were securely locked with guards standing outside them, but no-one was inside. They had apparently escaped. Confusion! Joel had never seen anything like it in all his time working for the High Priest. He looked over at Nicodemus who seemed to be stifling a smile. The two exchanged hopeful glances. Absolutely no-one in the room had known what to do next. Then a guard came running in saying the men they were looking for were in the Temple court teaching the people. Wonderful, thought Joel, they were in the very last place anyone would have expected to find them. How typical of Josh. The guards were dispatched again to bring them in with as little fuss as possible in order not to start a riot among the people.

"Didn't we tell you never to speak in this man's name?" the High Priest said when they were standing before them. "You've filled all Jerusalem with your teaching about him. And you want to make us responsible for his death!"

"Yahweh must be obeyed rather than human authorities," said Peter boldly. "He, the Yahweh of Abraham Isaac and Jacob, raised Jesus from the dead after you killed him by hanging him on a cross. Yahweh has placed him in the place of honour at his right hand as prince and saviour. He did this so the people of Israel would repent of their sins and be forgiven. We are witnesses of these things, and so is the Holy Spirit who is given by Yahweh to those who obey him."

Hearing this, the High Council became incensed and wanted to destroy them.

"Listen!" a pharisee called Gamaliel was standing up and beckoning to them. "Let's put them out for the moment while we discuss their case." Gamaliel was an influential teacher, an expert in the Law, and someone respected by all.

When they had left, he pled with them, "Men of Israel, take care what you intend to do to those men. Remember Theudas? He was thought to be great some time ago, and he gathered around him some four hundred followers. He was killed, and his followers dispersed. It all came to nothing." He continued, "Remember Judas of Galilee at the time of the census? He had followers but he was killed too. The same thing happened." He paused for effect. "Therefore, my advice is, leave these men alone. Let them go. If they are planning and doing these things on their own it will soon be over and done with. But if it is from Yahweh you will not be able to overcome them. You may actually find yourselves fighting with Yahweh!"

His advice was acceptable to them all, so they brought the apostles back in, and had them flogged.

The High Priest commanded them again, "Never again speak in the name of Jesus!" then he let them go.

Joel and Nicodemus made eye contact and communicated their relief and joy at the result. They couldn't wait to leave work that day and join up with Mikha who was only a minor official and hadn't been privy to what had happened, so that they could all be in the upper room when the apostles arrived.

News had spread quickly that the apostles had been released, and so Joel Nicodemus and Mikha were lucky to gain entrance. Everyone was ecstatic about this apparent and extremely visible answer to their previous night's prayers. The apostles were beaming and went over the events of the day. The gathering looked concerned when they learned they had been flogged by their religious leaders, but the apostles allayed their concerns. "We're so privileged," they said, "that Yahweh has counted us worthy to suffer disgrace for the name of Jesus!".

Judith found herself wondering if she had the same attitude as these men. She had had an intimate relationship with Josh, close encounters with the Father, encouragement from every quarter – but there she was at times lamenting Mikha's death, hankering after the past and her happiness with him. Was she being unfaithful? Disobedient? Did she count it a privilege to suffer disgrace for Josh and Yahweh? Sometimes the loss of her dear husband seemed so raw. In those moments, was she actually aware of thoughts inside her that blamed Yahweh and caused the overwhelming bitterness of the past to raise its ugly head? She couldn't afford to let them overwhelm her now and so she pushed her feelings and doubts away. She struggled off her mat onto her feet. She had to get away from these thoughts and her fear of letting Yahweh down. She wanted to be someone who rejoiced in her sufferings and overcame. She knew she would have to leave the room at that point if she wasn't to be overwhelmed. Judith remembered only too well what came next if she continued with these musings over the past. Yes, of course, the wonderful work of the apostles who continued teaching in the Temple and from house to house. Their message was simple, their message was glorious. It was, "Jesus is the Messiah!" It was a daily risk for them, but they ignored the dictates of the Council, and the word spread far and wide. But next! Feelings were running high in the Council, and it was only a matter of time before hatred and violence would break out, and this golden period would end. Next, came Stephen…and then Mikha! She really couldn't face these events just now. She had to leave, to get away. She quickly straightened her hair and smoothed down her robe, then left the room hurriedly and went to find Tabitha, Joel, and Mary. In their company she felt soothed, cared for and supported. She regretted having spent that afternoon rehearsing the past. It had left her feeling raw again. She had thought she was getting better, becoming stronger - but now…she wasn't so sure. She felt vulnerable. She found herself looking forward to the Upper Room meeting that evening, and the meal afterwards which Nicodemus and Barnabas had promised to attend. That would lift her spirit, she believed, and so she pushed her dark thoughts away.

Chapter Eighteen

"You were fortunate tonight, my dear," said Barnabas looking directly at Judith as he tackled his meal, "that the Holy Spirit was present in such a dynamic way."

Judith smiled back at him, "I know. I felt so bad, and suddenly I was on the floor."

"What was wrong, Judith?" asked Joel kindly. "I thought you were getting over things…" He apologised. "I mean…I know you'll never get over the loss of Mikha, but over the past few weeks, you seem to have come a long way."

"I have…thanks to you all," Judith said. "But there are times when I just cannot seem to cope. It all overwhelms me. Today was a case in point."

"What happened?" asked Mary.

"Well, when I was in my room this afternoon, I was going over the good times. You know, after Josh's resurrection, Mikha's, Tabitha's and my own involvement in the early days of 'The Way', the coming of the Spirit and the wonderful miracles. I felt so good, but then when the persecution started and Stephen…and Mikha…" She trailed off.

"Don't distress yourself, dear," said Miriam.

"No, it's all right. I need to face it. When I was about to think over these things, I just couldn't. I had to get away from them. And then the thoughts came. I've received so much from Josh and the Father, and yet, I still can't get over my feelings, my horror over Mikha. I'm not sure if I was blaming Yahweh."

"It's understandable that you would feel that way, Tabitha consoled her mother. "I sometimes have my days too."

Judith looked appreciatively at her daughter.

"So what happened at the meeting then?" asked Nicodemus who hadn't been there.

"I'm not sure," said Judith. "It's all a bit of a blur."

"Do you want me to tell it?" asked Joel.

Judith smiled gratefully at him. "Yes, I'd like to hear about it myself."

"Well," Joel said, "it was the time of prayer. Someone in the gathering was praying quite forcibly when it seemed as if they went onto another plane. It was pure prophecy. They said, 'My daughter, come to me, and I will release you. You are bound by fears and horrors you find difficult to express to others. I am here to heal you if you will allow me.' Suddenly Judith you were lying on the floor, screaming with all your might. It scared many of us, but two of the apostles went over to you and laid hands on you."

"I don't remember much," said Judith looking troubled.

"It's perhaps just as well," said Joel. "Your screams grew louder and louder. They must have been heard well down the road."

"I'm sorry," said Judith. "I didn't mean to attract attention to us."

"Of course not. Hopefully, it fell on deaf ears. All except ours anyway," Joel said smiling. "The apostles prayed authoritatively over you. 'My sister,' they said, 'you have suffered much and lost much, but I am with you. You are bound and need release.' The prayers of those around you rose to a crescendo, as did your screams. Then suddenly you were free."

"I felt free, for the first time in a long time," said Judith. "When I stood up, I felt clean and I had a strong sense of Yahweh's love in me."

"That's good," said Mary, "but did you hear the rest?"

"I can't say I did," confessed Judith. "I was caught up in how I felt."

"The prayer continued, and someone called out a word of wisdom. Do you want me to tell you it?"

"Yes please," said Judith, wondering what was coming.

"The word was this, 'My sister, my daughter, remember your smile. Don't let it go. You can choose life, or you can choose death. I have promised to guard your smile and to help you, but if you choose sadness, I can do nothing till you repent and return to me. Know that I am with you, O you of Little Faith.'"

Judith didn't know how to take this. It was comforting in one way, and not so in another. And the reference to 'Little Faith' wasn't lost on her either. She had remained faithful and loyal even in her suffering, and Josh had taken her and brought her to a place of overcoming.

This word, thought Judith, wasn't as comforting as she might have hoped for. It seemed to imply that her future was somehow in her own hands, and that she might make wrong choices.

"Was anything else said?" asked Judith feeling slightly unsettled.

"Only this," said Mary. "Remember your heart's desire!"

There were these words again. They had seemed to follow her down through the years. What was most important to her? Yes, it was her relationship with Josh and his Father. She shouldn't let even the horrors of Mikha's death supplant them. Something stirred in her pouch, and she knew instantly what it was. The green cross trinket she had found there after her experience in the garden, when Angel

Sophia had given her it. She put her hand into her pouch and held it. It seemed to give her the courage she needed to go on. Once again Josh was trying to gain her attention to help her.

The conversation moved on and she was grateful the spotlight was no longer upon her. She wanted to get on with her thoughts. She had much to digest. After their meal, they adjourned to the atrium where Nicodemus regaled them with details of his new job. In the meantime, Joel was out of the room talking to the servants who had indicated during the meal that they wanted to speak to him about something. When he returned, he looked quite grim

"I'm afraid there's some bad news," he said.

"What's that," asked Mary looking anxious. "Have the authorities discovered us?"

"No, nothing like that. I've just been informed by Jeremiah and Martha that they wish to leave our employ."

Mary looked stunned, "Why?" she asked.

"They apparently feel awkward in our service. They heard the screaming tonight. They've seen the large meetings over the months. They say they know what we're doing, and they're scared that the authorities find out and they get into trouble."

"Didn't you say that we would vouch for them?" Mary asked.

"That wouldn't do them any good, if we were caught," said Joel. "They just want to go."

"What have you agreed with them?" Mary asked showing some agitation.

"I've agreed to let them go…in return for their silence and a good reference from us."

"But what will we do?" Mary was almost in tears.

"I'm sorry Mary," said Judith, looking ashamed. "It's all because of me…and my screaming."

"No," said Joel. "That was only the last straw. They've been thinking of going for months they said. We won't be stuck. Yahweh will supply. We really need a believing brother or sister. That would be the ideal solution."

"Wouldn't it be good if you could have Esther back?" said Judith with a sudden spark of insight.

"Esther? But she's got so many family commitments."

"Actually, no she hasn't. She was with us as you know in our group for some time, and certainly then she had commitments. She used to talk of her husband not approving of her faith though and threatening to take the boys away when he got the chance. She told me recently that he'd left for the quarries in the Jordan valley. The work and pay are good there and he wanted the boys to learn a trade."

"So, she's on her own then?" Mary asked.

"No, her daughter Rhoda is with her. She's only thirteen."

"Do you think she might be willing to come back to work for us? It would certainly be ideal, as she's a sister."

"I think her daughter is too."

"They could both work for us then, if they wish," said Joel smiling. "I'm sure it would be a good combination, a bit like Esther and her mother were when she was a girl."

"Can you go and see them in the morning?" Mary asked. "We'll need help fairly quickly."

Tabitha spoke up, "I could help you too."

"No dear, you're family," Mary said.

"But we're living here rent free. I'd be happy to work for our stay."

"I wouldn't hear of it, dear," Mary said dismissing her great niece's suggestion. On seeing her disappointment, she added, "You could perhaps help out from time to time."

"That's settled then," said Nicodemus, who had been following the conversation which had interrupted his own.

"And yes, my brother," said Joel smiling, "you were going to tell us about your plans."

"Change is coming, and I need to get out."

"How do you mean?"

"You know as well as I do how things are in the Sanhedrin."

"That's true. It's difficult. It's getting more difficult by the day. There's so much political intrigue, and there's a definite hardening of attitudes toward 'The Way'."

"It's only a matter of time before we're discovered and excommunicated...or something worse."

"Do you think so?"

"Yes, there are rumours that the High Priest is planning a major purge."

"A purge?" Joel raised his eyebrows.

"He's got some of Gamaliel's hot boys," he looked apologetically over at Barnabas, "not you, of course, Barnabas," he continued, "to weed out sympathisers of 'The Way'. And we know who'll be first. Both you and I may command respect with the old guard, but these new men, they're lethal. Some of them I believe were responsible for Stephen...and Mikha..." he trailed off, realising Judith was in the room. "I'm sorry, my dear," he said.

"I know. I understand," said Judith graciously.

"That's why," said Nicodemus with a flourish, "I wish to leave, before I'm pushed. And if I were you, Joel, I'd do the same. You can't afford to attract more attention or have them find out about what goes on here."

"That's kind of you to arrange my career for me, my brother," laughed Joel. "You might be right. But what would Mary do with me around the house all day?" he smiled at her.

"I'd have another servant then," she quipped, with a rare flash of humour.

"Actually, the fact is Mary that both of us are getting quite old. Perhaps this might be a good time for me to retire. We could then work for 'The Way' more fully, without causing any suspicion."

"That's my thinking," said Nicodemus. "I'm still young enough to be of use. When I was a young man I worked in a commune, trying to get through to the poor. I had no success whatsoever. I'd like to try again. I'm sure I could do much more with Josh's help."

"You're a brave man," quipped Joel. "I might just join you." And noticing Mary's raised eyebrows, he added, "Not on the commune, just in retirement!"

They all laughed

"I've requested my resignation, and had it accepted by the High Priest."

"That was quick," said Joel frowning.

"Well, I think it's only a matter of time before they come looking for us. You'd do well to get out now too."

"Mary and I will discuss it and pray about it."

"Quite right," said Nicodemus smiling. "But don't leave it too long. I don't think we've much grace time left."

"So you think the High Priest is employing some of the men in my class to harm us?" Barnabas asked.

"Undoubtedly. Since Stephen and Mikha, he's choosing the most fervent, the most ultra-religious, to ferret out 'Way' sympathisers."

Mary looked quite scared now. "Don't worry, dear," Joel reassured her. "We'll find a way through this. The Father will help us out!"

This appeared to indeed be the case. The following morning Joel went to see Esther, and by evening Joel and Mary's household had two new servants. With her husband and sons gone to the quarries, Esther had jumped at the opportunity to work for her old employers. Her daughter Rhoda was to come with her, and both of them would live in the servants' quarters upstairs. They would relinquish their own house. It didn't look as if her husband and the boys would be returning, at least in the relatively near future, so there was no point in holding onto it. Also, a few days later, Joel secured a meeting with the High Priest to offer his resignation. He couldn't believe how easy it was. The High Priest accepted it willingly, commending Joel for his sterling service over the years, and wished him all the best for the future. "You've served us well, my son. Yahweh will reward you for your work. It's maybe right you're leaving now. We all have to make way for new blood. The people of 'The Way' are becoming more meddlesome and more prevalent. We'll have to do something about them soon. There's a new breed of 'religious' rising up. They've got the bit between their teeth. They're on a mission to eliminate these people and they have my blessing.

It's time things went back to the way they were. We wouldn't want Pilate imposing more Roman restrictions upon us because of them, would we?"

"You can't deny 'The Way' have done some good things," Joel countered. "More people seem alive in our faith, more money is being donated to the Temple…and there's the miracles."

The High Priest looked disconcerted. "You may be right in some of that, but these people are dangerous. They'll change the status quo if they're not stopped."

Joel decided not to argue the point any further. It might bring suspicion upon him. The High Priest smiled, "You sound like you approve of them, Joel."

"Well, they don't seem to be a threat to us. They seem to want to get on with doing their own thing."

"But they can't get away with blaming us for the death of their leader. What's his name…Jesus?"

"Well, we did throw him to the Romans, as far as I can remember," Joel said in a matter-of-fact way, trying to state the truth in as acceptable way as he could.

"Yes, if truth be told, I…we…did make that decision. With the nation in turmoil, it was better that one man die to save the rest of us."

"That's true, sir," replied Joel, able to agree with the double meaning in the High Priest's words. "What happened that day, certainly saved us all!" he said with feeling.

"You're a good man Joel. But don't let these people fool you in your retirement. We don't want to clamp you in irons!" The High Priest was laughing now. "Go and enjoy your house, your family. Keep the faith!"

With this the interview ended, and Joel, after almost forty years of service, was free to follow 'The Way' without anyone suspecting a thing…and he liked it that way!

At first, with Esther working in the house, Judith felt she had a friend she could rely upon. It wasn't as if she was a servant. To all of them she was a sister and they treated her that way…with respect. Often Judith would talk to her as she carried out her duties. Sometimes she would even help her with the work, just so she could enjoy her company and bend her ear. Judith found herself still unsettled though. She began to dread time spent on her own, because they always ended up with her going over the past and feeling guilty. She knew that she had been warned not to dwell on it, but she couldn't help herself. The dark feelings surrounding Mikha's death seemed to draw her into them, and she found great difficulty in telling anyone about them…except Esther. After all, they had not only been together for a short time as children, but also on that fateful day when Josh had been crucified. Both had stood at his cross, and wept. Judith therefore confided her thoughts to Esther, and Esther did her best to counsel her, but it was without success. The feelings were too strong for her, and inevitably Judith couldn't resist them. As the days went on, she became more restless, and her companions noticed she wasn't quite the person she once had been. She became moody, unpredictable and on some occasions, even sharp. Tabitha was extremely concerned, as Judith appeared to be becoming again the mother she had once known. She said nothing however, just prayed that her mother would eventually come out of her dark period, just as she had before.

This did not happen, and a month or so later, one spring afternoon, Judith was feeling particularly morose and so cooped up, that she decided to go against what she had agreed with Joel, and to venture outside on her own. She just had to gain her freedom again. What was the point in her hiding away in case she might possibly be recognised by those who had killed her husband? She felt as if she was in a terrible prison. Surely enough time had gone by for her to be forgotten about? She'd had enough of it anyway and decided to go out.

She took a coin from the bag of money she had hurriedly taken from her house the night Mikha had met his end, drew her cloak around her to keep out the nip in the spring air, pulled her hood over her hair so that she would look like most of the women around her – this would also make her less recognisable she thought – and stepped out of the villa without telling anyone. She walked smartly along the road to Mount Zion's main thoroughfare then down the hill to the lower city. She passed the street leading to her old house, but sore memories forbade her from entering it. She would like to have seen her house again, to see what had become of it, but common sense said it would not be a wise move. She continued down into the lower city and walked along the road leading to the Mount of Olives, passing the southern end of the Temple Mount. There seemed to be more Temple guards and officials on the roads, many more than she remembered having seen there for some time. She put this down to Joel's contention that the guards had been on heightened alert after Stephen's stoning, in order to deter and clamp down on the activities of 'The Way'. This didn't discourage her however as her cloak and hood offered her the same anonymity as other women.

How glad she felt to be out in the fresh air, no longer hiding away from her distant ghosts. She wondered about going into the Garden of Gethsemane, but her last journey there had been so traumatic, she decided to make do with reaching the bridge over the Kidron, then she would turn back. She was feeling much more confident now and so like some of the other women and girls around her she lowered her hood to allow the spring sunshine at her hair. On her way past the Temple Mount steps she became aware of a man on a horse staring at her. He seemed to recognise her and looked as if he was about to rein the horse into motion to follow her. She recognised him immediately as the man Miha had shouted at on his way back from Stephen's stoning, the man she believed had been responsible for sending the murderers to her house to kill Mikha. She panicked, and froze. Then feeling terror clutching at her heart, she ran. Fortunately a large cart was passing her at that moment and so she kept pace with it while at the same time pulling her hood back over her head. She heard the man shout in her direction, "Hey you! Stop!" but she ignored him and concentrated on keeping the cart between her and him. She knew she wouldn't be able to keep this up for long as he would soon be able to catch up with her. Then a brilliant plan came to her mind. She was about to pass her street. What if she could slip down it as the man was coming in line with the cart. If enough people were around her, she could slip into her street unnoticed, and the man would follow the cart until he realised, she had given him the slip. Her heart was racing as she executed her plan. It went smoothly, and after a minute or so, she was well away from the main thoroughfare and a good way down her narrow street. For good measure she decided to go into a shop she had often frequented when she lived there. If her pursuer retraced his steps and looked down the street, he wouldn't see any sign of her.

"You're Mikha's wife. Aren't you?" The stocky shopkeeper looked at her closely as she entered his shop. It was packed full of the grains and spices Judith had often purchased from him in the good times.

"Yes," Judith said quietly. "I used to come in here once. It was a while ago though."

"I remember well enough," he said ingratiatingly, putting on what looked to Judith like a forced smile. "That was a bad business…your husband I mean."

Judith just nodded and stole a quick look behind her out into the street to make sure her pursuer was nowhere to be seen.

"He was such a man of the community. We were all shocked to hear of his death…and in such a terrible way! We never saw you again either. We thought you'd left, or been taken. And that daughter of yours…"

"We've been away," Judith said, not wishing to make him more suspicious than he obviously was. "I had to get away from it all. It was terrible! Why would I have been taken?" She thought it best to put the ball back into his court to take the heat off her.

He looked down, unable to meet her eyes. "No idea really." She could tell he was lying. Most of the community knew of their house group and their affiliation to 'The Way'. Why shouldn't he?

He changed the subject abruptly, "What can I get for you?"

Judith thought quickly, "I'll take a bag of mixed spices." She indicated which of the spices she wished to have ground. Fortunately she had taken that coin with her! She placed it on the wooden table in front of him.

For a few moments, Judith browsed and examined some other goods, while he went into the back, and ground up her selection. She could hear whispering as he was doing so, and a moment or two later, a young boy hurried out of the shop, looking at her with interest as he passed.

The man returned seconds later and noticed Judith staring after the boy. "He's a good boy, him. I've sent him to exchange some coins." Again, he could not look Judith in the eye. Judith was beginning to feel anxious.

"How much do I owe you?" she asked trying to appear normal but feeling anything but.

"Five pennies," he said, handing her the bag. He nodded to the coin Judith had placed on the table. "I can't change that just now," he said. "I'm afraid you'll have to wait till the boy comes back with some change."

Judith now totally worried, dropped the bag and exited the shop quickly, the man shouting for her to come back. At the end of the street Judith could see the boy talking to the man on the horse and pointing in her direction. Once again panic set in and Judith fled. She didn't know where she should go. She just had to get away. She could now hear the shouts of the man on the horse, and the shrill cries of the boy as they came after her, the horse's hoofs clattering on the road. Suddenly her mind cleared, and she knew what to do. She was almost at her house now. She took in at a glance it had new owners. She would go further down the street then turn into a tiny alley between two houses. She thanked Yahweh that she knew the area well and should be able to outwit the man and the boy. She could hear the hoofs catching up with her when she suddenly turned into the alley. She heard the man curse. His horse was too big for the passage. She bargained on him being stuck there for a moment or two while he worked out what to do with his horse. He couldn't leave it there. She turned left, then right again in the maze of passageways between the houses and shops, and as she put more distance between herself and the man, she could hear his cursings, and his shouting at the boy to look after his horse while he gave chase. Judith was far enough away now to lose him. She heard his feet running on the hard ground, and his steps echoing between the buildings, but she had a good head start. She came out into the lane that ran behind the houses and shops, the very same lane from which she had entered her house the night Mikha had died. She sped along it and out into the main thoroughfare again long before he was out of the alleys. She knew he couldn't pursue her for long, as he would be afraid to leave his horse unattended or under the uncertain care of the boy. She picked her way through the people making their way up Mount Zion and was relieved when she saw the familiar figure of Joel riding his donkey on his way home from the city. She stepped up to him and walked beside him, assuming that her pursuer, if he happened to see them in the distance, might automatically consider them to be husband and wife, and not give her a second look.

Joel was surprised to see her. "Didn't we agree you would stay indoors until the current danger was past? Should you have been out? Is everything all right?" He looked concerned.

She told him what had happened and about her lucky escape. Joel did not look pleased. She hadn't seen him like this since the day he had come home to discover her, and Josh left behind in Jerusalem all these years ago. She felt just as she had felt then – like a little girl who had been naughty.

"I'm sorry, Joel," she mumbled. "It wasn't wise."

"You're right," Joel said, not mincing his words, his head furrowing. "That's an understatement!" He thought for a moment, then said, "We'll have to talk later. In the meantime, let's see about getting you home. You don't want to get caught now!"

Both of them quickened their pace and soon they had left the main thoroughfare and were making their way down the road to Joel's house, and safety.

Chapter Nineteen

"You were silly, Judith, to do what you did today." Joel was speaking. "You put yourself at risk, and I'm afraid to say, us too." The family with Barnabas and Nicodemus present, and Esther in attendance, were seated in the dining room at their evening meal, discussing the events of the day. Judith decided not to defend herself. She recognised she had been foolhardy to go out, with the possibility of attracting attention to herself, and to her friends. She might easily have compromised the work done by their group in the organising and training of the believers. She had no argument for them. She was already feeling out of sorts. The others were sympathetic to her position – of course they understood that in the period of time since Mikha's death she had been through so much., that she was having to cope with lifestyle changes, especially now she lived at Joel's and Mary's; and they could totally identify with her feeling oppressed and needing to regain some freedom. What they didn't understand was why she hadn't come to them. They could have accompanied her outside and perhaps have avoided this debacle. Nicodemus was speaking.

"This is not the best time to be rattling the cage of the authorities. They're beginning to find their feet, and more and more they want to stamp out 'The Way'. Weve had it amazingly good for so long. I suppose they've been dealing with matters of state – the governor's not making things easy, and there might even be an Imperial visit on the cards. That'll stir up the people. They were probably waiting to see if we'd go away, but with Stephen's death...and Mikha's too..." he looked at Judith sympathetically, "the gloves are off. They're coming for us!"

"You're right," said Barnabas helping himself to more vegetables. "Some people in my class are spoiling for a fight!"

"Those hotheads again," commented Joel. "I'm glad I'm out of it all now!"

"But not maybe for long...if they start coming for us," Nicodemus said. "We have to be careful." He looked over at Judith. "Do you think that man really recognised you?"

"It appeared so," said Judith dryly. She didn't like being the focus of attention, especially in such a negative fashion. As the others looked at her, she said, "He was the person holding the coats at Stephen's stoning, and he didn't take kindly to Mikha shouting at him afterwards. The ruffians enlisted to guard my Mikha's body talked about him as they kept watch outside our house that night. They said he had sent them to do the deed." Judith was now becoming angry as she outlined these facts to them. She felt resentment building up in her. The feelings were all coming back, and with a vengeance. She had thought she was over it all…but no. Anger was beginning to fill her heart and she wanted to explode. She allowed her ire to infect her words.

"I may have been wrong to go out, but I'd no idea that I was being sought after. Yes, I knew that they had been looking for me, but time's gone by. I thought they might have forgotten. And anyway, you've no idea what it's like being cooped up like a hen each day, unable to go anywhere. I might even do it again if I feel bad!"

This response did not encourage the rest who had been hoping for a fulsome apology and a promise not to do the same again.

Joel looked concerned. "Judith, you've placed us in an awkward situation. It would not be good if you compromise our position. You must understand that?"

"Oh, I do," said Judith with uncharacteristic crispness, "but I can't stay here all the time. I'm like a prisoner!"

"You're not," said Mary in a soothing tone. "We love you and want the best for you."

"Of course you do," said Judith getting into her stride, "you want the best for me, except for the very thing I want the most."

Mary and Tabitha looked down, but Joel continued to look straight at Judith.

"We have to face things Judith," he said calmly and quietly. "Things can't be as they were before – not for you, not for any of us. We're all at risk now. For instance, if that man was looking for you, and knows now you're still in town, he will continue looking. You just can't afford to go out at present."

It was Judith's turn to look down now. She couldn't argue against his logic, or spurn the kindness he and her aunt had shown her by letting her stay in their house.

Joel continued. "We'll have to do what we planned just after Mikha's death." He turned to his son, "Jonas, is the cistern sorted out."

"Yes, father. The carpenter's been in and the secret panel is ready. The only thing we've not done is practice using the escape route."

"Well, that will have to be done, just in case." Joel looked at Judith, "Are you all right with that?"

Judith nodded. He continued. "I'm not sure why he seems so keen to find you. If he's as incensed as you've said, it may be that he made enquiries about Mikha, found out he was working in the Temple, put two and two together and associated him – and therefore you – with 'The Way' – and wants to bring you to justice. He may also have found out from any number of believers that you operated a group. With the current clampdown on the go, he may feel he has a good excuse to pursue and apprehend you…as a prominent member of 'The Way'."

"Do we know who he is?" asked Barnabas. "Did you say Joel that he might be associated with Gamaliel's group, my class?"

"Well, from what I saw before I retired, quite a number of your fellow students were zealous for the Law. They were ready to challenge any 'unorthodoxy'."

"You're right there," Barnabas agreed. "But to go as far as to encourage a stoning? I'm not sure if any of my friends could do that."

"There's no stopping a man who feels he has right…or even Yahweh…on his side," commented Nicodemus grimly. "I've seen it so often. And if you want further proof, just look at what our religious leaders did to Josh!"

Barnabas looked at Judith, "You said I think, that this man was holding the cloaks at Stephen's stoning? I'm sure with a bit of probing, I can find out more about him. At least, if he's associated with my class."

"That's all very well," snapped Judith, "but while you're doing your detective work, that's not going to gain me any more freedom!"

The others looked awkward, and Judith stood to her feet, making as if to go.

"We know, we know," said Joel sympathetically. "But we all have to be safe too." He looked at Judith apologetically, "There are consequences if this epidemic of persecution persists."

Judith stopped in her tracks, delaying her exit.

"In the longer term, we may have to leave," Joel said. The others shot him a glance.

"If the persecution goes on and believers are being harassed and arrested, some of us will have to relocate. Judith, you're welcome to stay here as long as we're safe, but if things get too hot, you may have to prepare to go up country."

Judith looked shocked, "You'd throw me out?"

"No, of course not. Nothing like that. But if Jerusalem becomes difficult for the apostles, and us, we'll have to consider alternatives. Would Yahweh want us to stay here and be imprisoned, or even worse, slaughtered.?"

Judith sat down again. "I hadn't thought of that," she admitted. "I know you and Aunt Mary have been extremely kind and supportive to me. I couldn't have had better friends or family. I'm Just hurting and feeling constricted. I don't know that I'm making as good a recovery as I thought. I still feel the need of space."

"And you shall have it, my dear," said Joel kindly. "We don't want rid of you…but we must make contingency plans. It's clear Yahweh is moving things on."

Nicodemus nodded gravely. "As you know, I myself am moving south to work with a religious community. Many of us may have to leave…or die!"

This grim assessment had the effect of focusing everyone's minds. They were as one now as they sought to plan the way forward.

Nicodemus said, "It's important that we don't make any hasty moves. We must wait fully upon Yahweh for Him to move us, to show us where He wants us"

They agreed, and after some further discussion, they ended the evening in prayer, committing their ways into Yahweh's hands.

That night on her mat, Judith reflected on the day's happenings. She saw that she had been lucky to come out of it safely, and that she was extremely fortunate to have the support of her family and friends. She could not shake however her unsettled emotions. That day had stirred them up. Hatred, anger, and resentment laced with guilt and fear. She had been wrong to take a risk and go out. Had her actions opened up a can of worms? With Josh's and the Holy Spirit's help she had believed the bad days were over. But now…the past seemed to be fully in her face again. And why was she feeling a tinge of guilt? She assumed it was because she had allowed her baser nature to come through at the meal…but was that all it was? Deep down she felt troubled. She felt as if she'd done something wrong. The more she thought about it, the more she felt out of sorts. She felt cold. Her emotions felt numb. She hadn't felt like that for such a long time. She put her hand to her pouch and felt the trinket she had recently been given. She drew it out for moral support. She needed it. But no, something was wrong. It didn't glow or sparkle. There was no face of Josh, nothing to comfort her. She felt…actually…as if she was on her own. There was no deep peace. Something seemed to have broken it. It felt, the more she thought about it, as if Josh and the Father had withdrawn from her. What had she done! She decided to reverse tack immediately and pray. If she had let Josh down by going out that day, and by putting the others at risk, she wanted it off her conscience. "Father, I have sinned. I ask for your forgiveness for letting you down. I know you've done so much to reassure me and to support me…" she stopped. She felt nothing. Why? It had always worked before. NO assurance was spreading over her, just a cold sense of numbness, and a gripping panic that things weren't right. What was she to do? She lifted the green cross trinket up to her eyes and prayed again, "Forgive me Father…" Nothing. No flashing glow, no reassuring face. Instead, just an empty cross and…did she imagine a face of condemnation? Of sadness? She hadn't seen it, but the thought had impacted itself on her consciousness. Had she been disobedient? Was she being punished? She couldn't feel or trace Josh's presence. She felt flat…and that sensation didn't go away. She went to sleep experiencing it and woke up the next morning feeling exactly the same.

A turning point had been reached. For Judith she felt as if she was now looked upon with a degree of suspicion, someone who wasn't fully on side. She was aware of a strained atmosphere when she entered a room, and even Tabitha seemed to stop talking whenever she appeared. Added to this was her sense of having let Josh down, and although she sought forgiveness, for the first time in a long time, she felt adrift, apart from his presence, held at arm's length. This worried her the most, as she couldn't now trust her own judgment. She seemed to be at the mercy of many dark emotions, all of which conspired to make her behaviour erratic. For the next day or so she went through the motions of interacting normally with her hosts, but nothing seemed quite right. Her heart just wasn't in the conversations. Neither was it in the 'escape protocol' enthusiastically tackled by Jonas. Yes, she ran up the servants' stairs to the upper room; then out of it and up the stairs onto the roof; then into the cistern housing and squeezed herself behind the wooden panel, pulling it closed behind her...but none of it made any sense, none of it really mattered. She got to the point of thinking, if she got caught, she got caught. She needed to get things sorted out with Josh to make things go back to normal. The sad thing was that the upper room meetings, which up till then had been fairly regular, had been stopped for the moment. After her sojourn into the outside world, and after a warning from Barnabas the day after that a definite push was on to seek out and eliminate cells of 'The Way', it had been decided to relocate them in order to give Joel and Mary some respite. Judith's focus was in bits and she bore a sense of guilt for spoiling things for the others. The following afternoon she closed the door of her room behind her, determined to sort things out once and for all. She knelt on her mat and prayed intensely, if not desperately, for forgiveness, and for things to go back to normal. The atmosphere remained unyielding however. No matter what she said or thought, nothing seemed to cut it. She felt alone, and afraid. Had her disobedience of action in going out, and her disobedience of thought in allowing some of her dark feelings to return, cost her her closeness with Josh? No matter how hard she pled, there was just no respite. In frustration, she took out the green cross, rubbed it, stared at it, and longed for some comfort from it – but none was forthcoming. She was about to get to her feet and leave the room in despair, when she sensed a change, an opening in her spirit, an easing of the atmosphere. Did the cross flash? She kept looking at it, and her heart leapt as it began to morph as before. Then her heart sank as she saw Josh's face, but it wasn't happy, or encouraging. It was sad, and it seemed to engender in her a deep sense of sadness too, a strong sense of disappointment. She knew she had been given so much by way of comfort, much more than many others might have received if their husband had been martyred; and she had spurned it by entertaining her dark thoughts and espousing her selfish actions. What was she to do? She didn't feel that anything she said now would alter things. She was going to be in that situation for the foreseeable future, and this scared her, this depressed her. The face was now fully formed. She thought she saw the mouth move and felt something impress itself on her spirit. What was it? Was it a word? Was it a name? It seemed like the name of a past king she had heard when the scriptures had been read. She

153

struggled to form it fully in her brain. What was it? Then it was clear. 'Nebuchadnezzar.' Nebuchadnezzar, she thought. He was the king of the Babylonians which took Judah into exile. Why this word? It didn't make sense. It wasn't a command. It wasn't an encouragement. It wasn't even a reprimand. Just 'Nebuchadnezzar'. She couldn't make anything of it, and the more she tried to understand, the more her head hurt. Suddenly she felt sick. It felt as if all the energy had drained out of her, like water through a bag of holes. She had to lie flat. Her strength had gone. She felt absolutely weak and empty. What was happening to her? When she summoned enough strength to open her eyes and look at the trinket again, it had gone back to normal. There was nothing there to show there had been a face, and that it had been Josh's. She felt awful. Had she been rejected by Josh? Had she gone too far in ignoring and taking for granted Yahweh's help? She obviously had. And would she be able to be restored? All these thoughts flashed through her mind, but there was no resolution to them.

Suddenly she heard the clanging of the gate bell. It was loud and insistent. In line with Jonas's protocol, she left her room quickly, turning over her mat and straightening it before she left for the atrium. Mary and Joel were there when she arrived. They had been expecting Barnabas or Nicodemus, so weren't concerning themselves. Esther would get the door. As she passed the shutter, Judith looked out to reassure herself that the guest was a 'safe' one. She froze at what she saw. Through the closed black gate, she saw the figure of a man sitting on a horse, with another man at his side. It was none other than the man who had almost caught her just days before. She gasped, and at that Joel and Mary looked up.

"It's him!" Judith said hoarsely. They followed her gaze and realised that danger was at their door.

"Quick!" said Joel. Keep away from the shutters. Don't go near the door." Esther was about to open the gate. "Don't go into the dining room to get to the servants' stairs. You'll be seen as you pass the door. Go straight up to the upper room from here and get onto the roof that way!" His voice was urgent, and she obeyed without saying a word. When she reached the upper room she continued up the stairs that led to the roof, making sure to make as little noise as possible. From the roof, she could hear Esther and the men's words floating up to her. There was something about a search, then she heard Joel's voice welcoming his guests. She went into the cistern housing, pulled out the artificial wooden panel, got behind it and pulled it back into place. She was safe for the time being! Her hope was that perhaps her pursuer wasn't there because of her. Maybe it was just a routine visit, and soon she would be back down with her family and friends. She knew however in her heart of hearts that this wasn't so. She knew why he was there. He was looking for her, and she was scared!

"Saul of Tarsus, sir."

The balding stocky man had dismounted and was standing in Joel's courtyard. His assistant was holding his horse. "I'm here on official business, sir."

Joel acknowledged him. "I'm Joel," he said. "Welcome to our house. How can I help you, Saul?" His voice was even, showing no sign of agitation or anxiety. "We're at your service."

"Thank you, sir. Hopefully, our visit will be brief. As I said, we're here on official business."

Joel raised an eyebrow.

"Yes, we know who you are, sir, and this is just a formality. The high priest sends his regards."

"Please take mine back to him," Joel said, his even demeanour unflinching.

"Yes indeed. I know there's unlikely to be any problem here. Your reputation goes ahead of you, sir. You've been a loyal servant to the Council for years. In fact, the high priest said I could miss you out, but I want to be thorough, and be able to say I've done my job to the best of my ability."

"Of course you do," said Joel warmly. "It's what I would expect from a representative of the High Priest. What's it all about anyway, Saul?"

"I have to conduct a search in accordance with the clampdown. You have heard we're homing in on 'The Way'?"

"I had heard something of it, although I'm no longer in the know. There's been a bit of tension in Jerusalem because of it."

"Tension?"

"Yes, it's common knowledge that 'The Way' has been flourishing and growing in popularity. The more traditional of us have been wondering why nothing's getting done about it."

"It is now, sir," said Saul smiling. His eyes were hard though, as if he perhaps detected a criticism of his masters.

"So why are you here? Do you suspect us of something?"

"No, not at all, sir. We're just searching all the properties in this area. We've already got people who've pretty well thoroughly been through the lower city. I can tell you we've been quite surprised at the extent of the movement. However..." he looked satisfied, "many of them now are in prison! And there's many more left yet."

"I see," said Joel. "So, you want to carry out a search here then?"

"That's what we'd like, sir...with your permission." Saul's eyes remained hard. He was being polite, but he was fully intending to have his way.

Joel acquiesced, "No problem. Feel free to have a look around. We've nothing to hide here."

"As I imagined, sir. Shall we go in?"

"Yes, indeed. Follow me." Joel knew only too well that this man intended business. He might have been polite, but if he was to find anything amiss, he would bring down the full force of the law upon him. They went into the cool of the atrium and Joel introduced Mary. "How do you wish to proceed?" he asked.

"My assistant will go over the upper floors, while I stay on ground level having a look around and chatting with you, if that's all right? Can you provide someone to show my assistant around?"

At that moment Jonas came into the atrium from the back of the house.

"This is my son Jonas," Joel said. "He'll show him around."

"A fine lad," said Saul going through the motions of ingratiating himself with Joel. He instructed his assistant to take a good look around, and then the two of them left to inspect the upper floors.

"Your reputation goes before you, sir. I've long been impressed by you."

Why was he saying this, wondered Joel? It's clear he hardly knows me. Perhaps he's trying to lull me into a false sense of security.

"You hardly know me. I don't think I've ever met you."

"Once only, sir. I was in the meeting you gave a report to after that fellow, Lazarus's funeral. I seem to remember you were quite favourable to him…and to the miracle."

"It certainly was quite an event," said Joel. "It's not often a person is reported dead and seems to be alive afterwards." Joel was thinking quickly, trying not to appear flummoxed.

"Reported dead…These are the important words."

"Yes, that was the official conclusion," Joel said. "A few of us knew Lazarus though, from our years of working with him on committees. That's why we went to his funeral…or his reported funeral," he corrected himself. "It was quite a big event."

"Apparently so, sir," said Saul. "It seemed to affect quite a few of you. No-one can come back from the dead. Messiah figures always play tricks on the unsuspecting or gullible public."

"That certainly has been the case with many," Joel agreed, without compromising his views on Josh.

"I've also watched you from afar. Your devotion to the Law has been admirable. I know the High Priest has appreciated your support. How many years were you in service, sir?"

"Nearly forty in total."

"I'm sure there's no greater servant of the Temple than yourself." Saul's speech was fair, but his eyes were hard. He wasn't going to be won over by flattery or platitudes. "Shall we make a start then, sir?" Joel led him into the public areas first.

Jonas was nervous, but fortunately for him his companion was new to the job, and was also a bit uncertain, feeling slightly overawed at being in such a grand house. First Jonas took him round the outside of the house to the steps that led up to the upper room and the roof. Just that morning Jonas had gone around the upper room putting away any tell-tale signs of people and meetings. He was glad he had done so now as nothing could afford to be out of place for this inspection, nothing to make the investigators suspicious. After ascertaining the upper room was normal and just used for family purposes, the assistant asked to see the servant quarters which were also on the upper floor. They had to go down the internal stairs to the atrium and then from the dining room go back up to the other half of the upper floor which was occupied by Esther and her daughter. Again, finding nothing of note there, the assistant asked to see the roof. Jonas led him out of the house again and up the outer stairs, past the Upper Room and up to the roof. He had a look around, and it was obvious he saw nothing untoward lurking there.

"What's that?" He pointed to the cistern housing.

"It's for our cistern," Jonas tried to sound impressive. "We've actually got a pump in the kitchen so we can have instant water."

The assistant looked suitably impressed.

" Can I look inside it?" he asked. "Your cistern looks quite elaborate."

"Yes, we've tried to make it as weatherproof as we can. We don't want to lose any of the water once it gets into the tank."

"You've done a good job. It's certainly well protected and is quite appealing to the eye. You've made it into a functional room."

"Indeed. My father likes things to be just right. He doesn't cut corners or like makeshift work."

Jonas opened the door and the two of them went inside. He was thankful that the bulk of the tank being above them made things shady and dark.

"You've panelled inside the room too," the assistant was inquisitive, and quite awed.

"Oh yes. As I said, my father likes things just right. He wanted to cover up the pipes. It keeps them cool, and it looks better."

"Very good. It's almost a work of art!"

"You're right said Jonas feeling relieved. Suddenly over on the farther edge of the panelling, his eye caught sight of a piece of cloth poking through a crack. He assumed by its colour it was the edge of Judith's robe which she obviously hadn't fully managed to pull in as she'd closed the panel behind her. While the assistant was otherwise occupied, examining the structure, he walked casually over the room and placed himself directly between the cloth and the assistant.

"You've done a good job here," the assistant said admiringly. "One day I might be able to afford one of these myself." He had noticed nothing. He left the cistern and Jonas followed him, breathing a sigh of relief. Judith heard them leave and also allowed herself to breathe freely again. She felt faint at having had to hold her breath for so long, and because of the heat which had built up dramatically in her small hiding place. It looked as if she was still going to be safe!

The inspector had seemed satisfied by his tour of the public rooms, the kitchen, and the housings for the animals, but as soon as he entered the family areas his tone and attitude became more inquisitive, intrusive and suspicious.

"Don't you find this house too big for just your wife and yourself?" he asked.

"Not just us, Saul. There are our servants too."

"Yes, but the house is massive. You could hold meetings here." This seemed to Joel an open challenge. Did he know, Joel wondered. He continued in an even tone, "We often have guests, and sometimes our family visit. When I was working, we entertained colleagues regularly."

"Maybe I'll get an invitation some time," the inspector said, with an attempt at humour. "I've always wanted to spend some time in a house like this!"

"You never know," said Joel smiling.

They were in Judith's room when the inspector's tone changed quite abruptly. "I've seen your room. Who stays in this one? You're just on your own at the moment, aren't you?"

"Yes, we are, but from time to time we have guests."

"Even ones that leave pictures?" He was referring to Judith's image in centre place on the dresser. "The room looks as if it's in use." His eyes seemed fixed on the picture and he was frowning.

"Oh yes, we have relatives who stay up country who visit fairly regularly. They stay with us when they're in Jerusalem. Their daughter is with us at present. That's my niece you're looking at. She had it done when she was a bit younger."

"It's quite amazing," said Saul who seemed transfixed by it. "It's an unusual composition."

"It's a little girl smiling happily in Galilee. That's where they came from then."

"No, I didn't mean the girl. I meant the quality of the picture. It's so life like. You don't get many artists who can do that type of thing."

"Oh yes, you're right. We were all amazed when we first saw it. It's not your average drawing or painting."

Saul picked it up and turned it around. "Judith," he said, thoughtfully.

"That's her name," said Joel beginning to feel uncomfortable.

"It's a pity..."

"Why so?"

"It's a shame the artist didn't think to inscribe it better. Such a masterpiece is spoiled by the rough etching of the name on the back." He turned it over and looked at it more closely again. "Hmmph," he said.

"Something else wrong?" Joel was beginning to sweat.

"No. It's her eyes. They remind me of someone. I can't place who just now. It'll maybe come back to me." He paused, "It'll come back to me, but those eyes seem familiar. They're right, but the picture isn't."

At that moment they were interrupted by Esther and her daughter Rhoda who were coming in to clean the room. Joel breathed a sigh of relief as Saul put the picture back down and decided to speak to the women.

"Have you worked here for a while?" he asked.

Joel answered for them, "This is Esther and her daughter Rhoda. Esther's been with us off and on for more years than I can remember."

Saul looked directly at Esther, "Off and on?"

"Esther looked down as a mark of respect, "Yes, sir. I left to get married and have my family."

Saul seemed satisfied with her answer, commenting, "Good servants are hard to come by. It's good that your master and mistress were able to take you back."

"Yes, sir," she replied, then looking over at Joel, she said, "I've left Tabitha next door to finish off her room. She has the atrium to do next."

"Who's Tabitha?" asked Saul raising an eyebrow. "Another servant?" He looked at Joel, "You're obviously well served."

Joel was thinking out his answer when Esther spoke up again, "She's master's guest, sir. She helps us out when there's a lot to do. She's like a sister to us, Rhoda, isn't she?" Rhoda nodded shyly.

Joel found his voice and launched into the alibi they had rehearsed previously. "That's so. She sometimes stays when her parents are out of town and helps out in return for her board and lodgings. She's a good girl!"

Saul was ready to move on and so he and Joel left to let the women get on with their work.

In the next room they encountered Tabitha cleaning and polishing, as if she'd been doing so all her days.

"You must be Tabitha then?" said Saul.

"That's right sir," she said, pausing to look at him.

"Extraordinary," he said. "I've just seen a picture next door that looks like you. It's of a little girl, but the features are definitely similar."

"Oh, that was my mother when she was little. People say our family all bear a striking resemblance to each other.

"Very much so," Saul agreed, still frowning. "I suppose these things can happen. Whoever did the picture must have had the creativity of Yahweh!" He let it go at that, knowing that to say any more would have gone beyond his remit. The mystery was for later pondering. Joel took him through the remaining rooms then they re-joined his assistant when they were finished.

"Everything upstairs fine?" Saul enquired of him.

"Nothing to report at all…except for a wonderful cistern on the roof."

"Yes, we decided to build it so we could have running water downstairs," Joel said. "It's one of the first things we did when we took over the house."

"I'd love to see that" said Saul, looking interested. Joel and Jonas exchanged a glance when he got up as if intending to take a look. Instead, he made his way to the door, saying, "I'm afraid I won't have time though. We have other properties to check before sundown. Business before pleasure. Perhaps another day."

Joel smiled, feeling a great sense of relief inside, "Yes, perhaps another day. Feel free to come back if you wish the tour."

Saul and his assistant made their way to the gate where his horse had been tethered, and after a brief farewell they were on their way to the next villa a few moments later.

Everyone regrouped in the atrium once Judith was back downstairs again, and compared notes.

Joel started things off, "We were fortunate. Yahweh was with us."

"You're right there," Jonas said. The assistant was thorough, but he missed something."

"What?" asked Joel.

"Well, we were talking up in the cistern, and I noticed a bit of your robe sticking out of the woodwork," he looked at Judith. She looked horrified.

"I thought I'd managed to get it all in before moving the panel back into place," she said.

"Not quite all," said Jonas smiling. "Fortunately, he was more taken up with the structure of the cistern and its housing rather than small details. He really liked it!"

"We were fortunate then," agreed Joel. "Saul was a funny customer. He was ardent, absolutely focused and too inquisitive for my liking. I've met people before like him who are so fanatical, they would throw their own grandmothers in prison for heresy!"

"He seemed pleasant enough when he came in at first," Mary commented.

"His eyes gave him away though," said Joel. "He wouldn't suffer fools gladly, and he most certainly had it in for us believers. We were fortunate to come through this."

Judith had said little so far, but now spoke up, "You've described him just as I've imagined him. From the very day I first saw him at Stephen's stoning, there was something hard about him, something driven. And what he did to Mikha…" She broke off crying. "I'm scared. He's evil!"

They all looked on sympathetically until she had stopped crying.

Tabitha, still wearing a cleaning headband to hold back the sweat, said eventually, "He seemed nice enough, but he was persistent. I felt terrified as I spoke to him, especially if he was the one that came after you the other day." She looked at her mother.

Judith nodded, "Terrified is a good word. He was the one."

Joel said, "There's one thing that troubles me."

"What's that, dear?" asked Mary.

Joel looked at Judith, "It's the way he reacted to your picture."

"My picture?" Judith looked surprised, then clapped her hand to her mouth, "Oh, my picture! I totally forgot! In the rush, I forgot to put it away."

Joel nodded, "He was intrigued by it."

"What did he say?" asked Judith who was now visibly shaking.

"He mentioned the eyes, your eyes. He said they reminded him of someone. I told him it was of my niece, and that we had it here because your side of the family visit often. He couldn't work it out though. He said the eyes reminded him of someone. He's the kind of person who'll try to work it out. He said something strange, 'the eyes are right, but the picture's wrong'."

"Well, that's true," said Judith. "It's my eyes, but to all intents and purposes it's a different girl in a different place. Do you think he'll work out the link?"

"Seeing Tabitha might have complicated it for him a bit," Joel said. "He could see the resemblance in her. Perhaps there are so many links they might confuse the issue enough to throw him off the track."

"Do you honestly think so?" Judith asked.

"If I'm honest, no. He's a clever man who'll not be thrown off the scent easily. If he recognised you the other day from only having seen you once at Stephen's stoning, I think it's likely the link might just dawn on him."

"But that will bring danger on you," Judith whispered.

"He's clever, and he is driven by the looks of it. He'll make the link, but he'll have no proof if we deny it. It's only a picture."

"But a really good one," Jonas added.

"There's nothing for it therefore, but to plan on the basis that he'll be back. He may have been looking for evidence of believers today, but the next time he'll be looking for you." Joel scratched his head, "What I don't understand is why he's making you his mission. We'll need to investigate more. I'm going to ask Barnabas if he knows anything of this Saul."

"And in the meantime, father? We can't leave Judith here to be taken."

"Of course not," said Joel. "We'll devise a plan, but it will have to be quick. He could be back any time."

Judith felt a shiver go up her spine. She knew what was coming. It had already been discussed that she might have to leave. She now knew for certain this was the way Joel was thinking.

"There's a caravan of believers making for Galilee in the next few days. They want to get out of the city." He looked at Judith, "How would you feel about joining them? You could go to Galilee and lie low for some time until things cool down here a bit."

"Galilee!" Judith hadn't been ready for that. "Galilee...I don't know..."

"With the help of these believers, and any of your old links from the past, perhaps you could settle there for a while."

"I could go with you mother," said Tabitha, but for one of the first times in Tabitha's recent past, there seemed to be a reluctance behind the offer. Judith could see she wasn't keen to go, although she would have done her duty by her. Was it because of Jonas, Judith wondered?

Joel disagreed, "No Tabitha. If I may be so bold as to say, if he comes back, he'll be looking for you again. If you vanish,

As someone who has the likeness of the picture, it may bring further suspicion on us. If you're still here, then we've nothing to hide. The picture then is just a coincidence."

Tabitha nodded slowly. She didn't want to let her mother down.

"I've another solution," said Joel, and was about to launch into it, when Esther cut in.

"Can I suggest something?" she asked.

"Of course, Esther," Joel grinned. "I wonder if you're about to suggest what I was going to?"

Esther looked earnest. "I'll go with you Judith. You and I have been friends since we were even younger than Tabitha. We're sisters. We're friends of Josh. I'd count it a privilege to accompany you." She thought for a moment, "and funnily enough, I believe it's the right thing to do!"

Joel clapped his hands, "That's it! That's exactly what I was going to suggest. Well done, Esther."

"But what about me?" piped up a quiet voice. Until this point, Rhoda had been a silent witness to the conversation. Now she was concerned. Being only thirteen, she needed her mother.

"I'll be back dear. It won't be for long. I can help Judith get set up, and then return."

"You needn't worry Rhoda," said Mary kindly, "we'll take care of you."

Joel realising, he had forgotten about Rhoda, tried to make amends, "While your mother's away, we would promote you to chief housekeeper, and..." he looked over at Tabitha, "I'm sure Tabitha would be only too glad to help you. Isn't that so, Tabitha?"

"Yes, of course. I'd miss my mother...actually, we'd both miss our mothers. We'd have something to share. And you can teach me what you know, Rhoda."

This seemed to mollify Rhoda and her face brightened. "Chief housekeeper? I wouldn't have to do the cooking would I?"

Mary laughed, "No dear. We'll find someone," and she now looked at Tabitha, "and perhaps you might help out too, dear?"

"I'd be only too happy to," said Tabitha smiling. Judith noticed that Jonas was smiling too.

"How do you feel about all that?" Joel asked Judith. "I know it's a big change, especially after all you've been through, but it seems to be our best solution."

"I think you're right," said Judith slowly. "I just don't like the idea of putting you all out like this, especially you Esther. It's a lot to ask of you." Esther shook her head.

"It's no trouble," everyone assured her. "We want to do the right thing. We want to help!"

"I see that," said Judith, and managed a smile. "I'm not sure where I'm going yet, but I am sure Yahweh will sort things out." She looked over at Mary, "I don't want to be a danger to you all."

"No, it's fortuitous to have had this warning," said Joel. "We're fortunate that that person Saul came to us today. Not everyone's been so lucky I'm hearing."

Judith looked at him.

He continued, "Only yesterday I heard of three raids on our meeting places. People were dragged before the Chief Priests for judgment, and likely excommunication." Judith looked concerned. "We've been forewarned here therefore. Let's do something about it before it's too late!"

Everyone agreed.

"Joel went on. "It's evident Yahweh's doing a new thing, as he said he would in recent prophecies. Things are getting difficult here in Jerusalem. Perhaps we've had it too good for too long. He's shaking us up and making us go out with the Good News. I've heard that although the apostles have based themselves here and braved the persecution, it seems to be the intention of some of them, to go and make Josh real in other places. You'll be right in line with Yahweh's will, just like them, Judith."

Judith felt a twinge in her spirit. Remembering her experience just before Saul's arrival, she felt like a fraud. The Spirit had seemed to drain out of her. Was Yahweh still with her, she wondered?

Joel was speaking again, "I'll meet with some of the other leaders tonight and see what can be worked out for you both. Judith and Esther, you'll both be a loss to us, but we'll be praying for you both, every minute of every day."

They smiled at him and thanked him.

"I'll miss you mother," said Tabitha crying.

"It'll hopefully only be for a short time, if we're lucky," her mother said. "I don't want to miss any wedding!" She looked between Tabitha and Jonas who both looked down sheepishly, their faces going very red. Everyone in the room laughed. The secret between them wasn't very well kept!

Don Treader

"I also want to meet with Barnabas tonight. In fact, I'll ask him over for the evening meal. If he knows anything about 'Brother Saul' we need to know about it. It's a mystery to me why he should be pursuing you so hard, Judith."

The meeting adjourned, and they all went their separate ways. What a day, Judith thought to herself. In the moments before Saul had appeared, she had been clearly made aware of her disobedience toward Yahweh, her seeming ingratitude and lack of appreciation for the comfort and support He had so liberally bestowed upon her. Then she had hidden, fighting for her survival, in a cramped cistern while she was being hunted. Finally now she was about to leave the safe environs of this house of refuge and everyone she knew and loved – something she had wanted to do only yesterday - and was about to venture out on a perilous journey to who knows where. Was Yahweh in this? Had He actually left her? Would she be safe? She didn't know. She didn't feel she had the confidence to believe in anything! She seemed to be headed for disaster. Was she? And what about…'Nebuchadnezzar'? How did he fit into the picture?

Chapter Twenty

"Tonight's the night," Joel said, his face serious and concerned. They were all seated in the dining room waiting for their evening meal to be served. Around the table were Joel and Mary, Judith and Barnabas, Tabitha, and Jonas. Rhoda was bustling around, serving what her mother had cooked.

Judith felt a pang of fear strike her. "What do you mean, Joel?"

"I've managed to arrange passage up country for you, but the cart leaves at dawn. Esther and your self will have to leave here when it's dark. Jonas and I will accompany you of course to the departure point."

Everyone looked shocked.

"So soon," gasped Judith. "I hadn't thought…"

"Neither had I, but the leaders I spoke to said there was a definite push on, and people were keen to get out while they could. A caravan was set to leave at dawn carrying goods to Galilee, and some of our people had chosen to go with it to help, but primarily to escape. Given it was leaving so soon, and that your pursuer might return at any moment, I thought it best to put your names on the manifest."

Judith looked doubtful, and Tabitha was crying. Rhoda had stopped serving and was also crying.

"It's not ideal," Joel said looking awkward, "but if things are to get worse, you'd be best away."

Judith nodded and put her hand over Tabitha's who was sitting next to her. "Don't worry dear, I'll be back. It's probably for the best."

Tabitha hugged her mother and the two sat silently crying.

Rhoda in the meantime had gone through to the kitchen to tell her mother the news, and suddenly there was a clatter and shriek. Rhoda came running in, shouting, "Help, help! It's mother. She's collapsed. Come quickly!"

They all rushed through to the kitchen and saw Esther lying prone on the tiled floor, blood pouring from her head.

"She collapsed when I told her she'd be leaving at dawn," Rhoda wailed. "I couldn't catch her as she fell. Her head hit the edge of the table and started bleeding."

No-one seemed to know what to do. Should they send for a physician? Mary, Judith, and Tabitha gathered round her and tried to mop away the gushing blood from the unconscious Esther. The men prayed.

"She's going a funny colour," said Judith, "and she's not coming round. I think we'll have to get the physician."

The others agreed, and so Jonas was dispatched to fetch him.

In the meantime, they tried to make Esther comfortable but as the moments went by and the physician didn't appear, they grew more and more concerned for her safety.

Eventually Jonas returned with him. "You did right," he said, "to try and deal with the blood. It's good you didn't try to sit her up. The cut on her head is a deep one and she's going to have a roaring headache when she comes round." He took a small bottle out of his bag and proceeded to uncork it. He waved it under Esther's nose, and she began to cough and splutter.

"Where can we put her?" he asked. "She'll need to lie down for some time until she gets her strength back. She's lost a lot of blood."

Indeed, the kitchen looked like an abattoir. The men tried to lift Esther and carry her through into the atrium, but their feet were slipping on the blood. Eventually they managed to get her there and onto a couch. Rhoda had put a blanket over it to protect it from the mess, and another over her mother to help keep her warm, to avoid her going into shock.

Judith, Tabitha, and Mary dealt with the blood in the kitchen then came back into the atrium to see how Esther was.

She had come round and was saying, "I got a shock, when Rhoda told me we were leaving at dawn. I wasn't ready for that. I felt myself blacking out, and that's all I remember. I think I banged my head on something?"

"Yes, the wooden table, mother. Right on the corner."

"It's throbbing. I must have some size of bump."

"It's not stopped bleeding yet," Rhoda said.

"Yes, you'll need to stay in your bed for a day or two," the physician said. "I'm assuming that will be all right with you?" He looked at Joel and Mary.

"Of course," they readily assented.

"But what about tomorrow?" Esther protested. "I'm…"

"You won't be going anywhere," the physician interrupted her quickly. "You must rest until your strength returns. You've lost a lot of blood."

Everyone looked at each other. This certainly was going to create a problem.

"We'll make sure she rests," said Joel as he escorted the physician out of the house. "She had been going on a journey up north tomorrow, but…"

"It's out of the question, Joel," the physician said. "You'll kill her if you send her."

"We won't. Don't worry," Joel assured the physician as he left.

Esther was dispatched to her bed and the others went back to the dining room. Mary helped Rhoda with the food Esther had prepared, and they all sat down eating rather later than they had intended.

"What will we do now," asked Judith. "That's put a spoke in our wheel."

"Yes, that does make a difference," Joel said. "I can't see an easy way out of it."

There was silence for some time while they ate and ruminated over the problem. Finally, Judith put down her eating implements and said with an air of definiteness, "I'm still going!"

The rest looked incredulously at her.

"But you can't…" said Mary.

"A woman travelling alone…" Barnabas said, "it just isn't wise."

"But it's not impossible," said Judith determinedly. "I can't put you all at risk. I must leave."

Again, there was a pause, then Joel spoke. "That's not such a terrible idea. It's not ideal, but we all agree that Judith isn't safe here and neither are we if she is found out. She's travelling with believers. Why should harm come to her? We'll make sure she's on a wagon belonging to someone reliable, hopefully someone we know." Judith looked gratefully at him. "It's what happens to her at the other end that worries me. She'll be on her own in Galilee," he said.

"Not so," said Judith. "I still have friends there. There's Marius the retired centurion, and some of my friends from our synagogue days. I've got some money. I'll be able to pay for rent if necessary."

"You've obviously been working things out," said Joel. "Perhaps Yahweh is not closing the door on this enterprise after all. It's shut for Esther definitely, but not for you Judith."

She smiled. "We're all saying Yahweh is doing a new thing. We couldn't get any newer than this. There are many things I feel unsure about at the moment, but I feel quite certain that this is the way ahead for me. I'll be on that caravan tomorrow."

They prayed before eating, committing Judith's way to Yahweh, then they started their last meal together. As they were praying, Judith felt something vibrate in her pouch. She knew what it was and took comfort from it.

After the meal, and once Mary had checked on Esther, telling her she would in no circumstance be accompanying Judith in the morning, Joel tackled Barnabas on the other topic of the day, did he know Saul; was he training with him; and what was he like.

Barnabas looked concerned when he heard that their visitor had been Saul. "He's a hard man," he said. "He's probably the most dangerous person I've ever met. He's so focused on adherence to the law and our traditions, that he can't see anything else. Gamaliel has a flexible way about him, but Saul has often challenged him, and from a legalistic point of view has taken apart his every argument. He hates Josh with a vengeance, and anyone who follows him. He sees him as a heretic, someone working for the devil. We've all to watch ourselves around him. He would report us to the High Priest if he thought we deviated from the law one little bit."

"Certainly that's the impression I got, just talking to him," said Joel. "There has to be liberality in interpreting the Law, otherwise it can crucify you."

"And that's exactly what he'd do to every believer if he got the chance. He's ruthless. There's nothing but black and white for him."

"How dangerous is he to us?" asked Joel. "Can he do us any harm?"

"Well, he seems to have angled himself in with the High Priest, and been commissioned by him, to root out 'The Way'. He has the power to imprison or to bring believers before the synagogues to have them punished, and in some cases to have them excommunicated. Yes, he's dangerous. There are even rumours that he's training others to help him, and that he's been given licence to do the same in other towns."

"That's serious then," said Joel shaking his head. Others echoed this sentiment. The atmosphere had already been serious, but now it became quite solemn.

"Why do you think he should be focusing on Judith?" Joel asked.

"Well, I don't know for certain. But from what I know of your story Judith," Barnabas looked over at her, "you present a challenge to him."

Judith raised her eyebrows, "But I've done nothing to him. I don't even know him."

"But he takes things personally. Challenges don't sit well with him. You said that on the day of Stephen's stoning, Mikha challenged him, and what was being done. It seemed from what you said he organised the killing party to arrive at your home. He obviously got a good look at you too, if he recognised you in the street the other day, and again today when he went on about your picture too. Let's say he recognised Mikha as someone who worked in the Temple. He would have seen him as a traitor. If he made further enquiries, he might have found out that Mikha had been running a 'The Way' group in his house. He'd know you'd be involved in it as well. Therefore he'd want to get a hold of you too, as someone he considered to be an enemy of the faith." Unfortunately, he's not a man who forgets faces easily, or indeed for that matter wrongs he believes have been done."

"You've painted a damning picture of him," said Joel. "He's not a man to be trifled with or underestimated then. I think we have to assume he'll be back once he puts two and two together." He looked over at Judith, "I'm afraid it is inevitable you have to leave us, my dear. It would only be a matter of time…I'm sorry."

Judith nodded. "I agree, Joel. I hope I never meet him again. He scares me. I'll be glad to get away!" She looked around her, "If you'll excuse me," she said, "I'd like to go and see Esther before I pack my belongings. I'll have to be up well before dawn to get to the caravan."

"Don't worry dear," Joel said, "we'll be with you. Go now and do what you have to do. We'll call in for you at about 4am."

Judith left and went upstairs to Esther's quarters. She spoke to her for a few minutes till Esther fell asleep exhausted, then she went to her room. She was scared to pack. It all seemed so very final. She wondered if she'd ever be back. Of course she would. Tabitha was still there. Suddenly she felt very alone. For the first time in a very long time, she would be without Tabitha, and Mikha. She really was going to be alone, and she was scared. She couldn't let the rest see that, however, but that's exactly how she felt. N a matter of just a couple of days, things had changed radically for her. What was she doing going to Galilee alone? Was she mad? What would she do when she got there? She had precious few, if any, living relatives there. A few old friends from the synagogue might welcome her back, but she realised she was about to enter new territory, one that might prove quite alien to her. She started to pack. Clothes, shoes, important papers, and identification. She lifted her picture and gazed at it for a long time before putting it in her bag. Lastly, she felt behind the dresser for the little bag of gold coins she had taken from her home the night Mikha had died. She removed two coins from it and placed them on the dresser. Those were for Tabitha so she could pay for her keep while she was away. She then slipped the bag into her pouch beside her cross. When her fingers came into contact with the cross, she lifted it out and held it up before her eyes. It had provided much comfort for her since she'd received it; but she remembered though what had happened the last time she had taken it out, and she started back. She felt scared. Had Yahweh turned against her now? Had she gone too far in her disobedience? Would He help her? Would He go with her? Currently she felt as if she was at arm's length, as if she had offended Him. It was clear she had to leave…but would He be with her, would He protect her? She felt as if she was launching into the unknown and wasn't sure if there were arms there to catch her. She may have felt cold and numb, but she also recognised that Josh had spoken to her. He had communicated with her, however strangely, and it would appear that although she didn't feel His closeness at present, she sensed she could trust that he had engineered these events and that He would go with her and preserve her. She hoped so anyway.

Having done all this she lay down on her mat, still clutching her green cross. As she dozed off, she remembered the word 'Nebuchadnezzar'. Where did that fit in? She hadn't a clue., She was too tired at that moment to care. Tomorrow was going to be traumatic enough. She could worry about 'Nebuchadnezzar' another day!

Chapter Twenty-One

It was cold as Judith stood beside a long line of carts, wagons, and impatient animals, with Jonas at her side. She had her bag of meagre belongings at her feet, and a pack containing a water bottle and some provisions to last her on the journey hanging from her shoulder. She shivered and tried to draw her cloak around her but had difficulty doing so because of the pack. She gave up when she saw Joel coming back.

"Here's my father," said Jonas. "I hope he has good news for us."

Judith nodded, and waited for the verdict.

Joel was smiling, indicating a positive result. "It's fine," he said when he reached them. "They've no problem taking a woman on her own. Indeed, they've gone out of their way to be helpful Do you remember Elias and Joanna?"

"In the group that met in our house?" Judith felt relieved and looked more cheerful. "Yes, of course I do. They were good people. They have a little baby."

"That's right. The caravan leaders said you'd know them. They've assigned you to their wagon. In fact, the leaders told me they feel privileged to have you travelling with them. Mikha's and your reputations hold high with them. A bit of a celebrity travelling with them, you know."

Judith's spirit had now lifted, and had they been able to see it in the darkness, Joel and Jonas would have noticed her face was flushed. She didn't care about being a celebrity, but just that she had a safe ride with people she knew and trusted. She thanked Yahweh silently.

Joel picked up Judith's bag and all three of them made their way down the line to Elias and Joanna's wagon and found it at the end of the queue, the very last one. It was spacious, containing rather a large amount of produce at the front bound for Galilee, and adequate living space for a baby and two adults squeezed in at the back. Elias was a cheery man who welcomed Judith like a long-lost friend. "Go round the back, Judith. You'll find Joanna and baby Elias there. They'll settle you in."

171

She thanked him for his kindness and offered him a gold coin for the journey.

"No, not at all my dear. What Joanna and I owe you from just being in Mikha's and your group is payment enough. We were devastated to hear about what happened to Mikha. He was a really good man." He looked up. "He's with Yahweh now."

Judith nodded, and thanked him.

"A word to you," he said coming close and speaking quietly in her ear. "This is a legitimate caravan going to Galilee. It leaves regularly from here. As we go through the city gate, cursory checks are carried out on every wagon to see that we're carrying what we say we are. Our produce is for sale in Tiberias, Capernaum, and Nazareth – that is if we get that far. Recently believers have been leaving with us too, not in such great numbers as to cause suspicion. A few here, and a few there. If an official asks you, just tell them that you are Joanna's sister. There's no lie in that," he laughed.

She nodded again and made her way to the back of the wagon with Joel and Jonas.

"We're going to miss you, Judith," Joel said looking rather sad. "It does look though as if Yahweh will be with you. Hopefully, you won't be too long away from us. Things will move on in time. With any luck the persecution too…and Saul with it."

Judith hugged him. "Thank you for looking after me so well over the years, and especially since Mikha…"

"It's been our pleasure and privilege. Yahweh will be with you. I'm sure your relationship with Josh will carry you through. Try and get a message to us once you find a place to stay, so we know you're safe."

"I will. But if nothing gets through, you should send a message to Marius the Centurion in Capernaum. He's sure to get it, and I'll make contact with him when I get there to let him know that I'm there and where I'm staying."

"I see you've got it all organised then," Joel smiled.

"As far as is possible, in my mind anyway." Judith turned to Jonas, and hugged him too, "Please take care of my little girl. She's all I have now." She started to cry.

Jonas's face softened. "Of course I will," he said. He whispered so his father wouldn't hear him. "I'll let you into a secret, Cousin Judith. I love Tabitha, and hopefully one day when you return, I intend to gain your permission to marry her. I'll definitely take care of her for you! Don't worry."

Judith laughed through her tears, "That's no secret, Jonas. I've seen it in you both since the day you met. You're both young yet, but I hope to be at your wedding one day, Yahweh willing." She pulled away from him and made to get into the wagon.

As she drew back one of the flaps, a roar of greeting came from inside. Joanna, Elias's wife, was smiling broadly at her. "Welcome Judith!" she said. "Elias told me we were having a passenger. I'm really glad it's you!"

Judith climbed in and the two women hugged. Joel passed up Judith's bag to her,

"We'd better leave now," he said, "while it's still dark. We don't want anyone putting two and two together accidentally."

Judith agreed. "Take care yourselves," she said. "These are difficult times, but I'm sure Yahweh will look after you."

"You too," said Joel and Jonas together, and with a wave of their hands, they left.

Judith was glad to be in the company of friends. Joanna was a large woman, the motherly type, and someone who fussed just a little too much over her. Judith might have drawn away from that at one time, but now, she felt that was just what she needed as she reached out into the unknown. She felt welcome, she felt safe – exactly what she had been hoping and praying for since it had been agreed that she should leave. Joanna introduced her to baby Elias, and while they waited for the caravan to set off, and once Joanna had fed him, Judith got the chance to hold baby Elias. She hadn't held a baby for so long, and she felt just at home there. She had been dreading the journey away from Jerusalem, away from most of what she knew and loved. She was facing an unknown and uncertain future, but she was now faintly beginning to feel it might not be all bad after all. The excitement of a new start, an amazing challenge, a chance of renewal was filtering into her mind. But could she rely on Josh and Yahweh being with her? She had let them down, and was currently sensing their withdrawal from her. Their closeness normally with her no longer there, she felt in her darker more worried moments that she was all at sea, that circumstances were pulling her about. The confidence she usually experienced in the Holy Spirit was just not there. She seemed to be at the mercy of the elements. She needed clarification. She needed definiteness. But neither of these things were forthcoming. She had to content herself with waiting – hoping that illumination would come in time.

The caravan moved off just as dawn was breaking. As they passed through the city gate, an official waved them on. He had taken a cursory look at the produce, checked with Elias for occupants, and after looking in the back of the wagon to ensure Elias's wife and 'sister' were on board - and a squalling baby - he moved on to the next cart.

They left the city by the north road; a road Judith was unfamiliar with. Traders tended to use it to go up the west bank of Jordan to Galilee. It took in Samaria and its towns and villages, making for a slightly shorter journey to Tiberias and the Lake. Judith was glad she had people to talk to on the journey and so she involved herself as far as she could in their family life. She took turns at dealing with baby Elias which pleased Joanna who was grateful for the frequent breaks. During their fairly lengthy conversations, nothing was said of her reasons for leaving Jerusalem. She let them believe that she was just starting a new life, now she had adequately mourned for Mikha. Many of her roots were in Galilee and as far as they were concerned, she was going back to them. When they enquired about Tabitha -like many others, they knew about Josh's raising of her – she just told them that she had remained with her aunt in Jerusalem and might be getting married to their son at some stage in the future. Of course, she would return for that. But going to Galilee was something she had to do. It was necessary for her to do Yahweh's will. They accepted that, and no more was said.

Their first day of travel was through fairly rough terrain. Leaving the Jerusalem hills and peaks took some time before they entered the midlands. The rocky terrain gave way to valleys and grasslands, and the road often passed by orchards whose trees were starting to blossom, and grainfields which had not long been planted. Judith was impressed at what she saw. As she hadn't been that way before it was all new to her. She took it all in in the times she walked beside the wagon to give Joanna and the baby some peace. Elias spent most of the journey driving the cart or walking beside the beasts, and only rested in the wagon when the caravan stopped for short periods of refreshment. Judith was surprised that no time seemed to be scheduled for a full night's stop. She wondered how Elias would manage.

"We're all in a hurry to get our produce to Galilee before some of it goes off," Elias told her. "We only make occasional short stops to rest the beasts, to eat and take short naps. There'll be plenty of time for sleep when we get there."

Judith was unused to this method of travelling but tried to fit in with the schedule. She found that by the end of the first day, she was exhausted, and decided she would lie down as night was falling.

"It's a shame you're going to go to sleep," Elias had commented. "We're in Samaritan country now and we'll soon be passing Mount Gerizim and Mount Ebal, you know, where Moses gave out the blessings and cursings."

"Of course," she said. "Actually, I was schooled in things like that as a girl. But I've never been close to them before."

"We're also not too far away from Jacob's Well, if you're a student of our history. There's actually quite a lot of history around us."

"Are we stopping there?" asked Judith with a degree of interest.

"No, not likely," he said "We're in too much of a hurry, and it's a good way off our route. Hospitality around here is uncertain. It's Samaritan. They can be friendly on our way to Galilee, but on our way back...we're not so welcome. Anyhow we'll not be stopping tonight." He laughed, "And by the time you've slept, you'll have passed by all these historic places."

174

Judith laughed too, "There'll be many more of these where they came from. This is Israel after all!"

The two of them enjoyed the joke, then Judith went to the back of the wagon and re-joined Joanna and baby Elias who were already sleeping. She tried not to disturb them as she unrolled her mat.

Judith awoke feeling the motion of the wagon beneath her. Something had disturbed her sleep! The ground seemed harder and bumpier now. Was it that which had caused her to waken up? She had been dreaming of Josh and couldn't get the image of him hanging on the cross out of her mind. She could picture that day only too well. It had been one of the worst of her lifetime, watching her friend dying in such a horrible way right in front of her eyes. She remembered her overarching feeling had been how helpless she had felt. She would have done anything to have wrested him off the cross and restore things to the way they had been, but it was not to be so. She had had to watch until the end: to watch his agony; his physical wounds and the copious amount of blood; his mental torment as he had to say goodbye to his mother, his friends and life itself; and spiritually, to feel his Father's withdrawal from Him when he said, "Yahweh, Yahweh, why have you abandoned me?" That brought her up short. Josh had been abandoned by his Father! That's what He had said. There had been a time when he had experienced something…in a much bigger way of course…that she herself was now feeling. They had all believed at the time - and later when taught this by the apostles on the basis of the Isaiah scripture - that the sins of the world, of all of them, had been laid upon Josh, and that's why his Father couldn't look on him, and why Josh had felt bereft of his presence. It had had to be so for him to deal with the sins of the world decisively, and with the perpetrator of them, the devil, once and for all. In a small way, Judith thought, that's how she felt now…abandoned. The presence she had been so sure of for so long, was no longer there. She was existing at a level she didn't like and was being forced to for the moment. She was being upheld, she was alive - but that was all. She felt the need for comfort. Knowing that Josh had felt abandoned was one thing. What she was to do about her own sense of it was another. He had been abandoned for his taking on of the sins of the world, not his own. She on the other hand felt abandoned primarily because of her own. How she regretted them – her selfish disobedience and her lack of faith, her lack of trust that Josh would see her through. She began to weep silently, feeling so unworthy of all Josh and the Father had done for her. Would this break the ice, she wondered. Would her repentance be enough? No, she felt just as cold when the tears stopped. She needed comfort. How was she to get it? She dug in her pouch and took out her green cross. Suddenly she remembered where she was, and looked around her to see if anyone was watching, but no. Joanna and baby Elias were still sound asleep. She held the cross up to her eyes. Was it morphing? AS before, it seemed to grow bigger than itself, the green extending to the extremities of the four points, and the face beginning to form. She was glad that something was happening, but she didn't feel good. Indeed, she felt the same sickness coming upon her she had felt when it seemed as if the Spirit had gone out of her the previous afternoon just before Saul had arrived. She was glad she was lying down, as her strength had gone and she felt absolutely sick in the pit of her stomach. The face of Josh was fully formed now, and it had that same sad look it had presented to her on that afternoon. When she thought about it, it was the same face she had seen in her dream. Actually, there had been something different about her dream, she realised. On the crucifixion day itself, Josh hadn't looked at her. It was as if he was focused on other things. However, in her dream he had looked directly at her, and he was sad. He was sad now, and that's why she felt abandoned. How could she sort this out? She couldn't. Instead, she just felt worse and worse. Was she going to lose consciousness? Was she going to die? Was that what was planned for her? Because of her disobedience, had she forfeited her right to life? She was scared, really scared! In desperation she reached into her bag. She had been using it as a pillow. Out came the picture sitting on top of it, the one that always consoled her and made her feel better. No such luck this time however. If anything, she felt even worse. She was now aware of a girl's voice- not singing, but groaning as if in deep pain. She put it back hurriedly hoping she might lose some of the sickness or if possible, some of that horrible sound. The cross was flashing quite strongly now in her hand, and Josh's mouth was moving. It seemed to be roaring in her ears, "Nebuchadnezzar! Nebuchadnezzar! Nebuchadnezzar!" Sharp crippling pains shot through her, causing her to feel winded. She was absolutely terrified. Her body was in agony and she wanted to be sick. The girl's moaning and Josh's voice were strong in her ears and an overwhelming sense of panic and confusion swept over her. Thinking she was going to vomit she tried to struggle to her feet but the strap of her bag was wrapped round her wrist and made it awkward. She didn't know how she did it but she managed to reach the edge of the cart, her heavy bag hanging at her side. When she pushed her head through the flaps intending to be sick, they gave way. They weren't fastened properly, and as she pressed against them, the weight of her body and her bag together propelled her through them, and she fell off the moving cart and hit the ground with an almighty thud. Everything had taken place in the space of less than a minute. No-one had seen or heard anything – Joanna and the baby had been sound asleep, and Elias was sitting up front at the far end of the cart, driving. They had been the last wagon in the convoy – no-one was behind them to see or to help. Judith, winded and unconscious, was a prone figure lying sprawled on the road, her bag and its contents strewn all around her. As the cart pulled away from her on its way to Galilee, to all intents and purposes Judith might as well have been dead.

Sophia's Secret

Volume Two

Part Three – Reckoning

Chapter Twenty-Two

It was dark and cold when Judith came round again. She felt her consciousness returning and hadn't a clue as to where she was and what had happened to her. Whatever she was lying on was hard and unyielding. She put out her hand and felt dust and rubble. Where was she? She had a terrible headache and felt out of sorts, indeed she had great difficulty in trying to gather together her senses. She felt confused and terribly disorientated. Where was she? She had to open her eyes, but because her head hurt so much, she felt safer leaving them closed for the moment. A strong sense of fear also convinced her to keep them tightly shut. Afraid of how bad she might feel, and what she might see, she decided to concentrate on what she could hear for the time being. That was easier to deal with. Apart from the sound of a light breeze and other sounds of nature, there was nothing. She shivered. It wasn't cold, but she didn't feel quite right. She had a sick feeling in her stomach. She was shaking ever so slightly, and there seemed to be another pain – a different kind of pain from her headache. It seemed predominantly located on her face, her arms and chest, but when she thought about it, it even seemed to extend to her legs and feet. It was all over her body she realised. It wasn't a sharp stabbing pain, but rather more of a dull ache. When she touched any of these areas, the pain in them intensified, and also hurt her fingers. What was wrong with her?

Judith began to panic. She had to pull herself together. She must make sense of her situation. She should start by establishing her surroundings. With trepidation, she opened her eyes and took in the scene around her – and what she saw shocked her to the roots of her being. How had she got there? Why was she there? She was quite at a loss to understand.

First of all, she determined she was outside, and that it appeared to be nighttime. There was a large bright moon almost directly above her, surrounded by myriads of stars, which fortunately helped her gage her surroundings. The strong light was somehow comforting as it helped dispel the feeling of chaos and disorientation she had been experiencing. She was in the midst of a rugged landscape. She was lying on the ground, in the middle of what looked like a dirt track. It was more hard packed than the areas on either side of it, which looked more sandy, with occasional clumps of sparse grass sprouting from it. She could see quite some way into the distance on all sides of her thanks to the brightness of the moon; and almost as far as she could see this rugged landscape was punctuated by outcrops of rock, the occasional tree, or more accurately stunted gnarled bushes, and in the far distance what appeared to be high hills rising quite steeply out of the rocky terrain.

Her headache was beginning to subside now, and she started to pull herself together. She could see beside her what looked like clothes scattered on the ground, some fragments of food, and a patch of water which had emptied itself from a cracked water bottle at her side. Some of it had run under her body. It had probably been the cause of her coming to. There were also two or three documents strewn around her, some even off the track. The light breeze was causing them to rustle and flutter but wasn't strong enough to whip them away. She saw what looked like a large cloth object about ten feet away from her head. It too flapped slightly in the light breeze, or at least its top did, but it looked bigger and heavier than the other objects around her. Suddenly it came flashing into her mind - it was her bag. It was open, and the objects around her had come out of it. She sat up as her recollection returned. Oh, her head hurt something badly, and her body ached all over. The effort to sit up cost her her vision for a moment. Her head spun and her heart pounded trying to cope with the change of position. After some moments her vision corrected itself, and the queasiness affecting her stomach began to subside now that she was upright. Where was she?

Judith decided to get to her feet and try to gather what she assumed must have been her belongings before any of them might get too far away from her. It was her bag after all, so it was reasonable to believe that these alien objects in such a rugged landscape must be hers too. Her head swam again with the effort. She gritted her teeth and forced herself to stand, then to make her way to each of the objects, gather them up, and safely place them back in the open bag. She tried to shut it, but the strap was broken. It was going to be difficult to carry now, and this annoyed her. She sat down again, this time on a boulder at the side of the track. She had to gather her thoughts!

She remembered travelling in a wagon. This was her most recent recollection. She couldn't for the moment work out why she had been in it, or where she was going. She did, however, remember feeling terribly sick. She had been sleeping, and had stood up and tried to get out, to avoid vomiting inside it. The horror of these last few thoughts came back with a vengeance now. She had become entangled with the strap of her bag and as she had tried to push her head through the flaps, she had exerted too much body weight and had found herself falling through them instead and plummeting towards the ground. She felt again that sense of panic and fear at being unable to help herself, and was sure she was about to retch, but she managed to control the impulse and calm herself with the thought that she was now all right – or at least, as all right as she could be.

As her feelings and emotions steadied themselves and she settled down again, the memories came flooding back, and with them a sea of anxiety. Mikha, Joel and Mary, Tabitha, her disobedience, her pursuer, the escape, and night flight to Galilee – all of them surged back, and with them , her nausea. This time she did retch at the side of the road. She felt awful. Once she had dispelled the contents of her stomach, she felt slightly better, and sanity prevailed. Sitting upright on her rock, and breathing heavily to control the pangs of nausea, she realised she knew where she was now. She was somewhere between Jerusalem and Galilee, deposited in Samaritan territory, a woman alone in the middle of nowhere! As she looked around her, something glinted in the moonlight. She went over to it and realised it was her green cross. The pale light of the moon may have robbed it of its strong colour, but it was definitely her cross. She was glad to see it and picked it up. She was sorry to find that its chain had snapped. She had had it in her hand as she had fallen from the wagon. It must have broken when she hit the ground. She silently thanked Yahweh for helping her find it again and replaced it in her pouch. Then another thought struck her. She had been looking at her picture inside the wagon when she had suddenly become sick. Was it still in her bag, or had it remained in the wagon? She remembered having tried to stuff it back in before being sick, and the strap becoming entangled round her arm as she had struggled towards the flaps. She rummaged down the side of the bag and found her prize possession. It was still there, unharmed! She had now two things to be thankful for, no, three. She was still alive - even if it was in the middle of inhospitable country.

At this point, a dilemma hit her. What was she to do? Should she try to find some hospitality? There was absolutely no sign of life as far as her eyes could see. Should she wait where she was? Would Elias and his wife come back for her once they had discovered she was gone? Would they be likely to risk travelling alone through Samaritan country in the vain hope of finding her, with the possibility of being attacked by Zealot bandits? Neither of them had been aware of her leaving. It had all happened so quickly, and relatively quietly. Joanna and the baby had been sleeping, and Elias was up at the front of the big cart driving the beasts. He would have seen nothing because of the awning covering it. They hadn't known her plans. She hadn't shared them with them. She was just a passenger, a friend, to whom they were doing a favour giving her a lift. It had been assumed she was going to Galilee, but for all they knew she might have intended leaving them at a particular point on the journey suitable to her without telling them. And anyhow, by the time they found out she was gone, probably still some hours away yet, they would almost certainly assume that to backtrack would involve them in a fruitless search with little likelihood of finding her. All she could hope for was that in the morning they might ask another wagon travelling back that way to Jerusalem to look out for her. Should she wait there then? Probably not. She had no guarantee that anyone would come. What about waiting there for another wagon to come from Jerusalem? Yes, she could do that, but again, at that time of night the road wasn't looking too busy. It was desolate. How long might she have to wait to be rescued- and anyway, by joining them, she would be at the mercy of strangers. Was it worth taking the risk? She knew she couldn't stay there for long however. She was also at the mercy of unfriendly Samaritans or ruthless Zealots. What should she do?

She finally determined it would be better to keep moving. She would follow the track and hopefully might meet, if she was fortunate, the family coming back for her, or at least a wagon that had been alerted to keep an eye out for her. Then the sad truth hit her. Which direction should she take? She realised she had no idea which way she had fallen out of the wagon, and therefore which route might take her in the direction of Galilee. She could start walking and find herself going back to Jerusalem! She felt at a strong point of indecision. Keeping moving was her best option – but which way?

Judith decided to pray. It seemed the logical thing to do. She knew that although she had been disobedient and still felt at arm's length, Yahweh was doing something with her, perhaps even leading her, although she felt so bad. Yes, she had felt sick, but now that was subsiding. Her body still ached, as did her head, but she assumed that was the result of falling out of the wagon and hitting the ground heavily. She had been unconscious after all. However, she was still alive. Yahweh must want her alive for some reason. She began to feel better with this thought and decided to put what little faith she had at that moment into practice. She said, "Father, I thank you for sparing me, and for being with me, even here. I don't know what you want me to do, or where you want me to go, but please show me, and I'll try to do what you want. I'm sorry for letting you down, but whatever your plan is, please use me again when it is your will. I'm in your hands. Thank you." She had been praying with her eyes closed and now savoured the calmness, the peace, that entered her mind. She hadn't felt this peaceful for some time and so she held onto the moment. Did she sense an assurance creeping in, that she was in the right place? She couldn't be absolutely sure, but it felt that way. She would hold onto this by faith. She still didn't have any inkling as to what to do regarding which direction to take. The best thing to do she thought, was to sit and treasure the moment. When she opened her eyes again some moments later, she realised it was getting much darker now, and a tinge of anxiety began to gnaw away at her peace. She surmised that it wouldn't be long till dawn. The stars and moon were abandoning the night sky, allowing the darkest hour to reign before sunup. She could stay there, but the more the light faded the more uneasy she felt. Then she heard it. A scratching on the hard ground some distance away, behind a large boulder about one hundred feet from her. Was someone approaching? The scratching seemed too light to be of human origin. But what about an animal? There were numerous predators which could be harmful to a lone woman in a vulnerable state. She began to be afraid again, although deep down this time the fear didn't seem to be shaking her calm. What on earth was making that noise though? It sounded as if it was getting louder now, but as the darkness deepened and her distance vision shortened, she couldn't make out whatever might be approaching. It couldn't have been a snake, she thought. It was a different kind of sound. Rather it was as if a heavier animal was moving towards her. Could it be a desert hog or other creature, many of which could be quite vicious? It was certainly too small for a lion, she surmised, which at least did give her some relief.

It was pitch dark now and Judith could barely see a few inches in front of her. She hoped that the darkness might hinder the animal or whatever it was from seeing her. But no such luck. Just as she thought she might be safe, the scratching sound became more rhythmic, and it seemed as if the creature was accelerating in her direction. It wasn't hoofs though. It sounded more like a small animal's soft paws. Her only hope was that it wasn't something vicious. This would not be a good time to get bitten!

Seconds later as the animal neared her, she knew what it was. It was a dog. A wild dog? No. The realisation shot into her mind just as the animal reached her. It barged into her almost knocking her over, but she didn't care. She yelled and screamed with joy. Something very furry leaped up on her and was licking her face. Judith was ecstatic - as ecstatic as her furry assailant! Judith had had a few moments of ecstasy in her life - like her wedding to Mikha, like Tabitha being brought back from the dead by Josh, like meeting with Josh at the Sea of Galilee after his resurrection – and this one was definitely up there with them all. Faithie, Little Faithie, was there! Josh had sent her to her. What a marvellous sight for very sore eyes. She couldn't have wished for a better answer to her prayer! This bundle of fur was equally happy to see her, and both of them exulted in the moment.

"Faithie, it's you!" Judith's words were mingled with tears of joy that flooded down her face. "It's really you. I've missed you so much! I love you."

It's obvious that Little Faithie, if she could have spoken, would have said something similar. She contented herself instead with jumping up and down on her mistress, squealing with that yodelling sound that Judith knew so well, and licking her all over until not one square inch of her mistress's skin was dry. This reunion must have gone on for about five minutes until both of them were exhausted and gave up. Judith sat back on her rock to regain her breath and Faithie lay at her feet panting vigorously, looking up at her devotedly, and emitting the odd happy squeal.

Judith had to think now. It was so wonderful to see Faithie again, but why was she here. She must have been sent for a purpose. Was Josh here with her? She had relinquished Faithie very reluctantly to him at the Sea of Galilee when he had first asked to take her away. Faithie had been severely injured, and he had wanted to take her to help her. Judith remembered looking down at Faithie for that last time – as she believed it to be - misery clutching at her heart at the thought of losing her loyal little friend, who had been hurt in order to save her from a brutal attack. But she was also comforted by the thought she would be no longer crippled in Josh's hands. Now here she was lying beside her, squealing and reunited, happy to see her.

A thought imposed itself on Judith's mind, and she obeyed it by taking her cross from her pouch. It was flashing, now quite definitely green. There was no actual light from the moon or stars, but that did not seem to matter. It exuded its own glow. Josh's face was forming, and unlike the last time she had seen it, it was no longer sad. The word "Follow" seemed to form first on his face, and then in her mind. Very quickly, it was repeated once more before his face vanished and the flashing stopped. Judith now was in no doubt as to what she should do. She said a silent 'thank you' and pocketed the cross. Faithie who had been looking up at her with love, now stood up as if she too had received her orders. Judith noticed with great joy that Faithie no longer struggled to get to her feet. Neither had she heard her run toward her haltingly or seen her have any trouble standing on her hind legs when licking her face. Josh had been as good as his word and healed her, restoring her to her wonderful health. Once again Judith felt ecstatic. She got up off the rock, bent down and cuddled Faithie then readied herself to move. She quickly tied the strap of her bag, then slung it over her shoulder.

"Where are we going, Little Faithie? Go on, lead the way!"

Chapter Twenty-Three

it was dark now, so very dark. Judith could see nothing much in front of her. Nothing much, except for Faithie leading the way just a foot or two ahead of her. At times she seemed to dart from side to side as if to ascertain the best path, and at others she literally seemed to dance. She was obviously still overjoyed to be with her mistress again, and every so often she gave a little squeal of happiness. Judith noticed something unusual about her. She hadn't noticed it at first, but it seemed that Faithie was giving off an ever so slightly faint glow. It was almost imperceptible, but Judith was thankful for it. She wouldn't have been able to follow otherwise.

Judith often stopped in order to reappraise her position, especially if she sensed objects in front, or to the side, of her. She was not used to walking in the total darkness, or to putting her trust in a dog to lead her. She trusted Josh and Faithie however and did her best to follow. At these moments, Faithie came back to her and nuzzled into her leg, something she had done often before, and then backed away from her again looking at her, trying to encourage her forward in the direction they should take. Judith didn't feel worried. She was just so happy to have Faithie back. She would have followed her anywhere!

Judith had assumed Faithie would stick to the road. It would have been easier to walk on as it was hard under foot. But this was not the case. Very soon into their journey, Faithie left the track and headed into the sandy scrubland. It was much more uneven underfoot and occasionally Judith found herself stumbling over little clumps of rough spiky grass that scratched her feet through her sandals. This would not have been the route she would have picked if she had had a choice, but she was following a command and a wonderful guide. What right had she to object!

Judith was thankful for her little furry guide. At times she led her close to, but not into, huge outcrops of rock; and at others she appeared to be walking along the edge of something, with a drop at her side. She assumed it to be a dried-out riverbed, one she would not have appreciated falling into had Faithie been less conscientious. For some time, she sensed that she had been weaving in and out of various obstacles. At first her progress had been slow as she acclimatised herself to this new way of working, but soon as her confidence grew, she relaxed and allowed Faithie to increase the pace. After about half an hour of travelling this way Judith could hear that they were approaching running water. She trusted that Faithie wouldn't take her into it, and was right. She led her along the edge of it for some minutes then veered away into the scrubland again. There had just been enough time for her to bend down and splash her face in the cool flow, and to take a drink from it with her cupped hands. Her face ached, especially her nose, and as she splashed the water on it with her fingers, it became even more painful. It also seemed very rough, not like its usual smooth texture. She hadn't been aware of it so much when she was walking, because she had been so happy to be with Faith again, but now having stopped for a moment, it felt as if her whole body was aching. She wouldn't be able to go on much further like this, she thought. It would be daylight soon. Perhaps they would stop then.

The journey continued, Faith dancing ahead, leading her away from the water. How thoughtful of her, Judith thought, to consider she might be thirsty. The darkness seemed even blacker now, crowding in on her, and with it the cold. Judith wrapped her cloak closer around her as they walked. They wove in-between what Judith thought appeared to be larger bushes. She sometimes scratched her arms on their thorny branches. But Faithie was undaunted. She led on, a dog intent on carrying out her mission and keeping her mistress safe. Minutes later the terrain seemed to change, and Judith felt herself going uphill. The bushes were lower and closer together, scratching her even more ferociously. Her body ached terribly now and at times she sank to her knees, almost finding the pain too much to bear. Faithie stood patiently over her till she stood up again, then continued on her way. Was Judith imagining it, or was there just a pale streak of grey on the horizon? Dawn couldn't have been far off now, she surmised, and then got on with the business of climbing. It was hard going, and her body wasn't coping. There was an ache in every limb and joint. Deep stabbing pains in her chest arms and legs were intensifying. Had her fall out of the wagon really caused all that? She struggled to follow Faith now as the hill was steep. On her knees again, Faithie came back to her and nuzzled in. Judith cuddled her, allowing that soft fur to soothe her aching body. She was so grateful for it, and said again and again, "Faithie, I love you...I love you...thank you, thank you, thankyou." Tears of pain and of joy were streaming down her cheeks. Faithie gave one last nuzzle and licked her face. It was time to move on again and she stood in front of Judith encouraging her to get up and follow. Judith knew exactly what she meant and eventually raised herself onto her feet. She had the sense that Faithie was saying to her, just a little further. You can do it; so she made one supreme effort, and a few steps later, greatly to her relief, she reached the top, and stopped to catch her breath and gain her bearings. She had been right; it was almost dawn. The eastern sky was greying. It was still too dark to see much, but slowly out of the gloom she could make out a valley stretching into the distance beneath her; and as the light strengthened, was that a mountain she saw on the horizon? Looking further over she could see another one too. Could these have been the Mounts Gerizim and Ebal that Elias had talked about on the journey into Samaritan country? Interrupting her thoughts came a sharp stabbing pain that seemed to shoot through her whole body. Once more she sank to her knees. Faithie looked at her from a few feet away, impatient to move on, her task not yet completed. Judith was crying because of the pain, but she made one almighty effort to get onto her feet. She thought as she stood up, she could make out some shacks down the hill in the valley built on a flat expanse of ground. With the sun rising and bathing the area in a reddish glow, she was able to make out a structure which looked like an old-fashioned community well, set quite a bit apart from the shacks. There was also some kind of building just beside it. How was she to get down there? The hill was very steep, almost cliff-like, and her body was in too much agony. The pain was making her feel faint. She could see that Faithie was encouraging her to move on, but she just couldn't go any further. She wanted to sink back onto her knees, but felt herself blacking out before she could do so because of the intense pain. As she went into a dead faint, something registered in her brain. She recognised the scene spread out before her. She'd never been there, but somehow, she felt as if she had! Once more in almost as many hours, her body hit the ground hard and slowly began to tumble down the steep rocky grassy slope into the valley. It ended its trajectory when it reached the flat sandy ground at the bottom - some hundred or so yards away from the structures that had seemed strangely familiar to her. Faithie stood over her, protecting her mistress. She licked at her face trying to rouse her, but without success. Judith was dead to the world. For the second time that day, she was totally out of her misery!

"Where am I?" asked Judith weakly, looking up into the weather-beaten middle-aged face of a woman crouched over her.

"You're safe, my dear. Quite safe," the woman said, her rough lined face breaking into a reassuring smile. "You've appeared from nowhere and seem to have had quite a fall."

"Yes, the wagon..." Judith mumbled, closing her eyes again to shut out the pain.

"I don't think so dear," the woman said shaking her head. "A wagon couldn't get here, and certainly there are no tracks if it did. By the looks of it you've tumbled down the hill out there."

"Where am I?" Judith asked again. She was no longer outside, but inside in the shade, surrounded by what looked like big jars or pots.

"Don't speak for the moment," the woman said. "Let me dab your forehead with some water." She proceeded to do so, gently washing her face.

"A drink…" Judith gasped.

"Of course," said her soother and held a small container of cold water to her lips. This felt good, and Judith began to revive.

"Where's my dog?" Judith asked, suddenly remembering Faithie.

"There's no dog here. You're on your own." The woman paused, "Funnily enough when I first saw you from a distance lying at the foot of the hill, I could have sworn that something was standing over you. It was just getting light and when I got near you, there was nothing. No dog there, I'm afraid." The woman looked at her as if she believed she was hallucinating.

Judith moaned, and a tear rolled down her cheek. "Faithie, Faithie. I mustn't lose you again…" she mumbled and fell back into unconsciousness.

The woman continued to mop her brow, and soon Judith had revived. She tried to sit up to gage her surroundings, but the woman told her not to. "You're too weak," she said, "and no doubt quite sore. I'm sorry, but I had to drag you in here from the foot of the hill where I found you. I had to get you out of the sun and away from any inquisitive animals that might come along. No dogs though," she laughed.

Judith looked gratefully at her and allowed the woman to go on.

"I'm Rebecca, Becca for short," she grinned.

"Judith," said Judith, her voice rasping. She cleared her throat, "I'm Judith," she said again.

"Pleased to meet you, Judith," said Becca still grinning. "Even if you are a sorry sight."

"How did I get here?" asked Judith beginning to rally. "Did you bring me here?"

"Yes, and you're no light weight, I'm afraid. I hope I didn't hurt or bruise you on the way. I had to drag you."

Judith smiled wanly. She liked the directness of this woman.

"Where am I?" she asked for the third time.

"You're in a shed just beside Jacob's Well. Oh, I got your bag too."

Judith struggled into a sitting position with the help of her newfound friend and looked around her. She was propped up against a large clay water pot and was surrounded by more of the same. She noticed her bag was leaning up against one of them. One side of the building was missing, making it more of a shelter rather than a shed. Something stirred in her – a memory, a recollection – and at the same time she felt a sharp vibration in her pouch. Something seemed familiar about all this. When she looked out of the open side, it was plainly mid-morning as the sun was quite high in the sky. Some yards away was the old fashioned well structure she had glimpsed before she blacked out at the top of the hill. It all came back suddenly to her now – her falling from the wagon in the middle of nowhere; her being amazingly led through the desert scrubland by wonderful furry Little Faithie; the intense pain she had felt on the way there, culminating with the rising of the dawn and her sighting of the two mountains in the distance and the huge valley stretching out beneath her with its small village and this very well she was now looking at. Her pouch, or something in it, was vibrating quite persistently. She didn't need to look; she knew what it was. Something was trying to gain her attention.

She turned suddenly, thinking of something, and looked more carefully at her companion. After a moment, she said, "I know you; I know you, Becca."

It was the turn of the other woman to be startled and surprised now, "No you don't. I've never seen you before." She looked at Judith as if she was hallucinating.

Judith meanwhile was trying to make sense of things. Why was the cross in her pouch vibrating? It was indicating something to her that told her she was on the right track. The name 'Sophia' imprinted itself on her mind, and she could see her face as it came towards her in the garden that night an hour or two after Mikha had died. It was her, the one whom Judith had believed to be an angel, the one she believed had given her the cross. Was Sophia or Josh trying to tell her something? She didn't need to take it out to see. She just knew there was a link and that something was being told her.

She gazed into Becca's eyes, then voiced the thought that came to mind, "You know the Messiah, don't you! You've met him. Right here!"

Becca was shaking now. Her voice trembled, "Yes…but how do you know? I've never met you before. Did he send you to me? Do you know him too?"

Judith hugged Becca. "Yes, I know him. And I suppose in a sense he has sent me to you." She couldn't explain about the green cross or Sophia, but said, "I don't understand it myself, but I know I was here when you met him."

Becca drew back, looking scared. "There was no-one else here when I met him. I was in here before he came along. There was no-one else here. It was midday. No-one comes here then."

"But I was. I saw you from behind one of the pots. I saw you go out to him. I don't understand it myself – I just know that I was."

Becca looked at her strangely, "He was the most wonderful man I ever met. He told me everything I ever did!" Her face lit up as she said this.

"I know…" said Judith, a smile playing on her lips, "about the five husbands." Judith still had no idea where these thoughts were coming from, but she knew they were true.

Becca looked shocked, "You do know him. He must have told you!"

"In a manner of speaking," Judith half grinned, her face hurting too much to stretch any further. "That makes us sisters then!"

"Because we both know him?"

"Yes, those who follow him are his brothers and sisters."

The other woman was still puzzled and quizzed Judith further. "Have you been to our village before then? Have you spoken to or met anyone else from there who knows me?"

"No, only Josh."

"Who's Josh?"

"You probably knew him as Jesus."

"That was him. He stayed in our village for a couple of days before moving on with his men." She looked at Judith with newfound respect, "You know him?"

"I do...and I did. But that's a long story." Judith sank down against her pot. "I can't talk just now. I feel drained, very sore and exhausted."

"You poor thing. I should have been more considerate...but..."

Given their encounter, Judith wasn't surprised her agony had been overlooked. She said weakly, "I don't know what to do, or where to go. I'm lost, and far away from where I meant to be."

Becca looked at her sympathetically, "You're one of us. I'll take care of you."

"No, I'm not one of you. You're a Samaritan, I'm a Jew. I've been told all my life there's a huge gulf between us, a lot of bad feeling too. I wouldn't expect you to help me."

Becca grinned again, "But sisters help sisters, sister," she emphasised the word to impress it on Judith.

"I can't..." said Judith lamely.

"You can. We both know him, and I want to help. It's been a long time since he's been here. I want to know more about him from you - what he's done, what he's doing."

Judith closed her eyes feeling faint again. She didn't have the strength to argue. There were sharp pains in her face, her arms, and legs. She just wanted to rest.

"Anyhow, how could I leave you here when you're one of us?"

Judith opened her eyes again and protested, "But I told you, I'm not one of you. I'm a Jew."

"I don't mean that," said Becca pulling at the hood on her robe. Judith stared as it slipped off her head and revealed short hair with bald patches. "My face too. Look at my face," she insisted.

Judith looked carefully at her for the first time and saw to her horror small white blotches on her skin. She was shocked, stunned into silence. She drew back involuntarily.

"We're sisters, you and me," Becca said. "We must stick together, us sisters in suffering."

Judith found her voice, "But you're a…" She couldn't bring herself to say the word.

"A leper?" Becca helped her out, smiling at her as if it was something to be proud of "And what do you think you are?" Her smile broadened.

Judith wanted to shrink back but couldn't. "I'm…I'm not…"

"You surely are…" Becca's face straightened, and she said more seriously, "Didn't you know, sister?"

Judith couldn't speak and allowed Becca to continue talking.

"Look at your hands. I can see white marks on them. I daresay your feet and toes are the same."

Judith looked down at her hands and feet and saw the tell-tale marks. Touching them turned the dull ache she had been feeling in them into serious sharp shooting pains.

"I saw it in you when I was bringing you here. Your face is quite badly marked, isn't it?"

"I don't know," Judith sobbed. "I didn't have it yesterday." She thought back to the pains she had started to feel in the past few days – the nausea, the aching. Had this been coming upon her? But could leprosy happen to you suddenly? She didn't know, but preferred to think it didn't.

She put her hands to her face. Since falling out of the wagon and following Faithie, it had felt rough and painful to the touch.

"What do you see on my face, Becca?" she asked, terrified of what she might say.

Realising that somehow this was all new to Judith, Becca's face softened, "You've definitely got it, I'm afraid. There are marks on your forehead and chin…and your nose…" Judith put her fingers to where Becca had indicated the markings were, and again she experienced the shooting pains as she touched them. And when she felt her nose, it was rough, the skin peeling off it already. Indeed, it was one of the most painful parts of her body. How could this have happened? How could Yahweh have allowed this to happen?

"It goes for the extremities of your body, sister. The toes, fingers and nose are the first usually. They seem to die off. That's why they're white. There are people in our village who are quite disfigured…" She stopped as she realised, she was terrifying Judith. "It can take a long time though," she said, as an afterthought.

Judith was shaking and sobbing now, and Becca put her arm around her. She said quietly, "Us sisters, we must stick together."

Chapter Twenty-Four

Judith felt decidedly unwell. After her ordeal getting there, broken only by the joy of being with Faithie; and now the added knowledge and mental trauma of discovering that she had somehow contracted leprosy – she had no energy or desire to go anywhere. She felt like dying, like giving up. How was she to cope? Where was she to go? Lepers couldn't stay with others in society. Would she ever see Tabitha, and her family again? If she did, would she be able to hug them? Life at that moment seemed so unfair. She had hit a trough. Also, in her mind was Faithie. Where was she? Had she got lost? Was she somewhere outside the building waiting for her to come? Was she to follow her further, or had she been delivered to her destination? She wanted to see her again. She was the spark of hope that might just help her feel better. When finally she spoke, and asked Becca if she could see her anywhere, Becca said, "I told you earlier that I thought I'd seen an animal standing beside you, but when I got nearer, there was nothing there." She got to her feet and said in the kind of voice that sounded sceptical, "I'll have a look outside," but moments later she returned saying, "No, there's no dog there." Judith's heart sank, not for the first time that morning. Where had she gone? Had Little Faith been given back to her by Josh for good? Or had it been only to lead her there? She was thankful that Josh had sent her at all, but now the thought of living apart from her family, and also with the prospect of leprosy...if Faithie had actually been given back to her by Josh, it would have made life just a little more bearable for her. She sensed, however, that she was going to have to do without her for the time being, and suddenly this really deflated her spirit. She had had to give Faithie up once before, and it was hard. Now in the midst of major adversity, it was much worse. She remembered her promise made to Josh on that morning at the Sea of Galilee – she loved Faithie, but she had agreed to give her up to him wholeheartedly as he had wanted her to be with him, to take care of her and make her whole. She realised she was going to have to do so again. She should be grateful for having had her with her at all, and so slowly and painfully once more Judith yielded her heart to Josh. Somehow in doing so, it helped her face her other traumas. They weren't going away, but there was a peace there now, a deep one, which seemed to offer her a sense of stability. Her disobedience and ingratitude for Josh's help over Mikha, she knew, had led her into some terrible circumstances. She didn't want to add to her plight by being ungrateful for Faithie's help too!

At that moment she felt a slight vibration in her pouch, and simultaneously flashing into her mind came the word 'Nebuchadnezzar'. The vibration ceased, and instantly her brain rejected the thought. It was just too much for her. It was like an overload – she just couldn't cope with it at that moment. She had to get on with her life, whatever that held, at least for the next few moments anyway. She put aside the thought for another day therefore and tried to make it onto her feet. In the effort to do so, however, her strength seemed non-existent and she lost her balance. She fell backwards and crashed heavily into one of the pots. She was winded and decided to stay where she was for the time being.

"You're not going anywhere yet sister. You're far too weak." Becca's brow furrowed, "I'll have to get help."

When Judith had regained her breath she whispered hoarsely, "You stay over there?" pointing generally in the direction of the few shacks she could see in the far distance, hundreds of yards away from the well. "I think I saw them from the top of the hill just before I fell down it."

"No, I don't," said Becca defensively. "I used to, but now I don't."

Her answer surprised Judith and she raised her eyebrows. "I thought…"

"No, lepers can't stay there. I did…and had to leave when it was found that I had the disease."

"So where do you live then?"

"Down in the Valley of the Outcasts, as far away as the villagers could make it," said Becca, with a hint of irony in her voice.

"But we're in the valley, aren't we? It did seem a big one, fairly spread out."

"Yes, but on the other side of this shelter as far away from the village as possible, there's a smaller sunken valley big enough for most of our needs. It's ideal in that it's quite isolated. It has steep rocky sides, but it's quite flat once you get down into it. We are able to grow crops there, and there's a small brook running through it although the water isn't the best for drinking. It's an ideal place for us though. We've built some houses for ourselves - more like huts really."

"For us? Who's us?"

"Those of us who are outcasts, who all have the disease. We can look after ourselves there, and every so often the people from the village will shout to us from the top of the hill bordering our valley. They also leave food for us, and other necessities we can't make for ourselves."

"I see," said Judith.

Becca continued, "We all had to leave someone in the village. Most of my husbands still live there." She smiled at how irreverent that sounded. "And my last partner. Some of us have had to leave partners, but also children."

Judith looked horrified, "Did you...?"

"No, I was fortunate. I didn't have a child. For the others who did though, it was heart-breaking."

"I can imagine," said   Judith, looking sad.

There was a pause and then Becca said, "But all this talk won't get you down to the community though, sister." She seemed to like calling her that. She became more serious, "We have to get out of here before the villagers come to draw their water."

"Is that why you were here so early...to avoid meeting the others?"

"You're right. We have to keep apart. The villagers are absolutely scared they might catch what we've got. To be fair to them, they're decent people. We weren't thrown out in disgrace or anything. Most of them too are followers of the Messiah. They hated putting us out, and actually tried to ensure our community and living quarters were comfortable before any of us moved in. As I said, they still try to help with provisions etc."

"Are any of your family in the community?"

"No, I'm on my own." She looked at Judith sideways, "I'm assuming you won't mind coming there, that is, if you don't have anywhere else to go? I'd be happy to share with a true sister. I want to know more about our Messiah."

Judith nodded slowly. "I'd be happy to come with you...for the time being anyway. I haven't had a chance to think yet what I'm going to do...whether I can get home or not."

"Not likely," replied Becca. "But you're welcome to stay with me as long as you wish. I'm not going anywhere."

Judith smiled wanly, "It doesn't look as if I am either." The two women laughed momentarily sharing the joke.

"I'll go and get help," Becca said. "A couple of us will get a canvas cloth and we'll come back and get you."

"What's the cloth for?" asked Judith.

"To carry you of course. You're in no state to walk."

"What'll happen if any of the villagers come here while you're gone?"

"Just call out, 'Unclean', and say you're waiting for Rebecca to take you to the community."

Judith looked worried.

"Don't look so worried," Becca said. "They'll understand. They're good people – at least most of them are. But I'll have to go now. I'd rather we didn't encounter them here if we don't have to. We have the stream, but some of us use the well. The water's better here, and anyway…Force of habit, you know. They tolerate it, as long as we're not here when they are."

"Fair enough," said Judith. "Please be quick, won't you?"

"I'll be back very quickly. You'll meet another couple of us. Will that be all right?"

"Of course. I need all the help I can get at the moment."

With that, Becca left, and Judith got on with her thoughts.

It had been a lot to take in. The past two days had been hectic; being pursued by the man that had indirectly killed her husband; making the decision to leave Jerusalem for Galilee; falling off the wagon and being led through the desert by Faithie - and now discovering she had a serious life-changing illness from which she knew it was impossible to recover. Her whole life had been turned around far quicker than she could ever have imagined. What was she going to do? Ideally, she wanted to get back home, to be in the safe company of family and friends, but that was not to be. It might never be. She considered, were Yahweh and Josh in all this? Of course they were. They had to be. She had been confused, and doubtful, but now she could see a hand in it all. Her disobedience had led her to this spot. Now it was only Yahweh who could bring her out of it…if he wished. She would have to submit to him and relinquish her doubts. There was no other way, she thought.

The morning sun was heating the air now taking the chill off it, and she began to doze. Suddenly, she was rudely awakened by the sound of voices. Some women were shouting, "Who's in there?" They sounded scared.

"Unclean," the word seemed foreign to Judith's lips. She struggled to say it again. "Unclean."

She heard the women whispering, "It must be one of them."

"I'm Judith. I'm just waiting for Rebecca to come back for me. She's taking me to the…" she could hardly bring herself to say it, "the community."

One of the women shouted belligerently, "Get out of there, you leper. You'll contaminate us all! You shouldn't be there. You're filth! We don't want anything to do with you. You're a menace to our community."

Judith had never been spoken to like that before and was stunned into silence. She felt the tears returning.

"I'm not well," she choked, sobs beginning to rack her body.

"Who cares! You deserve all you get. You've ruined our community, you people. You're a curse on us all!"

The other woman tried to calm down her companion. "Leave her alone. She can't help it. If Becca's coming for her, we'd be better to draw our water and leave before she gets back."

"You're too soft," the other woman shouted, intending Judith to hear. "If she's not out of here by the time we return with the menfolk, we'll throw her into their community. These people don't deserve mercy. They've caused us too much trouble!"

The two of them carried their buckets to the well, and Judith could hear them being lowered then raised again. As they left, the belligerent woman shouted back into the shelter. "Just you wait. We'll be back, and if you're not gone from here, we'll make sure you'll be sorry, you and your type!" She laughed menacingly, and her loud guffaws seemed to echo all around Judith's head in the shelter.

So, this was her first taste of discrimination, she thought. Was she destined to a life of being hated? She couldn't bear the thought, and wept.

"Judith, sister, are you with us?" Becca's friendly but concerned voice broke into her tearful pity session. Judith opened her tear-filled eyes to see her face looking into hers. She saw that she wasn't alone. Two men stood slightly behind her and they were carrying a large piece of cloth between them. Both of them looked quite old. Judith wondered to herself if they would be up to carrying her in their makeshift stretcher.

"Yes, I'm here," she groaned. "I've just been visited by women from your village."

"We saw," said Becca. "We also heard them. Zenina and Keilah always come early. Zenina can be quite a handful, quite aggressive to us," Becca grinned. "She married one of my ex-husbands. If you mentioned my name, it would certainly have brought out the worst in her."

"I did, and it did," said Judith relaxing a little. "Are we going to go just now?"

"Yes, we'll have to. This place gets busy a little later on. I'll carry your bag."

The two men unfurled the wide canvas cloth and spread it out.

"Meet Ezra and Daniel, Judith," said Becca. "They're founding members of our community. Very highly respected."

The three of them laughed at her remark.

"Hello, I'm Judith. Pleased to meet you," Judith said weakly.

"Just try and slide onto the cloth, ma'am," said Daniel in a croaky voice.

Judith complied. The two men gathered up the ends and lifted the cloth. Her body sank into it as if she was in a kind of hammock. They lifted Judith out of the shelter into the hot morning sun. She couldn't see much, except the top of the well, as the walls of her hammock obscured her view.

"It's fine," said Becca, who was walking beside her swinging her bag. "This is the easy bit – we're on flat ground. It'll be more tricky getting you down the rocky slope into our valley."

Judith dreaded the thought, but she trusted that they knew what they were doing. After all, they'd lived there for a good time. They must have worked out ways in and out of it.

Don Treader

Two or three minutes later they came to the edge of it, and she began to feel herself going downhill. It was steep, and at times with Ezra below her and Daniel above, she almost felt as if she was about to stand up. Becca helped steady the stretcher by walking at her side, trying to cushion her from the bumps. It was clear the men were finding it difficult as they were breathing quite heavily and loudly. Two minutes or so later and they were on level ground again, and Judith felt safe.

"We'll take her to my place," said Becca. "She'll be staying with me." The two men complied, and it wasn't long before Judith was being carried through a squeaky door and then unceremoniously deposited on a rumpled, gritty mat that had seen better days. Her bag was set down on the far side of the room beside a large grubby one of Becca's.

"Sorry about the mat…and the mess," Becca grinned. "Our home comforts here are limited. I hope it will be all right for you."

"It'll be fine," said Judith gratefully. "I'm just thankful you rescued me this morning. I believe Yahweh sent you."

Becca smiled, "Your Yahweh sent me?"

"Well, you've met his Messiah," Judith reasoned with her. "Why couldn't he have sent you? He's helped me a lot."

Becca shrugged her shoulders. "The prophet's been saying we should expect visitors, but what does he know? Maybe he's got it right this time though."

"The prophet?"

"Yes, the prophet. He came to us some time ago, and he looks after our spiritual, and sometimes even our physical needs." She flashed a knowing smile at the two men who were straightening up, and about to leave. They laughed.

"Let's get you settled in," she said. "There'll be enough time to talk, sister to sister."

The men backed out carrying their makeshift stretcher. "Thanks for helping this morning, boys," Becca said. "You've been a big help." Judith echoed her thanks, and the two men left.

"Now how can I help you, Judith?" Becca asked. "Your face looks quite sore. Can I bathe it for you?"

Judith ran her fingers over her face and realised that her normally smooth complexion had become quite rough literally overnight. "If you give me a cloth soaked in cool water, I'll bathe it myself. Does it look really bad?"

"You've obviously been through an ordeal. Did you really not know you had leprosy? Some of the marks look quite well developed."

"No. Yesterday I was in Jerusalem, and as far as I knew, I was perfectly well. I have however been experiencing quite a bit of nausea recently and sometimes even an aching in areas of my body, especially my face arms and legs, but nothing's been evident outwardly. These blotches and rough spots seem to have

200

appeared overnight. And I see there's a bit of a swelling in my fingers. It's probably there in my toes too."

Becca looked at her feet, "You're right. You have a fully developed case of leprosy, I'm afraid."

Judith looked worried. "Is it likely ever to go away. Is it possible I've not got leprosy, but something else?"

"Not a hope, sister," said Becca, shaking her head. "All of us have it here, in varying degrees. The one thing I can tell you is that no-one has ever left here cured. You'd have to be like the legendary Ephron!"

"Who's he?" asked Judith curiously.

"Oh, a year or two ago he did a tour of the villages telling us how he had been healed by a wandering Jewish teacher."

Judith's ears pricked up. "Tell me," she said.

"Well apparently he and another nine people suffering from leprosy went to the teacher to ask him to help them. According to Ephron they were all healed by him and went off under his command to seek out a priest to confirm their recovery. Ephron apparently thought about it as he went, and he returned to thank the teacher. The teacher asked him where the others were. He seemed surprised that the only one that had returned had been a Samaritan. The rest had been Jews, you see. You'd need a miracle like that…and that's not likely."

"That would have been Josh," said Judith excitedly.

"No, his name was definitely Ephron. He travelled all round Samaria telling his story."

"No, I don't mean the leper. I meant the teacher. He went around all Israel healing and teaching. Thousands were healed, sometimes even in one afternoon. People who heard him felt as if his Father was speaking into their hearts."

"His father?" It was now time for Becca to be curious. "His father?" she repeated.

"Yes, he called Yahweh his father."

"The man that spoke to me at the well talked about Yahweh being like a father, and that he was doing a new thing. People were to worship him in spirit and in truth. He said there would come a day when it didn't matter where we worshipped him, Mount Gerizim, Jerusalem or anywhere. He told me he was the Messiah. Neither did he seem bothered that he was talking to me a woman, and at that a Samaritan one."

"That's definitely Josh," Judith said, her eyes sparkling. "That's exactly what he would have said and done."

"And you know him?"

"I knew him," Judith paused.

Becca looked at Judith questioningly. "Do you mean…"

"Yes, he's no longer with us. Josh was crucified!"

Don Treader

Becca turned white. "How could such a thing be? He stayed in our village for two days, he and his men. They changed us. After he had been speaking to me at the well, I went around the village telling everyone to come and see someone who had told me everything I had ever done. I was notorious. People knew about my five husbands and my living outside of marriage with a partner. They were curious so they went to hear him. We Begged him to stay and he taught us just the way you said. For two whole days he stayed in a Samaritan village - ours. That totally impressed us. When he left, people in the village said to me, 'Now we believe, not just because of what you told us, but because we have heard him ourselves'. We really did believe he was indeed the Saviour of the world. I don't think there was anyone who didn't believe!" Becca stopped to gather her thoughts. She looked sad and continued speaking her thoughts aloud as if she had forgotten Judith was there. She had a distant look in her eyes, "He was special. We had hoped he would come back to us one day and teach us again, especially when so many of us got sick. And now he's gone..." She looked bereft, a woman whose hopes had been shattered.

Judith had put down her cloth while Becca was speaking. She had listened carefully to her story and was itching to tell her more. Her own body pain seemed to be dissipating as she sympathised with this woman's grief. Becca continued speaking, in a more matter of fact tone now. "I suppose it's all we deserve. We're lepers, we're sinners. People believe we're bad news and avoid us. Hardly anyone comes to see us. It's not surprising he too has been taken from us!" Her tone changed again, "Perhaps if he had still been alive, he would have come back to us and helped us..." She looked directly at Judith now, "and if what you said about him was true, he might have healed us, like he did Ephron."

Judith nodded, her face now glowing, "I believe he could have...indeed he could..." She was about to launch into her story when someone knocked at the door. Becca answered it to another woman, "Samara, it's good to see you. Come in and meet our latest resident Judith."

Samara, a largish woman with a big smile stepped in, went over to Judith and somehow managed to hug her even in her lying position. Close up Judith could see her face was pocked and marked, but somehow her smile and obvious big personality seemed to make them less obvious. Judith felt a respect for this woman already. She had been prepared to hug her.

"Well, Judith, we've all heard you've fallen off the mountain and landed here with us. I'm so glad Becca found you."

"So am I," Judith said smiling. "I don't know what would have happened to me if she hadn't."

Becca broke in, "Judith, Samara's kind of our organiser. She gets things done in our community. She knows everyone and everything. Anything you want done you go to her. She's like a leader, a mother to us."

Samara laughed, "Don't listen to her, Judith. I'm just an ordinary member. I don't have these airs and graces." She paused, "but if I can help you, I will." She smiled at Judith, her eyes showing genuine concern. "You're a Jewish girl?"

This was more of a statement than a question, and Judith wondered how she should respond. Might Samara show some prejudice towards her if she agreed? Judith knew in her heart that if a Samaritan girl had entered a Jewish community, the welcome would not have been the same. She decided that honesty was the best policy, and said, "I am. And I appreciate your willingness to help me."

"No matter Judith. We're glad to see you We don't bear any malice." She laughed at her semi joke, then her eyes became serious. "We're glad to have you here. From now on, you're one of us. We may share a dreadful disease, but we love each other and look out for each other. Till death. The Teacher taught us that. It's how we survive.!"

"The Teacher's dead!" Becca cut in. "Judith's told me. She knew him too."

"Are you sure?" Samara looked shocked, as if someone had hit her in the stomach and winded her.

Judith didn't know how to proceed. She didn't want to be new in the community and the bringer of bad news which might take away all their hopes. She decided for the second time in as many minutes that truth was the best policy, and nodded her head. "He was crucified," she said softly. Judith thought the older woman was going to cry. She let out a great sob, and then said to Becca, "Get us all something to drink…and a bit of food for this poor girl." She looked at Judith, "You must be hungry?" Judith nodded. Samara continued, "We'll eat and drink, and sit down together. You can tell us your story if you like…and about the Teacher. No-one ever comes here. We get very little news." She smiled again. "We've got lots of time. We're not going anywhere!" She laughed ruefully.

Becca busied herself, and within a few minutes Judith was sitting up on her mat with her back against the wall, eating handfuls of cereal and drinking a crushed fruit drink. The meal might have been frugal, but it was welcome to her equally crushed body. The two women sipped at their fruit drinks while Judith spoke.

Chapter Twenty-Five

"I'm not someone who is used to talking like this, but I assume you need to know something about me, about my family and about my life."

"And about the Teacher," added Becca.

"No problem there. I'm happy to tell you all about him. There's a lot more to tell you, and if you've got patience, I think you'll be amazed, if not blessed."

The two women settled down to listen, their eyes fixed on Judith.

"I was born in a small village in Galilee thirty-seven years ago, and yes, I'm a Jew. We were a simple family, living in the hills above the lake. My life was shattered when my baby brother was killed, and he died in my arms. Roman soldiers were chasing Zealots and he got in the way of their horses. It was awful!"

Samara and Becca looked at her sympathetically.

Judith continued, "it was about that time that I first met Josh...the Teacher. I was seven and he was eight. He was wonderful – special – even then. He helped me through my brother's death..." she paused for a moment. "Where's my bag, Becca? I saw you carrying it for me as we came down here."

"Right here, Judith," she went to the other side of the room and brought it to Judith. Judith opened it, rummaged down the side of it and produced her picture. She passed it to the women. Josh did this for me," she said proudly.

"It's wonderful!" said Samara. "I can see you in this, even as a little girl. Your smile is quite captivating." She paused then added, "After your brother's death, you say?"

"Yes. Josh wanted to cheer me up. He tried to capture my smile, and he gave it to his friend Abbas to complete it. Abbas is his Father," she explained.

"Well, we'll have you smiling like that again. The Teacher...or Josh...did a good thing in capturing it."

"That's what he said. He told me I'd lose it, but I'd get it back again. I've lost it a few times, but he's always been there to help me through. He'll do it again, I hope. Even after this trauma!"

"But he's dead, my dear. That's what you said, wasn't it?" Samara reminded her. "He can't help you now."

"Oh, but he can…if he wants to…just wait until you hear the whole story." Judith continued, "I went to Jerusalem when I was twelve with my family and Josh's. We had our Obligation services there. It's a long story, but the two of us got left behind in Jerusalem, and Josh ended up in the midst of the Jewish Council, in the Temple, talking to them about his Father…and they listened. Even then he knew Yahweh as his Father. When his parents eventually found him there, he asked them, 'Why were you worried? Didn't you know I'd be in my Father's house?' We got into trouble for staying behind in Jerusalem and the two families never met again. I grew up a bit and married a fine man named Mikha. He was a synagogue leader. I'll cut a long story short. Things went terribly wrong for me and I lost a baby – she was stillborn, you know - and my next daughter Tabitha was terribly weak. I gave up on life, and them. My smile went downhill, and I treated them badly. When Tabitha was twelve, she died. It was one of the worst days of my life but listen – it became one of the best. My husband was desperate. He went to find a healer that was travelling around Galilee. I hated everything I'd heard about him. Miracles just don't happen I told Mikha. He came back with him though and took him into my daughter's room. I came in behind them intending to tear a strip off the healer and put him out, but…" Judith wiped away a tear at this point. "He spoke my name, and when he looked at me – it was so wonderful – it was Josh. I hadn't seen him for years, and here he was just at the right time, to restore my smile."

Becca was enthralled, but had to ask, "Did he heal Tabitha?"

"Yes, yes. He did. You should have seen it. He called her back into life and he helped her up off her mat and into our arms." Judith was crying now remembering how she had felt. The other two women brushed tears from their eyes too.

"That's amazing!" said Samara. "If he's the same person as our Teacher, then I can imagine him doing it. He also healed a Samaritan leper, you know."

"I do know," Judith dried her eyes. "Becca was telling me."

"Go on," said Becca, anxious to hear more.

"Josh did many miracles and taught about his Father all over the region. It may well have been about then that he healed your friend."

"Oh, he wasn't a friend. Just someone who came our way to tell us his amazingly good news," Samara said. "Go on though, Judith."

"Well, our association with Josh made us bad news in the synagogue. Eventually we were told to leave, and so we went to Jerusalem, to relatives, to see if they could help Mikha get a new job. It was while we were there – it was Passover week and we also intended having Tabitha's obligation Ceremony then too – it was at the end of that very week Josh was murdered."

"Both women looked shocked and stunned. Samara gasped, "How…why? Such a good man. The Saviour…how?"

"The leaders were jealous of him. They said he was a threat to Israel's stability. They handed him over to the Romans who killed him."

"You said, by crucifixion?" said Becca.

"Yes, that's right. I was there. I saw him die." Once again Judith had a tear in her eye. The other women too. "Do you want to know what he said?" Judith asked as the thought struck her.

They nodded.

"He said, Father forgive them. They don't know what they're doing."

"All three of them were crying now.

"Don't be disheartened though. The best thing is yet to come." Judith's eyes were sparkling now. The others looked at her as if she was mad.

"He came back to life on the third day after his crucifixion!"

They stared at her, disbelievingly.

Judith went on, "Before he died, he had taught that he would rise on the third day.!" She squealed, "And he did! I saw him!"

"No," said Samara, "You didn't?"

"Oh, I did. I hugged him. I spoke to him a week or two later…in Galilee when I returned there. He was seen by many, his men, and many others too."

"Where is he now then?" asked Becca, a little sceptically. "Do you think he might come this way?"

"No. After forty days, he was taken up to heaven by his Father. His men saw it happen. He's very much alive, and he's promised to come back one day from there."

"So, we might see him then?" asked Samara hopefully. "He made a big impression on us all the first time."

"I can't tell you that. He said only he and the Father know the time when he will return. But there is another way you can meet him."

"How?" the two women asked simultaneously, eagerly.

"It's a bit of a story," Judith said. "Are you sure you've time to listen. I don't want to bore you."

"You're definitely not doing that!" Samara said. "We'd never forgive you if you didn't tell us."

"Well, after he went to heaven, another promise of his came true. He had said, 'Unless I go, you won't receive the Holy Spirit. He'll tell you all about me and help you communicate with me. He'll also give you the power to do even greater miracles than you've seen me do. When I go to the Father, we'll send him to you.'"

"What's the Holy Spirit?" said Becca looking a bit worried.

"Well, you remember you told me of your conversation with Josh at the well. He said that the Father wanted those who would worship him in spirit and truth."

Becca's eyes were gleaming now. "He did," she said.

"Well, that's the Spirit you need to communicate with him. And you must do it in honesty and truth." Judith thought, then added, "Please don't ask me how I know this. I just do. You remember I told you I'd somehow been there. Perhaps the Holy Spirit told me, but there's something else you didn't tell me."

Becca looked at her quizzically, and Samara looked bemused hearing about all this for the first time.

"When you met Josh, he offered you living water. You said you wanted it to save you coming to that well every day."

Becca looked as if she was about to faint. "You…you're right! I'd almost forgotten that." She was breathing in and out quite heavily now, trying to stop herself from passing out.

Samara's eyes were wide open, hardly daring to believe what she was hearing. Judith went on quietly, "The living water he was offering you was the Holy Spirit, and you said you wanted it."

"You're right!" exclaimed Becca excitedly. "You're right! I don't know how you know, but you're right!"

"I know," said Judith. "I saw it clearly and heard him speak to you. I don't know how I know. I just do."

Samara now spoke. "Are we still waiting for this Holy Spirit? Has he come yet?"

Judith became enthusiastic. "He's here!"

"Here?" asked Samara. "You mean, here? In here?"

"Yes. I suppose so. He's come into the world and is everywhere where believers are gathering."

"I believe," said Becca. Samara looked slightly unsure.

"Josh told us where two or three believers are gathered in his name, he's in the midst of them. By his Spirit. So yes, he's even here. Because you and I believe."

Samara looked a bit unhappy at being shut out of the union.

"Let me tell you the rest of my story," said Judith. "It might help you understand. Just after Josh left for heaven, about ten days after, many of us - about one hundred and twenty of us - were gathered together praying, when there was the sound like a powerful rushing wind. The room was filled with the noise of it, and above all our heads were tongues of fire. Some of us started speaking in other languages as the Holy Spirit entered us, and we all went running out into the streets of Jerusalem to tell everyone the Good News about Josh. We were speaking in languages we hadn't learned, but people gathered there for the Festival of Pentecost from all over the empire, they could hear the good news in their own languages. It was supernatural. Our leader, one of Josh's disciples called Peter - you probably met him – he preached powerfully, and three thousand people became believers that day."

Both women's eyes were sparkling now. To Judith it looked as if their faces were burning.

"It was wonderful; and for the next while, the good News spread like wildfire. Miracles…teaching in the Temple. The whole of Jerusalem seemed affected for the good." Judith's voice dropped and her face saddened. "It didn't last though," she said softly. "The authorities clamped down eventually and started to persecute us. They killed one of our prominent believers by stoning him to death…" Her voice trailed off. "And my husband Mikha, my lovely, lovely husband…they executed him outside our own house and threw his body into our public room…while I was in the other room hiding." Once again, the tears fell.

The other two women looked at her now with great sympathy. Eventually Samara spoke, "Just because he was a believer?"

"Yes," said Judith when she had pulled herself together. "They're clamping down." She added, "That's why I'm here."

They looked at her askance.

Judith went on. "The man responsible for killing my husband seems to want to exterminate me too. He knows what I look like, and almost found me in Jerusalem the other day. He seems to be heading up much of the persecution of believers." She looked awkward now. "The past little while doesn't put me in a good light I'm afraid. When Mikha died, Josh came to me that night by his Spirit and comforted me. He told me what was in my future. And in the days after that his Spirit was with me and helped me overcome my feelings. My relatives and daughter Tabitha took care of the rest. I was in hiding. However, I began to doubt, and I suppose I was a bit complacent and ungrateful for all the support I'd received. I went out into town because I couldn't tolerate staying in the house any more, and as I told you, I was spotted by the man who's pursuing me, and he almost caught up with me again at my relatives' house. They helped me escape in a wagon bound for Galilee two days ago. Before I left however, I had the distinct sense I had disobeyed the Holy Spirit, by doubting and by taking myself out of Yahweh's protection. It was then I first felt the nausea and the aches in my body. The pains in my face arms and legs started then too. Perhaps I'm being punished for what I've done, especially after the wonderful things Josh and his Father have done for me."

The two women were now looking surprised.

"Will I finish the story?" Judith asked.

"Of course, my dear," said Samara.

"Well, I think I'm in a bit of a muddle. I know I've done wrong, and I've repented of it. But given the past two days events, it looks like Josh and his Father are still with me. You see, I felt so ill on the wagon, I wanted to be sick. In trying to get out of it, I fell off it. It was nighttime and the others were sleeping. The driver was too far in front to see. We were the last wagon in the caravan, and so when I hit the road, no-one noticed. Now this is the marvellous thing. When I came around, I had no idea as to what to do, but somehow the dog Josh gave me, then took away from me at our last meeting because it was ill – that little dog came up to me miraculously and led me here from the road. I am so grateful to Josh for sending her."

"You're fortunate," said Samara. "Some of the land between here and the road is quite treacherous, especially if you traversed it in the dark. There's a river there too. Some parts of it have steep banks. You could have fallen in and drowned, especially in your state!"

"Well, I was indeed fortunate, with Little Faith just ahead of me." Judith looked at Becca, "That's the dog I was talking about when you first found me."

"I had assumed that," said Becca smiling. "A good name for a dog!"

Judith nodded. "And the rest you know. Somehow, I've contracted leprosy. Yahweh has obviously led me to you, for whatever reason he knows."

"That's some story, my dear," said Samara sounding impressed. Becca's demeanour was similarly awed. Judith noticed that both their faces were still glowing.

"You've done something today for us we would never have thought possible," Samara said. "The last person who did so was the Teacher…Josh…himself."

"Yes, he helped us to believe," Becca said. "You've done the same. I really do believe – in what you've said…and in Josh, our Teacher."

"But I've made such a mess of things, and now I'm having to pay for my mistakes. How can you trust me, or believe what I say?"

"Because my dear, there's a ring of truth about it," said Samara quietly. "You mentioned the Father wants those who worship him to do so in Spirit and truth. Well, you've spoken in truth. Perhaps the Spirit – this Holy Spirit – is here too as you said he was. Who can help us believe? We want to believe!"

"Really?" said Judith quite surprised. "I do believe the spirit of Josh is where believers are. I sense him with us now. I'm amazed that he's with us after all I've done."

"My dear, perhaps you're seeing this from the wrong perspective. You say you're being punished by having leprosy and arriving here. I see it differently. I believe the Teacher…Josh…has sent you here to us. We need you…and we need him. Will you help us, pray with us and stay with us? We asked him to do the same thing."

Judith looked shocked at Samara's wisdom. She nodded slowly as the realisation of what her words meant. Instead of Josh and his Father having abandoned and punished her, they had been leading her all the time, bringing her to a place where she was needed…and where they needed her to be. This indeed put a whole new complexion on things. Her spirit lifted; her face brightened. She said, "I'd be glad to." They all smiled, then Judith said, "Well believers, shall we pray?"

Chapter Twenty-Six

Judith woke up hours later. It was dark outside, and Becca had a candle burning in the middle of a rough little table.

"Have I been asleep that long? It's dark!" she said, slightly groggily.

"You certainly have, sister," Judith could just make out that Becca was smiling by the pale flickering light of the candle. "You've been asleep for hours, but you needed it. We must have exhausted you by making you tell your story."

Judith shook her head, "Not at all. I was glad to tell it and get some of my misdemeanours off my chest."

"Well, you've done something wonderful for us. You've introduced us to a whole new world and reacquainted us with the Teacher. Not much happens here. Your coming has revitalised us. I can't wait till the rest of the community hear all you've to say."

"Will they believe me, do you think?"

"Did we?" said Becca grinning now. "If we could, they could too."

"I hope so," Judith was silent for a few moments, thinking over the events of the morning. Her two friends had readily agreed to pray with her, and they had spoken haltingly after she had started things off. Judith very soon had become aware of Josh's strong presence in the room, and the others seemed to be sensing something too. She then had felt constrained to ask them, "Do you believe...I mean, really believe?" Both women responded almost instantaneously, "Yes". Immediately, the atmosphere in the room had become charged with something, a sense of peace, a sense of power, a sense of love. Judith could hear both women crying. She heard them whisper alternately, "Sorry" and "thank you". Then there was silence and Josh's strong presence was evident again. She felt as if he was close enough to touch. Something in Judith's pouch vibrated, and she knew something was required of her. She waited expectantly, and then it happened. She had heard inspired messages in a few of the upper room meetings before, but she had never been one to give one out. Now however, she felt Josh imprinting on her mind words she felt she had to say. "You have heard my daughter's words today. They show you that I can do anything. Nothing is impossible for me. Do not disbelieve but walk with me. You received my words before when I was with you. I have not forgotten you or your community. I have sent my daughter to you to revive you, to remind you of my words. I will give my presence to anyone who believes. Do not think I cannot help you. All things are possible, only believe!" Judith stopped, quite surprised at what had happened. The two women were weeping tears of joy now. All three had hugged, each of them experiencing the same joy in their hearts. When Samara had left, Becca encouraged Judith to sleep, and had got on with some household chores before going out.

"Hungry?" Becca asked. "You haven't eaten since late morning."

"I am a bit. I feel I need to gain strength."

Becca brought out some bread she had baked that afternoon. She placed some cheese on it and handed it to Judith, who ate it greedily. When she had finished, and drunk some milk, she enquired where Becca had got the food and drink.

"Well, I told you earlier that the land in our valley is able to grow vegetables and fruit. We also keep animals on it, hence the cheese. One of the ladies in the village churns it for us. Milk is a luxury as there are not too many animals, but we do have the stream if we get stuck. The water's not all that good for drinking. It's fine for washing. As I told you, if we go early to the well with our own jars and buckets, our former village friends will let us draw water. We're well enough served – just a little frugal, but we survive."

"How many are in the community?" asked Judith.

"About fifty. Most of us help each other. We share. Some of us work on the land, some get the water, some build or repair. We're all busy, but there is a strong community spirit."

"That's not unlike what happened in Jerusalem after the Holy Spirit came," said Judith. "People helped each other. They sold their houses or lands and shared the money. We even gave it to the poor. We didn't use it all on ourselves. There was a real sense of love. We were happy to help each other, and so there was a strong bond of unity. We held meetings and had meals in each other's houses. We even shared the bread and wine there. No-one called anything their own."

"What do you mean, 'bread and wine'?" Becca asked.

"Well Josh, the night before he died, had a meal with his twelve men. He told them that in the future, as often as they ate bread or drank wine, they should do it remembering him. He said the bread represented his body which would be broken for them, and the wine his blood which would be shed for them. It was symbolic of Yahweh's new agreement with mankind. So, at every meal we do it and it makes Josh seem very close."

"We have wine every so often when we press the fruit. We could maybe do that too? You know, Judith, I really sensed the Teacher's presence with us today when we prayed. I felt just as I did when I listened to him at the well, and over the next couple of days he spent with us in our village. I want more of it, but let's have the bread and the wine sometimes too."

"Yes, that would be good. But what you were experiencing today was the Holy Spirit making Josh real to you. Remember when two or three believers are gathered, he's there with them. That's what he taught. You've now got those 'living waters' you asked him for all those years ago, and if you let them, they'll flow out of you and bless others."

"That's what I want, Judith. You promise you'll help us?"

"Of course I will. We can all share our gifts and talents, and hopefully make a difference to the community."

"You'll definitely stay then?"

"Of course. I can't see where else I could go. I'm a leper too. But I've seen today that rather than being punished by Yahweh, he's led me to you for a purpose. We'll be able to help each other."

"What you said today was so much more meaningful than anything the prophet says. It seemed so real. He seems to speak only religious phrases and moral commands. We need more than that."

"Yes, I've been meaning to ask you. Who is this prophet then? I certainly wouldn't want to set myself up in competition to him, or cause division in the community."

"I don't think you'd do that. He's our kind of priest."

"A real priest?"

"No, not really. He's a man of the people, quite a strong man. He came out of nowhere. Not long after we had come here having been expelled from the village, he just appeared one day and offered to help us on the land. He had the marks, and so we readily accepted him among us as we needed all the help we could get. He said he had had religious experiences too and would prefer to stay apart from us so he could be in communion with the spirits. We built him a dwelling at the other end of the valley, and every so often he comes among us offering help of different sorts," she laughed, "and the odd moral or spiritual pronouncement. I suppose that's why he was given the name 'the prophet'. He keeps himself much to himself and every so often seems to make journeys into the wilderness. When he returns, he sometimes distributes items of food or clothing he says have been given to him on his travels." Becca paused for a moment as if deliberating whether to say any more. She contented herself with, "He also provides us with other services."

Judith said, "Well, I certainly don't want to be in contention with him It sounds like he's quite aloof though. Maybe our paths won't cross."

"That's unlikely," Becca said. "He'll want to see you. He feels he has the right to vet anyone who joins us. There haven't been that many since he arrived, but he likes to get to know them, especially the young ones."

Judith raised an eyebrow, but Becca closed down the conversation. "He'll definitely want to see you. He knows you're here. It didn't take long for that news to get round the community. In fact, he's been saying for a while we should expect new people. Most people took that with a pinch of salt…until today."

"Well, I'll look forward to meeting him."

"Wait till you get your energy back and feel better. You'll meet him in due course, no doubt. It'll be interesting to know what he makes of your story. He knows about our encounter with the Teacher but says little about it, except that he believes he's been sent by the spirits to continue his work. We don't see it that way, those of us who met the Teacher, but he is a benefit to the community, so we just say nothing."

." Should I make an appointment to see him, or do I just go along when I wish?"

"Oh no. He'll send for you when he thinks it's the right time. He's particular that way. He'll call for you when he's ready."

Although she thought the prophet sounded a little strange, she decided to withhold judgment until she had met him. She might just get a pleasant surprise, and perhaps they might share spiritual experiences. The two women talked a little longer, then decided to go to sleep. Becca had the water to go for in the morning - at dawn as usual. As Judith drifted off, she thanked Yahweh for his protection of her, and for his bringing her to the community. She prayed for Tabitha, Joel, and Mary that they would be safe. She had no way of getting a message to them. She just prayed that if one day they heard she had disappeared from the wagon, they wouldn't be too worried. Would Yahweh help her get back there? She had no idea. At the moment it looked impossible, but she contented herself with Josh's words, 'With Yahweh, all things are possible'. She was glad she had new friends, and desired more than anything to be a blessing to the community she had dropped, or rather been dropped, into. As she dozed off, she felt a contentment, a happiness, that the Holy Spirit was with her, and had used her that day. She realised that she no longer felt at arm's length with Josh and Yahweh. She now had a strong sense of purpose and knew Josh was close to her to help her fulfil it. She fell asleep happy. Even her pain seemed to have subsided. She knew she was in the right place!

When she awoke, she felt really good. Becca was up and about, and it was her activity that had roused her. Judith struggled to her feet, and noticing this Becca said, "I'm up early to go and get the water we'll need. Just stay where you are and rest."

"Good morning," said Judith with a smile. "I'm coming with you."

"You can't, sister. You're not well. Stay and rest."

"I'm feeling much better, thank you. I want to pull my weight here. I'll help you with the water. And anyway, I want to find my way about. I didn't get much of a chance to see where I was yesterday lying deep down in that hammock."

"Are you sure?" Becca queried.

"Positively. Definitely," said Judith, straightening her robe.

"Are you hungry?"

"NO, not yet. I can wait till we get back."

"Oh, I didn't say there was any food," Becca said with a grin. "But we'll see what we can do. If you're up to it, I'll show you around after breakfast. I know there are a lot of people who want to meet you."

"Sounds good to me," grinned Judith. "I hope I don't disappoint them."

"Oh, I don't think so. Samara's been going around telling them all about you. They're keen to meet you."

"I've a lot of expectations to ruin then," Judith said smiling. "Come on, let's be going!"

The two women left the hut as dawn was breaking and walked past some other huts towards the hill Judith could see rising in front of them. At its base was vegetation, but as it rose steeply it became quite rocky. Becca led the way to some well-worn footholds, almost like steps carved into the rock, and very soon they were standing at the top looking down over the Valley of the Outcasts. Judith was amazed at just how big it was. It was reasonably flat, and just beyond a few small huts that were fairly spread out, she could see some fields sporting crops that looked more like vegetables rather than wheat. In one of the fields she could see a number of cattle and in another some sheep. From one of the huts, she could hear the sound of a cockerel crowing at the dawn. She assumed that the inhabitants also would have had chickens. Beyond the fields, near the edge of the valley, she could see rows of trees, which she assumed were fruit orchards. She recognised some straggling vines there too. As she looked into the distance, the valley narrowed. She asked Becca," Is it down there that the Prophet lives?"

"That's right. He keeps himself apart from us, except when he's working."

"Oh, he works too?"

"Yes. He takes his spiritual role seriously. He must spend hours praying and meditating, but he also joins us in the fields when labour is required. He's strong, perhaps not as strong as he once was, but he removes his normal prophet clothes and becomes like one of us."

"Will he be there today?"

"No, it's usually at planting and harvest. Of course, he's always present at the celebrations after. He blesses them." Becca paused, and said, "Are you still feeling all right? We'll have to be moving." She smiled, "Otherwise you'll be bumping into Zenina and Keilah again!"

Don Treader

Judith shivered, and hurried after Becca towards Jacob's well a couple of hundred yards away. She was in another valley whose sides were quite steep too. This was much bigger than the Valley of the Outcasts, and seemed to stretch far into the distance, reaching towards two major hills at opposite sides of it. Becca pointed them out, "That one' Mount Gerizim. Our Temple is there, you know - the Samaritan one. The other's Mount Ebal. In our traditions Moses had the blessings and the cursing shouted out from each hill, while the people stood between them listening."

"It's the same in our tradition," said Judith. "They're quite imposing the way they rise out of the surrounding landscape."

"True," Becca agreed, "And that's where I stayed, before..." She was pointing to a fairly large group of huts resembling a village not too far away from the well. Judith knew exactly what she meant. She had seen them from the top of the hill the previous day as she and Faithie had watched the dawn rise. She looked up at the hill she had fallen down. She marvelled she hadn't hurt herself more, and whispered a quick "thank you" to Yahweh.

The two women reached the well and Becca lowered the bucket into the water which seemed a long way down. It took some time for Judith to hear it splash into it, and an even longer time for Becca to pull it back up again. It was obviously heavy. Judith helped Becca empty the water into the container she had brought with her, and they took it in turns to carry it back to their valley, gripping the handle firmly to avoid spilling any of its precious contents.

"Tired now?" Becca asked. As they entered the hut.

"No, not really. Once I've had a seat, and a bit of breakfast – if you're offering it – I'll be ready to face anything."

"Good for you," said Becca and proceeded to bring out a container of cereal. "Help yourself to some of the water."

Judith did so and ate a handful of meal. It wasn't quite the same as breakfast at Joel and Mary's. They had platters and utensils – and a maid. But Judith didn't mind roughing it. After all it wasn't unlike how she had lived in her village when she was a child.

They finished their breakfast and were chatting when there was a knock on the door. Samara came straight in.

"We don't stand on ceremony here, Judith," said Becca laughing. "Samara's welcome in everyone's house."

Samara laughed too. "Not always true, but I do try to be discrete." They laughed again.

"Where are we going then?" asked Becca.

"Well, if Judith's able, I thought I'd introduce her to the village," said Samara grandly.

"What about me?"

216

"Oh, everyone knows you already," said Samara grinning." But you're welcome to come too."

"I hope so," said Becca feigning indignation. "I'm part of her story. I'm her sister!"

"Only at the end of it," said Judith laughing now. "I'm glad you're in it though. I don't know what might have happened if you hadn't come along yesterday!"

"We're sisters," Becca said. "We must stick together. Right!"

They all went out, and the grand tour began. First they knocked on the doors of most of the huts and acquainted Judith with their occupants. Next, they visited the vegetable fields and Samara introduced Judith to the workers, who at this time of year were mainly women. They were singing and appeared to be happy in their work. They welcomed Judith with open arms. Finally, they visited the orchards at the edge of the valley. The trees were well kept and even at this time of year were showing rapid growth, with many blossoms and even a little early fruit beginning to appear on them. It seemed mainly the men of the community that worked here. Some were tending to the trees while others were digging holes for new plantings. One end of this area was given over to straggling vines – the ones she had seen earlier as she had looked down the valley. Men were taking great care of them making sure only to pick only the grapes that were ripe and juicy. They dropped them into wooden containers which when they were full were carried to a small building   by other workers who would trample them in the winepress inside.

The sun was high in the sky when the tour finished and the three women made their way back to Becca's hut and a light lunch which echoed breakfast, except this time there was milk which Becca had been given at the place where the cattle were milked.

"I managed to get some grain today on our travels," said Becca triumphantly. "We'll be able to have something different for our evening meal. I'll make some bread and we can have it with cooked vegetables. We can finish it off with a little fruit. Today's been quite profitable. People were glad to see you Judith and were quite generous."

"That sounds great," said Judith trying to sound grateful. The meal would have been seen as frugal or sparse at Joel and Mary's, but in Judith's situation, it was wonderful.

After lunch, the women talked and prayed a little, before Samara left and Becca got on with her chores. They shared more of their lives, the two women asking about Tabitha, Mikha and Josh, and for Judith's thoughts on the community.

"It looks to me," she said, "that the people here are in different stages of the disease. Some look more ravaged than others."

Don Treader

"Yes, those who can work do what they can," said Samara. "As their illness progresses, we expect less and less of them. That's a given rule."

"What happens when things get too bad?"

"Those who are nearing the end stay in their huts and the rest of the community try to help as much as they can. It can be painful and quite horrible at the end. We've seen it so often. I think the thought of it eventually happening to us spurs each of us on to help the poor wretches."

They paused for a second or two as the gravity and horror of the situation took hold of them.

Becca said, "Hopefully that's a long way off!"

The others agreed.

Judith asked them how long they had been in the community. Becca answered first, "I contracted leprosy about two years ago. You've been longer haven't you, Samara?"

Samara nodded.

Becca continued, "Our village near the well was a happy community, especially after the Teacher had come to us. Most of us believed in what he had said, and we were looking forward to him returning some day. It was so refreshing to have a Jew amongst us that didn't criticise or condemn us for being Samaritans. He just stated things as they were. We were all equal in the eyes of his Father and we could all worship him wherever we were. It didn't matter where we were because his Father was everywhere. The big religious places didn't count any more. Neither were traditions important. His Father was doing a new thing and had sent his Messiah to get it going. We knew who he was and felt privileged he had come to us. When he left, we were sad, but his words held us together. We all talked about and longed for the 'new thing' he would bring us. We expected him to come back one day. We went on as we had been. I stayed with my partner, and you know about Zenina. I told you she married one of my ex-husbands. She didn't like me."

"That's an understatement," said Samara laughing. "She loathed you. Not only had you been married to her husband. You were seen as a bit loose, having been with other men and left them. You were a danger, a threat, to other women. It wasn't only Zenina."

"Becca looked uncomfortable, "I'm not proud of it now, but I wasn't alone. It was a small village, and we all knew each other, and sometimes…"

"Enough said," said Samara. "Tell Judith the rest."

"Well into this 'happy' situation came a stranger to our area. I got to know her. You see, as I was a bit of an outcast even then in the community because of 'my men'. I could only make friends with those who didn't know me, people like this stranger. I didn't notice at first the tell-tale signs. She covered them well. She must have left her village because of them before they had the chance to exclude her. Anyhow I got to know her, and we visited often. Unfortunately, it didn't take long for the marks to appear on me too. I couldn't understand it at first, but when it became clear, I was terrified. I knew what it meant. My partner and my neighbours were terrified too. No-one cared about relationships. I had to go. They didn't want me amongst them once they knew. The afternoon after I told my partner, I was unceremoniously dumped into this community with all my possessions – and they weren't much! The house my partner and I had stayed in was burned to the ground - and that was that. No-one was happy about it, but it was the rule. Leprosy can spread quickly and must be shunned. Society must be cleansed."

"That must have been a terrible time for you…and your partner," said Judith.

"Yes, it was. I was low for weeks. And so was my partner. He often stood at the top of the hill and shouted down to me, crying. But eventually his visits grew less and less, till he never came back at all. I tell you, I'm so grateful for this community. They know what it's like to be cut off, and they were able to rally around me and rescue me from myself. I did consider killing myself at first."

Judith looked shocked. "Did you ever try?" she asked with a worried look.

"I must confess, I did. Once or twice, I climbed out of our valley and went along the edge to a particularly steep rocky place and tried to jump." She started to cry at the thought. "I just couldn't. I didn't have the courage."

"I'm so glad," said Judith quietly. "Yahweh wouldn't have wanted that."

Samara continued, "Becca's not alone. Many people who live here have gone to that spot. Fortunately, few have ever jumped, but…it is a popular spot."

"You seem happy now, Becca," said Judith.

"I've grown used to it. You have to." She smiled. "With a death sentence hanging over you, you get to realise that you should make the most of every day…and anyway, these people here are my companions in suffering. Helping and supporting each other is a lifeline for us. It helps us make it through the day! And now…now sister, now you're here, I'm feeling great. You've made me see there's hope, and that the Teacher will come back to us one day."

"He's here," said Judith. "We experienced something of that yesterday, when his spirit came amongst us."

Rebecca looked radiant now. "I know." She turned to Samara, "Tell Judith about yourself, Samara."

Samara settled down, as if gearing herself up to tell a long story. "Well, Judith, I've been here much longer. This community has existed for generations, and local villages far and near send their lepers Here. It's convenient, and loved ones know that we take care of our own and we can support ourselves fairly well. They hardly need to supply anything once their relative is here. Sometimes our community can be large, sometimes small. It depends on how quickly the disease spreads in the area. We do our best for our residents. Well, I lived on a farm with my husband and our four children. We were relatively successful at what we did.

We grew different crops and sold them at market. I organised most things, as my husband spent most of his time in the fields. My story's not unlike Becca's. One day we hired a worker who was to labour for us throughout the summer. He stayed in our barn and gave us very little trouble. When he wasn't working in the fields, he kept himself to himself. Well he'd had a day or two off and when he was due to return to work, he didn't appear. I went into the barn and found him in a terrible state. He was in extreme agony and because it was dark inside, I didn't notice that much of the skin on his face had broken out in sores and white blotches. I tried to help him by bringing him food and gave him new straw for his mattress, much of which had been defiled. This continued for a few days until he rallied and reported for work. It was my husband that noticed it first. The man's face, arms and legs were covered in these marks. As soon as leprosy was determined, we had to get rid of him. We gave him his wages and let him go. Unfortunately, however some days later it was discovered I had similar marks appearing on my face. I hadn't felt well since I had helped him by giving him food and clearing out his straw. I must have got it by touching something of his. I don't know. All I knew was that I had it, and that my fate would be similar to his. My husband tried hard. He converted the barn for me, making it into decent living quarters, and it was planned that I stay there in seclusion. At least I wouldn't have to go away. However, his men objected to having a leper living so near to them. Some quit - and he was going to lose the summer crop if he couldn't hire workers. We talked it over, at a distance, and we agreed for the sake of the farm, and ultimately the family, it would be best that I come here. I would never have forgiven myself if any of my children had caught it off me. So, like Becca, I was deposited here with a few belongings and weekly visits from the family, which eventually tailed off too."

"How sad for you all," Judith said. She noticed Samara was trying to hold back a tear. This surprised her as she thought of Samara as a solid woman usually unflappable. She realised that she had lost much too and that even after all this time, it was still very raw.

"Yes, it was difficult being separated from my children. When they stopped coming, I realised that I would probably never see them growing up, getting married...my grandchildren..." She couldn't contain herself any longer. The tears fell. The others joined her as she spoke for them all.

Once these emotions passed, Samara said, "The only thing to do was to throw myself into the life here. I was good at organising farms, so I tried to put my skills to work where I was allowed."

"You can see much of Samara's handiwork as you walk about the community – the crops, fields, the animals, the orchards...you've helped make us more self-sufficient."

Samara nodded, "Well, I wanted to do something to help. Many here at that time lived in misery and squalor."

"And you have," said Becca proudly. "You go into homes and help the sick. You cheer us up when we're low…you're like a mother to us…and we appreciate it."

"I only want to help and to be useful."

"Exactly the qualities the Messiah is looking for," said Judith smiling. "Shall we pray?"

The others agreed enthusiastically, and once again they sensed Josh's presence with them, encouraging them.

As they were finishing, Judith felt a vibration in her pouch. She felt she should take out her cross and show it to the women. They marvelled at its beauty. "I often feel encouraged when I look at this," Judith said. She explained to them how she had come about it and how much it meant to her.

"It's not flashing now," said Becca.

"No, it usually does so when I need to know something. For instance, when I first met you. I don't know how I knew about your meeting with the Teacher at the well, but when I felt it pulsing, the thought seemed to come into my mind. Perhaps Sophia, my angel, knew about you. I don't know. But I do know that when this is with me, I feel encouraged."

"Just telling us about it makes us feel good too," Samara said. "You are indeed a blessing, a Messiah messenger to us. How would you feel about telling your story to others in the Community? They need to know Josh too."

"I'd be happy to do so. Why don't we make this time every day a time for people to come? For instance, each of you could bring one of your friends. We can have something to eat, then chat and pray."

They both agreed.

Becca laughed good-naturedly, "Who's going to supply the lunch? I'm only a poor widow woman!"

"It wouldn't be fair to put that burden on you. We can encourage our friends to bring something small to eat with them. I'm sure you could supply the water, Becca."

Becca nodded. "Great! I'm looking forward to it already. Whom shall we ask?"

The two women set about trying to agree on whom they could invite for the first week.

Judith said, "You know, this is how 'The Way' got started. People met in each other's houses and just ate together, and shared stories about Josh and their experiences. You never know, if our group grows as quickly, the whole community will be believers before long!"

"Let's hope so," said Samara. "Wouldn't that be wonderful!"

Once she'd gone and Becca was busying herself with chores inside and outside the hut, Judith settled down to rest. She found herself praying to Yahweh and thanking him for his goodness to her. Things were moving on fast, but that didn't worry her. Her renewed sense of purpose, and Josh's presence with her, inspired her, motivated, and enthused her. She wasn't going to forget Tabitha or her family, but thoughts and regrets at what she was losing were fading fast. In the back of her mind, she believed she would see them again one day…and even if she didn't, she would meet them again in heaven. For the moment she was in the right place, in Yahweh's will. What could be better than that…and she felt fulfilled!

Chapter Twenty-Seven

"The prophet's calling for you," said Becca a few days later when she came in after doing her afternoon chores. "He's heard you're much better and wants to meet you. I've to bring you to his hut tomorrow afternoon."

"That's good," said Judith. "I've been wondering when I'd get to meet him...and how."

"We'll leave after our prayer time," said Becca. "It'll take about twenty minutes to get to the other end of the valley."

"That's not long. We'll easily manage that. How will I get back? I'm assuming you aren't staying?"

"That's right. His audiences are usually private. He'll tell us when we get there what time he wants me to return for you. He might decide to bring you back himself."

"Fine. Is there anything I need to know, anything I need to do when meeting him?"

For the first time since she'd known her, Becca looked uncertain. She simply said, "He's the prophet. You'll know how to act when you're with him. Most of us do. Only do what you want to."

Judith thought this seemed a strange answer but decided to make up her own mind about the prophet when she got there. She was looking forward to discussing spiritual things with him. She wondered how much he knew about the Teacher and Yahweh. Becca had mentioned before that he talked much about the spirit. Was this the same Spirit she knew? She hoped there might be a meeting of minds. Then she remembered he was more than likely to be a Samaritan prophet. He might know little of the Jewish side of things. Jews generally believed that the Samaritans had perverted their scriptures to suit their own faith, beliefs, and traditions. This caused her to feel anxious, so she put the thought to the back of her mind and decided to leave the meeting in Yahweh's hands.

The following afternoon came, and again just before she left, it seemed to Judith that Becca was a little withdrawn or perhaps anxious.

"What's wrong?" she asked her. "You seem a bit pre-occupied, Becca."

"Oh, nothing. I was just wondering if you'd bathed thoroughly today? It really isn't any of my business, but the prophet likes his visitors to be spotless. Your robe is perfect. I just wanted you to know about his standards and requirements before you left."

Judith sensed a note of anxiety in Becca's manner, but it was clear she wasn't keen to continue the conversation by going into more detail. Judith put it down to the fact that probably like the others in the community, they seemed to have a respect, either reverent or fearful, for their prophet and wanted to show him off to strangers in the best light possible.

The two women made their way past the fields, and down the path that led to the other end of the valley, which narrowed quite markedly when they neared the prophet's dwelling. Judith had the impression when it came into sight that his hut was of slightly better quality than the huts of the other residents. When she commented on this, Becca said that the residents were proud that a prophet had come to their valley and had wanted to build him something befitting his status. The prophet had at first objected, being a humble man, but rather than offend the good will of the community he had eventually agreed to accept their kindness. "Even inside, you'll see it's not quite like our humble dwellings," Becca said. "But he's our spiritual leader, and he does much for us, in oh so many ways." She was looking at Judith strangely, which made Judith feel unsettled. She didn't know what to make of Becca's attitude that afternoon, so she simply put it down to the fact that she was anxious that she and the prophet would get on well and didn't want to spoil anything.

As they approached the building, the door opened and a man in a long robe came out to meet them. Becca," he said in a quiet, serene voice. "You've brought Judith, I see. Very good." He spoke slowly and deliberately as if every word had to sound meaningful. Judith wasn't sure what to make of him. He was fairly tall, and well built, but she was unable to see much of his face as he wore a hood that obscured everything except his eyes, which seemed to stare out at her from under it. He was carrying a large wooden staff in his right hand. If she hadn't known any better, she would have thought that by his demeanour and clothing she was meeting with an ancient prophet straight out of her own scriptures.

She noticed Becca lower her eyes and bow before him. She decided to do the same as an obvious mark of respect and submission to his status.

Again, he spoke, "Becca, please return for Judith about half an hour before sunset. We should be finished our communion by then." Judith thought this a strange way of talking, but she had been used to Josh, and put it down to the 'spiritual' way of talking.

Becca said nothing. She nodded then walked backwards for a few steps before turning and making her way up the valley again.

"Come in, my dear," said the prophet softly. He went in and Judith followed meekly. Once inside, it took a while for her eyes to adjust to the gloom. It appeared he thrived in shadows and low light. It somehow added to the atmosphere he obviously wanted to create. As her eyes acclimatised themselves, she was surprised to see the walls were covered with hangings, and some of them were drawn over what she assumed were shutters to keep out the light. In the middle of the room was a table on which a solitary candle was burning. The smell of it filled the room giving it a slightly musty air. The prophet stood his staff in a corner then went to the table and sat down while Judith remained at the door

The prophet looked at her carefully and Judith felt his eyes boring into her. He was used to this light she surmised and was making up his mind about her, or perhaps the Spirit was revealing to him something about her? After a few moments, he said, "Come over here my dear. Sit down."

Judith complied and sat at the other side of the table. He seemed to have accepted her, and she felt more at ease.

"Give me your hands," he said and reached over the table to take hold of them as she held them out to him. His grasp was gentle. He began to speak in a language she didn't recognise and seemed for a moment to get carried away. Suddenly he stopped and she was aware of his eyes boring into her again from under that large hood.

"Tell me about yourself, my dear. We're always glad to welcome new people into our community."

Judith decided to keep things short. She didn't want to exhaust the prophet's patience with much talking. "I left Jerusalem a few days ago. I was making for Galilee. Unfortunately, I took ill on the journey, and tried to be sick out of the wagon. It was the middle of the night and I fell out, rendering myself unconscious. As we were the last wagon in the caravan, and everyone inside it was sleeping, I was left behind on the road. By a miracle I somehow found myself at Jacob's Well where I collapsed, and Becca found me. I'm so grateful for your people taking me in. I don't know where I'd have been without your help!" Judith tried to sound as grateful as she could.

"You've been brought to us. We're happy to take you in. We are a haven for the unclean"

His gaze seemed to relax a little. He continued, "How long?"

"How long?" queried Judith, unsure what he meant.

"How long have you been unclean, my dear?" His grasp felt tighter.

"I had pains just before coming from Jerusalem. The marks only appeared on my face and my body when I reached Jacob's well. I didn't know I had it till I met Becca."

He seemed pleased with this answer and stood up. "I want to pray for you. Come round the table and stand before me." Judith dutifully complied, and the two stood looking at each other. Judith noticed that even at that close range she still couldn't see anything of his face but his eyes. He raised his hands above her head which she bowed. He began to speak again in a foreign tongue she didn't recognise. She believed a blessing was a blessing and so she allowed it to happen.

He stopped and Judith was readying herself to sit down again when he said, "My dear, in my understanding of your faith from the reading of the ancient scriptures – it's the same in ours – if someone contracts leprosy, they must go to the priest to have it confirmed or annulled. Am I right?"

Judith nodded.

"Will you then permit me to take down your hood to see the extent of your problem? I stand in the place of your priest." Judith thought for a moment and then accepted his offer. Up till that point she had just assumed that Becca and the other women had been correct in their assessment of her condition. She hadn't doubted that she had leprosy.

He lowered his two hands from above her head and put them on either side of her hood. He gently pulled it down, exposing her hair and face.

He looked into her eyes. "You are beautiful, my dear. It's such a shame that the disease has affected you in such a way. He touched her nose and the other places where white blotches were evident. Judith felt shooting pains under his fingers.

"And you say they're all over your body?" he enquired, his voice becoming lower.

"Not all over. Mainly on my arms and legs. I have pains in my fingers and toes."

"To be expected, my dear," he said. He moved his fingers to her hair and teased it out. "Yes, you have some markings there too. It won't be long before some of your hair will fall out."

Judith didn't know what to think; whether to be grateful for his confirmation or uncomfortable that she was being touched. The thought had gone through her mind that he might not have confirmed that she had leprosy, but perhaps some other minor skin condition. If this had been the case, she could have returned home to Tabitha and her family.

While she was considering these things, she was caught unawares. His left hand slipped down her body and deftly found its way through the slit in her robe. She tried to draw back from him saying, "What are you doing?"

He had been too quick for her though and his other hand held her in place while he searched in her pouch, then extracted the small bag of gold coins she had kept there since coming to the community. She hadn't been unaware however, that His fingers had taken advantage of his search to poke and prod at her body through her robe. She felt sick.

226

He pushed her back a little so he could examine the contents of the bag. He looked satisfied as he emptied the coins onto the table, counted them then bagged them again.

Judith said nothing. She felt intimidated and violated by his action.

"I'm sorry, my dear. When you were outside, I noticed the bulge in your robe, and forgive me, I assumed it to be something similar to what I've just found. It struck me that if you were journeying over our land, you would not have come unprepared. It was also likely you wouldn't have left any money lying around at Becca's in case anything happened to it. Logically, therefore, you would be carrying it on your person."

Judith stuttered, "I was going to give some…" She stopped, then finished her sentence, "for my keep."

"I know, and that's why I took it. The community will get the benefit, and believe me, we're grateful for your gift." His voice remained soft and quiet, "I know you're grateful Judith." He moved back towards her. She hadn't changed her position because she had been feeling petrified.

He put his face up to hers and whispered. "Just how grateful? This is a small community, much populated by women. Many of them have had to leave families and friends. They have needs. and they expect their prophet to meet them. It can be a long time here as an outcast with no prospect of getting back. Many of our women come to me to supply what they are missing and to make their lives bearable before they succumb to the disease."

Judith was horrified at what she was hearing.

"So, my dear, see this as an initiation ceremony, a baptism into our community of the unclean." He licked his lips. "Take off your robe. Let it down slowly."

Judith was shocked. She was still unable to move. It was as if she was some poor animal caught in the mesmerising stare of a wily snake.

"I won't hurt you, my dear," he started to pull at her robe and succeeded in pulling it off one shoulder. "We can examine those sores, and I can soothe them for you."

Suddenly she was galvanised into action and pushed him away forcefully. She knocked him off balance and he fell backwards. Judith tried to run to the door, but he was back on his feet and reached it at the same time as her. He spun her around so that she was facing him and pressed his body heavily against hers to stop her struggling. Simultaneously, his lips were upon hers and he was insistently kissing her. She tried to move her head from side to side to make it difficult for him to do so, but he was too strong for her. Judith panicked. She didn't know how to get away from him and his advances, but she knew she wasn't going to give in without a struggle. She lifted her hands and grasped at his head to push it away from her to stop him kissing her. She jerked his head backwards and in doing so his hood fell down.

Don Treader

Judith screamed. Terror, horror, fright, shock. Then the word came, as a gasp, as a strained cry, "Barabbas!"

Suddenly there was silence, and a total absence of motion.

"It's you. Barabbas! Isn't it!"

It was the turn of the prophet now to be silent. Indeed, he was speechless. Then carefully he stepped backwards, then spoke softly and deliberately, in an accent that was distinctly different from the one he had used earlier, "You think you know me? That's not my name." His face told Judith otherwise.

"You're lying. I know you. I've seen you. I know who you are, and all you have done!"

Judith was so definite, so sure, that he gave up the pretence for a brief moment. "I may be, but how…?"

"You're no prophet," said Judith scornfully. "You're a liar, a cheat and a murderer. You wait till the community finds out!"

There was a pause while he took this in. "You're wrong about me," he said flatly. "I've never met you before."

"Oh yes you have. Do you want me to tell you?"

"You can, but you'll be wrong."

"Oh no, I'm not. I watched you swagger out of prison while my friend Jesus was taken and crucified in your place!"

Another silence prevailed, then the prophet spoke again, "How do you know that was me?"

"Because you bumped into me on the way past and cursed me. You even tried to kick my dog." She added, "It was you all right. I saw your face all through the trial. You were proud of your actions, killing Roman soldiers. You know, I believe you'd have happily been crucified that day. You'd have been a martyr. Yet you allowed an innocent man to die in your place. You were a coward!"

This seemed to animate him, "No, I'm not." All pretence gone now, he said, "I believe in freedom for Israel. The other man deserved to die. He was weak and foolish. How could he and his people ever have freed Israel? He was the coward. He was wrong. You'll know the scripture well that says 'Anyone who is hung on a tree is cursed in the sight of Yahweh', well he was the cursed one, the wrong one, the misguided one. I at least fought for Israel."

His outburst stopped, and Judith spoke again. "No. I stood there in the crowd and wondered, how could such an act of injustice happen. How could the Romans let it happen? They mete out justice all the time. But you, a big man in Israel, a zealot of the zealots. You allowed an innocent man to die in your place. How could you? It's barbaric! He healed thousands, taught about love and peace, brought hope to our people, helped the poor. You've done nothing like that. Oh yes, you've killed Romans, you've terrorised the population, you killed my brother…" She broke off, realising what had come out of her mouth. She turned suddenly and ran out of the hut. Halfway down the valley she leaned against a

228

wall and rested. She was grateful that he hadn't pursued her. She was out of breath and wanted to cry. She couldn't however as her fury hadn't yet subsided. She was astonished, humiliated, traumatised at what had happened. It was unbelievable. What had Yahweh brought her into? As she started to walk slowly back up the valley, she wondered how her meeting with the prophet might impact upon her staying in the Valley of the Outcasts. Was she destined to be an outcast again? She determined she was not going to let this happen to her – at least, anyway, not without a fight. She quickened her step.

Chapter Twenty-Eight

When Judith got back it was still only mid-afternoon and Becca wasn't there. She was probably out working or visiting, Judith surmised. She was glad of that, as she didn't feel like talking to anyone anyway. What on earth would she say when she had to, she wondered. Her ordeal had taken a lot out of her and when she reached the safety of the hut, she found herself shaking. She sat down on her mat to think. What on earth was she going to do? She had been attacked by the leader of the community, a man who was supposed to be a holy man. Everyone looked up to him and respected him. If she said anything she wouldn't have been believed. She was the new person in the community – they didn't know her, but they did know him, and he was trusted. Her mind was in a whirl as to what to do. Her head hurt and she slid into a lying position to rest, and to try and think. Barabbas! Who would have thought it? Posing as a holy man? She couldn't get her mind around it. It had been so unexpected, so utterly unbelievable. He'd taken her money too, and almost humiliated her. She felt horrified, and a little scared. If she said anything to anyone, he would deny it, and might even have her removed from the community. Where would she go? She was in the middle of Samaria, a foreign land to her. She would be lost, and no-one would want to take in a leper. She would never get back to her family, but more than likely die alone and rejected. She now felt extremely low. She wanted to expose the imposter but realised that her best option was to say nothing in the meantime. Perhaps in the future people might believe her when they got to know her better. This option didn't appeal to her though. She didn't want to be silenced, or let Barabbas think he had got away with it. And what was he doing to that community anyway? He was preying on the vulnerable, taking advantage of their trust and generosity…and who knows what else with the lonely. If her experience was anything to go by, he seemed to expect favours from the women, many of whom would be unwilling to refuse him, or be unable to. She felt sick at the thought. The sight of his face leering at her when she had pulled down his hood traumatised her. It had brought back the horror and unhappiness of the day she had seen him pitted against Josh in that trial before Pilate and had watched as he had cursed at the soldiers when they had had to release him, getting one over them. He was a horrible man. Everything about him was unholy. She had in no uncertain terms made it clear what she had thought of him. The words had just flowed out of her. She had even told him he had killed her brother! Where had that come from? She had never made that link before…and yet…on considering the picture she now saw in her mind's eye, there was a similarity, perhaps even a resemblance. Was it Barabbas's face that she had seen on that horrible fateful day? She rehearsed the scene, and the image became clearer. The zealot threatening her with his dagger, his finger on his lips demanding her silence…was – she could hardly believe it, could she believe it – none other than a much younger version of the same loathsome figure she had just left. Why had she never made the connection before, she wondered? And why now? Something was being shown her that she evidently needed to know. It was so clearly, so definitely him. The trauma of Josh's trial must somehow have overwhelmed her brain and buried that childhood picture with it. Horror, confusion, recrimination for her stupid lack of insight – she felt them all – but slowly they were being replaced by another powerful emotion. Rage was taking hold of her. She so wanted to expose him in public, to bring him down for what he had done to Josh, for what he had done to Joe. She had done so privately to the man himself. What might he do now to silence her? She couldn't make up her mind what to do. She needed to get away from it all. It was just too much. She did the best thing possible - in exhaustion, she fell asleep.

It was dark when she awoke to Becca bustling about the room.

"I see you're awake," she laughed. "You must have had a heavy afternoon?" She looked concerned. "I went back for you just before sunset, but no-one was in. The prophet didn't answer his door, and there was no sign of you. I eventually gave up and came back."

"I'm sorry, Becca. I left early and found my own way home. You weren't in."

"That's all right. Just as long as you're safe."

Judith reacted involuntarily, "Why wouldn't I be?"

Becca looked embarrassed, and it suddenly hit Judith that she might have some inkling as to what might have gone on. Indeed, she might have expected something to have happened – all the things she had said about bathing and the prophet expecting cleanliness… She had been a fool not to guess what Becca had been hinting at!

"You know!" she accused her. Becca looked down. Judith took this as an admission of guilt.

"How could you…?"

Becca looked up defiantly. "How could I have told you? You wouldn't have thought much of me, would you?"

232

"But you could have warned me."

"I did try to, but if I'd said any more…there would perhaps have been consequences. Anyhow your meeting might have gone well, and I would have spoken out of turn." She looked down again. Judith suddenly realised it wasn't through embarrassment, but shame.

"You too?" she whispered. "You too!"

Becca spoke, her head still down, "Not me only. Most women in the community. He's had us all."

Judith was shocked. "Did no-one object, no-one expose him?"

Becca still couldn't look up, "He's our prophet. What could we do? He has certain rights."

"Not these ones though! He's taking advantage of you."

"Not really," Becca looked up now, a hint of defiance in her eyes again. "Some of us are glad of the attention. What have we left? No family to speak of no physical pleasure. He can supply it and make us feel like women again, even if our bodies are horrible and wrecked. No-one else would have us, and what else have we got to look forward to before we undergo a painful death?" She started to sob.

Silence reigned for the next few minutes. Eventually Judith spoke, "I'm sorry, Becca."

"It's not your fault. We all make a choice, don't we? It's common knowledge amongst the women here, but it's just never really spoken about. It's part of our lifestyle. No-one condemns anyone."

"But it's wrong, Becca. Surely you see that? He shouldn't be allowed to take advantage of the vulnerable."

"Perhaps we're taking advantage of him?"

"I don't think so. I found his attitude intimidating. He knew what he wanted."

"Don't most men?" Becca said dryly. "I was married five times and had a partner. All of them were similar. Now down here, what was I to do? Give it all up? Perhaps we don't like being taken advantage of here, but it does satisfy a need. Can't you see that?"

Judith thought for a moment. She looked at her own life – a stable childhood, a marriage to one man, a faith that forbad promiscuity – her standpoint was totally different from Becca's. It was a totally different country, a different culture, and a different religion. Still, she couldn't bring herself to condone it.

"But whatever the case, Becca, no matter how lonely or miserable you are, no-one has the right to expect these things of you or intimidate you into giving them."

Again, there was a pause, then Becca said, "I know that, but…it does happen in our culture."

"What about the Teacher, the Messiah? When he stayed amongst you did, he say anything about this sort of thing? Did he and his men expect favours?"

Becca looked horrified. "Not at all. When he spoke to me, he

was gentle. he knew about my lifestyle, but he didn't judge me. I suppose it was implied that I was notorious and perhaps not doing the right thing, but there was no condemnation."

Another silence.

"I suppose I do know it's wrong, but when you live in a community in which it's accepted, it's difficult, you know. He is ur prophet. He has the right to expect love and obedience from us."

Judith said slowly, trying to avoid sounding condemnatory, "That's not the way the Messiah works, Becca. You said it yourself – he's gentle and treats the vulnerable with respect. He would never intimidate or force people into believing and doing what he wants."

"I know, I know. Maybe you've been sent amongst us to help us change. I know we shouldn't be taken advantage of, but what else can we do?"

"We can change!" said Judith firmly. "The Messiah thinks of us differently and has different goals and aspirations for us. Things can be different for us if we want them to be."

Becca was finding the conversation difficult and so she changed the subject. "Did he harm you in any way? He can get quite carried away."

Judith shook her head, "Things didn't get that far. I left."

"Oh," said Becca. Up till then she had assumed Judith had succumbed and that was the reason for her reaction.

"So, you didn't…"

"No!"

"So how did you get away? He wouldn't have let you go without a struggle."

"Let's just say, I made my feelings known, and he had to accept them." Judith said wryly, "I don't know what position that puts me in though. He might put me out of the community."

"He's not a bad man. He wouldn't do that."

"I'm not so sure. He may see me as a threat…"

"Why?"

Judith had no intention of going into detail at that point. She liked and trusted Becca but didn't want to affect or sour their relationship by telling her what she knew about her prophet.

"Suffice it to say, I left him in no doubt as to my feelings about him. I do expect some kind of reaction from him though."

Becca looked genuinely worried, "I don't want to lose you now sister. I feel we've a special bond, even if we do have our differences. I hope you don't have to go!"

"Me too," said Judith. "But come on, let's have something to eat. We've talked enough. It's not been the best of afternoons, but hopefully something good will come out of it."

"Right, perhaps we can talk about it again when Samara is with us for prayer?"

"A good idea," said Judith. "There's nothing like prayer for settling differences and making things plain. We'll do that."

The two of them settled down to eat and put the conversation aside for another day. Judith couldn't help wondering if events might overtake them however and she might find herself excluded from the community before then.

"Waken up, Judith," said Becca shaking her shoulder. "Time to get up!"

Judith was groggy, but struggled into wakefulness rather grudgingly. She had been dreaming and felt she had been very rudely awakened.

"I believe this is yours," said Becca laughing. She tossed a small bag containing coins onto Judith's chest and grinned, "You must have done something special to be given this. We get nothing like that!"

"I told you, nothing happened between us – although it could easily have."

"I believe you," said Becca, becoming more serious. "I was just winding you up."

"Please don't. It was bad enough, without more being made of it. Where did you get this?"

"Oh, the prophet gave it to me. He seemed to think it was yours."

"It is. I left it there by accident. I left so quickly…"

"You're a dark horse, Judith! Having all that money, and not telling us."

"I would have got round to it Becca. I had fully intended using it to help the Community. You've all been so good to me, taking me in."

"I'm only joking," Becca said. "It's none of my business what you do with your money. We're happy to have you anyway, and what's ours is yours."

Judith looked appreciatively at her. "I fully intended paying my way, and still do. I told you about my leaving Jerusalem – it stands to reason I'd need to carry some money with me to make things work in Galilee."

"Sister, it doesn't matter. I believe you. Don't worry."

Judith felt the need to explain a little further. "I fully intended to use it to help the community, to pay my way. Given the leprosy, who knows if I'd ever get anywhere else to spend it. That's why I took it to the prophet yesterday – to show my good will. However, we never got to that point! I left before we got the chance."

"So how did he end up with the money?" queried Becca looking interested.

"I can't say," said Judith, her face reddening. "It just got left there. I wondered what to do about it. I certainly wasn't going back for it."

In the pause that ensued, Judith wondered how Becca had come upon it, and whether anything had been determined concerning her future in the community. Had it been given back to her in the expectation that she would leave?

Becca spoke, "You were sleeping just before dawn when I left to get the water. You looked so peaceful, and after yesterday's events, I decided to let you lie. I got to the well when I saw someone approaching me from the shelter. Of course, it was the prophet. It was quite a surprise. I'd never seen him there before. He asked for you. I think someone had told him you sometimes have gone there with me."

Judith looked worried. "Did he say anything…?"

"Relax. No…and neither did I."

"Why did he want me then?"

"He didn't say. He did ask if you were all right. Had you returned home safely. I said yes. Funnily enough, he asked what you just asked me, did you say anything about your visit. I said you had been tired, and we'd eaten then you'd slept. You hadn't indicated there was anything to talk about. This seemed to satisfy him. His privacy had been maintained. He put his hand into his robe and brought out the bag, and said, 'Judith left this with me by accident yesterday. Tell her, I'm returning it to her in good faith. She must do with it as she thinks best while she's with us in the community. I'm going on a retreat for a few days. Tell her, everything being fine and settled, I'd like to speak with her again when I return. There are things it would be good for us to discuss. She should feel under no pressure, however. I hope she'll be happy with us here.'"

Judith took from that, that he had been sounding out Becca to see if Judith had exposed him. On finding that nothing explosive had been said, he seemed to want to make it plain that if she said nothing, neither would she be excluded from the community. Their silence was to be a marriage of convenience – at least for the time being anyway. For the moment therefore, her future looked secure. But for how long? The two of them couldn't remain in the Community without ever meeting or speaking. It was inevitable that something eventually would give. Certainly, for her part, she didn't want to let him off the hook. She hated him for so many reasons, and she wanted more than anything to topple him from his pedestal, and gain for him his just desserts. She would bide her time however, and perhaps in the fulness of it…

The days that followed were a learning curve for Judith. She had much to contend with. She was having to adjust to living with a major disease, one that kept her apart from most of the world. The initial outburst and appearance of it had made her unwell. She had felt weak and sick, and as well as that, there was the pain. As she settled into the community and took reasonable periods of rest however, she began to feel stronger, the sickness subsided and the pain became more bearable. It was more of a constant ache in her extremities, more easy to cope with. Mentally she was resourceful. Hadn't she coped with tragedies in her life - the most recent being Mikha's death? She found that with the friendship of Becca, and other members of the community too, she adjusted quite well to her situation. And then there was her spiritual condition. It felt healthy. She knew that Josh had taken her there, for whatever purpose. He had made her, a Jew, acceptable in what was predominantly a Samaritan community. His Spirit was evident in her times of prayer, whether on her own or with the others. In fact, she felt his presence more strongly than ever before - and energised...how she felt energised! She had a purpose now, and she was going to live up to it. Somewhere in all of that was the anomaly of Barabbas. Was this part of Josh's plan too? Nothing seemed clear. The horror of her discovery still clouded her thinking. She was glad however her outburst and rejection of him didn't for the moment at least appear to be resulting in her having to leave. Apart from prayer times with an increasing band of women, she began to investigate the community, getting out into it more and seeking ways in which she might be useful. It was funny, she thought, that no-one really made anything of their leprosy. They seemed to accept it as their lot, and just got on with their lives without making it an issue. She discovered quickly that moaning and complaining weren't tolerated. Everyone was in the same boat, and it was better to be stoic, and help others when they needed it. A bit like the prophet's treatment of the women, she thought – it happened, it was known about, but it wasn't a topic of conversation.

In her acceptance of her situation, and the likelihood she might remain in the community till she died, Judith actively looked for something to do. She found that working in the fields suited her well – being in the sunshine helped her condition. She enjoyed being with the other women, and every so often she could talk to them about the Teacher. They all knew about his visit to the village, and had heard that she had known him. Often when they sat down to rest and eat, one of them would ask her about him, and seek her opinion on situations that affected them. She noticed however the topic of the prophet never came up. When spoken of, he was always treated with respect. There were times she wanted to say something but felt somehow restrained from doing so when she was about to open her mouth. This was not something for the present Time.

She often wandered with Becca to the milking area or up to the well to collect water, and soon these duties too became a part of her schedule. She liked the friendship and the routine they afforded her. Of course, she also eased Becca's burden by taking on some of the household chores along with the preparation of meals. It wasn't long before she had accepted her lot in the community, and it seemed she had been accepted by them as well.

On her travels up and down the valley, she often came across people who told her they had difficulties in doing their work: either the buildings they needed weren't there, or weren't fit for purpose; similarly the equipment they needed to make themselves more productive. The drive in the community was to be as self-sufficient as possible, and most years they didn't quite achieve that goal. They were still dependent on the generosity or charity of the village in the higher valley, or of their estranged friends and families in the other villages they had come from. The longer a person had been in the community, the less they received as they began to be forgotten about. This was a major reality, so Samara and those she worked with organising the community did their best to motivate everyone into making it try to pay its own way. When the women came together to pray, there was seldom a day passed when one of these issues didn't come up. Judith decided to bide her time. She would watch and take note of what was happening, of what was needed - and when she felt ready with the Spirit's prompting, she would offer her money to give the community a boost. She had lived in Capernaum and Jerusalem for quite a large part of her life, but essentially, she was a country girl. She could see with her own eyes what things the community needed. She determined to be the means of making it more prosperous and comfortable.

Chapter Twenty-Nine

"The prophet's back!" said Becca one morning a week or so later. "I don't think he's ever been away for so long, but he's been seen around his hut."

Judith felt a shiver run down her spine. She wasn't looking forward to any meeting or confrontation there might be. She determined to avoid this as long as was physically possible. She had no wish to compromise her stay in the community. Yet, at the back of her mind, she knew that one day a meeting was inevitable. She prayed for guidance as to what to say when that day came.

Judith had arrived in the community fairly early in spring, and so was joining it at the start of its yearly cycle. It was sowing time in the fields and pruning time in the orchards. She had already determined to help in the fields, to add her efforts to the other women involved in the planting. The men did the hard work of ploughing, and the women did the easier task of scattering seed and tending to its growth over spring and summer until it reached maturity. It was a good opportunity to talk to the women and to speak about the Teacher. Judith was a popular figure. People admired the way this Jewish woman had come amongst them, had coped with the onset of a major illness, and was prepared to throw in her lot with them. They also liked hearing about the Teacher who had once visited them, and they often sought her out when they needed help, guidance or comfort. Many of them joined the meetings which were still held in Becca's hut. As the planting season progressed, it became more convenient to hold them in the late afternoon or the early evening after a day's work. Some even brought something to eat and they shared it before talking and praying. Judith became quite pivotal in all this because she was the only one who had recent and abundant knowledge of the Teacher and they looked to her to follow in the steps of the Messiah and teach them. Often the Spirit's presence was evident, and faces glowed with inspiration.

Don Treader

One day in late spring, Becca came home and informed Judith, "Sister, the prophet's calling for you. He wants to meet with you again."

Judith stiffened, "How do you know Becca?"

"When I was down getting the milk, a message was passed to me by one of the women there. She had seen him, and he asked her to pass the message on to me when she saw me."

"I'm not going," Judith said, turning the request down flatly. "I'll never go into his hut again. Not after the last time!" The sudden image of his leering face came into her mind and caused her to freeze. "I'm not going."

Becca looked at her with concern, "You can't ignore him. It's a direct request. If you made your feelings plain to him the last time, as you said you did, it'll probably be all right."

Judith shook her head. "There are things… I don't want to go. You'll have to drag me there."

"I won't be doing that sister. Have you seen yourself?"

Judith looked bemused. "What do you mean?"

"Well living here in the fresh air with us and eating more abundantly…you're beginning to put on some weight. Living here's doing you good!"

The two women laughed. "Never," said Judith. "I've always been thin."

"Not any more, sister," said Becca, fully laughing now. "It's time you looked in the pool. You're filling out…and that's not a bad thing. But I'm definitely not dragging you there!"

The tension was gone now. Judith relaxed again and tried to think out ways in which she might be able to put off any meeting with the community leader. A day or two later, another message was received, and duly ignored by Judith. She knew this couldn't go on for long, so she made it a matter for prayer, asking for Yahweh to work things out so she didn't have to be on her own with Barabbas. She hated him and in her heart of hearts she knew she was scared of him, not just because of his treatment of her when she had visited him, but also because of his harsh and cruel Zealot background and his willingness to let Josh die in his place. She thought her strategy was working when two days later, Becca informed her, "The prophet's working in the fields today. His strength is required along with the other men to build something. You're working there today, aren't you?"

Judith looked worried. "I am. But he won't try anything in front of everyone. He's got his reputation to think about."

"Of course he won't," agreed Becca, "but remember, most people here know what goes on. They won't find it surprising if he comes over to you or talks to you. You would be seen as rude if you ignored him or refused him"

"I've already refused him," said Judith hotly.

"I know, I know. But you'll have to go. You can't avoid going. People are depending on you. Just act as normal. He may leave you alone anyway."

Judith realised that Becca was right. She whispered a mental prayer for strength and guidance before leaving for the fields, and then with great trepidation she prepared herself for the worst.

Judith worked hard all morning. The ground seemed more difficult than usual. It was back breaking labour. The women around her employed singing to alleviate the strain, and she found that when she joined in, it helped. Her mind wasn't really on what she was doing though. Every so often she looked to the end of the field she was in, to see who was working on the building - some kind of barn type shelter they were erecting. It was mid-morning before she saw him – the prophet, or as she knew him, Barabbas. It was becoming warm now with the sun climbing high into the sky, but her blood ran cold. It was the self-same man as she had remembered seeing at Pilate's palace, at the trial. Gone now were the prophet robes. He was now just a man dressed for heavy labour. His hair, his face, his build – it was all the same, and she felt a deep sense of loathing creep into her soul. This man had been responsible for the death of her best friend. Had he not been in Roman hands and indicted for murder, Josh might not have received his punishment. She knew this was not strictly true, as Josh's death had eventually been understood by people of 'The Way' to have been a part of Yahweh's plan. But remembering the sight of Barabbas swaggering, gloating cursing, totally unrepentant, along with her more recent experience of him leering, exploiting, abusing – she felt nothing but hatred for him. She felt sick to the pit of her stomach. She wanted to expose him. What right had he to take over a community like this – decent honest helpless people trying to eke out a living – and use it for his own ends! Here he was, the pride of the community appearing for work, garnering more of their respect. But she knew the truth, and she wanted to shout it out. Her emotions were boiling, and as she worked, she sensed something different going on inside her. She felt out of control. Her rage was consuming her. She felt scared of how she was feeling. Might it cause her to lose her place here, the only place that would accept her in her condition? She had to calm down, she thought. To let go would alienate her from the community and would also cause damage to her spiritual standing which was growing day by day in the meetings. Indeed, deep down she felt a check on how she was feeling. The thought struck her that as he was being crucified, Josh had forgiven his enemies, his accusers. Then more forcibly into her mind came the unwelcome thought that Barabbas would have been one of them. No, this didn't sit well with her at all. This man had done some awful things; killed Romans in cold blood; attracted the Romans to her village who had killed her baby brother; happily let Josh go to the fate which should have been his without batting an eyelid - and now here he was exploiting decent people abusing them under the guise of being a prophet. She hated him, but somewhere in her spirit she sensed that she should say nothing, she should hold back, no matter how righteous the anger was that she felt. As the break for food approached, she felt less upset and more in control again. She determined that as her Master had done at his biggest trial, the best policy was to say nothing. Certainly, this helped her feel better.

Judith wasn't prepared for what happened next. She and the other women were eating, sitting in the shade provided by the newly erected barn wall, when the prophet came toward them from the water trough where the men were eating. The break was almost at an end, and when he arrived, the women lowered their eyes in respect and said, "The Lord bless you, prophet." He responded, "The Lord be with you, my children." Judith felt her anger rising. The other women were showing signs of awkwardness, deference at being in his presence, and so with a motion of his hand, he dismissed them. "Work calls," he said, smiling. "But not for you, Judith. I have to talk with you. Our last meeting was too brief. Stay for a moment." The others saw nothing wrong in this. It was normal for the prophet to single out people to talk to. It was an accepted practice. He was perhaps passing on a blessing or word of wisdom. Some of the women knew of his 'other blessings' but in a public place like this, nothing like that was suspected. Judith was forced to stay therefore, as to disobey him would put her at odds with the community. He motioned for her to sit down again as she had risen to her feet with the other women. He sat down beside her, and although they were alone, he invaded her space quite deliberately in order to intimidate her and no doubt to avoid other ears hearing. The men were too far away to   hear anyway, but he wasn't taking any chances. Judith could feel his breath on her when he spoke and could smell the odour of the morning's sweat on him wafting up her nostrils. She recoiled, but he just moved his head nearer to her. It was obvious that her time of reckoning had come!

"You're avoiding me, Judith," he said quietly. There was a menacing tone in his voice. Judith said nothing. She was going to put her plan into action.

"You're avoiding me," he repeated. "That won't do."

Judith still said nothing. She looked at him coldly, loathing building up inside her.

"I sent messages to you. Didn't you get them?"

Still no response. His face hardened and his lips became set in a straight line. His voice was now angry. "You will not get away with ignoring your leader, your prophet."

"You're not my leader, or my prophet. You're an imposter!" Judith spat the words out. She couldn't help herself.

There was a silence for a few moments, then Barabbas spoke again. "How can you know that? I've never met you before."

"You have…and my memory's clear. I know you. I saw you there, and you allowed my friend to die in your place!"

"Really? You're confused. You know nothing. I'm prophet here, and someone who encourages peace, not violence."

"Oh yes," said Judith sarcastically, "you don't use violence with the women then? You almost got away with it when I visited you!"

"That's different," he said softly. "They want me to build up their self-esteem, to make them feel better. I do what prophets have done over the years - fulfilled the needs of women. Sometimes they can't have children, or their men can't perform. We all have needs, and the women here are needy."

"That's disgusting!" said Judith coldly. "And you a Jew too. You know the Jewish law!"

"Who said I'm a Jew?"

"It's obvious. Your features are quite definite. And anyway, it's clear that Pilate and the Roman soldiers believed you were a Jew."

"What have I to do with them?"

Judith's face hardened now. "Are you denying your name is Barabbas?" The power of her words seemed to put him off his guard for a moment. He said nothing.

Judith continued. She felt her policy of silence had helped her say the right things. "I don't forget a face. You are the same person I saw standing, gloating and smirking, before Pilate. You were playing to the crowd and they loved it. I'm not mistaken. You're a zealot, the worst of all Jews. You got off, and my friend died in your place!" He tried to interrupt but her words cut him off. They were firm and accusing. "You even cursed me as you bumped into me when the soldiers let you go. You tried to kick my dog. No, I'm not mistaken. You were as close to me then as you are now. Remember, you raised your fists high in a gesture of defiance!"

He looked taken aback. Her description had been too graphic for him and it was now his turn to recoil.

Judith pressed her advantage, "Am I right, or not?"

He did not reply, then twisting the topic away from himself, he said, "The zealots are not the worst of all Jews. How can you say that? They're fighting for freedom. Even Samaritans want freedom from Rome!"

"Do I take it then that you support the zealots?"

"I do. They're trying to make a difference while the rest of Israel is compromising."

"You're a zealot! I was right.!"

It's clear he did not want to deny what he believed in, so he said nothing.

They sat in silence for a few moments then Barabbas spoke again, "You are a threat to this community." His voice hardened, "You are dangerous. You can't be allowed to remain here while you're making those accusations." There was a strong threat implied in his words and Judith did not fail to miss it.

"I'm not wrong," she said. "And you know it."

He looked at her thoughtfully, "Even if you're right, and I am a murderer - a zealot – don't you feel afraid of me, and what I might do to you?" He was trying a different tack. Reasoned violence designed to intimidate and silence her.

Judith wasn't to be silenced. She had a burning hatred of the man and wasn't going to let him off so easily. "I'm not scared of you. Yahweh will protect me."

He laughed, scorning her, "Even as he did your friend! I don't think so."

Was this an admission, she wondered? It was as good as she was going to get at the moment. He may not have been owning up, but it was definite he was warning her one way or the other.

"You wouldn't dare harm me. You would expose yourself for who you are."

"That's a risk I'd have to take," he said carefully and deliberately. "But at the minute it looks to me as if the risk is yours."

Judith said nothing. She felt a deep loathing of the man, and although she had determined not to speak, she found the words coming to her naturally, "You too have a lot to lose. Your sway over this community, and your cover with the Romans – it would all be over if I were to say anything here."

He tried to look innocent, "What do you mean, my cover with the Romans?"

Judith was emboldened now, "Well, if you were exposed and had to leave here…you're using this place as a hiding place from the Romans. I'll bet there's still a price on your head, and that there are thousands of Roman soldiers who would only be too happy to capture you."

"I thought we'd passed all that," he said sounding less confident.

"No. You're a liar, an imposter – and a murderer. You and I both know it, even if you won't admit it."

He smiled at her, "But I just did. Don't you remember? And having done so, it puts your life more at risk." He paused. "Why didn't you expose me as soon as you returned to Becca's? If I'm that bad, why didn't you say anything to anyone?"

Judith looked awkward. He was calling her bluff.

"Was it because you weren't really sure of your facts…" he continued, "or was there something else?"

Judith looked at him, wondering what he was going to say.

"Perhaps it was because you knew you needed me."

She burst out, "Never!"

"No. I don't mean in that way," he said smirking at her, "I think you knew that you needed me to allow you to stay in the community. With one word I could have had you put out, and then where would you have been? I'd give you a week living rough – no-one willing to take you in because you're a leper. You know you'd be dead within that week. My job would be done." Her eyes showed her hatred of him. "You know I'm right, don't you?" he said, echoing her earlier words. He continued, smirking, "It seems that we both need each other., a kind of marriage of convenience, wouldn't you say?"

Judith said nothing. Her throat was choked up with anger.

"Perhaps we can live with this until one of us oversteps the mark. What do you think, Judith?"

She shook her head. Her emotions took over, and instantly she regretted it. "I hate you!" she said, "for all you are and for all you've done. And for the way you are exploiting these good people here!"

He smiled at her infuriatingly, "But they don't need to know, you know. If you don't tell them, we're both safe." His veiled threat was obvious to her.

"Compromise is important," he said. "I've learned in life to agree with my enemies when it suits me. It sounds like someone about to die might agree with his enemies the Romans to kill an innocent man, if it suits his purpose."

Judith now knew. He was telling her plainly that she'd been right all along…and he was using it as a threat against her.

"You are Barabbas!"

"Guilty as charged," he said. If a smirk could get bigger, his did. "But not guilty…set free by my enemies!"

Judith's emotions again got the better of her, "You are evil!"

"Aren't all zealots evil to you?" he taunted. "We survive by convenience and compromise…and so will you if you know what's good for you." Again he paused. "You said the other day that I had killed your brother. How are you managing to pin that on me?"

Judith was about to explode but felt that check on her spirit again. This man was dangerous. She would have to watch her step. However, she wasn't about to let him off with Joe. "You were responsible for my brother's death!" she spat out hotly.

Barabbas was taken aback by the venom in her outburst. "You're talking rubbish!" he said. "I don't even know who you are, or anything about you. Our paths have never crossed!"

"Oh yes they have!" Judith was almost shouting now, and the men working on the barn looked around to see where the noise was coming from.

"Be quiet!" Barabbas hissed. "If you attract attention to us, it'll be the last thing you do!" He was angry now, and the veins stood out on his head. Knowing his background, Judith didn't doubt he might kill her in the heat of the moment, regardless of how he would be affected. She calmed down again.

"When I was seven, you came to my village in the hills above Capernaum. My little brother and I were playing when suddenly you and your friends appeared round one of the houses. You may have been younger, but I'd have recognised you anywhere."

"I've never killed any little boys," he insisted.

"You looked at me, putting your finger to your lips, to make sure I stayed silent. It was obvious you were hiding from someone. You lifted up your dagger to make sure I understood."

"I've never killed any boys - Jewish or otherwise!"

"Oh, you didn't kill him, but you brought the Romans to our village. They were chasing you. On the way through, one of them, his horse trampled my little brother Joe to death. He died in my arms. I hate you!"

"I knew it!" he said triumphantly. "I've never killed children, especially of my own countrymen."

"You haven't killed them perhaps, but you've stolen from, threatened and abused your own countrymen, labelling them collaborators!"

"That's not our purpose. We're at war with the Romans!"

"Our people aren't helped by your antics. Few of them support you. Yes, they want freedom, but not the way you're going about it. You're making it difficult for them to live in their own country."

"Rubbish! You're wrong. Just as wrong as you were about me killing your brother!"

"You were indirectly responsible, and I'll never forgive you for it!" Judith felt a total check on her spirit. She sensed she'd gone too far. Why hadn't she just remained silent as she'd intended?

"We're getting nowhere here," Barabbas said with some irritation. "If you're intent on exposing me then, I'll kill you. When I spoke to Becca the other day, I realised that you had said nothing and so I gave her the money you'd left in my hut to give back to you…in good faith."

Judith burst out, "You took it from me!"

"Whatever," he said, shrugging his shoulders. "It doesn't matter now. You can stay in the community and use your money to help us…and I'll keep out of your way," He said with a false humility, mocking her. "These people are needy, really needy, and could benefit by your contribution."

Judith riled at this, but kept her mouth tightly shut. He continued, "One word from you about me…and my terrible past…" he was mocking her again, "and you'll be dead. So, Judith, do we have an agreement?"

Judith looked down. She didn't want to compromise, but at least for the moment she had no other alternative but to do so. She nodded slowly, feeling ashamed of herself.

"Good!" he was smirking again. "We have an agreement then. Sometimes we must compromise with our enemies." He stood up and made to go back to his work. Turning back to her, he said, "Oh by the way, you need to practice what your friend taught. It's not good to go around accusing people and refusing to forgive them. You might be called a hypocrite." He went on his way, leaving Judith fuming, but also feeling a little guilty.

Chapter Thirty

"It's no use," said Judith. "I just can't do it. I don't have the power."

Becca looked on sympathetically. "Your condition has progressed quite a bit since you arrived. Things don't usually move on quite so fast."

"It's so frustrating! A month or two ago I could have done this no trouble at all."

Judith had been trying to patch a hole in her robe but was having trouble holding the needle.

"I'll help you if you wish," Becca volunteered.

"No, thank you. I must do it myself. I'm not going to give up!"

"You know I'm happy to help you, sister. What's the point in being sisters if we can't help each other?"

"But what do I do for you? Very little."

"Not at all. You maybe don't realise just how much you've helped me. I was doing most of the physical things before and I do appreciate your help around this place. But your main contribution has been to lift my spirits. I was verging on depression before you came. It's a joy now to have a sister I can share things with. You've helped me to become reacquainted with the Messiah...and I know for a fact that you're appreciated by the women who attend the meetings too."

"But really, that's not so much. I need to be paying my way. Physical things are important."

"Yes, but we need more than that, and you're supplying it. You knew the Messiah, and that knowledge and experience is worth more than its weight in gold. Just look at the meetings. Everyone is thirsty for more. They're gulping down all you tell them."

"It's the Holy Spirit too. He's leading us. Josh does seem close when we all get together."

"That's it. And it was you who introduced it all to us. Don't do yourself down. You've given us a lot. Dare I say it, more than the prophet has. You've given us something real!"

Judith refrained from criticising the prophet. She had over the past few months held back from blurting out what she knew about him to Becca and now she was getting quite practiced at it. The benefit of spreading the word was far more important than decrying or exposing him. She had noticed that Becca was beginning to feel jaded about him, and since their conversation the day Judith had been abused by him, Becca had never gone to his hut again.

Judith put down the garment and rubbed her numb fingers. There just wasn't enough feeling in them. Where was it going to end? She felt a tear run down her cheek.

"Don't," said Becca sympathetically. "Sometimes the feeling comes back. Every day is different. We're all in the same boat. We all understand."

"I know. I'm being selfish and self-pitying. I'm sorry. It's just sometimes…it seems to get to me more than others."

"We all have our bad days. The thing is to pray and to keep ourselves busy, so we don't wallow. The best medicine I've found is to think of others and try to help them."

"And you're doing - you've done - a great job," said Judith smiling now. "You have been a real sister to me - the sister I never had!"

"That's good to hear, Judith. I'd never have guessed." The two of them laughed.

"That's better," said Becca. "We can't have you being miserable. Where would the rest of us be then?"

"But Becca, I need to do more. I'm not satisfied with what I'm doing. You know I've got that money, but apart from a few small things, I've not been able to determine much of what's needed. I want to help, but on my own I'm not seeing anything."

"Why don't you speak to Samara? She and those who work with her would be glad of your input. They're looking for ways all the time to improve the community. I think they're wanting to expand."

"How do you mean? How can they expand? We can't go around pulling people in and making them lepers."

"Of course not," said Becca laughing. "I didn't mean that. Expanding means making the community more productive and prosperous."

"I see," said Judith. "But how would we go about that?"

"That's the very point. That's what they're looking at. The valley is satisfying our needs for the moment, but we could do more. Look at the edges of it, the grounds rocky and arid. It's unusable, except by wild animals. And that's only one issue needing tackled. There are so many other ways we could make the valley more productive too."

"It's unusable because it's far away from the stream that runs through the valley. Has no-one ever thought about diverting it?"

"Ah, but then, the other fields would dry up and produce nothing."

"True. But there are bound to be ways round that. In my aunt's house in Jerusalem, they've got a cistern on the roof and the water is channelled into their kitchen. Surely we need to do something like that here?"

"Well take your suggestions to Samara and her people." Becca laughed, "I'm sure they'll be glad to hear them."

"I'll do that," said Judith, and when the next meeting came up, she made a point of attending it. In the meantime, she had worked out a plan which she hoped might inspire the committee to greater things.

"We want to welcome Judith to our meeting tonight," Samara said. "This is her first time here. She's told me that she wants to help us expand the community and has some ideas for doing so."

The three women and five men assembled smiled at her. "Every bit of help is welcome," said old Jacob. "We're needing young blood. I think we're running out of ideas sometimes."

"Hear! Hear!" said another elderly gentleman, and then started coughing. It seemed a sore cough to Judith. He did not look well.

"Would you like to tell us your thoughts, Judith? You've been here a few months now and you see how we do things."

"I'd love to," said Judith smiling at the gathered company. "If you really want to expand things, then this might just help to do it." She cleared her throat and rubbed her hands which were aching. "If we want to do more, we must go further - beyond the limits of our own valley. Do any of us still have contacts in the surrounding villages?"

Jacob said, "Quite a number of us do. Our relatives who put us here. They all profess they'll help us, but in truth, they forget us once we're here. They do come and visit sometimes, and we shout up to them from the bottom of the hill. It's not satisfactory."

"No. Definitely not," said Judith. "But as I said, if we're to expand, we have to think outside our valley, and make use of our contacts."

The others looked mildly interested.

Judith continued, "For instance, we should get our contacts to sell our produce in their towns. They could keep some of the proceeds and hand back the rest of the money to us, so we can improve the valley even further."

Another older gentleman said, "They're always complaining about having to support us. They wouldn't have to then would they."

Someone else chipped in, "And we'd be helping support them then." They laughed.

Don Treader

"Let's be realistic though," said Samara. "We barely harvest enough crops and fruit to keep ourselves going. If we sell to others, we'd go without."

"Not if we use the higher land at the left side of the valley," said Judith. "It's fairly barren and the rocky areas are inhabited by wild animals. We could change it."

"That's a big task," said Jacob. "It's been thought of before, but abandoned because it's too big a job for us lepers to undertake."

"Maybe not," said Judith. "All we'd have to do is divert the stream that flows through the valley to water that land. It would eventually become fertile."

"A good thought," said Jacob, smiling. "But that would leave the rest of the valley to become arid.

"Not if we divide the stream."

"Yes, but you'd have to divert it from inside the valley, and the stream flows through the lower part of it. The water would have to flow uphill to the land you're talking about."

"Don't do it there then," said Judith. "Divide it on its way down the hill into the valley, and channel it also to that higher barren area."

"Too big for us," said Jacob dismissively. "There's the equipment we'd need …and the labour would be too intensive, far too intensive."

"All right, people," said Judith more briskly. "Here's what I'm proposing. We decide to sell our produce in the open market. We'd be promoting the community, showing the outside world that we're not useless and hopeless, or to be feared. It might inspire many of them to think more positively about leprosy. If they were to catch it, it wouldn't be the end of the world for them. Then, after committing to that decision, we employ some of the surrounding villagers to cut down trees and fashion wood into what we need to make a viaduct and set it up starting at the top or near top of the hill to take the water to the arid rocky area and deposit it there. They wouldn't have to come into the valley at all or have to meet any of us. The water would fill a pool there which we would dig. We can then make trenches to let it irrigate the surrounding land so things could start to grow in it. We would harvest the produce and get our relatives to take it to their markets and sell it."

"Very ambitious," said Jacob. "It's not something we could afford. There's the wood, the labour, the construction – all of it needs paid for, and the promise of some produce just wouldn't be enough."

Judith threw her bag of coins on the table. "I'm prepared to donate this as my contribution." There was a gasp as the bag burst open and many gold coins spilled out, some of them dropping to the floor.

"I'm fairly new here, but let's be serious now. Do you think my idea has any possibility of working?"

"The money makes all the difference," said Jacob more kindly. "Do we think it could work?" he looked around at his friends. Slowly they nodded, smiling.

He continued, "You've convinced us, Judith. I daresay some of us would contribute to it too. We haven't a lot of money, but what we have would certainly be worthwhile investing."

Judith beamed. "You're all terrific," she enthused. "Don't you see, it would give us something to live for, and let outsiders see that we're not just a worthless bunch of people that sponges off them. We'd be able to hold our heads high with dignity."

The little group clapped enthusiastically.

"What about a time frame, everyone?" asked Samara.

One of the gentlemen who'd spoken earlier said, "Well, it's late spring now. Let's start by putting the idea to the rest of the community and our prophet. At the same time, let's sound out our relatives in the villages and give them a chance to respond. Once harvest's in, if they want to be involved, we can get them to sort out the wood. We'll pay them for what they bring. It'll be winter then, and they'll probably be keen to get the opportunity to work. They can start to build the viaduct, so it'll be ready for spring sowing. We'll also make sure we have the pool and the trenches dug by then. It'll all be hard work, but it'll be worth it. I like the idea of supplying a service to the outside world. In some ways we've been quite selfish up till now. Everything we plant is for ourselves. We haven't thought of others."

"Quite right," said Jacob. "This project might just kick new life into our ailing community."

"I believe it would," said Judith, trying to pick up the spilled coins with her numb fingers and put them back into the bag, "and we'd be thinking more of others, rather than of ourselves. It's a good thing to give. And if we reap what we sow then who knows what the result for the community might be. Blessing!"

Again, a ripple of clapping went round the room.

"Who'll keep the money then and pay the outsiders?" one of the women asked.

"I'm giving it to Samara for safe keeping," said Judith. "The money's no longer mine. It belongs to the community, and is therefore for the benefit of the community."

"That's generous of you," said Jacob appreciatively.

"It's the least I can do," said Judith. "You've all made me so welcome here, taking me in and supporting me. I'm totally in your debt."

"Well, my dear," said Jacob grinning, "you've maybe done something tonight to put our community firmly back on the map. They won't be able to ignore us or forget about us now!"

Judith's status in the community was rising. The news of the major change coming to all of their lives spread rapidly and was met with general approval and appreciation. She was an innovator and heralded as someone who might well transform their lives from the humdrum to the meaningful. There was an excitement in the air as people geared up to working over the summer till harvest, and then the prospect of a winter of major construction and innovation. This had a knock-on effect upon the evening meetings. More and more people were attending them and becoming believers, so much so that the newcomers had to be divided up and meeting places increased. Judith, Becca, and Samara presided over the burgeoning numbers and by the end of the summer, there were four healthy groups meeting twice weekly for sharing and instruction. Right in the middle of this was Judith, whose knowledge of the Teacher Messiah was in great demand. Her own experience of him was known to all, and her dedication to the cause legendary. Unfortunately, as her status rose, her health decreased. Her energy lagged and the aching in her extremities crippled her at times, so much so that she had to take to her mat regularly. The others looked on helplessly, willing her to improve, but knowing from bitter experience that this was unlikely to happen. Judith's prospects were looking poor. If her leprosy increased at the rate it appeared to be doing, then in a year or so she would have great difficulty in getting about; and two or three years after that she herself might no longer be around. In the times when she felt low, these thoughts disturbed her. If her life was to be terminated early, she would never see Tabitha or her family again. That scared her. The counterbalance to that was that daily, her sense of Josh's presence and the Spirit's leading seemed to increase. When she was able to surrender her fears, and her horror at possibly having a grim end, she felt a deep peace which helped sustain her. Those around her could see what she was going through and were encouraged themselves by her response to her plight.

"You're an example to us all, sister," said Becca one night as they were both settling down to sleep. Judith had experienced terrible pain that day but had still struggled to a meeting in someone's hut further down the valley in order to share the good news.

"But I'm helped by the Spirit. I'm not doing it myself," said Judith almost weeping with the pain. "I can't take the credit and neither do I want to. If he didn't help me in my weakness, I'd be lying on this mat all day. When I feel weak, that's when he seems to strengthen me most!"

"As I said, sister, you're an example to us all," said Becca seriously. "What you're experiencing with your rapid deterioration, will come to all of us one day. The knowledge that the Teacher will help us encourages us, spurs us on." She paused, then asked with trepidation, "Have you given much thought to how the future will be?"

"Oh, the community's set for great things," said Judith enthusiastically.

"No, I don't mean that," said Becca choosing her words carefully. "I meant your future."

"Oh," said Judith, taken aback for a moment. She really didn't want to confront her fears head on, but was now being asked to. "I believe Josh and his

Father will take care of me." She looked over at her picture which had long since vacated her bag to sit on top of a shelf near her mat. "They give me comfort. They did say that my smile would go, but it would return one day. Well, if that day is in heaven, so be it!'"

"You're very brave, sister."

"No. I'm not. Many other believers have had to face similar challenges – my husband Mikha for instance – but they overcame because of their hope of being free one day and reunited with Josh and his Father in heaven. If I die here, so be it. Don't think of trying to contact my relatives, or anything like that. Just bury me, and rejoice in the fact that you've known me, and that you know the Messiah. Your strength will come from that."

Becca looked sad and concerned.

"Don't look like that, Becca," Judith said sympathetically. "We all know the truth of our situation. It's not how or when we'll die that counts; it's how we live our lives; it's what we do with them in the meantime. When it's our time, I believe the Messiah will meet us, reveal his great love for us, and help us through. Remember the way you felt - the expectation, the excitement, the love - when you first met him at the well? Get ready for another meeting like that one day. It'll be even more glorious and wonderful!" A thought struck her, and her eyes seemed to twinkle a little as she spoke, "And Becca, on that day, we'll be reunited with those who've gone before us, those we've loved." Judith decided to say no more as Becca was crying.

The two women shed some tears before Judith said, "It'll be worth it all when we meet Him and see His face. Our eyes will close here on earth for the last time, and in the blink of an eye, they'll open again in heaven…and our weak pathetic bodies will be renewed! We'll be whole again. And that added benefit will be ours too – we'll be able to meet each other again."

They hugged, and went to their mats, both dealing with their personal thoughts and hopes. Judith was surprised at the strength of her words. They were encouraging, but if she allowed her mind to think on her future, there was a gap between her thoughts and her hopes. This was something that truly needed faith. She didn't feel she was there yet, but hoped that when the time came, she would be able to deal with it. Had not Stephen claimed to see Josh coming to him before he died? His face had been enraptured, and he had seemed to fall asleep as the stones rained down upon him. Her own dear husband Mikha in his last moments had seemed to face his fate with fortitude. And Josh had even made it possible for her to speak with him again later. What right had she to doubt therefore? With Yahweh all things were possible. All she had to do was to believe, and keep believing!

Judith felt a slight vibration in her pouch and knew instinctively what it was. Becca was sleeping, so she took her cross out of her pouch to look at it. It had been a source of comfort to her on many occasions, and she felt the need of it now. She had never quite worked out the significance of being given it by the one she had called her angel, Sophia, but it was at times like this she appreciated it with all her heart. As she gazed on it, it began to morph again. Slowly but surely Josh's face was appearing, filling the whole area from tip of cross hand to tip of cross hand. Judith felt comforted and her peace returned. She felt more assured now. Then something unsettling happened. Josh seemed to be speaking to her, and into her mind came the word, "Nebuchadnezzar". It unsettled her because she couldn't determine what this meant. It seemed a random thing for him to say, to tell her. What did it mean? Flooding back into her mind came the confusion, guilt, fear, she had felt when she had first heard the word in Jerusalem. It seemed somehow linked to her disobedience. For a moment, she was thrown off balance, but as the morphing subsided, so did her discomfort. She slipped it back into her pouch, and pondered for a little while, but could come up with no specific answer. As before, she would have to resign herself to waiting to see what Josh would reveal to her. In this, she had no doubt. She believed more strongly than ever now that all would be revealed in time. As her peace returned, so sleep too put its arms around her, and acted as a soothing balm, eliminating all her cares.

Chapter Thirty-One

"So it's the woman who thinks she can take over my job," Barabbas was standing over Judith as she sat with her back against the barn wall. He was smiling.

It was three months after her proposal to the community's improvement committee, and harvest was in full swing. Judith had worked in the fields over the summer when her strength had allowed her to do so, being keen to throw her lot in with the workers. She had just spent a strenuous morning in the autumn sun and was now feeling exhausted. She did not respond to his words.

Barabbas motioned away the two women she had been talking to and sat down beside her. "Not talking to me?" He laughed. "Not ready to forgive me yet?" he mocked.

Judith determined to stick to her policy of silence unless she felt prompted to speak to him. After their last meeting, she had felt guilty because she had said too much and had opened herself up to the charge of hypocrisy.

He tried again, "I see you're beginning to take over the community. You're the flavour of the month, and everyone's talking about your Messiah."

Judith still refused to be drawn.

"You're indebted to me Judith, in case you didn't realise it," he said, a threatening note entering his voice. "You can't afford to ignore me!"

"Why not?" Judith asked coldly. "We don't see eye to eye, and you're a criminal, an exploiter, a fake. You're no prophet, and we both know it."

He feigned sadness, pretending to be hurt. "You still surely don't see me that way. Where's your compassion?"

Judith snorted, "For a common murderer, a fugitive, an imposter. Definitely not. You have treated these people shamefully and fully deserve to be exposed."

His face hardened and what he said was sharp and biting, "You are wrong! You know nothing about me. I'm your greatest benefactor here, as I am to the rest. You wouldn't be here unless I had allowed it. Your suggestion to expand the

257

community was ratified by me, and your 'holy' meetings sanctioned by me. I've kept my word and still you treat me this way."

"You're not alone," Judith said curtly, "I've kept my word too. You're not exposed, are you!"

There was silence between them for the next few moments, then Barabbas spoke. "Seeing that we've both kept our sides of the agreement, it's maybe time that we went one step further."

"There's no way I'm coming anywhere near you," Judith retorted. "I'm not like the other women you've exploited!"

"No, I don't mean that," Barabbas said laughing at what she had assumed. "How about a truce?"

Judith was horrified. "A truce," she said. "Between us? You must be joking! I've nothing to say to you, nothing I could ever agree on with you, and I certainly don't want to be anywhere near you. The thought of a truce is an anathema to me!"

"You are bitter, Judith," Barabbas said, sighing loudly. "Here I am coming to suggest peace between us, and you the bringer of peace to the community reject me. You're totally blinkered aren't you? You can't see past your own prejudices!"

"They're not prejudices, they're facts. You're a murderer, and you're pretending to be something you're not to these good people."

"You may be right, Judith…but can't people change? Is there no room for that in your religion?"

Judith was taken aback. She hadn't been prepared for that challenge.

"Not for you. You are evil!"

"How can you be so sure? You don't know the full facts. You're judging me without evidence."

"Don't make me laugh!" exclaimed Judith angrily. "No evidence? I saw you at Pilate's…and the way you treated me when I first came to see you – it was barbaric, gross, and abusive. There's evidence a-plenty!"

Barabbas shrugged his shoulders. "You think so…"

"I know so!" Judith said vehemently. "You'll never get me to agree with you, or to forgive you."

Barabbas was conciliatory now. "Before the community embarks on your project, I wanted to talk with you to see if we can resolve some of our issues. You need me to continue supporting your venture, and…" he paused to choose his words carefully, "I need you to make sure the people still come to me."

"You need me to what…?" Judith was shocked.

"The status quo must be maintained," said Barabbas crisply. "Your faith meetings might be seen as being in contention with me and what I stand for."

"What you stand for!" said Judith incredulously. ", I see. You want me to support you!" she said bitterly, "when you were responsible for killing the one who is at the root of my faith – the Messiah."

"Come on," said Barabbas, "there's no way he was the Messiah. He was just a poor deluded fool who happened to get in the way - to be in the wrong place at the wrong time – and I just happened to be fortunate!"

Judith riled at his explanation, but said nothing

"I didn't kill your friend," Barabbas insisted. "It was the Romans, not me."

"But you allowed it to happen."

"I'm a zealot. What else could I have done? What would you have done – volunteered to die to be honourable?"

Judith had no answer for this. The way she felt, it was safer to say nothing.

" No, we zealots believe in freedom, freedom from our oppressors. We believe in standing up for our faith when others would do us down, like Daniel with Nebuchadnezzar or the Maccabees with Antiochus Epiphanes…" He laughed, "or me with Pilate. It was my right to take the freedom I was being given!"

Judith hadn't fully heard all he'd said. The word 'Nebuchadnezzar' was filling her brain. He'd mentioned it in the same breath as 'freedom' to justify himself.

"You're nothing like Daniel," she said. "He was a diplomat. He preserved our traditions while supporting people like Nebuchadnezzar."

"If you say so," Barabbas said. "He was a patriot and would have overthrown the system if he could have."

"No, you don't know your history. Daniel might have been fighting for his faith from the inside of that system, but he chose to uphold the system and work for its benefit. Look how he treated Nebuchadnezzar. He won him over when he interpreted his dreams, and his three friends survived in the fiery furnace. He even felt sad for the king when he had to tell him he was going to be humbled and live with the animals for a time until he realised and accepted that Yahweh rules from heaven…" She broke off as something clicked in her thinking.

Barabbas was speaking again. "I don't think so. Daniel would have supported insurrection if he could have. As it was, it took at least seventy years for our people to get free again by your methods. We haven't time to wait. We want rid of the Romans now…to take our freedom when we can get it. That's what I did."

Judith looked at him coldly, disbelief showing in her eyes at his re-writing of history for his own ends. He wasn't speaking for all Jews, only his narrow band of freedom fighters.

"I've had time to think since then," he said. "As a zealot freedom fighter, I got away with it. I got my freedom. Perhaps your Yahweh wanted to free me so I could help these people."

"Never!" contradicted Judith. "He would never espouse your plans or methods."

"And yet, I'm the one alive. Your friend isn't! I've been given a second chance."

Judith looked at him, horrified. She hadn't thought of things this way. Was he mocking her, she wondered? She most certainly didn't want to think of things this way…and yet…there was a glimmer of truth in what he said. She knew about second chances. People she had known had benefitted from having been given one. If she was honest, she too had been the beneficiary of more than one, her current state being the consequence of one of them. What right had she to deny him the possibility? She rejected this thought immediately. It made her feel uncomfortable…and anyway, he was only playing with her. She said nothing.

"You're angry with me and maybe aren't seeing straight," he taunted. She bit her tongue. She so wanted to respond.

He continued, "It's time you knew the whole picture. Things aren't as black and white as you suppose." He sighed, and then rallied, anger now in his voice, "I'm just like you."

The words came flooding out of Judith's mouth, "You're nothing like me. I couldn't live with myself if I was you."

"Maybe not," he said evenly. "But in many ways, I'm just like you." He looked into her eyes, "Do you think I wanted to come here?"

"I don't know, or care!" she said sullenly, waiting for him to give her some pathetic excuse designed to get her on side.

"As soon as I was set free, I got out of Jerusalem. I assumed the soldiers would be keen to get a hold of me again after the governor's stupid mistake. I would be sought after up and down the country. I hid in Galilee for a while, getting on with my life the way I had done before. I had a band of followers who helped me. We decided to come back down to the Judean hills to be nearer the action with the Romans when I had a stroke of misfortune. There was a great storm, my horse took fright because of lightening. He tripped and fell, damaging his leg. As he was limping, I told the others to leave me there and go to the nearest town. I'd join them later. I felt bad, and the horse was also in a bad way. The shock seemed to have terrified him. He lay down and didn't recover. He died just before dawn. I hadn't noticed it at first as I was tending to him, but I myself must have been hit by the lightening. I had an aching all over my body and nausea swept over me a couple of times. My hands felt wrong and my legs too seemed different. They felt leaden. When dawn came up, I saw it. My hands had white blotches on them, and there was pain in my fingers… I knew what was wrong immediately. I'd seen leprosy often before. We'd passed by villages of the unclean too many times to be ignorant of it. These wretches had come out toward us, and the sight of their disfigured bodies had spurred us on to get away from them in great haste. I Couldn't move for a while. I sat beside my dead horse and wept. Yes wept. Me a zealot, a hardened criminal according to you. And yes, you'll be glad to hear this. For the first time since my lucky escape I began to wonder, was I being punished for my lifestyle? When you're low, you think the weirdest things. I saw the face of your messiah looking at me. It pitied me. The sadness in the eyes haunted me.

It was too much for me. What with my horse dying, my body showing signs of leprosy, and now this image – I had to somehow get away from it all. I picked up a stick and started walking aimlessly. I needed it to support myself. Still, I couldn't get away from those eyes! I'd been glad he'd been given my punishment. It had let me off the hook and I was happy about that. But those eyes – they really haunted me. They wouldn't let me go till I'd realised that he bore me no malice. I'd been given a second chance, and what was I doing with it? I was delirious, with the pain, the nausea, and the deep sense of unease I felt. I stumbled about for a while before I spied a narrow valley. It had a stream flowing through it. I needed a drink. On my way down into it, I must have fallen. I came round and found a group of lepers standing around me. I heard them say, 'he's one of us. Just look at his skin. It's a miracle. His robe, his staff. It's the prophet. He's come to us at last.' I'd no idea what they were talking about, but as I felt so bad, I allowed them to take me to a place they'd apparently prepared for the coming prophet and let them tend to my wounds. I said nothing at first, because I was so unwell, and didn't know what I was getting into. They seemed certain as to who I was, and so at least for that initial period I decided I wouldn't try to dissuade them of what they believed. It was in my own interest and so the zealot in me adjusted to my new circumstances and sought how to make the most of them. I discovered in the coming days that if I said little, they took this for spirituality and wisdom. And when I did speak, I tried to sound holy. It worked. They seemed to get benefit from me being there, and I…I had a refuge, a hiding place. I was accepted without question and took on the mantle of their leader. If I wasn't to live out my life with normal people because of my leprosy, I might as well make the best of my situation. Slowly but surely, I became a fixture here, and met with little or no resistance." He paused, "Until you!"

"You expect me to believe all this rubbish?" Judith asked, with not a trace of sympathy or warmth.

"Believe what you want," he said, sighing again.

"You're nothing like me!" Judith scoffed. "All you've done is take advantage of these people since you've been here. It's the zealot way!" she mocked. "And what about the women you've taken advantage of. How does that fit into your role as prophet?"

"It's what they do. The women expect to give themselves to the prophet. They need me, and I suppose I need them too in this miserable life. We help each other out…and it's spiritual."

"You're deluding yourself, while taking advantage of the vulnerable!"

He shrugged his shoulders. "We're all happy, and there's no complaints. You don't have to participate."

"You're right, I won't. You're despicable! And please don't bring my friend into your story to try and win me round. He'd never deal with the likes of you!"

261

Suddenly Judith felt a check on her spirit again. She'd said the wrong thing. She'd gone too far. She started to cry with frustration. "Get away from me!" she hissed, trying to hold back her tears. Barabbas looked uncomfortable. He was aware that their conversation had been getting louder and that others were noticing. "I will," he said, "but we'll speak again soon." He left Judith to her tears and thoughts. The other women came alongside her and tried to comfort her. She got to her feet though and started to make her way back to the hut before she would have to explain herself. All she said was, "The pain's been bad recently. I'm going back to my mat. I need to rest. I've done enough for one day." They looked sympathetically after her slow-moving, shuffling figure, then went back to their work.

In the hut, Judith lay down wearily and struggled with her emotions. She was tired, and this added to her distress. She had been accosted by her enemy; mocked and chided by him; made to listen to a string of lies - and to add insult to injury he had had the audacity to ask her for a truce. How could she side with the devil even if it was for the benefit of the community? There was turmoil in her mind. Not only was she angry at having been treated this way, but she sensed through it all, she wasn't in a good place. She didn't feel fully justified in her anger. She felt a duty to defend Josh from this brute...but justification when she did it? No, she knew deep inside there was something missing, something wrong. There was no peace. She felt jangled. If she had been speaking truth, she would have sensed that peace, but it just wasn't there. Josh could defend himself, and her efforts didn't seem to be hitting the mark. And what about his story? And his having claimed to see Josh's face bearing him no malice. It had to be lies. Josh wouldn't have revealed himself to him...or would he? While he had been with them, Josh had said he had come for sinners. A doctor doesn't go to the healthy, but the sick. But Barabbas? A murderer, someone who'd been happy for Josh to take his punishment and didn't blink an eye? He said he'd thought about it, but had he really, or was it said just to gain her sympathy and get her on side? But through all of this, something bigger was filling her mind, "Nebuchadnezzar". What had she said? Something had registered at the time. It was as if the Spirit inside her had put it into her mind and then hit her with the implications. She went over what she knew of the scriptures concerning Daniel and his place in the court of Nebuchadnezzar, the king of Babylon. He had been an exile, taken to Babylon as a youth and selected for the king's service as a wise man and advisor. He was known for interpreting the king's dreams which were mainly about the future. The one about someone being judged and made to live as an outcast for some time was the one that fascinated her. The king had been proud and then judged by Yahweh. He had been made to live apart from everyone like an animal for a period of time until he recognised and submitted to the King of Heaven - and then he had been restored. Daniel had predicted that, and had been rewarded for it. Suddenly she knew what 'Nebuchadnezzar' meant. It was about her. She had been proud. She thought she had known best as to what to do. She had ignored or even disregarded Josh's comfort and leading and had chosen to go her own way. She had doubted him, and even had gone out into Jerusalem putting herself and her family at risk. She was the one made to be an outcast. She was the 'unclean' one. She was the one suffering because of her disregard of Josh and his Father, and because of her disobedience. But another thought gripped her too, causing her to exult. Nebuchadnezzar had been restored! He had been given back his kingdom, all that he had lost. It was as if he had come back from the dead. Would she be restored? Would she get back to Tabitha and her family one day? Would she be released from all this? She didn't know, but should she dare to believe? She'd said it so often before, 'Anything, everything, is possible with Josh! 'Was this her way out? Circumstances were indeed bleak, almost without hope. But the fact Josh had mentioned 'Nebuchadnezzar' hadn't been by chance. Even her speaking to Barabbas that day when the name came up, none of that was by chance. She had been disbelieving before and had allowed herself to disregard Josh and his support. She wasn't going to do that again. The consequences of her last mistake had been catastrophic. No, she would throw herself into believing that someday, somehow, she would escape from all this, and find her way back to civilization. She fell asleep comforted and happy.

Chapter Thirty-Two

It was winter and the work on the valley reclamation had begun. The outcasts had successfully enlisted their friends and family members who lived in the nearby villages, and progress was going according to plan. The work was being done with great enthusiasm, families, and friends happy to be helping their outcast neighbours, in the knowledge that they would receive remuneration not only for their winter labours, but also for their eventual aid in selling the expected produce. It was a venture that everyone threw themselves into.

The wood had been gathered and deposited at the head of the valley in the spot that was nearest to where the work would commence. Some joked that the hillsides around Jacob's Well were now bare having been stripped of trees. It was winter, others reasoned, and things would grow back when the spring came. A squad of men worked on the pile of wood, cutting, and shaping it to what would be required to make a viaduct and the trestles it would stand upon. Others more skilled in building and quarrying laid out the track from the stream to the area where the water would finally be required. The splitting and diverting of the stream would happen later once everything was in place. While their friends and families were involved in this, the outcasts busied themselves in preparing the ground the water was intended to irrigate. The stronger men dug a deep pool at the end of the viaduct, and once a satisfactory depth had been achieved, they proceeded to dig channels all over the arid ground to make sure the water would irrigate their crops. It was heavy work, and for a while it was every man on the job. The women helped by bringing the men sustenance during the day, while at the same time doing the winter work in the fields that the men had been taken away from. Weeding and clearing stones could be backbreaking work, and keeping the soil in a good state to make the spring planting easy was demanding. Judith helped where she could, but often her failing energy levels precluded her from participating. As the recognised 'founder' of the project, the others were content to let her watch or supervise their efforts. Her contribution had been her ideas, and her money. That was quite enough.

It was on one of these winter days, a few weeks away from the spring planting, Judith was up at the pool which had just been completed, admiring the network of channels spreading out from it, when she spied Barabbas looking at her. He had been working with another man on one of the main channels taking the water to the extremities of the area, digging a trench away from it. He had stopped work, obviously in need of a rest. Although the air was cool, he was visibly suffering from the heat of his labour and was resting on the stick he always carried with him. She turned away and proceeded to retrace her steps when she heard him call her name. In full view of the others, she couldn't ignore him, and so she turned back and looked at him enquiringly.

"Stay for a little longer, Judith. I'd like to talk to you about how we're progressing with your project."

There was no way she could avoid it, as he was showing support for her idea in front of all the others. He motioned for her to sit on a convenient rock and he came and sat down beside her. They were just far enough away not to be in earshot of the others.

"Your work is progressing well," he said. "I think we'll get it finished in time."

Judith said nothing, looking away from him into the distance. She had determined that the best policy was not to acknowledge him or speak to him unless it was absolutely necessary.

"It won't work," he said, jibing at her. "It's your work, and you should be glad to speak to your prophet about it. The others will notice."

She realised that he spoke the truth, and so she looked at him quickly and said, "I want nothing to do with you."

"That's a shame," he said in a mocking voice. "Especially when I'm here to help."

Judith spoke quietly between clenched teeth, "I don't need your help! I despise you." Suddenly she felt as if she'd said something wrong. She looked down, hoping to avoid any further conversation.

"Aren't you being a bit harsh? I'm willing to help. It's benefitting my community."

"It's not your community. You've just come into it and taken advantage of it. The community belongs to these poor people putting their backs into the work."

Barabbas changed tack, "You know, Judith. I admire you."

Judith was taken aback. "You admire me? Why?"

"Because you're you. You're straightforward. You're doing a good job, and everyone loves you. They know exactly what they're getting when they deal with you."

"And they don't with you?" it was Judith's turn to mock.

"True. I'm not hiding it, at least, not from you." He sighed, "I see what you're doing and how the community have taken to you. Your motives are good and you're giving people hope with your Messiah."

This was a strange confession from him, Judith thought, but decided to say nothing in response. He continued, "Yes, Judith, I'm impressed with you and what you're doing."

"What are you after?" she asked suspiciously.

"Nothing," he said, looking offended. "Can't your prophet give you a compliment?"

"I don't need any from you," she said gruffly. "And there's no point in trying to get me on side, as you did the last time with your lies about my friend."

Barabbas looked surprised, "Lies? Didn't you believe me?"

"Of course I didn't!" she snarled. "You have no thought or consideration for me or for my friend. He died taking the blame for you. You're making a mockery of him."

"That's where you're wrong," he said quietly. "I'm not. I wasn't lying. I told you the truth, the way it happened to me."

Judith didn't know whether to believe him or not, so decided to say nothing.

"You're very judgmental for a believer," he said. "The little I heard about your beliefs before I came in here was that they majored on love and forgiveness. Let's say I was wrong to allow your friend to die. Can't you forgive me?"

The word was wrenched out of her. "No!" Barabbas seemed surprised at the vehemence of it.

There was a pregnant silence between them, then Barabbas said, "Because you hold me responsible for your brother's death too?"

Judith felt he was hitting home. She hated him because of what he had allowed to happen to Josh, but she was filled with absolute loathing for him because of Joe. She didn't want to go there. She said nothing and felt absolutely numb inside.

"I am not responsible for either of their deaths," Barabbas countered. "I was there, but it was the Romans who did the deeds."

"You can't excuse yourself as easily as that," spat out Judith. "By being there on both occasions, you were indirectly responsible...and..." She felt something vibrate in her pouch and with it a picture came into her mind. She had to speak the words that came, "You almost killed him before!"

While she was dealing with this thought, Barabbas responded, "What are you talking about? Who? Your Messiah or your brother? Perhaps it was both!" His tone was sarcastic.

Judith was grappling with thoughts and pictures filling her mind. She spoke slowly, "The Messiah, my friend."

"Rubbish. I've never met him except on that one occasion in front of Pilate. I think you're mad!"

"No, I'm not. You met him in the woods above Nazareth a long time ago." As the thoughts came, Judith was reaching out for more.

Barabbas looked baffled. It was his turn to say nothing as he waited for Judith to speak.

"Your zealot friends had captured two little boys and brought them to you." Judith looked into the distance as if envisaging the scene. The cross in her pouch was still vibrating. "You were sharpening a knife."

"Well, that's what we 'knife men' do?" He was still mocking her, but it was clear he was contemplating what she was saying. "Go on, let's hear more!"

"I can see you're asking their names. You were pleased with one of them as he told you he wanted to be a zealot just like you when he grew up."

Barabbas was beginning to look uncomfortable now.

"You tried to kill the other little boy." Barabbas was thoughtful as his memory of the event seemed to be returning slowly.

"Don't you remember?" Judith said, "you asked the other boy his name and he told you he was the son of Nazareth's carpenter."

Barabbas remained silent.

"He stood up against you, didn't he? He told you zealots shouldn't be responsible for murdering little babies, as you were."

Barabbas looked astonished as the facts came out.

"You turned on him, didn't you? You gave the knife you were sharpening to the little boy who wanted to be a zealot like you and told him to kill his friend."

Barabbas's mouth was now open amazed at what he was hearing.

"He walked away," he said as if he was now sharing in what Judith was seeing. "He just walked away, as cool as you please. Right out of the camp. He wasn't scared of us."

"Do you remember his name? He gave it to you."

As the realisation came, Barabbas spoke the name involuntarily, "Josh. It was Josh."

Judith nodded, amazed herself at what was happening. She had no idea where all this was coming from. It seemed linked somehow to her trinket given her by Angel Sophia, and therefore from Josh himself.

"Another name for Josh?" she queried.

"Now the realisation hit Barabbas fully, "Jesus." He said wonderingly.

Judith's voice took on a hard note again, "And you tried to kill him, even then, and…" she paused, before speaking more deliberately, "the baby he told you that you had been responsible for killing…was my baby brother Joe!" She felt an absolute hatred of him now.

For the first time she saw Barabbas's normally hard and mocking face look stunned.

Silence reigned.

Eventually Barabbas said, "How do you know all that?"

"Is it true?"

"Yes, all of it. I don't know how you knew but it's all true. But how did you know? Were you there? You must have been there!"

"I was, in a manner of speaking. I wasn't there myself, but someone else..." Judith didn't know where she was going with this, "But someone who knows me was!" Going through the forefront of her mind was the name 'Sophia', but she had no idea why.

"Did your friend the Messiah tell you?"

"Not exactly, although I believe he's allowed me to know, and to tell you."

Both sat in silence again, wondering where to take the conversation next.

"It's not surprising then why you hate me so much," Barabbas said, as if giving vent to his thoughts.

Judith wanted to say, "I don't just hate you; I despise you," but the words wouldn't come. Somewhere deep down she felt they were inappropriate for the moment; and also a sense of guilt for thinking them. She wondered what Yahweh was doing in this situation. Why was he letting her say all this to Barabbas, an enemy of the faith? Was it to condemn him, to make him feel bad and wretched? Instinctively she knew she was wrong. Yahweh and Josh didn't work that way. There had to be a purpose. She waited for the clarification.

"If you weren't there, and you knew nothing of this beforehand, then..." Barabbas struggled for the words.

"Then what?" asked Judith unrelentingly.

"Maybe...your friend's trying to speak to me through you..."

"Don't hold your breath," Judith said, and instinctively regretted it. She knew she was wrong and was curbing the work that Yahweh was trying to do through her.

Barabbas wasn't listening. He was caught up in his thoughts. "I'm sorry," he said.

"Sorry for what!" said Judith, not minded to let him off the hook.

He looked at her seriously, "For being involved in the death of your brother...and of your Messiah. I've done many bad things in my life, but I never considered myself fully responsible for some of my actions...it was the Romans."

"Well now you know!" said Judith. "Yahweh's found you out." She tried to get up off the rock and leave him.

"Not so fast," he said, holding her arm. She expected him to be rude to her or to make a fool of her, but he didn't. She shook him off. "Will you forgive me?" he asked quietly.

"No! I can't!" Judith said, forcing the words out. She looked down, avoiding his gaze.

"Can't...or won't?" he asked, his voice very close to her ear.

269

"Leave me alone!" she spoke loudly, causing those working nearby them to look up.

She said it again, more quietly, "Leave me alone!" and rose to go. This time he let her get up, but as she went, she heard him say, "I admire you Judith for all you're doing and for all you've done. We'll speak again. Pray for me."

On her way back to Becca's hut, Judith's mind was in turmoil. Her conversation with Barabbas hadn't gone the way she had expected. She had intended saying nothing, but it was obvious that Josh and his Father had had other plans. What were they doing? Talking to Barabbas? How could they? He was an enemy. The thought struck her, he was her enemy, but was he theirs? He had been right. Josh had taught love and forgiveness. But love and forgiveness for Barabbas? Next to Judas Iscariot he was Yahweh's next greatest enemy, or was he? All her competing fears and thoughts – she didn't know how to deal with them. And what about that revelation she had had. It had seemed linked somehow to her trinket. There was just too much for her to think about! There was also her underlying feeling of guilt. Too much, too much, she thought! On her return to the hut therefore, she lay down on her mat and sought solace in sleep.

A man's face was pressed against hers, and it seemed to Judith that it was very like Barabbas's. It was, but it wasn't quite. It was disfigured, deformed and grotesque. It leered at her out of the darkness, and she cringed. It was so horrible, and she felt petrified. It was dark all around, and the face seemed to be extremely bright, dazzling her and making her want to close her eyes because of the glare. His eyes were malevolent. They were bright and glistening, exuding evil. She wanted to push it away but couldn't make her arms rise to do so. They seemed stuck by her sides, and she felt very vulnerable, totally at the mercy of his relentlessly gloating stare. She wanted to run, but neither would her legs work. She was horribly transfixed, and she could do nothing about it. Added to this scene was the background sound of howling and moaning, with Barabbas's cursing in the foreground. She felt sullied by the experience. Her skin crawled as if evil cruel fingers were exploring her body. She wanted to scream, but her mouth wouldn't open, and no sound would come. She had no way of protecting herself from this attack, this invasion of her privacy and space. She had to submit to the humiliation of it all and she felt filthy and corrupted. Barabbas's face now changed and she saw demonic figures approaching her, bright red and grinning grotesquely. They carried fiery torches and seemed intent on burning her. She could feel the heat as they came close, and they howled with diabolical enjoyment as they taunted and terrified her by making the flames lick at her face. The pain was intense as her flesh burned, and it didn't stop either. She couldn't collapse or become unconscious to get away from it. The experience of burning just seemed to go on and on for ever; she still couldn't scream; she could only endure. The smoke, and the sickly smell of her burning flesh filled her nostrils, and she struggled to breathe. Her throat kept closing and there was a constant choking sensation in it which made her want to vomit. Her clothes were burning, and she saw her nakedness. Burn marks were appearing all over her body but they didn't increase; they didn't consume her. They remained there smouldering and glowing – only the pain increased. There was no escaping even for a moment. Looking around her, the darkness illuminated by these demonic torches, she saw others like herself, burning and howling in pain. Curses filled the air, and she heard words she had never used before coming from her own mouth. She didn't need to think about where she was. She knew. She was in hell! Could it get any worse?

Suddenly she felt something crawling up her legs and up and over her body leaving a horrible foul-smelling trail of slime. She couldn't get away from this either but had to submit to the indignity and awfulness of the experience. It looked as if her body was being taken over by tiny miniscule mucus-secreting worms, sliding and slithering over her skin, so much so that she could barely see a patch of white. At a given signal they started to burrow into her body, and the pain became excruciating. She was being eaten alive! Her flesh crawled, and blood was oozing out of the wormholes. She felt nauseous, and reeled from the pain, but nothing she could do helped her escape the ordeal. It just went on and on without ceasing. She wanted to die but couldn't. The smell of decay now filled her nostrils, odours of faeces and the most awful rotting fungus she had ever experienced. Nausea swept over her but again, not enough to allow her to become unconscious.

The red demonic creatures were back wielding sharp instruments which they plunged into her skin. There were no wounds this time, only cripplingly severe unbearable pain. They laughed horribly as they carried out their torture of her. Their laughter penetrated her brain so much that she could hear nothing else. In the midst of these demons a face appeared and came rushing towards her stopping only inches from her nose. She felt its hot rotten foul-smelling breath enveloping her. It wasn't Barabbas's face this time. This face was intrinsically evil and glowed with malicious intent. It was the face of a goat, grinning horribly at her. Out of its mouth came the foulest curses she had ever heard. She couldn't cover her ears or shut them out by any other means. The words echoed around her brain. She didn't understand them all as they were distorted and sometimes in another language she couldn't make out. However, before the scene closed, amidst a volley of demonic laughter, the face leered grotesquely at her, and its insidious voice snarled at her the words, "the last penny", and for good measure, it repeated them "the last penny" before it was engulfed by darkness.

Judith heard her name being called out of the darkness, and she felt her shoulder being shaken violently. "Go away!" she shouted. "Leave me alone!"

"Judith! Judith!" the voice was insistent now. She recognised it as Becca's. "You've been dreaming. Come on, wake up!"

Don Treader

Judith opened her eyes and saw Becca's face close to hers, exhibiting great concern. "You've been having a nightmare, I think," she said.

Judith glanced around and looked relieved to find she was lying on her mat in the hut. "You're right," she said. "I've been in hell…" She was shaking. Becca took her hand and tried to stop the tremors.

"You've got it bad," she said. "It must have been some dream!"

"It was," Judith said, and before she could stop herself, she added, "I saw Barabbas…and the devil. I was burning, being eaten up by worms tormented by demons…I was terrified!" She was crying now.

Becca hugged her, trying to ease the effects of Judith's nightmare.

"Who's Barabbas?" She asked.

Judith held back. She didn't want to say anything to Becca about the prophet. She clammed up and Becca took it that she was still feeling frightened.

"It's been awful. I've never known anything like it. I felt as if I'd been abandoned by Yahweh and was doomed for eternity!"

"That sounds awful," Becca agreed. "But remember, it was only a dream."

Judith didn't feel so sure. She knew it had been a dream, but it had seemed so real. Her flesh was still crawling, and her mind felt shattered by the horror of it all. "It was just so real, that's all," she said lamely, feeling stupid at being affected so badly.

Becca continued with her soothing tactics. "It was only a dream. Put it out of your mind."

Judith looked troubled though, "But why would Yahweh let me go through that? I felt as if I was being punished for my sins."

"A dream," Becca soothed again.

"But it was so real," Judith was crying now. "Horrible words. Terrible threats. And I'm sure I saw the devil." Her face straightened as she remembered, "His last words to me – they were strange…"

"Don't think about it. Just put it in the past. It's all over now."

"I don't think I can. His words are haunting my brain. What were they again…" Judith thought hard? "He said something about a last penny."

"Look Judith, it makes no sense. Put it down to a nightmare and think no more about it."

"It was so real though. Why would Yahweh put me through that unless there was a message in it for me?"

"You're reading too much into it," Becca reasoned. "Let it go!"

"The last penny…what did he mean?" Judith wasn't listening but was intent on discovering any meaning that was to be found in her experience.

Eventually she shook her head and gave up. "I don't know. I suppose you're right. It was only a dream. If anything's to come out of it, I'm sure Yahweh will let me know in due course."

"You're probably right," said Becca bringing Judith a drink.

They sat in silence for a few moments, then Becca said, "Perhaps you're doing too much at the minute. Scale things down a bit. Rest more. Then your condition might improve a little."

"Do you think so?" asked Judith thoughtfully. "I'm not so sure. If I do nothing, I'll be bored out of my mind. I enjoy watching the progress of the viaduct."

"Yes, but it's taking too much out of you. One of the things about our condition is that given some rest, we can sometimes gain periods of respite. You'll be of more use to us if you get into one of these periods."

"I need to feel useful," Judith said determinedly. "I'd vegetate if I sat around."

"Don't then. Why don't you put your efforts more into the meetings? People really do appreciate your input. The numbers are growing. It's a good sign. So many people are now talking and thinking about the Messiah. Your experience is precious."

"I'm not the only one who can do this. Many of you have received the Spirit."

"Yes, we knew him for a few days, but you...you spent years with him and are his friend. No, your experience is invaluable to us."

"I suppose I could spend more time praying and preparing. I did find today's outing quite tiring." Judith was also thinking that if she was to take up this opportunity, she would be able to avoid seeing Barabbas again, at least for the time being, until her strength improved.

"And that's probably why you had such a terrible nightmare," Becca chided gently.

"During the day?" Judith laughed. "It must have been a devilishly bad daydream then!"

They both laughed, the atmosphere lightened, and the two women prepared their evening meal.

273

Chapter Thirty-Three

The days wore on and Judith true to her word devoted herself to the practice of prayer and preparation for the evening meetings. She avoided strenuous exercise and going to the viaduct to check on its progress. She made a point of only visiting it once a week, and with each trip she marvelled at the dedicated work of the able-bodied putting together the structure, and the energy of the less than able as they dug the pool and the irrigation channels. It looked as if they would achieve their goal – to have everything ready for the spring plantings. She was satisfied that things were going according to plan, and that she didn't have to interact with Barabbas.

The big day came when she had to be present for the splitting and diverting of the stream: the day the water would take its first journey down the wooden structure to its final destination; the day it filled the pool and its irrigation channels. The two groups of workers took their places where their work had been done. The able bodied stood where the viaduct began. It had been sunk into the ground before it made its way down the hillside. It was on the same level as the stream, so that when they broke down the artificial bank they had constructed between the stream and the wooden channel, the water would start to flow along the viaduct. They had made an island in the stream to divide the flow, one channel continuing on its natural course down into the valley, while the other made its way to the viaduct entrance. The not so able-bodied workers with just about every one of the other outcasts in the valley stood by the pool, just under the end of the viaduct, awaiting the arrival of that precious flow. At a given signal the bank was broken down and the channel blocked just after it. The water began to make its way down the artificial structure, gurgling and swishing as it went, until it reached its journey's end. It splashed out of the channel into the waiting pool below to the sound of an almighty cheer. The project had been a success and the rejoicing of the outcasts knew no bounds. They leapt up and down cheering, and once the pool was of sufficient depth, many of them jumped into it their faces radiant. Some of them positioned themselves under the viaduct's exit and allowed the cool clear water to fall on them. They were excited and happy. The majority of the able bodied looked on from the top of the hill. They too were shouting and clapping, entering into the spirit of the day. Some of them with buckets of pitch in hand made their way along the viaduct route plugging any places where water was escaping from joints or flaws in the wood. The venture had been completed in good time and once the able bodied had gone back to their villages and their own celebrations, the outcasts lit a huge bonfire near the newly created pool, and their festivities began. The outcasts had outdone themselves in preparing for the day. Food and drink were in abundance, music was played, and the people sang and danced well into the evening. Some however chose to spend their time watching the water falling into the pool then trickling along the irrigation trenches and being soaked into the arid ground. They could see that the sand was slowly becoming muddy and would soon be able to support the crops they hoped to plant. When it became dark, the light from the main bonfire, and the little campfires that individuals had built, allowed the party to continue until exhaustion took its toll. There was a real community spirit and those who weren't engaged in the singing or dancing chose to sit and talk, enthusing over what had been achieved. Many came up to Judith and congratulated her, thanking her for what she had enabled them to do. She was indeed everyone's favourite person and she basked in their praise.

It was a couple of hours after sunset and people were still singing and dancing when Judith spied a hooded figure approaching her and making to sit down beside her. Those around her had scattered for the prophet, who loudly congratulated Judith as he sat himself down.

"You've done our valley proud today, Judith," he said loudly, then more quietly when those around had moved far enough away to give them privacy, "You are flavour of the month here." Did Judith sense jealousy here? She said nothing and awaited his next utterance.

"This can't go on Judith. You treat me with no respect and others can see it. You should see your face."

"What's wrong with my face?" asked Judith coldly. "Is it not to your liking!"

"No, it's not that. I admire you. I've always thought your face had good qualities...but whenever I approach, it's clear that you dislike me."

"I do!" said Judith.

"Well, this can't continue," Barabbas said. "On such a special day, when we're all celebrating, I'd like you to try to like me."

"Never!" Judith said.

"Well, I'm amazed. I come to you in a spirit of peace. I've spoken to you about my experiences, my encounters with your Messiah - and still, you spurn me."

"You're a seasoned liar, thief and murderer. Why should I trust anything you say?"

"Because your spirit is telling you."

"My Spirit is telling me nothing!" Judith knew that this wasn't quite accurate. She felt cold and numb.

"I've been thinking over everything you've said since our last meeting. I can understand why you hate me – what with your brother and your Messiah – but I don't think they hate me."

"How dare you speak for them!" Judith spat out. "You know nothing about them and what they think."

"Then why did your Messiah appear to me when I was at my lowest ebb, just before I came here?"

"I don't know!" Judith said dismissively, not even considering seriously that Josh might have appear to him. "Perhaps he wanted to warn you or punish you." She mocked him.

"That's not the spirit," he chided her softly. "He looked sad and disappointed, not angry."

"Well, he should have been!" As in her previous conversations with him, she now felt she had gone too far.

"You're hard." He said. "If your Messiah can forgive me, why can't you?"

"Who said he has forgiven you?"

"I know it. I've had much time to think. Do you think you're an island here, that whatever you do doesn't get to me?"

Judith looked at him questioningly.

"I meet people in this valley all the time. They speak very highly of you, and occasionally they tell me what you get up to in your meetings."

"What I get up to?"

"Yes, the way others are falling under your influence, and the influence of your Messiah."

"Really?" she said sarcastically.

"Yes, I know what you're teaching and how it's influencing others."

"So then, how's it affecting you?" Judith didn't try to keep the scorn out of her voice.

"Well," he said hesitantly. "I like what I hear. Your friend was a good man. I don't regret that he was given my punishment because I'm free. But I am sorry. And I think he knows it."

"What makes you think that?"

"Because of the Spirit. You teach about the influence of the Spirit. I've heard that at your meetings there's a reality, there's a presence. Well, I sense that I'm not being held responsible by your friend. I don't know how, but I sense it."

Don Treader

Judith stared at him in unbelief. "How can you say things like that? You know nothing of the Spirit."

He looked at her with disappointment. "I don't feel it's me with the problem any more. I think it's you. You're hard, Judith, not the person they say you are."

This stung Judith. There was truth in what he said. Whenever she spoke to him her hackles rose and she wasn't the person she wanted to be. Up till this time she had believed it was his fault for goading, for mocking her. But now...was he right? Was she somehow to blame too? She didn't want to countenance this thought, so she decided to leave. She wanted no more of this conversation, or of the feelings of condemnation she was experiencing.

Barabbas looked directly at her. "I've told you Judith, I admire you. Indeed, I feel quite drawn to you. You set a wonderful example in this valley and you've helped lift us out of mediocrity. I want to know you more, but every time I'm with you, you reject me. Is this the attitude your Messiah would want?"

Judith couldn't say anything. She felt stung, right to the quick, by his words. His avowal of admiration and of being drawn to her, was just too much for her to cope with. She felt sick and horrified all at once. She had to get away from him. He made no effort to stop her as she rose to leave. He wasn't angry or mocking. He simply said, "Please remember what I've said. Think about it. Don't let your beliefs about your brother or your Messiah get in the way."

Judith's head was spinning now. Her emotions were running high as she started on her way back to the hut. It was fortunate that Becca saw her stumbling and lurching away. She was crying quietly to herself. Becca took her by the arm and led her up the valley.

"What's wrong?" she asked. "How can you be unhappy on such a wonderful day as this?"

"Nothing," said Judith resolutely. Oh, how she wished she could have shared everything about Barabbas with Becca, but she knew she could not. It might end her days in the community. Instead, she settled for saying nothing, except that the efforts of the day had exhausted her, and she was ready for her mat.

Becca nodded understandingly and said no more. She wanted her friend, her sister, to get what she needed and deserved. Sleep would work its magic on her and in the morning light, whatever had affected her would have melted away. The future could begin again.

Judith's time was limited. She knew it and prepared her heart for it. She had never imagined that she one day would end her life in a leper colony...and so soon. But she accepted that Yahweh had made that her lot, and so she submitted to it. She remembered how her Lord had surrendered to his Father's will the night before he died. Not only had he said the words, but the next day, the day of his crucifixion, he put those words into action. She recognised that unless Yahweh intervened, it was unlikely she would see the first harvest of her project. A number of conflicting thoughts passed through her mind over the next weeks and months. She felt at peace where she was; she knew she was in the right place. She had made a valuable contribution to the community and she was happy with the results. She still spent evenings in the meetings, and more people were coming, more people were talking about the Messiah. In her lower moments however, she was scared at the speed her illness seemed to be progressing. More marks had appeared all over her body. Some were turning into sores and many of her toes and fingers were now totally numb, so much so that standing up could be precarious. She was rubbing at her numb little toe one day when the nail and part of the toe itself came away in her hand. She was surprised to realise that she felt no pain. Her condition was in an advanced state and she worried; would she die in pain; die a gruesome death? She struggled to put these thoughts aside, and to allow Yahweh's will to be done, but with the support of her friends and also because of the example they expected from her, she generally managed to overcome. But other thoughts unsettled her and at times gave her a strand of hope. Death looked inevitable, but what about Josh's promises to her to be with her and to restore her smile after the dark days. Maybe these weren't her dark days though. She was happy and felt more fulfilled than she had ever felt before. Could she expect a deliverance? Her situation was so extreme she thought it very unlikely. But then again, there was the 'Nebuchadnezzar' situation. Was she to take from that, that she might be restored back into society just as he had been? As the days went on and her condition worsened, she deliberately allowed this thought to become a distant memory. This was her lot in life and she should face it and accept it. Maybe her skirmish with hell in her recent nightmare might actually be more relevant than she had imagined. On subsequent occasions she had wakened up to find herself sweating and crying, having relived the nightmare in her dreams. She contemplated at those times that perhaps she might actually be bound for hell because of her previous ungratefulness and disobedience – but…Yahweh had brought her here and hadn't forgotten her. Her work was being blessed - but Then again, perhaps on the other hand, she might just be deceiving herself because she didn't want to face the truth!

And then there was the mystery of Barabbas! Why was he here? Why was he targeting her? He even had said he admired her and felt drawn to her. The very thought turned her stomach. She had become good at blotting him out of her thoughts, of numbing herself from thinking about him. And yet, as the days progressed, she found herself wondering why Yahweh had placed her there - in the valley where Barabbas reigned. She knew that nothing Yahweh did was by coincidence. She had to be there for a reason, but she couldn't countenance the thought. It was too much for her brain to contemplate. Barabbas's claims about forgiveness and seeing the Messiah just couldn't be true. He was working on her to get her on side, to prop up his waning influence as the prophet, and perhaps even to take some of the credit due to her. She hated him with a vengeance because of her brother and Josh. There could be no reconciliation with him, let alone forgiveness. Yet when she thought this way, she felt uncomfortable, and if she was honest, she knew in her heart she would have to face and confront her feelings one day - just not that day!

Spring planting had gone well, and the outcasts rejoiced. Very quickly the arid ground became quite fertile, and in weeks only, vegetation and crops were sprouting. A fairly large area had been set aside for vines and fruit tree planting, cuttings having been taken from the best of the orchards below, and although it might take a year or two to gain a high yield from them, the ground was lush and the promise of abundance good. A community effort promised to make the community prosperous. Many of the outcasts had a new spring in their step. They looked forward to working in the fields and orchards, and put their backs into the strenuous labour. Judith on the other hand did less and less, and finally took to her mat. She hated lying indoors as the spring moved into summer and so she had Becca put her mat outside in the mornings and she stayed there for most of the day soaking in the sun. It also gave her the chance to speak to others as they passed. She felt content with this; if she could not work, she at least could encourage those who could. In the evenings when she felt able, she got off her mat and Becca helped her to a hut where a meeting was being held. She was always prepared and always ready to speak about the Messiah. She was totally glad that these limits placed upon her meant she would never be likely to encounter the prophet. Indeed she hoped she had seen the last of him before she died. As the summer wore on, she did however hear rumours that he had attended at least one of the meetings she hadn't been at. She dismissed this as a ploy on his part to get at her, and wiped it from her mind. Let him do what he wanted as long as he didn't come anywhere near her!

It was late summer and near to harvest time. The fields were green and the crops full and healthy. The trees and bushes in the newly created orchards were growing quickly and strongly. There was a sense of excitement in the community at the expectation of a wonderful harvest and all the profits that might bring in. Judith had seldom seen the community so buoyant, and rejoiced with them. One night about a week away from the start of harvest, Judith forced herself to attend a meeting. Although it had been a painful day for her, she was determined to go, and so she arrived at it leaning heavily on Becca. She relished the thought that she had to do nothing there that night except to pray with the rest. It had been agreed that different women would speak about their time spent with the Messiah when he had visited their village for the first time so many years before. The speaker wasn't someone Judith knew well. She had been in a few of the meetings, but Judith had never bumped into her anywhere else. She was middle aged and quiet.

She wasn't one for saying much, and Judith wondered why she had been chosen to speak as she hardly ever said more than a few words. Darkness had just fallen, and everyone sat in a circle in the hut. A candle was set in a pot on a table in the middle of the circle. As it flickered, people's faces took on different hues and shapes, making it quite an eerie scene. The middle-aged woman started to tell her story, hesitatingly at first, but as she got into her stride, her words became more confident and flowing.

"Some of you know my story, but most of you don't. Since I've contracted my illness and had to leave my husband and sons, I've kept myself to myself, and just done what I had to. I'm not a mixer. I've always hated the thought of being in a gathering like this, but a few weeks ago, curiosity got the better of me and I came along. I'm a believer now thanks to your prayers…and you know something – it's all beginning to make sense to me now. You'll understand when you hear what I'm about to tell you."

The rest of the gathering smiled and looked interested. Most of them knew each other's stories, but this woman…she was new to many of them.

"When I was young, barely into my twenties, I had been working in the fields near to the village where most of us used to stay. It had been a quiet day and only a few women were picking. I'm not going to say who it was – some of you might know him although he's moved on since then. He was in charge of the workers, and when evening came he dismissed the others but told me to stay as he wanted to speak to me about my work. When the rest were gone, and it was almost dark, he propositioned me and asked me to lie with him - right out there in the field. When I refused, he hit me again and again until he had me lying on the ground, barely conscious, and…" the middle-aged lady paused, "he had his way with me. He threatened me if I told anyone, my husband or family, he'd deny it and say I'd asked him and had pursued him. He'd find a way to kill me if I spoke up."

The other women looked sympathetically on her. Before their leprosy, most of them knew what it could be like to be abused in this way.

"I went back to the village and said nothing. I wanted to but I was scared. I hated that man with a vengeance for what he had done to me. I had a husband and two baby sons. I couldn't tell him. Yet as time went on, he noticed I had changed. I felt cold and numb. I couldn't respond to him. I was neglecting my sons. I didn't want to be alive, because of the terrible secret I was forced to hide. I tried to take my life twice but couldn't go through with it. My hatred was getting the better of me and I was losing my family because of it."

She looked over at Becca and smiled. "Well, you came along and altered all that, and I'm grateful to you."

Becca looked surprised.

The woman continued, "We all knew what you were like, and most of us avoided you then!"

Don Treader

The others laughed, knowing what she meant.

"You had had five husbands and you were staying with someone who wasn't your husband. I was there when you came rushing into the village telling everyone to go out to the well. You'd met someone who had told you everything you had ever done, and you believed him to be the Messiah. I found myself thinking, if he'd known everything you'd been up to, he would have had to be the Messiah - or someone who'd been intimate with you."

A ripple of quiet laughter went round the room.

"I went out to see Him, with just about everyone else in the village. I didn't get a chance to speak to Him, but by the few things I heard him say, I felt impressed. I didn't know though about your claim that he was the Messiah. Also, if he was the Messiah, surely he wouldn't have had such a rough band of followers with him. Most of them didn't look a bit religious!"

Some people in the group were nodding in agreement. They'd obviously had the same thoughts.

"Well, as most of you know, they stayed with us for a couple of days, before going north to Galilee. They really ought not to have been staying in our village at all, being Jews, but they did. Some of you might remember that on their second night with us we had some food round a campfire and listened to the man you claimed was the Messiah." She looked again at Becca, who was nodding. "He told the story I'm about to tell you. He told a lot of stories. He didn't teach like the other religious leaders or prophets. As he spoke, I found myself fixed on his words. He said, 'A great king had a servant who owed him a great deal of money. There came a day of reckoning and the king asked for his money to be repaid. The man was terrified as he knew he couldn't pay it back and was going to be sold with his wife and children into slavery. He pled with his master to forgive him and wait till he could repay the debt. The king took pity on him and freed him from his debt. He didn't have to pay it back. He was totally free from it. That servant however decided to go to one of the other servants who owed him just a little money and demanded he repay his debt to him immediately. When he couldn't pay him back, the servant who had been forgiven the great debt had him imprisoned. His fellow servants were unhappy with him and told his master about it. The king was angry and called the servant in. He told him, "I forgave you your huge debt, but you treated your fellow servant despicably, having had him imprisoned because he couldn't pay back the tiny amount he owed you".' The Messiah went on to say, 'if you refuse to forgive others the sins they have committed against you, how can you expect Yahweh to forgive the greater sins you have committed'."

The woman stopped for a moment to let the story sink in with her audience.

"It's the next bit that shook me. He went on to say, 'If you will not forgive someone from your heart, you will be placed in prison till you have paid the last penny'."

282

She looked around and saw everyone was waiting to hear how his words had shaken her. Judith had been slightly dozing till that point trying to cope with the pain that was racking her limbs, but suddenly she had jerked into attention at hearing the last three words. She found herself speaking. "What did you say?"

The middle-aged woman smiled. "The whole story, or just the end bit?"

"Just the end bit," Judith said apologetically. "Just the last few words."

"I said, the Messiah said, 'If you will not forgive someone from your heart, you will be placed in prison till you have paid the last penny'."

Judith mumbled, "the last penny...the last penny..." and her mind went into overdrive. The self-same words from her nightmare were hitting her hard. She had to force herself to calm down, and to listen again as the woman spoke.

"These words shook me right to the core of my being. The Messiah seemed to be talking to me, right into my heart. It seemed so clear. I hated the man that raped me, the man who had destroyed my happiness with my husband and my children. AS the days had gone on, I had wanted to kill him. I knew it was a fantasy – I'd never have managed it. And fortunately for him he had moved away. But I was numb and cold. I couldn't even forgive myself for having allowed it to happen to me. I knew I wasn't the cause but somehow, I felt dirty and disgraced. I was in the prison the Messiah talked about, being tormented by my hardened heart and my unwillingness to forgive. I saw it so clearly. I needed to forgive my attacker, and I didn't know if I could. I waited till most of the others had gone and spoke to the Messiah, thanking him and telling him his words had meant something to me. He said quietly but firmly, 'You must forgive in order to be released. My Father wants to forgive you, but your own actions are causing a barrier to this. You must not hold grudges, no matter how justified you feel. My Father's forgiveness is worth much more to you than living in a prison.' He said no more, but as he had spoken, I felt within me that I had the ability to forgive my abuser. Up till that point I hadn't or wouldn't have contemplated it, but...his words, his voice, his presence seemed to make it possible. I tell you, from that moment I was healed, I was released. My prison bars were gone. I could love my family again."

The woman was crying now, and there were a few sniffles in her audience too.

"I nearly ruined my life and the lives of those in my family because of my lack of forgiveness. I was in torment and I put them through it too. I had learned that there was no point in holding my assailant accountable, and withholding forgiveness from him. Yahweh would hold him accountable. It was my responsibility to get out of the prison I had created for myself and get back to the life I'd known. Yahweh would catch up with him in the end. It was my duty to live my life the best way I could."

While the woman was speaking many things were whirling through Judith's mind. Some things she liked the sound of...and much she didn't. Clear focus had been thrown on her dream now. She understood what 'the last penny' meant now.

It was linked to forgiveness. Her forgiveness…or the lack of it. She realised that she had been in torment, not only obviously in her nightmare, but also in her thoughts. That numbness she had felt at times, that coldness, that sense of not being right in her judgments or words – it was the prison she had placed herself in because she was unwilling to forgive. Forgive who…or what? She knew the answer instinctively but couldn't bring herself to face it. It would have to wait until she could rationalise it.

Samara had taken over the meeting now and was encouraging the gathering to pray as they always did after the speaking. Judith looked around the group and saw everyone had been quite affected by the middle-aged woman's story. She had been too, but couldn't vocalise her thoughts and anxieties. She waited and listened to the others as they opened up. She felt she was just an onlooker. She didn't feel part of the meeting at all. It was as if she was an observer but an unwilling participant. The coldness and hardness she felt seemed to be increasing with every minute. It was as if they were coming to a head. She didn't know what to do about it. She had seldom felt so alienated from others in a meeting. She knew why. She was going to have to deal with it now. She couldn't put it off any longer. The expectation was that she would have to forgive. Once again, who or what? She knew this time, and she didn't like it. She wanted to shy away from it, but she knew she couldn't unless she wished to deny the Holy Spirit and his leading. She saw the face of Joe in her mind. It was smiling at her. If he was in heaven and happy, why should she deny forgiveness to those who had killed him? Then the thought struck her - or those she held indirectly responsible for his death? The thought chilled her, but she knew she wasn't finished. What had Barabbas said? He felt forgiven, not being held responsible for Joe's or Josh's deaths. This was too much for her. She felt sick. She didn't want to forgive him. How could Josh have forgiven him? Quite happily and smirking, Barabbas had allowed him to go to his death in his place. Surely forgiveness didn't fit this crime? Barabbas didn't deserve to be forgiven! Now the face of Josh came into her mind, and at the same time the trinket in her pouch vibrated. The face was just as Barabbas had described – sad and disappointed, not condemning. Was she seeing what Barabbas had seen to convince her he had actually seen it? The horrible truth hit her. Josh was sad and disappointed with her, not Barabbas. Sad and disappointed at her hardness of heart, at her refusal to forgive. Into her mind came his words just after he had been crucified. "Father, forgive them. They don't know what they are doing." She had been there that afternoon. He had forgiven those around him, those who had crucified him, those who had accused him and whipped him. And Barabbas? What about Barabbas? Her mind came into sharp focus now. Barabbas was one of the 'them'. Everyone who had conspired or contributed to his death, Josh had forgiven…and had asked his Father to forgive too. What right had she to deny it if Josh had so freely given it? "Father," she said in a whisper that was barely audible, "I don't feel I want to forgive Barabbas, but I know I have to, to be released from the prison of my hatred and the torment it's causing me. Please help me! I'm wrong to hate, I'm wrong to deny forgiveness. I ask you to help me cope, and try…" she almost choked on her words, "to show love…to…" She couldn't say it, but persevered. "I'm wrong, I know I am, and I know you're disappointed in me," Again Josh's face on the cross came back into her mind, and she felt guilty. "You're not condemning me…and you should. But I'm sorry I've disappointed you for so long. I promise I'll speak to Barabbas and…" the words couldn't come, "…and try to forgive him. Please help me! Forgive me."

Suddenly it was all clear. She had been brought to the Valley of the Outcasts for a purpose, one she hadn't considered. She hadn't been there to condemn Barabbas, but to lead him to Yahweh's forgiveness. All the time she'd been hating him, Yahweh had been speaking to him - even if she hadn't believed him. She was repentant now and felt the surge of the Holy Spirit as she opened herself up to him. A weight was lifting from her, and the ache in her body diminished radically. She felt herself beginning to faint and so she lay down. Moments later she revived, and found the whole group standing around her. They were praying, and she felt at one with them again, and enlivened. She tried to get up from her lying position, and found it much easier than she expected. After pushing herself onto her elbows and drawing her feet up under her, she made an effort to rise. Willing hands grasped her arms and pulled her to her feet. She felt strangely different. The aching in her body she had experienced for a long time, had subsided and she felt able to stand. She did so - and for a moment, things seemed precarious. Then she started to walk forward and found things much easier than before.

"Do you think you're healed, my dear?" someone asked her.

She looked at her hands and feet. Still the white blotches and the damaged skin. The numbness however seemed less, and certainly the pain much reduced.

"No…or at least, not fully," she said. "I certainly feel much better than I did when I arrived here though."

"Then perhaps we've experienced a bit of a miracle tonight," Samara said, and hugged her.

"Perhaps," said Judith, carefully. "I certainly found tonight's message helpful"

Others agreed with Judith, the expressions on their faces showing that some of them might have had a battle like her.

"It's given us much food for thought," Judith added. "I believe Yahweh's been in our midst tonight, and working on our hearts."

"And on some of our bodies too," someone wisecracked.

"Yes, and we've all been given much to think about. I know I have."

The meeting broke up and Judith felt confident and well enough to walk home unaided by Becca.

Don Treader

"You know," said Judith, "I'm glad I was there tonight. The way I felt earlier, I might easily not have gone at all!"

Chapter Thirty-Four

Over the next few days, Judith took time to think about her position and what she should do about it. Her experience at the meeting had been intense. The challenge, and her response to it, had happened at whirlwind speed - and she felt the need to appraise things, to take time to make balanced choices. She thought it funny that she had been in the Valley for almost a year and a half and it was only now that she was beginning to understand. It wasn't surprising it had taken her so long to work things out, she reasoned, as many things in her life had conspired against her, putting barriers between herself and Yahweh to make her blinkered. It was a big list – first her removal from Jerusalem caused by her disobedience, then her discovery of having leprosy. These would have been big enough to throw anyone, she thought. Then her mind went back to her first meeting with the prophet, her almost being abused by him and discovering he was Barabbas – that was something else to have contended with. The emotions, the feelings, all these things had released in her were extremely deep seated. She had tried to get on with her daily life doing what Yahweh wanted as she coped with her illness, and in many ways she had been successful – for example, the meetings, and the viaduct project. But there was the bigger picture. While all this had been going on, Yahweh was doing something else with her. Feelings and attitudes which had for long been buried deep down in her were coming to the surface - and Barabbas had awakened most of them. Two of the major traumas of her life were being exposed – Joe's death in her arms and Josh's death on the cross. She had been oh so present at both, and whether she liked it or not, they had led to attitudes being developed in her. She had thought Josh encouraging her after Joe's death, Abbas's trinket, and their picture of her –these things had helped alleviate her plight. But the sight of Barabbas had awakened the hatred she felt for the perpetrators of Joe's untimely horrible death; and the sight of Barabbas's smirking face as he had tried to take advantage of her, brought into sharp focus the fact that Josh had taken his punishment, while he had got off absolutely free – and didn't care. Only once before in her life had she hated like this - and by comparison that hatred hadn't been as bad as this. Mikha, poor Mikha, she thought. What she had put him through – and now he was no longer with her! She just hadn't seen the bigger picture, and now she was being forced to make changes. How like Yahweh it was to lead people step by step. If they were to see the end from the beginning, they would run away from making the journey. Having known Josh over the years, she could see that it was only bit by bit his purpose and destiny had been revealed to him by Abbas. And what about Stephen, she thought. He had had the joy and privilege of working miracles and testifying before the Sanhedrin, but the next step for him had been death. Her spirit lifted as she thought of his face shining like an angel as he saw Josh coming for him. Yahweh might ask difficult impossible things of us, she thought - but he makes sure he's with us when we need him. Mikha too. He had thrown himself into the work, ever since Tabitha had been raised from the dead. He had known the joys of doing that work - but to whom much has been given, much seemed to be required of them. His death had not been expected and had left Judith a widow, but Yahweh and Josh had been with them even in that terrible event. Now much was being expected of her. She had repented and made her vows before the Holy Spirit at the meeting…and now she was going to have to make good on them. She had humbled herself and renounced her hatred. She had sensed it coming to the surface and being skimmed off. Now her prison door was open and She was released, she was free. Her body even seemed to have benefitted from her confession. No more torment any more, she was ready and willing to face her task. The debris of her life's experience having been lifted from her and her vision restored, she was now prepared to see things the way Yahweh and Josh saw things, and she realised that she had been given a glorious purpose. She was privileged to be where she was, to bring Barabbas to them, to be the one that would help him on his path to faith. Somehow now, her suffering seemed minimal in comparison to the enormity of the task. It had been worth it all, and she would have gone through it all again if asked. All these days of doubting, depression, and disobedience – Yahweh and Josh had been planning this very task for her through it all. Had they not told her there would be dark days, but that she would smile again. She felt stupid for not having understood this before now. It's not as if I haven't been in a similar position in the past, she thought. It's taken me a long time to learn my lesson. But now her heart was unburdened, excited and focused. Josh had entrusted her with a major task, and she wouldn't let him down!

Having come to that understanding and decision, she now had to work out how she would go about things. She realised she was going to have to speak to Barabbas and tell him the conclusions she had come to. Would he laugh at her? Had she been right all along, and he had been stringing her along, trying to get her on side. That thought didn't sit well with her and so she put it aside. After all, if the Holy Spirit had been revealing all this to her, she would have been wrong to doubt again. She would tell him that she accepted his story and that she believed Josh wasn't condemning him, but wanted him to become a follower, a believer. Again, the doubts came. He was a zealot. He would just mock her. But she discounted this too. After all, even if he did, she should be prepared to suffer for her faith. Her experience of the past days encouraged her to believe that this would not happen though. If Yahweh and Josh had been speaking to him and at the same time speaking to her, she believed that eventually only good things would come from it. So, with this in mind, she determined to meet with Barabbas at the earliest possible moment. With her diminished pain and renewed energy, she could be seen the next day making her way down to the fields where the men were preparing things for harvest. There was no sign of him there, and after looking in the orchards, she determined to go to the new reclaimed area at the side of the valley to see if he was working there. She was disappointed. No-one had seen him for a few days. One of the women she knew who attended the meetings said that she had heard he was on retreat. "He'll be back for the harvest," she said confidently. "He always is."

Judith retraced her steps, but his non-appearance only served to make her more determined to accost him when he returned. She mentioned it to Becca that evening as they ate, and Becca confirmed that he was on retreat. "Someone told me that he had seemed quite excited about going. He had told them he had expected to meet with some important people. I can't think who they'd be. That's one thing that always intrigued me about him. When he went away on retreat, he'd have to meet with lepers like us, wouldn't he?"

"I suppose so," said Judith, who wasn't really interested in the nature of the retreat or its participants. Her main focus was on her own meeting with him, and what she would say to him when it happened.

"I can ask when he'll be back, if you like," said Becca, smiling, knowing that her sister would prefer to run a mile from him.

"Please do," said Judith. "Who would you ask? Who'd know?"

"Oh, that's easy. His group leader."

Judith looked surprised, "His group leader?"

"Yes, didn't you know? For a week or so he's been attending the group near his end of the valley. He seems to be becoming interested."

"I had heard he'd been to a group, but I thought it was only a one-off, just to see what we were doing."

"No, apparently it's a bit more than that. He scares the others in the group I believe. He says very little but takes note of all that's going on. Someone said they saw him smiling."

"Oh, that is worrying," said Judith laughing. "Try and find out when they think he's due back and let me know."

"A change of heart, Judith? I thought you didn't like him?"

"I just want to speak to him, that's all. Nothing more!" Judith said defensively.

"Of course," said Becca laughing now, amused at her sister's reply. "I'll do what I can."

The result of Becca's enquiries informed Judith that the Prophet was due back for harvest, the following week. It had been a hot dry summer and the crops were ripening perfectly. They had been blessed by the former and latter rains and it was expected that the harvest in all areas of the valley would be a plentiful and lucrative one. All the able bodied were to be recruited for the task. It would take more hands and more time to bring it in this year. As usual the prophet would be expected to join them. Although he was getting older and his body seemed marked badly with leprosy, he was still strong and vigorous, and a great asset to the work.

Judith took the days before his return to go over in her mind what she would say to him, to imagine what he might say in response and to formulate her responses to his responses. She became quite excited as she anticipated their encounter, but trying to work out how things might go gave her a headache, and eventually she gave it all up as a bad job. She would just have to trust in Yahweh, that he would show her what to say at the right time. If it was too pre-planned, she sensed it wouldn't work.

When the first day of the new week came around, Judith went down to the fields in full anticipation, but there was no sign of him there.

"He's up at the new harvest area," a man told her. "He's helping with the scything."

Judith thanked him and made her way to the side of the valley and climbed up to the higher level. She saw with satisfaction that he was busy with a group of men cutting the crop and placing the sheaves into bundles. She decided to wait till an appropriate time arose to speak to him, probably when work stopped for refreshment. She sat with her back against the wall of a wooden shelter which had been erected for the workers. From here she could get a good view of the whole valley and its myriad of labourers. It was a luscious and green scene, and it made her heart glad to see the results of her project coming to fruition. She was silently giving thanks when she was startled by a voice beside her. "Judith." She jumped visibly.

The prophet was standing beside her, looming over her. "You're a long way from your hut."

"Yes..." she stuttered. This wasn't quite the way she had wanted their encounter to begin, she thought. She had been caught off guard, and was looking stupid.

She pulled herself together and said, "Yes, I wanted to see how the work was going. I thought it would be good to see the harvest and the valley before everything was gone. I also wanted to talk to you."

He looked interested, and a bit surprised. He sat down beside her, and she could smell the sweat off his body. All her good intentions vanished for a second or two as she felt the old revulsion rise up in her. She moved away from him.

"What's wrong? I won't eat you," he said, laughing. She flinched and felt her hackles rising. Her negative reaction was being compounded. "I wanted to speak to you too, Judith," he said, and waited for her to respond.

Judith couldn't. She was struggling with her emotions. His arrival had put her on edge. Had she been stupid, she wondered, to even think things might improve between them?

"I want you to come away with me," Barabbas said.

Judith was stunned. What on earth was he doing? Why was he playing with her like this? She gasped, "Sorry?"

He looked deadly serious. "I want you to come away with me. I have something I want you to know."

All thought of reconciliation and forgiveness was gone now. Judith spat out, "Get lost! I'd never go anywhere with you. You're despicable! You're a monster - preying on vulnerable women!" Judith never cursed but at that moment she almost swore at him. She was so disappointed, so angry, so surprised at his audacity.

"No, not like that," he said, looking quite hurt and surprised by Judith's outburst. "There's something you need to know, but I can't tell you here. I need you to come with me."

"I'm going nowhere near your hut…and you can forget any thought of what you're thinking about!"

"I'm not asking you to my hut," he said. "I realise I was wrong before. I need you to go away with me – beyond the valley."

Judith's jaw dropped open. What was he suggesting? That he escape with her? That they run away together? Why was he saying this? Did he like her that much? What exactly was he talking about? Words escaped her! She only said, "You're mad!"

"It must sound that way," Barabbas said gently. He put a hand on her arm, and she shook it off angrily. "I want nothing to do with you. You're horrible!"

"Oh, that's a shame." He looked solemn now. "And I had some good news for you."

"What's that?" said Judith mocking him with heavy sarcasm in her voice.

He sighed. "I wanted to tell you this in a quieter spot, but it'll have to be here, if you're so afraid of me."

"I'm not afraid of you," Judith spat out again. "You just disgust me." She wasn't holding back now.

Don Treader

He sighed again, "Look, Judith. I believed we had a truce…" Judith glowered at him, but he continued. "When I was on retreat, I met some people who want to meet you."

Judith's jaw dropped open again.

"I told these people about our valley and your efforts to make it pay for itself. I told them about the wonderful harvest we hoped to produce, and about our intention to hit the markets with it every year from now on." He looked at her with concern in his eyes. "I spoke very highly of you, you know."

"Of me?" Judith said, startled. "Why would you do such a thing? We're enemies."

Remembering her reason for being there and how now she was so badly falling short of her goal, she looked down awkwardly.

"Because I like you, Judith. I admire you. How you've coped with your illness, adapting to our valley, and how you've raised all our spirits and hopes…" He added, "and brought the Messiah to us."

Now she really felt bad. Was he making a fool of her? But one glance at his face told her otherwise. He seemed to mean what he was saying. She cringed. She didn't want his attention. She wanted this conversation to stop

She rallied, "I thought you didn't care about the Messiah?"

"I told you before about my experience. I've come to a number of realisations since you've been here, and one of them is about the Messiah. I told you I didn't think he was condemning me for what happened, for what I did. Only you did!" He paused again. "And I understand why."

Judith squirmed at what he was saying. She knew it was the truth and she didn't like how it made her feel. "I don't need you to patronise me!" She tried to change the subject.

"Who're these people you talked about? I thought you were on retreat."

"I was," he smiled. "But over the years when I've gone away, I've sometimes met with some of my old companions, or other people in the towns."

"But you're a leper!" Judith protested.

"My compatriots know it and we keep our distance. However sometimes I cover up and go into the towns. I often meet people there, and sometimes even important ones like these people."

Judith looked interested. "So, you're not on religious business then?" Her tone was half mocking, half inquisitive.

"You've guessed it. You know very well I'm not religious. Why would I meet with anyone of that ilk? No. I do things that will benefit me, and sometimes the community."

Judith's tone was totally mocking now, "Another way you're deceiving and taking advantage of the community then."

He looked hurt. "I may not be the religious person they think I am, but I do appreciate them in my own way. After all, just like you, they took me in."

292

"I find it difficult to believe that. You're out for yourself."

"Not quite true," he sighed. "I said I'm not religious, but recently I've found my self thinking about your Messiah. The community has changed - and in some ways, so have I."

Judith looked at him. He continued, "It may surprise you, but I went to a few of your meetings before I left. The experience made me think."

Judith wondered what to say next. Was Yahweh leading her into the conversation she had intended having with him but had singularly failed to achieve? She held her peace for the moment.

Barabbas went on, "You want to know about the people I met? Well, I spoke so highly of you," he looked apologetically at her, "they insisted on meeting you. You see, they're influential in markets throughout many of the towns in Samaria, and before they place a substantial order with us, they want to meet the genius behind it all. I told them that was you."

Judith didn't know what to say. She didn't feel she could cope with this high praise coming from Barabbas. Was this just a ploy of his to entice her away from the valley to either have his way with her or to kill her...or both? She found herself reaching out in her spirit and sensed that she was on the wrong tack. It was disturbing her peace. She focused again.

"I know nothing of business. What could I tell them?"

"It's not business they want to talk with you. They simply want to see the person that's invested her time, effort, and money into the project, to see how genuine we are about exporting our goods to them. They're very sympathetic to our cause. They want to help lepers, and I thought you'd want to meet them."

"But I can't," said Judith reluctantly. "I'm a leper. I couldn't leave the valley."

"So am I," said Barabbas grinning. "If I can do it, so can you. It would benefit the community," he cajoled.

"I can't!" Judith looked distraught. She had been ill for so long and knew her limitations. Then she remembered her recent experience at the meeting, and how since then her leprosy seemed to have gone into a measure of remission. She wondered, had Yahweh allowed that to happen for a time, for a venture such as this? She felt confused. There were too many objections and difficulties.

Barabbas seemed to know what she was thinking. He smiled at her. "You're worrying if you're able. I can solve that problem by getting a donkey supplied to us. You needn't walk." He looked meaningfully at her, "If you're worrying about being alone with me - or whether I'm being genuine - you can take Becca with you. She can come with you to keep you out of harm's way." He laughed, "Meaning me."

"What would the community say?" Judith asked, wondering why she was contemplating it at all.

"They know sometimes when I return, I bring benefits from the outside world and any contacts I make. They won't be surprised at this current time when we're trying to break into markets, that potential buyers might want to meet the person behind it all." He paused, "And no-one will suspect anything if Becca comes with us."

Judith nodded thoughtfully. "I certainly want to help the community. I wouldn't like to hold things back for us. Can you definitely guarantee our safety, and all you've said about the people wanting to meet with us?"

For a moment she thought she caught a flicker of doubt in his eyes. He hesitated for a second then said, "Of course. I am the prophet. You should know that!"

Judith sensed she was dropping back into doubt because of this, but at the same time she was aware of a strong impression telling her that she should go. She decided to take the risk, and said, "Well if you can persuade Becca to go, I'll be there too."

"He seemed genuinely pleased at her response, and said, "Thank you, Judith. We can be friends?" Judith felt her doubts rising again in her. She wondered why she was even considering it. She wanted to continue hating him. She couldn't bring herself to say 'Yes'. Instead, she said slightly more coldly, "We have a truce." She got up to go, struggling to get to her feet. He tried to help her by taking her arm. She pulled away.

"I'll make sure I get good mounts for us," he said. "Oh, by the way, when I arrived you said you had been wanting to talk to me? What about?"

"Nothing. Nothing at the moment anyway," Judith said, keen to get away before she allowed her negative feelings to take over again. She had wanted to be humble and talk of forgiveness, but the conversation hadn't gone that way. Instead, some of her baser feelings seemed to have been exposed again. Now didn't seem just the right time to open a new avenue up. "Perhaps we'll have time to talk on our trip." A thought struck her, "You haven't actually told me where we're going, and how long we'll be away for."

"I didn't, did I," he said. "We'll be going to a small village about two miles outside Samaria. It's on the road between Samaria and Jerusalem. These people do a lot of travelling in the area, and they say if we get there in two days' time, they'll be spending the night there on their way to Jerusalem."

"How long will it take us to get there?"

"A good day by donkey, if we leave tomorrow morning early."

"Well, before anything happens, you'll need to see if Becca wants to accompany us. If she can't, I won't be going. "

"I understand," Barabbas said. "It's in all our interests to make the journey. We owe it to the community."

He allowed her to go, and returned to his work after taking a drink from a pitcher of water in the shelter. As Judith made her way back down into the lower valley and home, she wondered what she was letting herself in for. She sensed she was doing the right thing, but was also aware that she had almost ruined things by her initial attitude towards him. The main topic hadn't been broached yet, but she had taken from their conversation signs that Barabbas might not be the totally evil person she had believed him to be. There was some good in him after all…and he seemed to be warming to the Messiah.

Chapter Thirty-Five

Daylight was beginning to appear in the east when Judith and Becca left their hut to meet with the prophet. Both women were tired, as the previous day and night had been hectic getting things ready for leaving, meeting with well-wishers from the community, and trying to grab what little sleep they could in the remaining hours of darkness. The prophet had been as good as his word and had asked Becca if she would accompany Judith and himself on their mission. At first, she had been reticent. Since becoming a leper, she had never left the valley or its environs, preferring to keep herself separate from others and avoid being ostracised by them for compromising their health. The prophet had been persuasive and eventually she had succumbed to his pressure.

"I'm doing it for you," she told Judith that evening. "I know how you hate being in his company and I thought you might need a minder to keep the two of you apart." She grinned when she saw Judith's face. "I'm only joking sister," she said. "I thought you'd want a sister there with you for no more than company if nothing else. The prophet seemed keen that I come. He didn't seem to want you to feel worried about being on your own with him. I assumed you would never have agreed to go if you'd been in any way doubtful about his motives, so I signed up for the trip. Us sisters should stick together!"

Judith looked gratefully at her. "You're a good friend, Becca."

"That's what sisters are for. Since you've come to the valley you've helped me a lot – in many more ways than you think – it's my turn now to take this opportunity to help you…and the community. The prophet seems quite enthused by this chance to benefit the community. It's only right I get involved too. Anyhow, you're not in any fit state to travel distances."

"I have felt better since the meeting the other night," Judith said. "I have more strength than I had a week ago, and the pain isn't as intense. Travelling though – I just don't know. All three of us are at a disadvantage. The more people on the trip, the better. We can at least help each other."

Becca nodded. "We'd better get ready for the journey then. He says we might be away from the valley as long as three or four days. You must take your best robes. I'm taking mine." A mischievous grin spread over her face. "You never know what parties we might get invited to. The opportunities might be immense once we've left the valley!"

Judith looked horrified. "That's not why I'm going."

"Me neither," said Becca laughing. "But we will have to take some provisions and a change of clothes or so."

Judith went over to her bag and put in it what she thought she might need. She didn't want it to be too heavy and so she took only the basic essentials.

"Have you got room for a water bottle and some bread and fruit?" Becca asked her. "We'll take just the bare minimum. We might be able to pick up some things from the places we pass through. Did Samara see you?"

Judith knew what she was referring to. They had had a stream of visitors in the latter part of the day. Well-wishers who had heard they were leaving to help the cause of the outcasts. She had learned in her days in the community, good news, or bad news, somehow travelled fast in their little enclave. Samara had been one of them. She had been so enthusiastic about what they were doing.

"I want you to have this," she said, pressing two gold coins into Judith's hand. "This is the remains of the money you gave us to get the project up and running. I had kept it aside in case we had further expenses, but now we're about to sell our harvest, and you're on a mission to promote the community, it seems right that you take this in case you need to buy things. You won't be able to purchase anything if you go without any money."

Judith had seen the good sense in this and thanked her. "It might be useful, but if we don't use it, I'll bring it back. The community needs as much as it can get."

"Perhaps not for much longer, if you, Becca and the prophet are successful!" Samara smiled.

The three women had spent the next hour or so in prayer, asking that their mission bring good things to bear on the community. As they had talked and prayed, they had shared in an excitement at what was happening, at how the community was starting to flourish, and at the fact that the Messiah was having a stronger influence on them all.

"The numbers are growing, and whatever happens we'll keep the work going," Samara had said. "We've come too far now."

Becca for the first time seemed anxious. "What do you mean, Samara, 'Whatever happens'?"

"I'm sure it's nothing," Samara said, trying to alleviate the tension she could see in her friend's face. "It's just when I was praying, I had a deep sense that change was coming. I'm sure the Messiah will bless your journeyings and your mission." She looked fixedly at Judith. "I just want to say thank you for what you've done for us, for your kindness, your friendship – and for bringing the Messiah to us again."

"You sound as if I'm going away for good," Judith laughed. "I'll be back in a few days. You can't get rid of me that easily." The two women had hugged, but somehow Samara's words had engendered a sense of unease in Judith. Perhaps Samara had caught wind of something that might go wrong. After all, no-one really left the valley, for other towns in Samaria. She had no idea of what dangers she might face. Perhaps the prophet might not be all he seemed. She knew from past experience that he couldn't be trusted. Wy was she trusting him now? Maybe his motives were suspect. Perhaps he had plans to harm herself and Becca. This would be an ideal opportunity for him to get them out of the way, have some of his compatriots kill them, and then return to the community with a sad story about their fates. She had to pull herself out of this speculation. She had just felt a sense of oneness and excitement during their time of prayer. Why was she allowing Samara's words to unsettle her and make her think this way? She mentally shrugged her shoulders, "I'm sure Yahweh and the Messiah will be with us. They'll give us success."

"I'm sure they will. May they bless you both in all you do!" With that Samara left, after hugging them again.

Judith looked at Becca, "That was a bit strong, wasn't it?"

Becca smiled. "Haven't you noticed? Since coming to the meetings, Samara's become more intense. She's become more serious. That's not a bad thing. I'd ignore the dramatic. She means well, and only wants the best for us."

Judith agreed and got on with putting the final objects into her bag. She swithered about taking her picture. Her sense of unease made her wonder if it would be safe while she was away. She had never known there to be any crime in the community since she had been there. Everyone was in the same position - poor and diseased - and no-one wanted to make the lives of their friends any worse by stealing from them. She would however be away for a few days, and there was always a first time. Now she was being ludicrous. It was more likely, she felt, that she didn't want to be parted from it, as it had always been with her and had afforded her comfort when she had needed it. Who knows what she might encounter while she was away? She took it from the dresser and stuffed it inside her bag just in case. Becca noticed, but said nothing, and after a quick drink they both settled down for a night of fitful but excited sleep.

Judith was already breathing heavily as she carried her bag up the steep path that took them out of their valley. The early morning air was cold, and she shivered. It had been agreed that they would meet the prophet at Jacob's well and Judith was glad that she wouldn't have to walk much further than that. The prophet had indicated to Becca he would make sure they had some form of transport as the distance they would have to travel was no small one. They would be going to a village just south of the city of Samaria, on the road to Jerusalem, and it would take them a full day, if not more, to get there.

They arrived at Jacob's well to see the prophet standing beside a cart and two donkeys. "Our friends have provided well for us," he said as he checked the animals were harnessed properly to the cart. "Nothing but comfort for you both! Feel free to walk or to get under the awning, especially when the sun gets up."

The two women were impressed. He had obviously gone to much trouble to pull the strings that had secured them their ride. Both decided to get aboard so they could stow their bags away and avoid doing too much walking. The donkeys would be able to take the strain.

The morning passed fairly uneventfully, both women feeling a sense of excitement, and if truth be told, a degree of exhilaration from being out of the Valley of the Outcasts. It was an adventure to be going to another village and to meet with people who wanted to help the community. Yes, they knew they would have to stay apart from them, and probably not enter an enclosed area because of their condition, but still, doing something different, being somewhere different, made them feel good.

"I've never negotiated with anyone except for cloth for our clothes," said Judith somewhat abashed. "I'm not sure if doing a deal for our produce is something I'll be good at."

"Nonsense, sister," Becca said encouragingly. "Just look at how you got the committee to take on the project. It's only right you help us promote the community."

"Maybe, but this is such a strange situation. Why could these people who want our goods not just deal with the prophet, or someone from one of the other villages?"

"My guess is as good as yours. But the prophet seems to believe in you and in what you'll be able to achieve."

Judith looked unsettled. "Why? We've never been on the best of terms, and we're totally different people." She wondered if she should say any more to Becca about the prophet seeing as they were embarking on what might have been a dangerous mission, but she decided against it. He was sitting up front and might have heard what she said. "Well, we'll have to make the best of it. As long as the community benefits." She thought for a moment. "How should we disguise our leprosy?"

"We'll keep our hoods up, and make sure our hands and feet aren't too exposed. But you're forgetting something…"

Judith looked at her questioningly.

"They know we're lepers. We come from a leper colony."

"I know that. I was just wondering how we should take precautions from causing possible dissention…especially if we go into a village or town."

"We just cover up and hope," said Becca smiling.

"And suppose at the end of the day they take one look at us and say they aren't interested?"

"Their loss," said Becca, "but the prophet seems quite confident of their sincerity. I don't think he'd bring us here unless he was sure."

Judith nodded. She still felt unsure about his motives though. She continued, "But what if things aren't the way he says they are? What if he's brought us out here for another purpose?"

"Have you seen the way he looks at you?"

Judith was startled, "No. What do you mean, Becca?"

"He likes you. You can tell he admires you. He softens any time he is near us, sister."

"Maybe it's you he likes," Judith countered.

Becca shook her head. "My money's on you. You've kept away from him. Maybe he sees you as a bit of a challenge. This deal might be his way of getting you to warm to him."

Judith thought for a moment. "We did hear he had attended one or two of the meetings. Maybe they're softening him up!" She didn't want to admit it to herself, but that thought had occurred to her too on a few occasions.

"What are you two women talking about?" came the prophet's voice from the front of the cart. "Do you need a break?"

"No," said Becca nudging Judith. "It's just sister talk."

They heard a short laugh from the front …and the cart trundled on.

They stopped for something to eat when the sun was high in the sky. The donkeys were unyoked and tied up to a tree beside a patch of rough grass, which they started to munch. After eating and saying very little, the prophet asked if they minded him lying under the awning to take a short nap. They arranged themselves in the cart to give themselves adequate space, and each of them tried to doze. It was hot, they'd eaten well, and sleepiness was setting in. Becca was the first to snooze, her gentle breathing coming in short bursts. After a little time, Judith became aware of being watched. She looked over Becca's body to see the prophet propped up on one elbow staring at her.

"What do you want?" she whispered coldly.

"Nothing," he whispered back. "I'm just interested in what makes you tick. You're not like the other women in the community."

Judith said nothing. She wondered what was coming.

He continued, "I've come to appreciate you – your attitude, your work and your efforts. Following the Messiah has made you different."

"That's what it's all about. He came to change us…if we let him."

"But not me?" he said, a hint of sarcasm in his voice.

Judith said nothing for a moment trying to work out her response. Was this her time to talk about forgiveness, she wondered, but put the thought aside. She didn't want to talk about it over Becca's sleeping body. It could wait. Instead, she said, "You sent him to his death, the one you should have had." She felt a numbness beginning to spread over her spirit because of her words. She added, "I do believe he came to forgive those who're really sorry and want to come to Yahweh."

"So do I," he said. She was taken aback at his agreement with her. Was he just playing her along? Was he just trying to melt her resolve?

He changed the subject, "Yesterday morning you came to find me. You said you'd something to say to me. You never did say."

Was this her chance to tell him what she had intended to? She might have said something if Becca hadn't at that moment woken up with a jerk and a loud snort. She looked groggily at each of them. "You've been talking?" she said.

The prophet laughed. "We couldn't sleep because of the snoring, Becca."

Becca looked apologetic. "I'm sorry," she said. "I was hot and tired. Have you both worked out your strategy as to how to deal with the buyers?"

"I'm leaving that to Yahweh and Judith," the prophet said smiling. He sat up. "No more time left for sleep though. Unless we start now, we'll not make the appointment in time." He took a drink from his water bottle, left the cart to harness up the donkeys, and soon they were on their way again.

Judith noticed that the terrain was changing. They had been travelling along a flat arid piece of scrubland, but now as the mountains, Ebal and Gerizim, were being left far behind, the ground became more rocky and rough. The cart bumped along more unstably now and was making a good number of creaking sounds. It was clear that the prophet knew where he was going and was taking a shortcut over the scrub to get to the Jerusalem Samaria road. He said as much. "I'm trying to make for the Jerusalem road. Apologies if the ride is becoming more uncomfortable. It won't be long until things get smoother again. We may be late though. I hope we don't miss them. It would be a journey wasted then."

"I thought we were making good time," Becca called.

"Come out of the cart for a moment and look up," came the prophet's response.

Both women got out once the cart had slowed down and stopped. What they saw amazed them. They were used to cloudless blue skies, but now in the distance, in the direction they were travelling, black clouds seemed to be building up.

"We might get hit by a storm," the prophet said. "They can be quite vicious at this time of year. It's the build-up of heat. We'll need to go faster if we can, so we get to the village before it breaks."

Within half an hour there was a strong wind blowing, and the black clouds seemed to be moving their way rapidly.

"Do you think we'll make it?" Becca asked.

"Not at the speed these clouds are moving. There's a lot of rain with them…and did you hear that thunder?"

The women had assumed the noise they had just heard far away in the distance was perhaps something to do with the increasing wind.

"I'm afraid we won't have time to stop if it hits us," the prophet said wryly. "We have to make that appointment."

The two women looked at each other, got back under the awning, and gave some moments to prayer.

An hour later, the prophet shouted, "That's us on the Jerusalem road now, but I'm afraid we're going to have a rough ride."

The women knew exactly what he meant. The awning was flapping madly in the wind which was getting stronger by the minute. Peals of thunder were getting closer, and although the cart was on a flatter road, the wind was causing it to be unstable. Although it was only mid-afternoon the sky was dark with looming clouds. Then the rain came, large drops bouncing off the awning and running down the sides of the cart. The prophet continued driving, his hooded robe sodden with the rain. The donkeys didn't like it and slowed down, but they kept moving with the goading of the prophet.

Judith took a chance to look out and saw that once again their landscape had changed. They were going uphill now, and the road had more bends in it. There was still scrubland on either side of them, but from time to time the road seemed more elevated to negotiate the rocky ground, and there were furrows and deep ditches on either side of it at particularly high spots.

"Shouldn't we stop?" she asked the prophet. "The clouds are making things dark…and the rain doesn't help either. It must be difficult to see where you're going."

"Why do you think we've met no-one else on the road? It's been deserted for miles. Everyone must have seen the storm coming and stayed where they were." The prophet looked grim. "We'll keep going though."

Suddenly there was a flash of lightening followed by a loud burst of thunder. The donkeys squealed and brayed, but the prophet kept them moving.

"Hopefully it'll pass soon," he said.

"It doesn't look like it," Judith said, beginning to worry. "The clouds are even blacker than they were earlier – and the road's getting steeper. Are you sure you can see where you're going? The rain's driving right into us."

"So far so good. I have left the road a couple of times but that was on the flat. We'll just have to trust your Messiah to help us."

Judith didn't know whether he was mocking her or not. She put her head back under the awning to keep dry.

Don Treader

Seconds later, there was a powerful flash of lightening which lit everything up under the awning. It was immediately followed by an almighty burst of thunder which shook the cart. The donkeys squealed in terror and tried to bolt. They were frantic and the cart sped up, regardless of the efforts of the prophet to calm them down. Suddenly there was a crashing sound and a sense of falling. The noise was tremendous and the two women screamed. The cart seemed to be turning over onto its side and the contents of it were scattered everywhere. The women were thrown into each other and then found themselves lying on the awning which now seemed to be resting on the ground. The cart was on its side, the donkeys were shrieking , and water was getting everywhere. Judith and Becca crawled out through a huge tear in the awning, and found themselves in a deep ditch, the road a good few feet above them. They were lying in a pool of rainwater and mud. There was a groaning coming from the front end of the cart, and they assumed it must have been the prophet. His groans were overshadowed by the frightened brayings of the donkeys. One of them had managed to get out of its harness though, the yoke having snapped leaving bits of wood hanging from him. As they watched, he bolted into the scrubland. The other donkey hadn't been so fortunate and was still connected to the cart. The yoke was twisted round him, and he was showing signs of major trauma. They made their way to where the prophet was groaning and heard him say, "I'm all right. I'll live. Go and release the donkey from the yoke. He'll die of shock if you don't." Becca who had had a farming background went over to the donkey who was kicking and lashing out hoping to free himself. She positioned herself carefully and loosened the restraints. The donkey struggled to his feet, brayed loudly, shook, and then bolted into the countryside after his companion.

Judith who had been left with the prophet tried to help him to his feet. He was still groaning, and said, "Don't pull at me. I'm trapped I think."

Becca was back now and the two women inspected their surroundings. It appeared that when the cart had sped up when the donkeys had bolted in panic, it had been dragged off the road and fallen into a deep ditch. The prophet must have fallen off as the cart was turning over, and part of it was now lying on top of him.

"I can't feel my legs," he said. "I think they're caught under the wheel."

"You're right," Judith said. "We'll try and lift it off you."

"You won't manage. It's too heavy," he said, groaning loudly again. "The pain in my chest is getting worse too."

Both women looked at each other. "We'll try to get you out," Becca said. "Don't give up!"

"It'll take a lot more than this for me to give up," he rasped, and Judith thought she saw some blood at the corner of his mouth.

Both women struggled to position themselves at points where they might be able to lift the cart off him, but no matter how much they strained and pushed, the cart was too heavy for them and eventually they had to give up. "We can't do

304

anything at the moment," Becca said, giving up. "Perhaps another traveller will come along and help us."

"No hope of that," the prophet rasped. "We've seen no-one on this road since we joined it. There'll be no-one till morning now. It might be too late!"

Judith knew what he meant. He knew how badly he was injured. Perhaps he even thought he would die. She didn't know the extent of his injuries, but if his legs were crushed under the cart, his chest had been wounded and there was blood coming out of his mouth, he may indeed have been dying.

"Look," said Becca. "You stay here and help the prophet. Do what you can to make him comfortable. Try and keep him dry. I'll go and try to get a hold of the donkeys before they get too far away. I think I see one of them standing over there." She pointed. "I'll be back if I can get a hold of them. We may need them to get the prophet to the nearest village."

Judith nodded. "I'll do what I can for the prophet. You go. Do your best!" Becca left.

"Well, now you've got your way," Barabbas croaked, his voice crackling.

"My way?" Judith raised an eyebrow.

"You've always wanted me to be punished. I missed out the first time! Remember?" He looked a pathetic figure, the rain running down his face and his robe sodden.

"We'll have to get you out of here. You can't lie in this water."

"You're not going to get me out of here fast," he said. "Leave me to what I deserve."

Judith felt sorry for him. She could see he was suffering and trying not to show it. The rain was heavier now and was bouncing off them. She had to constantly wipe her face so she could see. Was the water in the ditch rising, she wondered? At the rain's current rate of downfall, the ditch would soon be full. He'll drown, she thought.

"We have to do something to get you free," she said. "If we can get you out of here, there's an overhanging rock over there we can keep you dry under." She tried to lift the cart on her own without success.

"You go to the rock," he whispered. "Leave me alone. It's all I deserve."

Was he beginning to worry about his fate, she wondered? She felt pity welling up in her heart. She may have hated what he'd done, but no-one deserved to die this way. An image of Josh hanging on the cross flashed into her mind. He did, she thought. If anyone deserved a horrible death, he did after what he'd allowed to happen to Josh! Josh's face was sad, and his eyes stared at her. Could she hold onto that anger under that stare?

Barabbas groaned again and let out a cry of pain. "I'm not going to make it," he said. "Save yourself!"

Judith knew she could have gone away and left him, and maybe if this had been an earlier time she might well have done so. But now...she couldn't bring herself to do so. She couldn't leave him lying there, any more than she could have left Josh to die on his own. She had stayed to the bitter end with Josh. She determined to stay to the bitter end with Barabbas too. Maybe this was her chance to talk to him - perhaps her last chance. She knew she had been instructed to forgive him, but now...when he was dying? Did Josh want her to speak? What better time than this!

She noticed blood was still coming from his mouth and was being washed away as fast as it appeared by the ever-falling rain. His face looked strange in the dim light and she wanted to wipe it dry to make him more comfortable. She took the loose corner of her hood and moved her head close to his to allow the cloth to wipe his face. It was the least she could do for him in the situation. A second later she gasped and started back. "You're not..." She had trouble speaking, "You're not..."

As she had dabbed at his face with the cloth to take away the wetness, she had seen that the familiar white blotches of leprosy were different. They seemed to have run in the rain causing them to streak. She had never looked at his face in great detail before, but she was sure it hadn't been like that. She had rubbed at one of these blotches and had found that she could wipe it away, wipe it off.

"I'm not what?" he said, struggling to speak. He coughed and more blood appeared. "I'm not a leper?"

Judith was too traumatised to speak. She just nodded. All her thoughts of forgiveness were gone.

When she could speak again, she said, "You're despicable! You never were a leper. It's the final insult. You led all these people in the valley to believe you were one of them. You deserve all you get. I didn't think anyone could sink so low, but I was wrong. You're the worst!"

"No," Barabbas rasped, his voice coming in short bursts now. "I was a leper until your Messiah..." His head fell back as he lost consciousness.

Judith didn't know what to do. Had he died on her? Died while she had been railing at him? She didn't feel quite so good now. She could still see Josh's face staring at her. She hadn't done what she had been told to do. She had been justified to feel annoyed. He was a fake...but was he? What was he going to tell her about her Messiah? She suddenly felt very sorry and very empty. She had missed her opportunity. Would he be consigned to hell because she hadn't forgiven him? Would she, for having been disobedient? She started to weep, tears rain and mud being her only companions. His body moved ever so slightly as it racked in pain under the weight of the cart. He wasn't dead! Was she too late? Could she, even after discovering he was no leper? She decided that if she didn't do something now, she might lose her chance forever. She kissed his forehead, and whispered close to his ear, "I forgive you; I forgive you."

Suddenly around her there was a powerful blinding flash of lightening. She heard it crackle as it hit something. She was terrified and a terrific pain went through her body. She felt sick and drained. A split second later came the thunder and it deafened her ears and shook the ground. It was directly overhead. Then a blue tinged flash of white lightening again followed by another clap of thunder. The ground was moving! Was it an earthquake? Whatever the case, she heard a creaking and crackling, not unlike that of a tree beginning to fall. The cart was shifting its position as it settled deeper into the ditch. It seemed to have settled in such a way that the wheel pinning Barabbas's legs had been raised up and was no longer crushing him She tried to get her hands under the wheel to see if she could push it further, but in doing so she noticed it was raised enough to let her slide Barabbas's legs from under it. She managed to free them with an almighty struggle, just before the cart moved again and the wheel sank into the mud. She was fortunate to have pulled her hands out of the way in time. Barabbas was still unconscious, but she determined to drag him away from the ditch and get him under the overhanging rock. She didn't think she would be able to pull him out of the ditch, but she was amazingly surprised at how light he was. For a big man he didn't carry much weight. After about ten minutes or so of expending a great deal of energy, she had him propped up under the rock, and gave thanks for the fact they were both out of the driving rain, even if they were soaking. On reflection, she wondered how she had ever managed to get this burly man away from the ditch at all, especially in her condition. She had seemed to have superhuman strength as she manoeuvred him, puffing badly. The rain didn't let up, but thankfully the lightning flashes were further apart now and the thunder seemed to be passing. She wondered how Becca was getting on.

"I'm not dead then?" Barabbas's voice came from beside her. She looked at him and saw his eyes looking straight at her. "You've forgiven me!" he said, his voice strengthening. "I don't deserve it, but thank you."

"I was coming to tell you that yesterday morning," Judith said. "That's why I came to find you. I was instructed to do so."

"Instructed?"

"Yes. I wanted to. My Messiah…"

He cut her short, "Our Messiah!"

Judith looked at him incredulously.

"I know him too!"

"How? Where? When…?" Judith was stunned and lost for words

" I believed…" He fell into unconsciousness again, leaving Judith with her questions and thoughts. Was he claiming Josh as his Messiah? It seemed like it. But what about all the lies, all the deception? What about how he had treated Josh? Judith couldn't get her head around it. She would have to wait till he came round again. It would appear he might have been telling the truth about Josh appearing to him and not condemning him. But what about him lying about being a leper? He surely couldn't have stayed in a leper colony untouched by it, especially if he had been having relations with the women? Her head hurt. She couldn't work it out. Fortunately, the rain was beginning to ease off now and the cold air that had accompanied the storm was being replaced by warmer air.

Barabbas came around again. "You're still here," he said, as if he had expected she would leave him.

"Of course, where would I go?"

"I thought you would have given up on me. How did I get here? Where's the cart?"

She told him about the lightening, and how the cart had moved just enough for her to drag him free.

"And you managed to get me to this rock?" he looked surprised. "In your condition?"

Judith heard a scuffling on the other side of the rock, and she called out, "Becca. We're round here!"

The scuffling came nearer. Judith called out again, "Becca!"

Suddenly around the rock came something that hurled itself at her, and almost winded her as it hit her.

"Faithie!" shouted Judith, amazed and overwhelmed. "Faithie!"

The reunion was wonderful. Both of them were soaking but that didn't stop them showing their happiness at seeing each other again. "Faithie, I can't believe it's you!" After the trauma of the day, Judith was crying now. Everything had just been too much, but it had ended in joy.

"A dog. You know it?"

Faithie was licking the tears away from Judith's face. "Yes. It's Little Faith."

"Little Faith? It can't be your dog! You never…"

"She was my dog. I'd know her anywhere."

"But how's she here? How could she find you…if it is your dog?"

"Not my dog, but the Messiah's. He gave her to me, then he took her away again when she was ill."

"So, he's sent her to you just now?" Barabbas looked sceptically at her.

"Yes. Why not? He did so before." Judith explained how she had arrived at the community.

"I wouldn't believe you. It's so farfetched. But because of everything that's happened to me, nothing's impossible!"

At that point they heard a voice calling from some distance away. "Judith…prophet!" Becca was trying to find them. Little Faith barked. And ran round the rock to greet her.

They heard her exclaim as Faithie jumped up on her to lick her. They heard her laugh.

"Over here, Becca!" Judith called. "We're under this rock."

Becca came in under it, escorted by Faithie. "I've found a dog!" she exclaimed. "Friendly."

"Definitely. Meet Little Faith!" said Judith proudly.

"The Messiah's dog," said Barabbas dryly, but trying to smile.

Becca looked bemused, but passed on the explanation and asked, "How on earth did you get the prophet out of there?"

Judith explained and Becca looked impressed. "It's fortunate the lightning struck at the right moment," she said.

"Indeed," said Judith. "At first I thought I'd been struck by it. It was all around us and it was crackling. A pain shot through me. I'm glad it's gone now."

"I had a similar experience," said Becca. "The lightening was bright, and it lasted long enough for me to see the donkeys were nowhere near. It felt as if I'd been hit too by one of the flashes. I landed on the ground. I got up and kept looking, but I'm afraid I've come back empty handed. I just can't find them."

"Maybe they'll come back by morning, when they are less frightened," suggested Barabbas.

Becca looked doubtful. She changed the subject, "How are you now? You definitely took the brunt of that accident."

"Now I've got the cart off me, I'm feeling better. My legs and chest are painful, but I'll live."

"There's no blood now," said Judith. "You were bleeding from the mouth earlier."

"I think I bit my tongue when I hit the ground. It's stopped bleeding now, although it's extremely sore."

"Good," said Becca. "Can you walk?"

"I don't think so. I've been trying to move my legs, but they're very painful. We can't walk anywhere now anyway. It's dark. We're best to wait here till morning. Someone will pass then. I'm sorry."

"What for?" Becca asked.

"For not getting us where we were going."

"Don't we still have time?" asked Judith. "One of us could walk, while the others stay here. We wouldn't be letting down the community then if a deal can still be done."

"It's dark," said Barabbas.

"But once the clouds go there'll be a bit of daylight," Judith said.

"No. The storm's gone, and it's dark now. We missed the sunset," Barabbas said wryly. "Anyhow, I've not been quite straight with you. There's no appointment - at least, not the one you're expecting anyway."

Judith suddenly felt fear rising inside her. She felt sick in her throat and terrified. Had her doubts been right all along? Had he been planning to harm them, to get them out of the way? Had she been mistaken to trust him and the Spirit?

"Don't, Judith," Barabbas said. "Don't do that. It's not what you think. Nothing's what you think."

Judith found her voice, "Just like you're not a leper? You deceived everyone for all these years!"

Becca looked worried. "You can't say that to the prophet!" she rebuked Judith. "He's as much a leper as we are."

"Oh no! Just take a look, Becca!"

Becca peered at Barabbas's face, and gasped. "Where's the leprosy? What's happened to you?"

"He's deceived everyone all along. Just as he's deceiving us now. I wiped off some of the white he'd painted his face with."

Becca looked stunned. Deceit on this level had never occurred to her. "Why…why would anyone want to live as a leper if they weren't one?"

"If they had a reason to hide from the authorities and get away with exploiting women," said Judith angrily. She looked at Barabbas, and said, "Go on. Tell her!"

Barabbas looked awkward, but said, "I can explain. Please give me a chance."

Both women looked at him sceptically awaiting his explanation

"I was a leper. Everything is as I told you Judith. I arrived in the community having somehow just having contracted it." He looked apologetically at Becca. "You people accepted me as one of your own. You somehow thought I was a prophet, and I didn't deny it. Yes, I did take advantage of some, but most of them wanted me to. I was wrong."

"Meet Barabbas, Becca. He's one of us," said Judith dryly.

"One of us? What do you mean? A leper?" Becca asked. "I'm confused."

"No, Barabbas claims to be a believer now too."

Becca looked bewildered, "Who's Barabbas?"

"This man who's been living among you is a robber, a thief, a zealot. Oh, by the way, he's also a murderer!"

Becca was struggling to take this in. "How…?"

"I recognised him," said Judith triumphantly. "You remember how when I told you how Josh the Messiah died, a murderer had been exchanged for him. The murderer was set free and Josh got his punishment. Well, now - meet the murderer!"

Barabbas looked down ashamedly.

"He was hiding from the Romans. Your community was a good place for him to lie low. Who would have thought of looking for him living with lepers? The retreats he went on were to meet with his compatriots. You've been deceived, well and truly."

"No wonder you kept away from him," said Becca, looking thoughtful. "But why didn't you tell us?"

It was now Judith's turn to look ashamed. "I couldn't," she said. "Who would have believed me? I was new. I was unknown. He would have had me put out of the community, and I had nowhere else to go in my state. I needed to stay."

"Yes, we came to a truce," said Barabbas unhelpfully. "I promised not to throw you out if you didn't expose me." He looked at Judith, "I'm sorry."

Little Faithie had been lying partially on Judith's lap sleeping. She now raised her head, expecting strokes.

"You've not got the whole story," said Barabbas, looking pained. "I was a leper till a few days ago. I didn't deceive you about that."

Both women looked at him disbelievingly.

"I did try to benefit the community in my own way, but I did take advantage of you. I'm sorry about that. In your own way Judith, you helped me to see It. The community has changed over the months. Your project, and the influence you've had for the Messiah, has warmed me to you…and to Him. But that's not all. You need to hear this."

Faithie fell asleep again and Judith stroked her head gently.

"Last week I was on retreat from the community. Yes, you're right, Judith, I took these times of retreat to meet with my friends. We kept a safe distance because of my leprosy, or I would cover up and go into towns without people knowing I was unclean. I could keep in touch with what was going on then, and it was a welcome release from having to be 'the prophet'." He looked apologetically at Becca. "It was the end of my trip and I was about to return to the community when I went into one of the markets in Samaria. Yes, I managed to infiltrate there. I saw a big man speaking to a crowd. I thought I'd join them and see what was going on. He was laying his hands on some of the people and praying for them. They actually seemed to be getting better. I saw a blind man walk away seeing., a lame man walk, a man with demons screamed and the demons were gone. Then he was calling to the crowd, 'Does anyone else want to be healed. Jesus the Messiah has power to do it. Only believe.' When I heard the name 'Jesus the Messiah' I knew exactly who he was and I wanted to slink away, to melt into the crowd and be gone. I would love to have been healed, but you Judith taught me that I didn't deserve anything from the Messiah, who had been crucified because of me. I couldn't expect anything from him after what I'd done. I was leaving the crowd when another of his followers - a younger man - accosted me and started talking about the Messiah. I tried to pull away from him, but he grabbed my arm and looked into my face. I saw him gasp, then recover himself. 'You're a leper,' he said quietly. 'Jesus can heal you.' I tried to wrench my arm out of his grasp. If only he'd known who I was, he wouldn't have bothered about me. I felt so guilty. I had to get away. Perhaps he saw something in me that wanted to be healed, and he didn't let go. He simply said, 'In the name of Jesus Christ of Nazareth, be healed.' I can honestly say I felt nothing. I was just so desperate to get away. But he led me to the front, to where his friend was speaking, and said, 'This man's just been healed of leprosy.' And a huge shout went up from the crowd. I was annoyed at being put in this position. I stood there cursing and shouting. I said, 'Look, these people are deceiving you!' I pulled down my hood for all to see the blotches, my leprosy. Again, another yell went up, and people started clapping and praising the Messiah. I was bewildered. Why were they doing this? 'You're healed, brother!' the man beside me said. 'No sign of the leprosy now.' I didn't believe him and ran out of the market Feeling greatly humiliated. I ran until I saw a piece of metal and looked at my reflection in it. The blotches were gone! I was healed! I couldn't believe it. How could this Jesus whom I'd consigned to death have healed me, and forgiven me? I assumed he had forgiven me if he'd healed me. I felt so unworthy. I felt so guilty. I went to the room I had rented, and wept. I didn't deserve this. Twice in my life I had encountered this Jesus and been helped by him. First, he had taken my punishment for me, and now my leprosy. Why? While I was weeping, I saw his face. It was the same face I had seen the night I had contracted the leprosy and found the community. This time it wasn't sad, but full of joy. I felt good. I felt forgiven. I hadn't realised it, but I must have been carrying a lot of guilt. I now felt absolutely free. I didn't have to deceive anyone any more. All the discomfort I had felt from the leprosy was gone too. I really had been healed - outside and inside. I wanted to give thanks, so I decided to go back to the market and see if the healers were still there. They were, and I thanked them profusely for what they had done for me. I was overjoyed, and they were happy too. Their work had been going well that day. Of course, I didn't tell them who I was. Neither of the men seemed to recognise me, and I decided it would be best to leave it that way. They might have somehow wanted to take back my healing had they known, I thought. The crowd was thinning, and I was about to leave when the younger of the two came up to me and said, 'You live in these parts. I wonder if you can help us.' 'If I can,' I said, only too glad to be of service after what they had done for me. 'We're looking for a woman who went missing somewhere in this vicinity we think, between here and Jerusalem, about a year and a half ago.' 'I'm sure I can't,' I said. 'I lived in a leper community.' He smiled, 'Of course you did. I should have known. Anyhow if you have met her, or come across her in the future, remember, her name is Judith. It's not a common name in these parts.' I tell you, that fairly shook me, and so I described you to him. 'It sounds like you know her,' he said. 'Where is she?' 'She's living in my leper community,' I told him. 'But she's not a leper,' he said. 'She never had leprosy.' 'She is now,' I corrected him. 'She tells our people about the Messiah.' 'That's Judith!' he said. 'I must meet her.' 'But she's a leper,' I said. 'And so were you,' he laughed. 'I want to meet her. Can you bring her to me? Her family will want to know if she is still alive.' 'You mean they don't know?' I said. 'No. She disappeared on a journey to Galilee. We presumed she was dead, when we heard that she'd disappeared on the way there and didn't reach Galilee. You know, a woman alone...' 'It's the least I can do for you, after what you've done for me,' I said. 'I'll go back to the community and bring her back to meet you in two days' time.' He told me they were due to return to Jerusalem in two days, and in the evening they'd be staying in a friend's house in the village we were making for. I'm sorry Judith, I'm not able to get you there. I really wanted to help you." He looked genuinely sorry.

As he was speaking, Judith had gone from the depths of fear and anger to the heights of joy and appreciation. Barabbas looked relieved as he saw her face brighten.

"Why didn't you tell us this?" she asked, "instead of inventing all these lies about buyers of produce."

"I didn't think you would believe me," Barabbas said. "I didn't think you would trust me or come with me. The story about doing a deal for the community seemed a better bet."

"I probably wouldn't have," Judith admitted. "Most people in the community know my story, and no doubt it had reached your ears too. I would have thought it to be a ploy to get rid of me as we were both enemies."

"That's why I invented the story. And blotched up my face too."

Judith nodded slowly. "And now I've missed the opportunity to get home." She shrugged her shoulders. "It doesn't matter anyway. I'd never have been able to go back with them. I'm a leper. There was probably very little chance they'd let me near them, but at least they can tell my family now that I'm still alive - for the moment anyway."

Becca had been listening and looked at her sympathetically. "Sister, you're going to meet them!"

"How can I?" asked Judith looking deflated. "I don't know where they are, and we're stuck here."

"Let me think," said Becca. "You told the prophet a few moments ago that the dog led you to our community?"

Judith nodded.

Barabbas said, "He's the Messiah's dog, you said."

"Not he..." Judith said. "Faithie's a girl, a good girl!" She gave her a hug which ended up with Faithie squealing in appreciation and burrowing into her.

"Well if that happened then, and the Messiah sent her to you, why's he sent her again?" asked Becca. "Are we being shown something here?"

Judith took up the thought, "You think she's here for a purpose, just as before? To take me to them?" She recoiled from the thought. "Surely not. It's dark, the ground's difficult, and I've no idea where I'd be going."

"That didn't stop you before!" Becca was smiling. "I'd stay here with the prophet, and you could go and meet these people. You could also bring help."

Judith looked dubious. "It's not the same," she said. "And I can't go into a strange village, knocking on doors and asking to speak to people travelling to Jerusalem, saying, 'I'm a leper, are there people here expecting to meet me?'"

At that moment the moon appeared through a hole in the clouds. They looked up in surprise as it lit up the landscape around them.

"Well, that's one of your problems gone," said Becca. "You'll be able to see where the dog's taking you."

Judith looked scared. "But, I can't…" She began to cry. The challenge was just too much for her. She brushed away her tears realising she was being selfish. Not only was she indulging her fears, but she was also denying all of them the possibility of help. The cart broken, the donkeys gone, one of them injured and the other two of them weak…and lepers – it was unreasonable for her not to go for help. She became aware that the other two were staring at her and felt embarrassed at her show of emotion. "I'm sorry," she said.

But her companions didn't appear to be listening. They just kept staring at her as if she had grown horns.

"Judith," Barabbas said, looking stunned.

"What!" she said impatiently, feeling awkward under their gazes.

"Judith!" he said again. She looked at him, wondering why he was saying her name like that.

"Your face!" he said. "Your face. Feel your face!"

She wanted to tell him to leave her alone. She had decided to keep the appointment even if it was against her better judgment. But because the others appeared mesmerized, she decided to humour him and put her hands to her face. She didn't know what she was looking for, but it was clear they were seeing something in the light of the moon. She felt for a bruise, a lump, or a cut. Nothing. She was about to say, "Stop it. There's nothing wrong with me," when she felt it, or more accurately, didn't feel it. Her skin was smooth. It wasn't rough in patches, lined and pocked as before. It was soft and smooth, baby smooth. Her hands went instinctively to her nose. It was perfect, no longer rough and wasting away. She squeezed it. She could feel it. There was no numbness now.

"You've been healed!" Becca gasped. "Your leprosy's gone. It's really gone!"

Judith was having trouble believing. Her next thought was to examine her hands. She held them up to her face, and then out to her companions, "The blotches are gone. The white patches – I can't see one. I can really feel my fingers again! See!"

Next, she looked at her feet and saw that the same story could be told. She felt for the toe which had partially fallen off. It was there! Fully restored! She could barely believe it, but it was true. All of it was true!

314

"I can't believe it," she said. She looked at Barabbas, "That flash of lightening and crash of thunder – you know, the one that made it possible to get you out from under the wheel – I thought at the time I'd been struck by it. It crackled all around me, and I felt an intense pain." She paused, "But since then…with all that's happened – getting you under this rock, Faithie arriving and Becca returning without the donkeys – I've not felt any pain or ache since then, I think. I feel nothing now. In fact, I feel strong." She paused again, "I wondered how I'd been able to drag you here!"

While she'd been talking, Becca had pulled down her own sodden hood and was feeling her face. She let out a shriek of joy. "I'm healed too! I can't feel anything – I mean, the pain. It's all gone too." She smiled at Judith, "My face is as smooth and as pure as yours! When that crack of lightning knocked me to the ground …I felt a sharp pain going through me the same as you…" She didn't need to finish her sentence. "We've been healed!" she yelled.

Faith, who had been dozing on Judith's lap till that point, jumped up and started to bark, happy to see them happy. They were up and dancing now, Little Faith bounding between them. Shouts of joy filled the night air. Even Barabbas was thanking the Messiah. When the two women sat down again, they noticed he had been crying.

"I'm so glad for you both," He said. "I struggled with my own miracle and forgiveness the other day, but now I'm struggling even more! It's so wonderful, I believe. I believe!"

They were indeed a beleaguered sodden little group, but anyone coming across them would have thought they were having the party of a lifetime. The rejoicing was loud and real!

"Let's pray!" said Barabbas. "I want to pray. We need to pray – to thank Messiah for his goodness."

Judith and Becca sat down beside him again, Little Faithie sitting in between them.

Becca looked at Barabbas and said, "You realise you're our brother now!" They all laughed.

"I couldn't have two better sisters." He looked down. "I'm sorry for all I've put you through…and the community. I was wrong…"

"That's in the past now. You may have taken advantage of me, and the others, but you've been forgiven." Judith looked directly at him, "I forgive you, brother."

He looked at Judith. "Do you?"

"I've done so already," she laughed. "You passed out as I did so – in the ditch!" She became more serious. "I treated you awfully, blaming you for the deaths of my brother and the Messiah. I couldn't get rid of my hatred for you. I wanted to hate you, even although I sensed it was wrong. However, Yahweh as dealt with all that, and I forgive you." She paused as a thought came to mind. "Do you realise that it was just after my forgiving you that the lightening came, and Becca and I were healed!"

"What's this about your brother?" asked Becca.

"It's a long story, Becca, but Barabbas here has figured in my life a number of times. Maybe we should pray first though. I believe Yahweh's not finished with us yet."

All three of them sat in silence for some moments, before Judith started to speak. "Father, you work in mysterious ways. We can scarcely believe your love for us, and your great kindness. Each of us has something to be thankful for tonight, and we surrender to you, to let you do with us as you will. Your Son said all these years ago, 'Not my will but let yours be done' and the following day he submitted to an awful death, the death that had been decreed for Barabbas here. But his death that day didn't only release Barabbas – it released all of us who believe - from sin, from sickness, and from death itself. We are so grateful to you. You have released us for a purpose – to serve you, to do what you will, and to tell the world about your love for us…and them. Help us to be faithful and obedient – and to promote your Son, the Messiah, wherever you take us."

Judith stopped for a moment, as an image came into her mind. In it she saw herself and Becca taking Barabbas by the arms and helping him to stand up. This was so far out of her realm that she rejected it at first, then slowly, deliberately, she got to her feet. She motioned Becca to stand up too, and told her to take Barabbas's arm. She'd heard these words before as they came into her mind, and so she said them out loud, "Barabbas, in the name of Jesus of Nazareth, rise up and walk!"

Barabbas shifted uncomfortably as the two of them stood on either side of him grasping his arms. "I can't…" he tried to say, but he seemed overtaken by another spirit, another emotion. His legs jerked, and his body went into spasm. He was shaking - slowly at first, then uncontrollably. He almost shook himself out of their grasp, but they held on, and the shaking eventually subsided. He said, "I…I can…I think I…I feel something…" He moved his legs and as he did so, it appeared that strength came into them. The women took their cue from this and gently lifted him up, till he was crouching with his feet underneath him. They hadn't the ability to lift him higher, but with a bound and a leap he was standing fully on his feet, his legs taking his weight. "I'm healed. I'm healed!" he shouted. "Thank you, thank you!" Now nothing could hold them bac! All four of them were leaping and dancing like mad things in the moonlight- Little Faith wasn't going to be left out!

Once calmness prevailed and they were again sitting down, they put together a plan. Now none of them had to remain there…or anyone else have to go it alone to the appointment. They could all go together, being led, they hoped, by Little Faithie. So many miracles had happened that night - why should they doubt that a little furry wet dog could lead them?

"I don't think we've that far to go," Barabbas said, "but I don't know this stretch of road. I think we're a mile or two away from the village."

"What time do you think it is?" asked Judith, now beginning to feel a sense of excitement at what was before them. She didn't want to be disappointed at this late stage.

"Judging by the moon, I'd say it's almost mid-evening," Barabbas said. "We need to move on now, if we don't want to get them off their mats."

It seemed that Faithie had the same idea. She ran to the end of the overhanging rock as if to encourage them to follow her.

"What about our belongings?" said Becca with a sudden flash of inspiration. "We can't leave them here. Anyone passing might take them if they see no-one's around."

"You're right," agreed Barabbas. "Just take essentials and valuables," he smiled, "if you've got any!"

They managed to find their way into the upturned cart getting wet again in the muddy water. Judith retrieved her bag and the others similarly took what they could carry with them. Barabbas paused for a moment to pick up a water bottle, and before they started to follow Faithie, each of them took a long drink from it. Somewhat revived they allowed Little Faith to do her work and followed her into the night.

Chapter Thirty-Six

At first, they followed the road up and down hills, Little Faith dancing ahead of them. If they slowed up she turned towards them and barked as if to hurry them on.

"She'd have made a good sheepdog," commented Becca on one of those occasions.

"She's keen to help us on our way...and to do her Master's bidding," Judith said. "We're privileged to have her here. I hope she doesn't leave this time!"

"As long as she gets us to our destination - that's what counts," said Barabbas.

They walked in silence for about ten minutes and began to pass more and more trees. Barabbas groaned. "I think I remember this part of the road," he said. "We're further away from the village than I thought. There's at least eight miles to go. At this pace we won't be there before midnight."

Judith and Becca looked disappointed. "Are you sure?" Judith asked.

"Fairly sure. I remember when I passed this stretch of road on other occasions, it took me two to three hours to reach the village we're going to."

"They won't appreciate being wakened up in the middle of the night," Becca said.

"I know," said Judith. "But we have to assume if Yahweh's brought us this far, he wants us to go there - and he'll make sure we get there. Just look what he's already done for us today. We've an appointment to keep!"

At that point Faithie veered off the road into the trees.

"What on earth is she doing?" asked Barabbas. "We need to follow the road to get to the village!"

"That's been great so far," said Becca, "but if we were just to follow the road to the village, we wouldn't have needed her. Maybe this is why she was sent to us."

"Perhaps she knows a short cut," said Judith, then corrected herself. "Perhaps Yahweh is taking us on a shortcut. Are you willing to follow us and take the risk that we might get lost?"

Both of them nodded and followed Faithie and Judith into the forest.

It was difficult to see where they were going under the canopy of trees. The moon's light was almost being filtered out. However, Faithie could be seen as a faint ghostly figure running ahead, and if they stayed close to her they seemed to find the easiest paths through the trees and undergrowth. Judith was surprised at just how well she guided them. Never did any of them stumble or bump into an obstacle. I should have guessed, she thought, that having been sent by Yahweh, no harm would come to us.

Suddenly they were out of the forest and a vast desert scrubland faced them, looking eerie in the moonlight.

"What now?" said Barabbas. "There's no sign of any habitation anywhere!"

"We have to keep going," said Judith. "I believe we've been led here. We must go on."

"The village could be miles away…and we might be going in the wrong direction," Barabbas complained.

"No. Let's not waste time. Yahweh knows what he's doing…and by the looks of it, so does Faithie. Look! She's going far ahead of us We'll need to hurry!"

The ground was more pitted here, and there was a danger they might sprain their ankles. Faithie was unrelenting in her pace and they struggled to keep up.

"We'll have to call her back," suggested Barabbas. "If she gets too far ahead, we might lose her."

"Link arms!" Judith said, a note of authority in her voice. "We should try to run."

"That's ridiculous," said Barabbas. "We'll never keep up, and one, or all, of us might get hurt, and then where would we be – lost in the middle of nowhere."

"Link arms!" Judith said again, that note of authority still in her voice. "We're going to get there - right, reason or none!"

Becca and Barabbas complied, and they started off again. But this time it was different. Linking arms seemed to have given each of them a boost of energy, so much so, that they started to run after Faithie. Faithie's pace altered too when she saw they were following her. She absolutely shot forward over the rough ground, her pack following her in hot pursuit.

"What's happening?" asked Becca. "I'm running but it feels effortless. Look, I'm not even breathing hard!"

"Me too," said Barabbas. "Our feet are barely touching the ground. There's no way we'll trip this way. "I believe I could even go faster!"

"Get ready then," said Judith. "Let's up the pace!"

They were traversing the terrain at a speed none of them had ever managed before. Their feet simply flew over the rough ground, and the more they thought of reaching their destination, the faster they ran.

They were laughing and bubbling over with joy. They were like children excited about achieving some new ability, and exploiting it.

"What do you think is happening to us?" Becca asked. "I've never run like this before…and I'm a leper in her latter stages."

"You were a leper in your latter stages," Judith corrected her, and they all laughed. Judith thought for a moment, then said, "Do either of you know the story of Elijah and the prophets of Baal?"

Becca said, "There's something about it in our writings. Didn't he kill them, and the queen was furious."

"I remember the story from my childhood," said Barabbas. "Israel, the northern kingdom, was following idols here in Samaria, and Elijah challenged the prophets of Baal to a contest. He was a nationalist, you know. He wanted to restore Israel to Yahweh."

"That's right," said Judith, still running. "The part of the story I'm thinking about is after he had killed the prophets in front of the king and made it rain again after three years. He told the king to get into his chariot and get home as fast as he could. Remember what happened next?"

No," said Barabbas. "They got wet?" Realising that a joke wasn't appropriate he said, "I learned the story in the synagogue school. The main bit was the defeating of the prophets of Baal."

"That's true, but it's the next bit that applies here." Judith laughed. "The king raced off in his chariot, and it says Elijah lifted his robe and started running before the chariot; and beat the king back to the city."

"You're saying we have the speed of Elijah?" said Becca.

"Well, if not, then we must be superhuman! No, Yahweh is, and he's with us, helping us to get to our destination."

"You know," said Barabbas laughing, "I've waited all my life for miracles to happen, to see evidence that Yahweh is with Israel helping us in our struggle for freedom. I became disillusioned and decided to set up my own miracle with the zealots. But this beats everything. I wait for miracles, and they all happen to me in one night! It's wonderful! I was wrong all these years. I should have trusted Yahweh."

Faithie was slowing now and their pace diminished appropriately.

"Look, over there!" said Becca pointing. "Do you see houses in the distance?"

"I tell you what I do see," said Barabbas. "We're about to join the road again. I'm assuming it's the same road we left about half an hour ago."

"Little Faithie's led us across country to help us keep our appointment," Judith said. "She's taking us back onto the road."

Having reached the road, Little Faithie stood in the middle of it and wagged her tail.

"Thank you, Faithie. You've done a great job!" said Judith, and held out her arms to her. Faithie almost bound into them, and ended up standing on her hind legs yodelling in happiness as her whiskers brushed Judith's face gently. "I love you, Little Faithie. Please don't go!"

Little Faithie dropped again onto her four paws and pressed herself into the crook of Judith's knee, as she had done so often before as a mark of affection. She whined softly. It wasn't so much a whine of sadness, but a sigh of complete satisfaction. Judith bent down and took her face in her hands and kissed her on the top of her beautiful soft furry head. "I love you Faithie," she said again. Faithie rubbed her head on Judith's knee, then nodded her head up and down in order to keep Judith's hand stroking her.

Barabbas tapped Judith on the shoulder, "The village is just ahead of us. We'll need to be going."

In the moment she took to look at him, her hand suddenly felt nothing under it. Faithie was gone. Judith had anticipated that this might happen, but she wasn't ready for it. She wanted to weep. For the third time in her life now, Faithie had been withdrawn from her.

"She's gone!" said Barabbas, "the Messiah's dog."

"Gone back to him," said Becca.

Judith tried to stop the tears from coursing down her cheeks. "Thank you, Little Faithie. Thank you, Josh," she whispered. Becca put her arm round her shoulder, and the three of them made their way into the village.

"This is the right place," said Barabbas, looking around him. "I've been here before. Faithie's done her job well."

Judith looked gratefully at him for acknowledging her.

"I was told to enter the square, and that the house they would be staying in was at one corner of it."

"Do you know where the square is?" asked Becca.

"If we keep walking, we'll no doubt come across it. It's fairly near the centre in most places like this."

True enough after about five minutes walking past a line of houses and huts, they arrived in the square. Like all villages at night, there was no-one about, and on this night in particular, most would have stayed indoors to shelter from the earlier storm.

"Which corner?" asked Judith feeling a little impatient. Since she had discovered the real reason Barabbas had brought them there, she was keen to meet those who had been asking for her.

"There's light coming from that house over there." She pointed to the far corner.

322

"We'll start there first then," said Barabbas leading the way to it. He rapped on the door with impunity. Having come so far, under extreme circumstances, he saw no point in showing timidity. Indeed, he seemed almost emboldened by his experiences.

Someone could be heard coming towards the door, and then unbolting it. A buzz of voices came from inside. It sounded like praying to Judith.

"Yes?" the elderly man said. "What can I do for you?"

"I've come to see the healers," said Barabbas in a strong voice. "Are they here?"

The man said, "Please wait," and immediately shut the door on them.

Barabbas would have knocked loudly again being unappreciative of the treatment they had received, but Becca persuaded him not to. They waited in silence and mounting expectation.

After a few moments, the man came back with a lantern, and beside him stood the two healers. The elderly man held up the lantern to Barabbas's face, and the two healers scrutinised it.

"Yes, he's the one," the big man said. "It's him all right." He looked over at the others and said, "Would the two of you mind stepping back a little? You're taking a chance coming into the village like this. Fortunately, the streets are empty. Being unclean is not looked upon favourably! My friend here will come over to you with the lantern and find out what we need to know." The smaller and younger of the two healers took the lantern from the elderly man and walked over to the two women. He held it up to Becca's face first and peered at it. "You're not Judith!" he exclaimed disappointedly.

"It's the other one," said Barabbas, a hint of impatience in his voice. While this was happening, Judith was almost beside herself with excitement. She had recognised the two men as Peter and Jonas, Josh's disciples.

"Jonas!" she said as he came towards her and raised the lantern. His hand was shaking, and the light from the candle inside it flickered and almost went out.

"Judith?" he said, hardly daring to believe it might be her.

"Yes, Jonas…it's me!"

He recognised her, and would have embraced her, but quickly stepped back, remembering Barabbas had told him that she was a leper.

"Yahweh be praised!" he said. "We thought you were dead. We'd given up hope for you. We had your burial service."

Judith was shocked, taken aback that she might have been thought of as dead. She knew the family may have considered she was dead…but to actually have carried out her funeral!

She was lost for words for a moment, then they came tumbling out of her, "Tabitha, how's Tabitha?"

"Well," said Jonas.

"Joel and Mary?"

Jonas's face showed concern for a split second, but he said, "They've had their troubles, but they're fine for the moment." He held the lantern up to Judith's face again, "Let me have a look at you again. It's so good to know you're alive..." He broke off abruptly and held the lantern as close to Judith's face as he dared. "Where's the leprosy? He said you had leprosy."

"It's gone!" said Judith triumphantly. "It's gone! Yahweh healed me tonight in the storm." She pointed to Becca. "This is my friend Becca. She was at the community with me. She was a leper, but Yahweh healed her too tonight. We're both clean!"

"I can see that" said Jonas thrilled. "I saw none on her, and I see nothing on you."

"It's been some day getting here," interrupted Barabbas. "Yahweh has certainly met with us in so many ways, it would be difficult to tell you everything out here."

"Peter, come over here," said Jonas. The big man obliged. "Take the lantern and confirm what I'm seeing."

Peter first went to Judith, and then to Becca. "They're clean," he said at last. "I'm assuming no priest has seen you to verify it?"

They nodded.

"I'm going to pray, and we'll see how to proceed from there." He smiled at Judith. "It's wonderful to have you back...back from the dead." All of them laughed.

"Father," he said, "your daughter has come back to us and we give you thanks. We thank you too for her friends and your goodness to them in bringing them here." He sighed and went on. "They have endured much to come to this point. Let them count it all joy as they have suffered much. You have helped them overcome and for that we are grateful. We thank you that you have chosen to heal our sisters as you healed our brother the other day. Be with them and bless them and let your face shine upon them. Make them true witnesses for you." He looked at Barabbas, "You have found forgiveness, and I wish to say to you what Jesus said to me the night before he died, before I denied him three times. 'Satan has desired to sift you as wheat, but I have prayed for you, that your faith fail not.' Wherever you've been, whatever you've done, know that there's no condemnation in the Christ. You are forgiven. Keep the faith!"

Barabbas seemed to sink under the weight of these words. He smiled. "Thank you, sir. You don't know how much these words mean to me!"

"I do!" Peter said. "I was given them for you." HE looked around the little group and guffawed. "Bartholomew, can they stay with us for the night - before we leave in the morning?"

The elderly man smiled, "Our house is your house. We'll gladly have them to stay. You've brought so much blessing to our village. One or two more guests will make no difference. We'd be glad to have you all!" With that, he turned around and went into the house. The others followed him, glad to get out of the cool night air and have a chance to rest after the day's traumatic, but momentous, events.

Chapter Thirty-Seven

"It's really good to see you again, Judith," Jonas said as they sat over refreshments. The room was small, and with three extra bodies in it, rather cramped. Far from hindering conversation however, this aided it. The light from the candle was dim, but each person was able to be seen clearly.

Peter exclaimed in a loud voice, "Yes, we thought you were dead. The people who had taken you in their wagon got a message back to us saying that they had reached Galilee, but you hadn't. It appeared you had left them somewhere in Samaria. They didn't know if that had been your plan all along, but you had vanished overnight without sign or trace. When time went by and we didn't hear from you, I'm afraid we assumed the worst."

Judith looked distressed. "Tabitha…the family…they must have been devastated."

"Yes," said Jonas softly. "There was an atmosphere of mourning for quite a long time. Tabitha, losing her father and then her mother in quick succession, took it all very badly."

Judith wept. "I never wanted to cause them such distress. I couldn't get a message to you. I was a leper and lived in a leper community. I couldn't do anything about getting a message to anyone. I'd resigned myself to living there and dying there."

"Yes, we were indeed fortunate to meet this man here who told us about you." Jonas looked at Barabbas. "Yahweh obviously helped you when you couldn't help yourself, Judith!"

"Yes, he and my friend Becca here, we all lived in the Valley of the Outcasts near Jacob's Well. The community was good to me and took me in."

Jonas looked at Barabbas and Becca, "Thank you for looking after our sister, and returning her to us. We'll be forever in your debt."

The atmosphere eased, and stories were exchanged. Judith told them about her experiences and how that very night she and Becca had been delivered from their conditions.

"All three of you in a matter of days…that's a wonderful miracle," said Peter beaming. "Yahweh is indeed doing a new thing."

"I haven't told you the whole story," said Judith. "I've kept the best till last. There was, I think, another reason why I contracted leprosy and ended up in the community."

Peter and Jonas both looked at her with interest. "What was that?" Jonas asked.

"I want you to meet Barabbas here!" she said. Barabbas looked awkward.

"We're thankful to you, my friend, for all you've done for our sister," Peter said warmly. "We knew of another Barabbas once, and he wasn't a decent fellow. He was a murderer, and on the day of Jesus's crucifixion, Pilate allowed him to go free and gave Jesus his punishment. He was a zealot, the worst of the worst."

"I am he!" Barabbas said. "I was that man."

There was a stunned silence while Peter and Jonas took it in. "You are the self-same Barabbas that allowed Jesus to take his punishment? That's difficult to believe. How can this be?"

Barabbas then told his story. Judith was impressed that he left nothing out. He told them of his becoming a leper and joining the community, of being made their prophet, of how he had exploited them for his own ends, of how Judith came and recognised him. He also told them of his journey to faith, of his vision and his sense that Jesus was not condemning him but was willing to forgive him, of how Judith had challenged him and hadn't believed him, of how he had invented a story about meeting buyers to get her to come with him to meet them. He ended by telling them everything that had happened that day, including the accident, their healings, the strange happenings concerning the Messiah's dog and their sprint to the meeting. He held nothing back.

"Welcome Barabbas!" said Peter seriously. "We would never have recognised you. Neither Jonas nor I were at your trial…but we heard all about it," he said grimly. "Had we done so, we might have been prejudiced against you the other day. I see now that Yahweh has mercy on whom he wishes to have mercy. We are so limited in our understanding. Jesus answered a question of mine one day. I had asked him, 'How many times should I forgive my brother if he sins against me?' I thought I was being generous by suggesting 'seven times?'. Jesus said, 'Seventy times seven'. As he was being crucified, he forgave everyone responsible for putting him there…and that, my brother," he smiled, "means you! Welcome to the Kingdom!"

"Talking of forgiveness," Judith said. "I had my own struggles. Barabbas was involved in the death of my little brother thirty years ago. He wasn't only involved in Josh's death. I had been at the trial and had seen Barabbas swaggering and taunting the soldiers as Pilate overturned his punishment and gave it to Josh.

When I recognised him just after I had joined the community, I hated him with all my might. We came to an uneasy truce. He wouldn't put me out, if I didn't expose him. This totally went against the grain. I wanted to tell everyone who he was, but I was restrained from doing so. Still my hatred of him grew and grew, and when he told me of having had a vision of Josh who wasn't condemning him, I didn't believe him. Yes, I got on with my everyday work, and we did help many to believe in the Messiah, but my hatred of Barabbas consumed me, and it took my deteriorating leprosy and the Holy Spirit to get me to confront my sin. One night at a meeting, a lady shared with us about a time you were all staying in her village. Josh had told a story about a king who forgave his servant a great debt, but that servant had had a fellow servant imprisoned when he couldn't pay his tiny debt to him. When the king heard about it, Josh had said he imprisoned the unforgiving servant and that he would be in torment there till he paid the last penny."

"Quite right. Josh did tell that story most places he went," Peter agreed.

"Well, I was in torment because of my inability to forgive Barabbas. I kept away from him as my condition deteriorated. That night the Holy Spirit challenged me and said I had to forgive Barabbas, otherwise I would stay in torment. I determined to do so and sought him out a few days later. In the meantime, Yahweh had been speaking to him, and when he met with you, he was healed. He said nothing of this when I went to find him and instead told me a story about coming with him to meet potential buyers for our produce. I had been partly responsible for setting up the project. I didn't get around to telling him that I forgave him till the accident tonight, when he was lying in the ditch under the cart. I thought he was going to die. At that very moment, there was an almighty flash of lightening and crack of thunder which sent a terrific pain through my body, and although I didn't realise it at the time, I had been healed."

"Me too," chipped in Becca.

"Little Faithie…you remember her?" Judith smiled. They nodded. "She appeared at that moment."

"The Messiah's dog," Barabbas said smiling too.

"She came, and we realised that she had come to lead me to you. It's a convoluted story, I'm afraid. You see, when the lightning and thunder came, the cart had moved enough to let me drag Barabbas from under it, and over to a place of shelter. He went and spoiled it all," Judith grinned, "when he told us he hadn't been quite straight with us…about meeting the buyers. At that moment, I believed the worst of him. All my fears and doubts, including my hatred of him came back with a vengeance. He told us however that he had met with you and that he had been healed. He said that you were looking for me. You can imagine how I felt then. We agreed that I would go with Faithie and that Becca would stay with him as he couldn't walk. I would bring back help in the morning. Well, we prayed, and again Yahweh was with us. She looked slightly embarrassed at telling them this, as they themselves had often been used to heal. "I felt we should pray for Barabbas in the name of Jesus, and we did so."

Barabbas took up the story, "I felt power and strength coming into my legs, and with their help, I got to my feet, and the rest you can see. We, all three of us, danced and leapt for joy!" He added, "I've just run for miles to get here. We had the feet of Elijah. Yahweh is amazing!"

"Faithie led us here, over rough country so we didn't have to take the long way round by road. And as Barabbas said," Judith laughed, "Yahweh gave us the feet of Elijah! They hardly touched the ground."

"Amazing," said Jonas. "Truly amazing. I'm sure the scriptures say somewhere, 'they shall rise up with wings as eagles, they shall run and not faint'."

"So," said Judith, "why are you here? I thought you intended staying in Jerusalem to pray and to teach the believers."

"That was our intention," said Peter, "but Josh had told us just after he had risen, that we would take the message out beyond Jerusalem to the rest of Israel and to the world. He would go with us, he said."

"I remember hearing about that in one of the meetings you held in Joel and Mary's, after He was taken up to heaven."

"Well, the persecution that kind of forced you out of Jerusalem, and killed your dear husband, intensified, and many believers started to leave the city. I suppose it was a way of getting us to leave our comfort zones to make us do what Josh had told us to do - to tell the rest of the world. Philip came to Samaria and helped make believers of many people. He healed and taught in their cities, and the Samaritans came to Josh in droves. It was quite a surprise that Gentiles were coming to faith, so when we heard about it in Jerusalem, it was decided that Jonas and I should come to Samaria to see what was happening. When we arrived here, we certainly met many believers, but up till then they had only been baptised in the name of Jesus. They needed to receive the Holy Spirit too. When we laid hands on them, the Spirit came, just as he did with us. It was clear to us that Yahweh was blessing the Gentiles too." Peter digressed, "There was one fellow there, a Simon the sorcerer. He had gained a great reputation with the people for his magic, but when Philip had preached, he had become a believer. When I met him, I told him he was full of bitterness and jealousy and that he'd better watch or he might suffer Yahweh's punishment."

"Why?" said Judith looking astounded at the severity of Peter's words.

"Well, the fellow had watched us laying on hands and imparting the Holy Spirit. He tried to offer me money to give him the power to do the same. As far as I know, he repented though."

"So, I'm assuming that's when you met Barabbas, and healed him."

"That's right. It was amazing timing. We were about to leave for home, calling in at a few Samaritan villages on the way. We told him where we'd be in two days' time and he promised to bring you with him. Of course we were expecting to see a leper," his smile broadened. "Unless you were to be healed by us, we couldn't see a way of taking you back, but…Josh has done the work for us. We'll be glad to take you with us…all of you."

For the first time that night, Bartholomew spoke up. "You're welcome to stay here overnight. It's a bit cramped here but we'll manage. In the morning I'll go with all of you and we'll try and find your cart. Maybe we can repair it. And you can use it to get to Jerusalem."

"Our donkeys ran off, I'm afraid," Becca said.

"No matter. We might come across them. If not, we'll improvise," Bartholomew said. "We'll do everything we can to make sure you'll all get there safely."

"Thank you," said Judith. "You're going well beyond what we can expect. We're in your debt."

"The Lord provides!" said Bartholomew smiling.

"I've got some news for you," said Jonas, who was also smiling. "It's about Tabitha."

"What?" asked Judith with a pang of fear that it might have been bad.

"When we get back, we've timed it so that we can get back for her wedding!"

Sophia's Secret

Volume Two

Part Four – Homecoming

Chapter Thirty-Eight

"She's coming round now," Peter said.

"Thank goodness," said Becca. "That gave me quite a scare."

The others nodded.

"Where am I?" Judith whispered. She saw Peter and Jonas's faces looming over her and her memory came flooding back.

"Tabitha...she's getting married?" she said weakly, looking concerned.

"Yes, Judith. She's a young lady now. Quite grown up. And she's found happiness," Jonas said.

"Who to?" Judith asked, still looking concerned. "Who's she marrying?"

"To whom else," said Jonas smiling. "Jonas of course."

Judith's mind blocked for a moment. "Not you!"

"I'm afraid not. She's marrying Jonas, Joel and Mary's son."

Judith looked happier now and struggled to her feet. "I must have fainted. I wasn't expecting to hear that news. I'm sorry."

"Don't worry yourself," said Jonas. "I should have been more careful in giving you the news. It must have come as a shock to you. There's been a lot to take in – your death, at least the finding out that everyone's had your funeral; and then to discover that your daughter's getting married."

"And in a day or two's time, you said?"

"Yes, we decided to make our way back from Samaria taking in a few villages and making sure we were back for the wedding in two days' time."

"I'm overcome," said Judith wanly but smiling. "I'm so happy for her. I knew she liked him, and he her. I had expected in a matter of time they would get together, but not this soon."

"Well, you have been away a long time. What is it – about a year and a half?" Jonas asked gently. "after your death, unfortunately Tabitha went to bits and hid herself away from the rest of us. She mourned for you deeply. Jonas was there for her and he slowly encouraged her back into life. Joel and Mary were a great help to her too. They supported her and brought her through the worst. Tabitha needed something to look forward to, to help her through her sadness - and as she grew closer to Jonas, it seemed only natural that the two of them should get married." He smiled. "It seemed inevitable. In fact, we'd all thought that for a while."

"You're right," said Judith. "It was looking that way even before I left. I'm so glad for her that she's found love - and that it's Jonas. They'll be a wonderful match!"

"It'll be a wonderful day for her," said Peter. "Just think, she'll be marrying the man she loves, and getting her mother back from the dead – all in the same day!"

Judith laughed. "It sounds funny, but yes, it will indeed be wonderful…and I'll get my daughter back too." All of them were smiling now at the thought.

"It's getting late," said Bartholomew. "Peter and Jonas have had a busy day, healing and preaching in the villages – and there's a long journey ahead of you all tomorrow. There's a couple more places we want to bring the good news to before making the journey proper back to Jerusalem. We should get some sleep."

"Yes," said Peter, explaining. "Bartholomew is a brother we met while in Samaria. He has a fruit stall in the market there, and some in the surrounding towns too. He offered us lodgings and hospitality on our first night there – we're not too far from Samaria itself here – and he also promised to take us around the local area to spread the good news for as long as we needed. We should be finished tomorrow, and as he has to collect goods in Jerusalem before the weekend for his business, it coincides with our need to be back for the wedding. Yahweh is good! He always provides. He never lets us down!"

"I'll put out some mats for you. I hope you don't mind but…if all three of you can sleep in here, we'll use the other room. My house is yours, but it's small."

"No problem at all," said Barabbas. "He looked at Judith and Becca, "Is that all right with you?"

"No problem for us either," said Becca.

Judith sighed, "I'll be glad to sleep anywhere. I'm quite exhausted after today. It's been wonderful…but it has been challenging since the moment we left the community this morning." A thought struck her and she smiled, "I got to see Little Faith once more! Josh has made everything so right for us again. I could never have imagined all this happening – and all in one day! And now, there's Tabitha – I'll be there for her wedding!"

"It's been a great deal for us all!" said Becca.

Barabbas nodded, and thanked Bartholomew for taking them in.

"We'll discuss how we're going to get you all home in the morning. Give me a night to think about it and I'll work out something."

"You're very kind, sir. We are indeed deeply in your debt," said Barabbas warmly.

They decided to end such a momentous day with a time of prayer, thanking Josh and his Father for their goodness to them all. Each of them then went to their mat and flopped down on it tired and exhausted, Judith Becca and Barabbas particularly contemplating what the future might have in store for them as they started their life anew.

Bartholomew wasn't slow in getting them up with breakfast the next day. He needed to set things out, and the three former lepers were in the way. He apologised for waking them up so early, but grinned as he told them an early start was required.

"Peter and Jonas are already out in the back field praying. They've been there since dawn. They'll be keen to get moving soon, I've no doubt."

"Where can we get cleaned up?" asked Judith. "We arrived here quite dirty yesterday after falling into the ditch and walking over the scrub land."

There's a trough of clean water in the back. The animals use it, but I always fill it up with clean water at the start of the day. It's good for washing. Have you got any clean clothes with you? I imagine you will have something, as you had planned to be away from home for a few days."

"You're right," said Becca. "We have them in our bags."

"Well feel free to wash your robes and other things in it. They can dry, hanging on the side of the cart as we go along."

"Good idea," said Barnabas. "We'll look like a portable laundry!"

They laughed as they fetched clean garments from their bags and went to the trough to wash. Barnabas went first, leaving the two women behind. Judith came across her picture as she rummaged in her bag. She took it out.

"Yes, I saw you putting it in there before you left," said Becca. "Did you have any inkling that you might not be going back for it? It's just as well you brought it with you!"

"None at all," said Judith frowning. "It was just an impulse…and I'm glad I did. I would have hated to have been parted from it - especially as it was given me by Josh and his Father. It's been with me for as long as I can remember."

"I understand. You'll be so glad to get back to your family. I envy you."

"You mustn't do that, Becca. We're sisters. You're my family, and I know you'll get on well with Tabitha, Joel, and Mary. We'll be one big family together, you'll see."

Becca looked dubious, "But I'm a Samaritan, and you're all Jews. We don't mix, especially in Jerusalem."

"But we're sisters now," Judith said, brushing her objection aside. "You're a believer. You'll be welcome among all our believer friends. You needn't worry. There's no such thing as Jew and gentile now - at least in Josh's eyes."

Don Treader

"I'm not so sure," Becca said sadly. "That worked well in our community as we were all in the same condition." She paused. "In Jerusalem, it'll be different."

"I won't let it. Look Becca, the first day you met me at Jacob's well you called me your sister. You looked after me and took care of me as my leprosy worsened. I'm not about to let you loose in Jerusalem to your own devices. I'm going to take care of you, look after you and make sure you get all the benefits you deserve. You've been a leper so long, and now you're clean. We're going to have a great time together in the big city."

Becca looked unsure, but Judith didn't pursue it. She knew there'd be much more time ahead of them for her to convince Becca that a wonderful new life awaited her.

Barabbas came back at that point and the two women left for the trough.

Behind the house there was quite a large field, which led in turn to a series of others. The immediate one not only contained the water trough and a stable, but also three wooden carts used to ferry Bartholomew's produce. Beyond it, through a rough wooden gate, they could make out a number of fields containing rows of vegetables, and a thick proliferation of fruit trees and bushes. Bartholomew's business was obviously blooming, Judith thought. They were extremely fortunate that he had offered his services, and that she would be back in Jerusalem for Tabitha's wedding. This thought captivated her mind as she did her washing, and so she said little to Becca. As they were finishing wringing out and shaking their garments, Peter and Jonas came back through the gate from the adjacent field where they had been praying, and passed them by on their way to breakfast.

"Glad you're nearly finished," Peter said. "We've a busy day ahead of us and we must get going."

When the women joined the men around the table for breakfast. Judith noticed that Peter looked slightly uncomfortable, and moved down to the end of it when Judith, Becca and Barabbas took their seats. This fact didn't go unnoticed by Becca either, who whispered to Judith, "Doesn't he like sitting with Samaritans?"

Judith played it down. "You've no need to worry, Becca. Jonas and Bartholomew don't seem bothered."

Becca still looked troubled but said nothing.

After praying over the food, Bartholomew told them of his plan for them that day. They had Bartholomew told them of his plan for them that day. They had to be in Jerusalem by the following morning, and so the intention was to allow Peter and Jonas to preach in two villages in the vicinity, and once this was done, he would take them all overnight to the big city so they could arrive early morning and be in good time for the wedding.

He looked at Barabbas, "Your cart is in a ditch? How far away?"

"I'm not sure, sir, as we were led here cross country. I would estimate about five miles or so down the road – perhaps more."

"Good. We're going that way anyway. What state is your cart in?"

"Difficult to say. It turned over, but it came to rest on mud. It may not be all that badly damaged. With all of us there, we might be able to pull it out."

"We've also got the donkeys," Bartholomew said.

"True. But how do you propose we all get there?"

"I'm going to suggest that we take two of my carts and some donkeys. Where are your donkeys? I'm assuming they didn't hang around in the storm."

"Once again, I don't know, sir."

Becca cut in, "While Barabbas was injured in the ditch, I went after them. It was dark apart from the occasional flash of lightning. I certainly didn't see them there. They could have run for miles. They were frightened."

"I understand," said Bartholomew. "Well, here's what I suggest. Let's get to where you had the accident, try, and see what we can salvage, and then we can be on our way to Peter and Jonas's villages. Your donkeys might have returned. They may have made their way back to the cart once the storm was over, knowing that that's where their food would be. If your cart is too badly broken, we'll just continue as we were." He looked at Barabbas, "You could proceed with one of my carts, and once I get back I'll get help to retrieve yours, which I'll repair and keep. Does that sound good to you?"

"More than generous. You're too kind, sir," Barabbas smiled at him. "And the donkeys?"

"Well, if they're back, we'll take them with us, and if not, we'll just continue as we were."

"But I'll have two of your donkeys?"

"Well, I've two alternatives then," laughed Bartholomew, "I'll either come back and find two stray donkeys, or you'll have a gift. I'm happy either way. It's all in the Messiah's work!"

"You are too kind, my friend. Thank you." Barabbas looked quite touched by the man's generosity.

"You've been a fine friend indeed," said Peter. "The Lord will reward you. He is no man's debtor."

"I know that," said Bartholomew, smiling broadly now. "He taught that if you give generously, you will receive back pressed down, shaken together and running over. Whichever way, I win!"

They all laughed, and the conversation moved on to consider the day's spiritual events. In due course, when breakfast ended they committed their ways to the Lord with a time of prayer.

As they went out to the two carts, Peter remarked to Judith, "I imagine you can't wait to get back to Jerusalem. How about Barnabas and Becca?"

"Oh, they'll be fine. Becca as you know is a Samaritan, but we're sisters. I've promised to take her in. She did that for me for so long. I'm indebted to her. She'll be a wonderful friend and asset to the family – to my family, and the family of believers." She thought for a moment, "And Barabbas…I haven't thought about him. I just assumed that as a Jew he would have contacts and perhaps family. He seems happy enough to come to Jerusalem with us, at first anyway. I'm not sure about afterwards. He would be an asset to any believer group."

Peter had a serious look on his face, "You have to be careful, Judith. When you return to Jerusalem, you'll find things aren't as good as they were. You left just as the clampdown was beginning. There are those in the Sanhedrin imprisoning, beating, killing, and excommunicating believers. Some believing priests have been vilified. There's a strong air of repression, and believers aren't safe. Don't imagine Barabbas will be welcomed into every or any group. They know what he did, and they might not be as forgiving as us. You have known him and have seen how Josh has worked in him, but most believers are suspicious now and are careful whom they trust."

"What happened to Josh's teaching on forgiveness?"

"You're right, they should. But it's more difficult to show in a climate of fear. He may well find he fits into a group, but I would hazard a guess that he might find things easier away from Jerusalem, perhaps in Galilee." Peter stopped for a moment, but Judith could see he had more to say, "Becca too, Judith. You and she will have to be careful. Because 'The Way' is consolidating, it's beginning to lose its first flush of enthusiasm and freedom. There are those now who are being more careful, and who will take a more legalistic approach to the scriptures and to Josh's teaching."

"How can they do that?" said Judith. "Josh tried to get us away from all that. If we love one another, and Yahweh…all the law hangs on these two commandments."

"You're right again…and I believe that…the other apostles too. But there's a move to discredit gentile believers. Up till now we've been happy to enlist Jews into the faith, but with the Samaritan revival started by Philip, there's a section of believers unhappy that gentiles are coming to faith. They don't believe it's possible. Yahweh is for Jews only – we're His chosen people. Jonas and I were sent to investigate these unbelievable goings on – gentiles just can't become believers some think. However, we've got news for them!" he smiled, "but unfortunately, many aren't ready to hear it. It'll take time. That's why you and Becca should be careful. Some will accept her, and others won't."

"I'll do everything I can to make her acceptable to every believer I come across. If they have the witness of the Spirit, they should know it for themselves!"

"I agree, but sometimes people's laws, fears and traditions get in the way. I'm not absolutely clear myself as to what to do with the issue yet, but I am convinced that gentile believers are possible. Josh gave them the Spirit when we laid our hands on them. Our testimony will carry some weight…but we'll just have to see what the outcome is."

Judith nodded. "Thank you for warning me. I'll be careful, and I'll tell the others when I get a chance."

Peter said, "I hope you'll find things great in Jerusalem. Tomorrow will be a big day – for you and for your family."

She grinned, and he strode off to his cart.

Chapter Thirty-Nine

Once their bags had been loaded, along with an adequate supply of food and drink for their journey to Jerusalem, the two carts left in rapid succession and joined the road that would lead them to the wrecked community cart. Bartholomew led the first one and was flanked by Peter and Jonas who said they preferred to walk too rather than ride before the sun became too hot. Barabbas drove the other cart and under its large capacious awning, Judith and Becca talked about recent events which they were only now just coming to terms with; and how they saw the future for each of them.

"Have you been to Jerusalem before, Becca?" asked Judith.

"No, never. I've never been out of our locality in Samaria. I had no reason to go there. We Samaritans tend to stick together. We don't always feel welcome outside our area…you know, the Jewish Samaritan thing."

Judith nodded, "Oh, I know only too well. But I felt none of that from you or your people when I came to Samaria."

"You arrived in the community though, sister," Becca said smiling. "We were all in the same condition. There's no benefit in treating each other badly. We needed each other."

"That's true. But what you did for me - taking me in and all the rest - you'll never know how much I appreciated it! If it hadn't been for you, I might have died." Judith thought for a moment, "It's funny to think that up till yesterday, both of us were edging ever nearer death because of our conditions, and now…just look at us. Look at what Yahweh has done for us."

"And for me too," came a voice from the front of the cart. "This past week has been amazing for me too. I never imagined that I might live anywhere other than the community all my days. My condition seemed like my death sentence, the community my grave. And now all that's changed. I am so grateful to Jesus, my Messiah, for what he's done in me. I know I don't deserve it…I never will. But I

343

want my life to count for something now. I want to pay back the debt I owe him for dying in my place."

"We all do," said Judith solemnly. "I remember thinking at the trial when you were let go, that a great evil had taken place that day, a terrible injustice. I couldn't believe that Yahweh had allowed such a travesty of justice to happen - and yet he did. You didn't deserve to get off, and Josh didn't deserve to die, but I see now that an amazing exchange took place. Josh took your punishment while you were given his freedom, to do with as you wished. But you weren't alone, Barabbas!"

Barabbas's voice came floating back to them, "What do you mean, Judith? I was alone. No-one else was freed that day. Only me."

"That's where you're wrong, Barabbas. We all were. When Josh died on the cross that day, we were all freed. You weren't the only criminal involved that day. All of us have sinned – we were no less criminals than you were – he was taking the punishment for our sins too, not only yours. I was wrong to see you as responsible for his death. I was equally responsible - but the wonderful thing is that he was willing to give up his life for both of us, for all humanity, to make us free." Judith was almost crying at this realisation. "When he asked his Father to forgive those who put him there because they didn't know what they were doing…that's us! He was prepared to forgive all of us who were blindly going through life as though there was nothing wrong with us, totally uncaring about him or what he wanted for us. We're now free to do what he wants, to live our lives fully for him. All three of us - and every true believer - have the possibility of a brand-new start. You've just said that yourself – it's your choice, and you want to live for him. We all do!"

"I do - and I'm going to start right now. I'm not going to hold back!"

Becca said, "It's amazing. I hadn't thought of it that way before, but the Messiah came to us so long ago and offered us…offered me…life. He had to die to give it to me. It's so precious. I don't want to let him down. The living water he promised me – I want it, I need it…to pass his life on to others."

"We all need it," Judith agreed, "all the time!"

Becca changed the subject, "What do you think lies ahead in Jerusalem? You've got Tabitha's wedding, but what else?"

"I'm going to make sure that as my precious sister, I'm going to introduce you to all my friends, and make sure you're taken care of just as much as you took care of me. You mustn't be frightened, Becca. It may be a big place and greatly different from your country, but you're a believer - you're my sister - you'll fit in well. You'll be a great asset."

Becca looked unsure. "It's not that I don't believe you, Judith - and I trust you as my sister to make sure that things go well for me - but…"

"But what…?" asked Judith smiling. "It's a whole new start for you…for us. Don't you find it exciting, Becca?"

"But it's so different. I'm having trouble getting my mind around it. Yes, I relish a brand-new start, but…"

"You'll feel much better about it when you're there," Judith said, trying to reassure her friend.

For a while, they journeyed on in silence, listening to the rumbling of the wheels and the occasional snorting of the donkeys. Judith could hear Peter and Jonas talking to Bartholomew, but they were too far away for her to make out what they were saying.

After they'd been just over an hour and a half into their journey, she heard Barabbas call out. She looked to the front of the cart and saw he was pointing, "It's just over there!" he called to the other men.

It wasn't long before the carts slowly ground to a halt and they looked into the ditch.

"We can't stop here," said Bartholomew. "We're on a hill and we're almost blocking the road for other travellers. We should move to the bottom of the hill and park the carts on the flat ground there. We can tether the donkeys there too." The little company moved off again until they had achieved their goal. Judith wondered why they just couldn't have stayed at the scene of the accident - there had been hardly any traffic on the road since they had started out that morning. But then, she reasoned, they might have become a major obstacle if it took them too long to sort things out.

The men made their way along the ditch, which was now empty of water, to get to the fallen cart. The women however preferred to look on from the road above. After a cursory inspection, Bartholomew said, "It would be impossible to get it up on the road just now. I can see parts which have fallen off the chassis. They probably sheared off when the cart hit the ditch. One of the wheels is buried in the dried mud too. It's not a job for today, I'm afraid." He looked at Barabbas, "I'm sorry, you're just going to have to drive my cart and keep it. I can see your cart is solid and quite similar to mine. When I return, I'll get some of the villagers to help me get it out of here and I'll repair it. Would you be happy with that arrangement?" He asked, smiling.

"Most certainly, Bartholomew - if you don't feel I'm taking advantage of your generosity?"

"I don't…and you're a brother. What else would the Lord expect me to do? It's settled then."

Jonas was looking towards the overhanging rock, the one which his friends had sheltered under from the storm the previous night. He seemed to be listening. "I hear something," he said. They all cocked their ears, and then burst out laughing when around the edge of the rock came the community's two runaway donkeys, trotting as if they'd been out on a fine morning's run.

"There they are, my friends," said Bartholomew. "They've come back to you as I suspected they might. They will have been hungry and have returned to the scene of the crime to see if any food was forthcoming. They must have heard us talking and decided to re-join us. They say donkeys are stupid, but I'm not so sure. Mine aren't!"

They all laughed and proceeded to catch hold of the donkeys and take them to where Bartholomew's carts were standing.

"What are we going to do now?" asked Becca, as they stood around taking some refreshment watching the donkeys eat before moving on. "We've too many donkeys."

"You can never have too many donkeys!" said Bartholomew laughing. Then more seriously, he said, "I suggest, Barabbas, that you harness up your donkeys to my cart. They'll be more used to you. I'll find a place beyond that rock to tether mine. I'll leave them adequate food, and come back for them - and the cart - as soon as I return in a day or so's time. They're used to me leaving them for a while on a long tether. They know I'm the one that feeds them!"

This settled, they were about to leave when Barabbas stopped them. He looked serious. "I want to thank you for your kindness and generosity," and looking at Peter and Jonas, "and for my healing and forgiveness; and for the fact that you haven't judged me as you easily could have done."

"You're our brother now, Barabbas. You must live as a brother…and accept good things from your Heavenly Father," Peter said. "You have something to tell us I think though," he smiled.

"I have - and it's important you understand." Barabbas looked concerned about what he was going to say. He struggled for a moment before he could get the words out, "I can't go with you! I appreciate all you've done for me, but I can't go with you. It's not right! I have to go my own way. Jerusalem's not for me!"

Judith who was in the process of climbing on board her cart almost fell off it again when she heard what he said.

Peter looked at him, "What will you do, my brother? Where will you go? Galilee?"

"No," replied Barabbas quite definitely. "I have other plans."

All of them now were looking at him. "Where will you go, Barabbas?" asked Judith. "We thought you were coming with us."

For a moment he looked sad. "I truly would like to have joined you, but…it's not for me."

"What will you do then, my brother?" asked Peter, speaking gently to him as if to tease out his thoughts.

"Since last night, I've been feeling Jerusalem's not the place for me. You all seemed so keen for me to accompany you, but I didn't feel it was right for me. I want to serve the Messiah , but not there. It's not right for me."

"Well, where is then, my brother?" asked Peter again.

"I think...in the community - my place is back in the community. A work's been started there - thanks to Judith - and I want to be there to finish it... or at least to continue it." He opened up a bit more, now he had managed to get his news out. "I started wondering, you see, what the community would think when the three of us didn't return. It didn't seem right, or feel right. They need us, or at least one of us, to help them with the project...and even more important, to know the Messiah. The work has well begun there but it needs to be continued, it needs to be nurtured. I believe the Lord would want me to do this. I can be an example to them of how Yahweh forgives, and how he blesses; how he heals. I've taken so much from them. It's time for me now to give something back!"

Judith cut in at this point, "But you'd be going back there clean! You'd catch leprosy again if you live there!"

"Not necessarily," Barabbas smiled at her. "I might not catch it again as I've been healed. But Yahweh's will be done. If I catch it again, so be it. I want to serve him there! If some day he lets me do something else, go somewhere else, I'll do it."

"You seem convinced that this is for you, my brother," Peter continued. "Are you absolutely sure? Have you any doubts?"

"None at all. The more we talk about it, the more I feel convinced this is the right path for me."

"You're a brave man," said Peter, looking admiringly at him. "None of us would ever have consigned anyone to live in a leper community, but your choosing to do so voluntarily does you credit. The Lord's will be done! I think you're making a good decision."

"Me too," came a voice from inside the cart just beside Judith's head.

"Becca!" said Judith, startled.

"Me too!" Becca called out louder, looking past Judith to the others.

"What's that?" asked Peter looking over.

"I want to go back too!" Becca said loudly and emphatically.

Judith nearly fell over again at hearing her sister's words. "You can't, Becca!" she said weakly. "You're my sister...we had so many plans about what we would do for the Messiah now we're clean and free."

Becca looked at Judith sorrowfully, "I know. We had plans...but they weren't me. The more I thought about them...I'm not a Jew...I belong in Samaria amongst my own people. People in Jerusalem might not take me seriously, but amongst my own people, I can speak about the Messiah. After all, they listened the last time after I met him, and told them, 'Come see a man who told me everything I ever did'. Now I've so much more to share with them. I know they'll listen!"

The company struggled to recover from the surprises they had just received. They had been unexpected and had caught them off guard.

Judith was crying. "I don't want to lose you, Becca! I was so looking forward to spending our time together. You're my sister!"

Becca looked sad, but determined, "I'll always be your sister, Judith - we're inextricably linked in the Messiah. But for the moment anyway, you're losing a sister, and gaining a family. Your daughter needs you. If Yahweh wishes, our paths might cross again in the future. Only He knows. And rest assured, I'll look forward to that day as much as you will. If not, we'll meet again after." She set her face. "I have a different family, a different community, that needs me more. I promise I'll continue what you've started there!"

Both of them were crying now. The little group looked on, savouring their sadness, but encouraged by the bravery, the self-sacrifice, both Barabbas and Becca were showing. After a few moments, Peter said, "We should pray, brothers and sisters."

They all stood together beside the carts and bowed their heads. Peter spoke. "Jesus sent us to Samaria to deal with the Samaritans who had become believers under Philip's preaching. We were amazed at the thirst and sincerity of these people. As we prayed for them, they received the Holy Spirit. Up till then they'd only been baptised in the name of Jesus. I feel strongly that Jonas and I should pray for the two of you to be filled with the Holy Spirit. He will guide, protect, and empower you as you seek to work for the Messiah in your community. He will comfort you when days are difficult, and strengthen you for the task ahead of you. He will be your ever-present link to Jesus and the Father…and to us. Becca, when Jesus first spoke to you, he promised you those streams of living water. You've known something of that over the past year or so. Now he's keeping his promise to you and giving yourself and Barabbas what your hearts desire." He motioned to Jonas, and the two of them laid hands upon Becca and Barabbas. "You shall be free now to bring the good news to your people, to bring them to a knowledge of their Messiah and King, to help bring the Kingdom of Heaven to earth. We empower you with the Holy Spirit to give you all you need to draw people to Jesus. By his death he brought freedom from sin and sickness. We give you the power to pray for people's sins to be removed, and their sicknesses to be healed. Living water is yours, and streams will flow out of you as you seek to lift up the Messiah. So be it in the name of Jesus. Amen."

When Judith lifted her head, she saw that both Becca and Barabbas were shaking; their faces glowing and smiling. Peter continued, "Remember, use your gift well!" He then prayed more generally, "Lord, we thank you for bringing us all to this point. You know each of us individually. Even the hairs of our heads are numbered. We trust you to go with us today, to whatever future each of us faces. Glorify your name, and the name of your holy child Jesus. So be it."

Quick farewells were now made before the little group started along the road again.

"Becca, I'll never forget you!" Judith said as she hugged her. "You've indeed been a sister to me, the sister I never had. You are the person who brought me through the past months when I was ailing. You encouraged me and lifted me up when I was low. You'll be a great proponent of the Messiah when you return to the community, I know it. Please tell the rest…" she broke off as emotion got the better of her. "Please tell them I loved them, and I wish the best for them. I'm sorry…" Judith broke down. the two women were now crying. "Tell them, I'd have come back too, that I'm going to miss them, and the flourishing of the project…but I have a family to see. Tell them what the Messiah has done for us, and what he can do for them. Pray for them. Let Jacob's Well and the community be known far and wide as the place of Living Water; where Living Water can be found. You and Barabbas are like the viaduct we built. Let the living water flow through you."

"You'll always be my sister, Judith, the sister I never had too," Becca spoke through her tears. "I know I'm doing the right thing, going back. It was wonderful knowing what it was like to be whole again, even if it was only for a little while. Whatever Yahweh wills for me will happen. You taught me so much. Thank you for sharing the Messiah with us again, for bringing him to us after his first visit. Indeed, Barabbas and I have a story to tell, and yes, I sense that Jacob's Well may now be an area known for living water." She paused and sobbed, "Maybe…maybe one day we'll meet again. I hope so."

"I hope so too, sister. Who knows what Yahweh has in store for either of us? But one thing we do know - it'll be good! And whatever happens, we will meet again one day!"

They hugged again before pulling apart. Judith went over to Barabbas, "Brother," she said with a smile on her tear-stained face. "I'm glad I can call you brother."

He smiled back at her. "I didn't appreciate you coming into our community and recognising me. If I'm honest, you worried me. Whether you knew it or not, you made me consider my position. I'd been in the community for some time, a confirmed leper. I had no hope except to make the best of a bad situation, and perhaps to exploit my situation a little. It gave me time to reflect. At Jesus's trial I was intent on being the hard zealot before the Romans. I didn't care what happened to Jesus. It took a while for him to get to me, but that night when I got leprosy and saw his face, it shook me. I was hard. It wasn't going to affect me. But when you arrived and started telling the community about the Messiah, and then encouraged them to take on a mammoth project far greater than their ability, I became interested in a distant kind of way. You were good for me, Judith - and just look, your efforts have brought me into the Kingdom. I owe my life to you and to the Messiah today."

"Well, it wasn't just one way, you know," Judith said, grinning. "You brought out the worst in me."

He looked at her askance. "It's all right. I mean it for the best. You made me think too. Seeing you brought up old wounds – my brother and Josh – I absolutely hated you with a vengeance! And if I'm honest, I didn't know how to square it with the Lord. My feelings ran parallel to all the other good things going on - but to see you was like inflaming a bull's temper. It took time - just as it did for you - for Yahweh to reach me, and to get me to forgive." She stopped for a moment, then said, "Brother, we've been good for each other - and the Messiah's been good to us."

Barabbas nodded, and kissed her on the cheek. "I'm glad you're my sister, and I'll always treasure our friendship. Who knows if we'll ever meet again, but if we do, I know we'll be blessed!"

"I think what you're doing is amazing, Barabbas. Not many people would choose to go into a situation that might bring them harm, as you're doing."

"Our Lord did," said Barabbas simply.

Judith was radiant now, "He did. And just look at what he achieved. You'll do the same, if you become a zealot for him!" They both laughed. "The Lord bless you, brother! Let the living water flow through you."

"The Lord bless you, my sister. Enjoy your family. They deserve someone like you, to encourage them and build them up as you did us. You've been through some dark days, and now it's time to smile again."

Judith looked at him, wondering if he somehow knew about Josh's predictions for her in the past. He was probably just expressing a hope, she thought, but...

Becca climbed into her cart and Barabbas sat up front to drive the donkeys who seemed glad to be in harness again, unaffected apparently by their previous night's upset. After saying goodbye to Peter, Jonas, and Bartholomew they were about to set off, when Becca called to Judith, "Aren't you forgetting something?"

Judith went over to her to give her a final kiss. "Not that, sister, although it's very welcome," Becca laughed. "Your bag, your picture. You're not surely going to leave your smile behind!"

They both laughed, and Becca handed Judith her bag.

"Thank you, Becca…for everything. I won't forget you."

They embraced again, then Barabbas shook the reins and the cart started to move forward.

Peter said, "We'll have to be going too if we're to preach in two villages before starting for Jerusalem."

Judith climbed into her cart, closely followed by Jonas. Peter and Bartholomew preferred to walk, leading the donkeys.

The two carts followed the same route for a mile or two before Barabbas veered off the main road to drive over the scrubland to get to the community. Final farewells were shouted, and then Judith had her last view of Becca and

Barabbas. She wondered at the fact that it hadn't even been twenty-four hours since they had joined the road at that point. So much had happened since then. She had thought she was going with Barabbas and Becca to secure a deal. And what a deal she had secured…her healing! Now here she was travelling back with old friends to be with her family…and there was Tabitha's wedding too! Everything suddenly got on top of her. She began to cry quite piteously, and Jonas did his best to comfort her without success, until she exhausted herself.

"I must seem stupid to you," Judith said. "I've been given my life back, and here I am crying."

"You're not stupid, Judith," Jonas said soothingly. "You've been through a lot. Tabitha suffered much, believing you were dead. You must have suffered too. Yes, you would have known that she was alive, but because of your situation, she might as well have been dead to you. You made close friends where you were, you even helped Barabbas to come to Josh. It's difficult to leave people we love behind when we have to. Take comfort from the fact we've all had to do this – with Josh…our families…and those who have died serving Josh…like Mikha and Stephen. Josh promised us that if we leave family, friends, houses, lands, fathers, mothers, children, and even sisters and brothers –if we leave them for him, well, in the Kingdom we'll receive back a hundred times what we've had to give up."

"It doesn't help at the time," said Judith sniffing.

"But it does in the long term," Jonas said. "There's always hope for every believer."

Judith looked at him gratefully and dried her tears on the sleeve of her robe.

"Can I tell you something?" she asked.

"Of course," he said gently.

"I didn't think I was coming back…but somehow behind everything I knew Josh was speaking to me." She didn't feel it necessary to tell him about her trinket.

"Josh wouldn't have left you there without comfort."

"That's true, but…" Judith had intended trying to make sense of all the events that had happened to her. Perhaps now was as good a time as any. "I felt I was there as a punishment."

Jonas looked at her quizzically.

"Before Leaving Jerusalem, I had been disobedient. I put the others at risk by getting bored and going out. I was nearly caught. Also, I had been ungrateful for all Josh had done for me after Mikha died…not deliberately at first. It was just easy to take it for granted. Well, I had the feeling that contracting leprosy so quickly and finding myself in a community of lepers was my lot, my punishment. The day before I left Jerusalem, Josh implanted a word in my spirit – the word 'Nebuchadnezzar'."

Jonas looked puzzled.

"I didn't understand it either at first. I just knew he was speaking it to me and that it had some meaning. Well, I became involved in community life, some people became believers. But you can imagine, the day I met Barabbas there masquerading as their prophet, I nearly went mad, it threw me."

"That must have come as a shock. None of us would have recognised him. We weren't at Pilate's trial, and he'd gone by the time we got there."

"It really threw me. To make matters worse, as I mentioned last night, I had known him from the past in Galilee when he had been involved in the death of my baby brother. The Romans came for him and his zealot friends and accidentally trampled Joe to death trying to catch them."

"I didn't realise …"

Judith became emotional again, "I really hated him. I could hardly bear to talk to him on the rare occasions I bumped into him."

"I understand that."

"I didn't see it then, but I do now. Yahweh was preparing me for something, and apparently he was preparing Barabbas too."

"His ways are past finding out sometimes," Jonas said, smiling.

"You're right. And it took me a long time to find out. It was during one of my conversations, or should I say arguments with him, that I discovered what 'Nebuchadnezzar' meant. Barabbas tried to tell me Daniel was a kind of freedom fighter who would have overthrown Nebuchadnezzar given half a chance. It made me think of the stories concerning him. You'll remember the one in which Daniel predicted Nebuchadnezzar's fall and his exile from society, until he humbled himself and was restored?"

"I do," said Jonas. "Before we left Jerusalem, the apostles were studying Daniel, to try to get his understanding of the end times."

"Well, I was Nebuchadnezzar. I had to be humbled before I might return. It's all so clear now! Of course, at that time I had no indication my situation might be reversed. I lived in hope, but there didn't appear to be any avenue of possibility."

"Yes, but with Yahweh all things are possible! It's at times that these you need to wait, and to have patience. If Yahweh makes a promise, he keeps it - even if we don't know or see how he's going to do it."

"My hatred was getting the better of me, I'm afraid. I couldn't stomach the sight of Barabbas, and what he was getting away with. Last night I also talked about a woman who'd met Josh when you all arrived in her village those many years ago - you know, the one at Jacob's well. At our meeting, she told one of Josh's parables that had meant so much to her, about forgiveness. I realised this was just for me, and that Josh wanted me to forgive Barabbas. You know something…" Judith's eyes sparkled, "I humbled myself when Barabbas was lying in the ditch. I thought it might have been his last moment. I had to forgive him…and I did. It wasn't until that moment, I was restored. Josh kept his word!

And now, here I am going back to Jerusalem and Tabitha, something I never dared to dream I'd do. Trust Josh to keep his word. I'm so blessed!"

"You're right," said Jonas. "And it's time to start looking forward, to what's coming. I can't say what Josh has in store for you, but it must be good! He's brought you through so much."

"I believe it," said Judith brightening up. "And there's a wedding to attend!"

"Exactly! You're going to make Tabitha's day."

"It'll be so good. I can't wait!"

Jonas took advantage of Judith's sudden upturn. "Do you mind if I leave you just now?" he asked. "I need to talk to Peter about what we're going to do when we get to the villages."

"Not at all. I've got a lot to think about."

With that Jonas left, and Judith could hear him talking with the two men as they walked beside the donkeys.

What was she going to do, she wondered? It was a second chance indeed! She was privileged, as she had been in much of her life. She would grasp her new situation wholeheartedly. She felt an immense surge of thanks welling up in her to Josh. She wouldn't let him down. She dug in her bag for her picture. She needed to see her smile, and feel all that she felt when she looked at it. Becca and Barabbas were gone. They had been such major players in her recent past, and she wouldn't forget them. She hoped she might meet with them again - but for now, she must focus on the future and leave sad farewells in the past. She had a life to live, and she would lead it as she had done in the community – with all her heart, for the benefit of others. She smiled to herself. She was going to get the chance of seeing her lovely daughter again. Tabitha was marrying Jonas! And now she could do something she thought she would never have had the opportunity of doing. She had believed that perhaps one day the two of them might get married. Now she could be fully involved in their lives...and maybe see her grandchildren if they were to have any. No longer was she going to wallow in the past with its sadnesses. She was thankful for all that Josh and Yahweh had done for her. She wasn't going to take their help for granted any more, or be complacent. She was going to live life to the full. She had been humbled, and had learned her lesson. No going backwards now, only forwards as fast as she could! She felt a vibration in her pouch and she took the green cross from the folds of her robe. As she looked at it, she saw the familiar morphing into the face of Josh. He was smiling at her and she felt a glow of satisfaction, as if she had done something that had pleased him. His mouth was moving, and the words came into her mind, "I have loved you with an everlasting love. You are mine. Your smile must return, for I am with you." She felt that a response was needed from her and so she said, "Thank you Josh – for humbling me, for helping me survive through my illness, for showing me how to help the community, for healing me, and...for

353

bringing me to Barabbas. I didn't deserve the chance of bringing him to you but thank you for making it part of your plan. You've always kept your word to me. You've always caused me to smile - even through it all." A sudden thought struck her, and she added, "Thank you Josh for lending Faithie to me again - not even once, but twice. You don't leave us comfortless, and you know just the right things that will encourage us, that will lead us on your paths. Thank you for Little Faith whom you sent. I give her back to you now and look forward to meeting with her again…in the same way that you're letting me meet with Tabitha again. Thank you. I don't deserve your kindness or love, but you have once again met my heart's desires." The pulsating stopped and the face receded. One word filled Judith's mind - "Go!" It remained until she responded in her heart, "yes Lord!"

The sun was now high in the sky, and after a little while they came to a village a hundred or so yards off the main road. It obviously benefited from the through traffic to Jerusalem, and Judith could see that its market square was thronging with people milling between the stalls. Peter and Jonas would have a captive audience as they preached the good news to them. They positioned the cart in a highly visible area and asked if Judith would mind vacating it so that they could stand upon it to be seen more easily by the people. Judith said it would be a good chance for her to explore the market. She hadn't been in one like this for such a long time. She had noticed as she had put the cross back into her pouch that there were two gold coins nestling in it too. They had been given her by Samara before she had left the community. And now this seemed an ideal opportunity to purchase a gift for Tabitha. Judith threaded her way through the market looking for something appropriate - looking in clothes, pottery, and novelty stalls. Nothing caught her attention, and after a good half hour's browsing, she felt disappointed and disillusioned with her search. She had worked her way to the farther edge of the market and was faced now by a row of small houses. She could hear in the distance Peter's voice calling people to repent and believe. She assumed that healings were happening as every so often a roar arose from the growing crowd. At one stage she was passed by a man and a woman who were excitedly praising Yahweh. The man was telling everyone he came across that his blindness had been healed. His face was radiant, and he kept telling his wife not to hold onto him - he didn't need guided any more. Both of them were laughing and rejoicing. Judith smiled at them and joined in their praises.

It was just at that point that she noticed out of the corner of her eyes something blue at the other end of the square. It was slightly taller than the other stalls and looked remarkably like the top of a tent. Her heart leapt. It surely wasn't likely…but she had to check. Could it be…could it possibly be Abbas's tent? She started to walk in its direction, and sure enough when she had passed most of the other stalls, it became absolutely clear that she was looking at a blue tent the spitting image of the one that belonged to Abbas. What was she to do? Should she barge in? If it wasn't Abbas's tent, she could imagine the welcome she would get! She decided to get as near to it as she could without actually going in. As she approached its entrance, it seemed to Judith that the street around her had become strangely quiet. The market had been packed, as were many of the roads onto it, but this end of the market was empty and she was the only person there. At least, it seemed so, until she spied someone coming out of the tent itself. The movement was swift but definite. The figure was beckoning to her. It was walking quickly towards her - actually not walking, but floating an inch or two off the ground. Judith tensed. Was the figure actually beckoning to her? The nearer it got, Judith froze, stunned almost to the point of fainting. The person she was looking at...there could be no mistaking it...was...herself! How could that be? There was no trick mirror anywhere about. The figure did not mimic her in any way. It was a separate individual...and it was her! On closer inspection, she saw it was not quite like her - it was a younger version of her. The figure stopped about ten feet away from her, and now that recognition had occurred, it was clear that the person expected her to follow her through the flaps of the tent. Judith gritted her teeth and moved forward, not knowing what she might find when she went in.

"Hello again, my dear. You have returned," the familiar voice of Abbas greeted her from further inside. Her eyes had not yet adjusted and so she could not see him at first.

"Come in, and rest!" he said. "Your journey has been long and hard, but now you can rest."

Judith quickly glanced around her once her eyes had adjusted. The tent was as before, filled with bales of clothes - and beyond them an area with cabinets and counters bathed in a yellowish glow. Something she hadn't seen before was a hanging or curtain on the far side of the tent just beyond the cabinets. She took it all in in a second, then followed her image further in to where Abbas's voice had come from.

"You are welcome, my dear Judith. You have endured much and served me well. Those who have been faithful in little will be entrusted with much."

"You...you helped me, although I...I didn't always know it," Judith said haltingly. "It was all of you. I don't deserve any credit."

"You are blessed, Judith. My Son loves you and has spoken to me on your behalf. We both want your smile and your image to survive."

While he was speaking, her younger image had positioned herself just behind him to his right and was smiling at her. Judith was captivated by this, but asked nothing.

"We need something from you now, and you mustn't hold back. Those who give willingly shall freely receive much more from me. I am more willing to give than you can conceive."

"What can I give you?"

"Something I entrusted to you when you lost your dear one. You were in distress and my angel passed it to you and deposited it with you for your safekeeping. I would not see you comfortless. Sophia needs it now for her survival. She has lent her strength to you through your dark days and now she is exhausted. She needs to take her rest for a time and gather her strength for living. Her dark days will come, and she will need what you have."

The green cross in Judith's pouch was throbbing.

Abbas turned to her angel image standing beside him, "Well done, Sophia! You have indeed strengthened my daughter as I asked. You have lent her your thoughts and experiences in her time of need, and now it is your turn to return. My strength and the image of my Son will go with you. Be faithful to Me as you grow and embrace life. Do so to the full and I will be with you. Your image will be required again in your latter days. Be ready when I call."

Sophia smiled at him, and then proceeded towards Judith. Judith half expected her to stop when she came close, but that didn't happen. Sophia kept on coming, as she had done in the Garden of Gethsemane years earlier, and seemed to pass through her. There was an enlivening as she did so, and then a diminution of her spiritual awareness and happiness as she left. Judith looked around quickly, but Sophia was gone. She was nowhere to be seen.

Abbas was talking again. "Your image strengthened you in your time of need. She shares your thoughts and experiences - and one day you will need each other, and your images will meet for the last time. I told her to be ready for the call. You must also remain ready. The two that are one are separate for now, but the day of reunion will be a glorious but awful one. Both of you will cling to each other and only your smiles will help you overcome. I have spoken, and it will all come to pass. Now follow me!"

He moved beyond the bales into the softly glowing cabinet area, and Judith followed. He put his hands on her shoulders and held her at arm's length, looking straight into her eyes.

"Many do not get a second chance, but I have plans for you. I told you that when you were making your Obligation Ceremony with my Son. His plan has been fulfilled, but yours is yet to mature. We gave you an image to sustain you, and I gave you a trinket in your early days to help you with Joe's passing. Mikha's passing was painful for you and led to your struggle with life. Sophia has now taken the cross I gave you to remind her of me through her own life struggles, and she will survive as you have done until the day of your joining. Now, you have to make a choice, and the choice you make will determine your path from this place and time."

Judith looked worried.

"Do you remember, when you came to me at first, I placed you before this cabinet?" he pointed, and walked towards a cabinet containing strangely glowing objects. Judith followed. As they stood before it, Judith's eyes were drawn to a

356

yellow pendant that glowed and sparkled eerily in its setting. She was so glad to see it again!

"You have to make a choice again and make it your heart's desire. You must want it with all of your heart, as all your heart will be required for the path you and your image will take. Choose now and choose well!'"

Judith was terrified. What if she made the wrong choice? She remembered experiencing something similar almost thirty years ago when she had first entered his tent in Galilee. The wrong choice might determine for her a horrible path! She sensed though that even her choosing was part of his plan. If she was to trust to her heart's desire, she would choose the right one and the crisis would be averted. She surveyed the cabinet shelves and their settings. Stones and gems of all colours were glowing and shimmering. After some moments, her eye was drawn to a setting on a high shelf. Two objects glowed together in that one setting. They were like earrings but when she looked more closely, she saw that they were matching silver rings. The most beautiful blue glow emanated from each – Judith had never seen such a beautiful blue – her eyes were utterly transfixed.

"You have chosen well, my dear." He reached up and took one out of the setting. "This shall be yours until you don't need it any more. Unlike my other gifts, it will not need to be hidden away. Wear it well and be proud of its link with my Son and myself." He placed it upon her wedding finger. Faintly at first, and then more strongly, she could hear a girl's voice singing coming from behind the hanging a little further on. It was beautiful and solo. "Your lifesong has been restored to you, my dear. It too will sustain you in times to come." Another fainter girl's voice joined it and the two blended in perfect harmony. "The other voice, Judith, is that of your image. When the two become one, you will both be with me for ever. Other images will join you too."

Judith looked at Abbas with questioning eyes. She looked up at the other glowing blue ring.

Abbas anticipated her, "Yes, my dear, you're right. This is reserved for your image when she is ready. An indestructible link will be forged at that time which will bind you both to my Son and myself. It will span heaven, earth and the ages, and we will be one."

He sat down on a stool at the edge of the hanging and clapped his hands. The hanging seemed to dissolve in front of her and in a split-second Judith was standing in the street again. She looked around and the tent was no longer there. The street was as empty as it was when she first arrived. She looked down at her finger to check she still wore the ring. It was there…but the stone wasn't as shapeless as she had at first thought. It still sparkled and glowed even in the strong sunlight - but it had a shape all its own. Was it a fish, she wondered? On holding it close to her face she could see a head which came to a point and a tail that fanned out behind. It was beautiful, a precious work of art…and there were two of them! She felt somehow privileged to be wearing it, and could sense that Sophia her image would also come to appreciate it in time. She thought back to Abbas's words, and thrust her hand into her pouch. The cross, her faithful companion over the past months, was gone - as were her golden coins. Judith shrugged her shoulders. What could they compare with her ring, and that marvellous meeting with Abbas? She felt so alive, so happy. She felt her whole spirit enlivened. She felt ecstatic - and with it, a sudden impulse to sing. She might have indeed broken into song if she hadn't been brought back down to earth by Bartholomew.

"Judith! Judith! Are you ready?"

"She looked quizzically at him, as he stood at the other end of the street nearest the square. "Ready?" she asked.

"Yes," Bartholomew replied, "ready to go. We have to move on to our next village. Peter and Jonas are finished here."

"Yes. I'm finished here too," Judith said, and walked towards him. "I couldn't find anything for Tabitha's wedding though. But no matter. I had a wonderful time looking."

"Yes, amazing things have been happening at the cart. Miracle after miracle. The donkeys were getting scared as demons were being cast out. It's been a glorious time - and many more Samaritans have become believers."

"Wonderful," said Judith enthusiastically. "Yahweh is in this place!"

"He most definitely is!" agreed Bartholomew, and they both walked back to the cart praising Yahweh for His goodness.

Chapter Forty

Back at the cart, Peter and Jonas were ecstatic. They had witnessed many miracles and were caught up in the excitement of it all. A small group of new believers remained and wished them well as they packed up and started to leave. Judith and Bartholomew joined them and the journey to the next village was begun.

"It's always exciting to see the Holy Spirit work!" said Peter, walking with Jonas and Bartholomew beside the donkeys.

Jonas nodded in agreement. "To my mind there's no question that Yahweh is moving amongst the gentiles."

"I agree with you, Jonas," Peter said, "but it's going to be hard to sell to the believers who want strict adherence to the Law."

Judith sitting in the cart near the front couldn't help hearing their conversation, and decided to contribute to it. "Surely they can't argue with experience? I've experienced it; you've now experienced it – Yahweh is doing a new thing, just as Josh said. I've lived amongst them for over a year and a half. The Holy Spirit's only too glad to get involved if people will open their hearts."

Peter still looked a bit dubious, "It's not that I don't believe it, but the scriptures tell us that first and foremost, we Jews are Yahweh's chosen people. The gentiles don't really figure. In fact, there are some Jews who believe that the gentiles are Yahweh's fuel for hell!"

"That doesn't make them right though," said Judith." Sensing anger rising in her. "They are people just like us, equally deserving of Yahweh's goodness."

"Look Peter," said Jonas, "Look at what Josh did. He treated gentiles with respect. He didn't discriminate. Remember these ten lepers he healed, and one of them was a Samaritan? The Samaritan one was the only one who came back to thank him!"

"I heard about that," said Judith. "It was all over our community. That man toured Samaria telling everyone what the Messiah had done for him."

Don Treader

"But Josh was careful to consider the Law," argued Peter. "He didn't go out of his way to break it. He respected our customs."

Jonas snorted, "He was careful, but I can't totally agree with you. He made a point of getting round the Law. Look at the people he healed on the sabbath. He allowed us to pick grain on the sabbath and eat it. He got angry with those who limited Yahweh from working by invoking the Law, contending with them, and showing them by what he did, Yahweh was on his side of the argument."

"Right then, what about the woman from Tyre?" Peter countered. "He wouldn't even talk to her when she begged him to heal her daughter. We tried to get rid of her…but what was it he said, 'I was sent only to help Yahweh's lost sheep, the people of Israel. It isn't right to take food from the children and throw it to the dogs'."

"That's what he said all right," agreed Jonas, "but don't you remember what she replied, 'That's true, Lord, but even dogs eat the scraps that fall beneath their master's table'. And the result? Josh told her, 'Your faith is great. Your request is granted', and instantly her daughter was healed."

"But he was sent to the Jews first. We have some say in the matter," Peter protested. "Yahweh chose us first."

"But the results, Peter. Don't ignore the results. Josh may have had his priorities, but he had compassion he had mercy on the gentiles. He wasn't all that happy with you at one point…remember?"

Peter looked askance at him, "What do you mean?"

"You surely haven't forgotten the time we were travelling through Samaria on our way back to Jerusalem - just like we are now? A Samaritan village refused to give us lodging because it looked as if we were going to Jerusalem. You asked Josh if we should call down fire from heaven to burn down that village. Josh told you he was come to save the lost, not to destroy them."

Peter looked humbled by Jonas's repetition of Josh's words. "I was wrong then," but in defence of his position, he came back with, "but there is an order…Jews first and then gentiles!"

"I don't disagree with that," said Jonas smiling. "After all, when he met us after his resurrection, when he was about to be taken to heaven, he told us that we'd be witnesses for him in Jerusalem, throughout Judea, in Samaria and to the ends of the earth. I believe he had a plan, but his intention was that eventually the gentiles would be saved too."

"I agree, Jonas!" Judith interjected excitedly. "It's time to get out of our comfort zones. Apart from the persecution, it's been quite easy for us to witness to our own people. They have the Law; they know the scriptures. Josh as Messiah could resonate with many of them. Perhaps the persecution was for a purpose though. I'd never have wanted the deaths of Mikha or of Stephen - but they woke us up, even shook us up. Many of us were forced to leave Jerusalem and go to the

360

gentiles. And just look at the results. The Holy Spirit's making, and filling, gentile believers! It's so exciting. And Yahweh's involving us in it."

Jonas eyes indicated he agreed with Judith's enthusiastic assessment. Peter on the other hand was going to need more convincing. He said grudgingly, "I can't deny these things. I've been involved in them too. But there are differences between us and the gentiles. Yahweh made them different...and chose us first."

"But brother," Jonas said, "it doesn't mean that Yahweh can't change the rules. Josh realigned them. Perhaps it was Yahweh's will all along to save the world. He just chose us to pass on the message, and we didn't do so well. He's doing a new thing now!"

Peter replied, "There are differences, but perhaps our testimonies and the testimonies of others who've witnessed to the gentiles will sway the legalists in 'The Way'," he looked at Judith, "and drag us out of our comfort zones."

Judith felt quite bold now, "Yahweh's doing that already. We should keep up!"

A water bottle was passed around for them all to refresh themselves. They weren't far from the second village, and so as Bartholomew steered the cart into its square, all of them prepared themselves for dealing with the anticipated crowds.

Peter came over to Judith. "We're going to talk to the people about Josh. Some of them will have already heard of him from Philip who passed through here some time ago. I'd like you to tell them that it's not a faith just for Jews. It's for everyone, including Samaritans. Tell them of your experience, and your healing. I want them to know that Yahweh is real, that Josh is their Messiah too, and that they can be saved and healed today by just listening and receiving."

Judith's face glowed with appreciation. Peter had asked her to speak! Apprehensive she might have been, but in her last viewing of the green cross, Josh had told her to 'Go!'; and implicit in what Abbas had just told her was the fact that she had a plan to fulfil, part of which was to spread the Good News. She accepted Peter's invitation with a full heart. She felt excited, and a sense of expectation that the Holy Spirit would work with her.

Peter started talking, telling the people about the Messiah who had been sent from Yahweh to them. It was clear he was having a hard time convincing Samaritan non-believers. They were steeped in their own customs and traditions. People were drifting away, and most of the remainder heckling him, when he asked Judith to talk. She stood up on the cart and faced a curious but hostile crowd. Women didn't often speak in public, and so those who remained decided to give her a hearing. The sight of her drew others and soon the little gathering had swollen to a large one.

"Friends, brothers and sisters. I want you to look at me." She did something unthinkable for a woman in that culture. She pulled down her hood and bared her face before them. Some gasped, others fixed their eyes on her. "What do you see?"

she asked. "It may surprise you to know that until yesterday, I was a leper with full blown leprosy. It was in an advanced state. I was covered in blotches and sores, my nose was disintegrating, one of my toes had partially fallen off, and my fingers and toes were numb. I was having trouble getting about, and spent most of my time on my mat. What do you see now? Do you see any leprosy? Of course not." A murmur of agreement swept through the crowd. More were joining it all the time, surprised to see a bare headed woman speaking. Judith continued. "I was healed yesterday by Jesus the Messiah."

Someone shouted from the crowd, "But you're a Jew, lady. You believe in that stuff. Yahweh's for you, the Messiah's for you. They're not interested in us. We're not good enough for you. Why tell us your good news? It's not for us…and anyway, it probably didn't happen!"

"No, my friend," said Judith feeling the Holy Spirit surge inside her and help her be bold, "That's not true. Yahweh and Jesus the Messiah are absolutely interested in you and we've come to prove it to you today."

"Where are they then?" sneered a middle-aged burly man in the crowd. "Why aren't they here with you today. We could then see them…and maybe they could heal us too!"

The crowd laughed and seemed to be turning against Judith.

She stood her ground, "Actually they are here today, and we'll prove it to you soon. But first, listen to my story. Please believe me that I was healed. You shouldn't say that Samaritans aren't deserving. I've just spent a year and a half in the leper community down beside Jacob's Well. There are many good people there, all of whom are my friends. They could testify, if they were allowed to be here today, that I spent a year and a half working amongst them as a leper."

"Well, they're not!" someone else shouted.

Another person, a woman this time, said, "Leave her alone! Let's hear her story."

The crowd quietened, and Judith continued.

"I want to tell you, that you're no different from us Jews. You live in poverty, you suffer, you die. You have the same concerns – how to do our best for our families, how to make ends meet. In my year and a half in the community, I found them the most wonderful people to be with, and they became my friends."

"How did you get healed? There are lepers near our village – our friends and partners – they need it too!" The woman who spoke had tears in her eyes. "My husband's there. I want him back!"

Judith looked sympathetically at her. "Yahweh is able. Listen!" Judith paused, and when she had their full attention, she continued. "First of all, let me tell you what happened. A few years before I got there, Jesus of Nazareth and his friends passed through the village. Many of you will have heard of him. Some of you may have come across a Samaritan leper whom he healed. He's apparently been travelling through your communities telling you about Jesus the Messiah. Jesus

362

told these villagers then that one day, there would be no need for Mount Gerizim or the Temple Mount in Jerusalem. People, all people, would be able to worship Yahweh anywhere as long as they worshipped in spirit and truth. Well, I was in Jerusalem the day the Messiah was murdered. He was the most perfect man who ever lived. He healed thousands, and spoke into people's hearts as if Yahweh was speaking directly to them. The authorities were jealous though and had him face a trumped-up trial, then had the Romans execute him. That was the worst day of my life. He had done so much for me." She said as an aside, "he'd even brought my daughter Tabitha back from the dead." Now some in the crowd scoffed, but others silenced them. "He lay in the grave three days, but on the third day he came back to life. Yahweh couldn't leave his Son there. He'd done nothing worthy of death, or of his punishment. Only good things, only wonderful things. Even as he was being nailed to his cross he said, 'Father, forgive them, they know not what they're doing'. He was crucified because of our sins, and all of us have sinned. Who hasn't? But he pled with his Father to forgive us, and as a sign of this forgiveness, his Father raised him up from death."

"Where's he now then?" the burly man shouted again.

"After forty days of appearing to his followers – three of us here actually met with him, and even more than five hundred people witnessed him alive at one stage, many of whom are still alive and you could check out - anyway, after forty days he was taken up to heaven by his Father, but he will return again at the end of days."

"How does that help us then?" The burly man was in the mood to be obstreperous.

"Because he's given us his Spirit; and the promise that wherever his message of good news is spoken, he'll be with us. You'll see people become believers because his Spirit will convince their hearts; and you'll see healings like the one I experienced yesterday." She pointed to Peter and Jonas. "These men can tell you more…they'll pray for your sick later."

Judith sat down, a sense of exhilaration filling her. She had felt the Spirit moving and she knew that Josh was mingling with, and speaking to, the crowd.

Peter got to his feet. "It's true, my friends. All that Judith has told you is true. Jesus the Messiah has come to you today to make Yahweh his Father real. If you'll open your hearts to him and believe – the only way to do so is to repent of your sins, turn from them, and accept his forgiveness which was freely given to you by his suffering the punishment for our sins on the cross. You can know in a split second that he's alive, if you'll open your hearts."

Peter gave them time to think about it and to comply. Not a great deal had been said, but it was enough for Josh and the Spirit to work on the crowd. Judith could see many changed faces.

Peter spoke again, "The Messiah wants to make himself real to you. If you want this, then come forward to us and let us lay hands on you so you can receive his Spirit. I guarantee you that things will never be the same again. Yield your hearts and your lives to the Messiah and he'll give you living water. You won't hunger and thirst for the paltry things of life again. You'll feel satisfied for ever and experience abundant life. When he was with us, the Messiah said, 'I have come to give you life, and give it abundantly'. Yahweh wants to give you good things this day. Don't hold back."

Peter and Jonas got off the cart and stood beside it. They prayed for those who wanted to become believers. The woman who had expressed the desire to have her husband back asked to speak to Judith. Judith came down too, and talked with her.

"Your husband is in a leper community?" she asked.

"Yes," the woman said crying. "And it's so hard. I've got four children, and it's difficult to bring them up without him. I miss him."

Judith nodded sympathetically, but she sensed that the woman had more to tell her.

"I'm living with a man now, and I can't bring myself to tell my husband. I don't feel right."

Judith told her about Josh's dealings with Becca, her five husbands and the man she had been living with wasn't even her husband. "You have needs, but Yahweh knows, and can help you. Jesus didn't condemn her, but he offered her something better - this living water. It would satisfy her."

"I want it too," the woman said, sobbing.

"Can I pray with you?" asked Judith with trepidation. She had never been in this position before, in front of a crowd. The woman nodded, and the two women bowed their heads.

"Father, your daughter before you wants to believe. She has acknowledged her sins and wants your Spirit to come into her life and give her the living water you promised to all who would believe. Do so now, I pray you!" Instantly the woman's head jerked backwards as if she had been hit by a strong gust of wind. Her mouth seemed to utter words that Judith couldn't make out, but most impressively her face was transformed. It became radiant. Judith felt amazed at the sudden transformation, but she felt she had to reach out further. "Father, you know her heart, how heavy it has been. I pray that you would heal her husband and restore him to his family. Show her that her heart has been hardened, and that until she acknowledges its state and willingly corrects it - and her actions - her husband will remain where he is."

The woman looked horrified. "How did you know that I was struggling? I do want my husband back - but at times I've given up that idea. I like what I've got now."

"Yahweh knows your heart. He's telling me what you need to do. Put him first and he'll work out the other things. You'll get your husband back if you seek him with a pure and whole heart." The woman looked conflicted and left. Judith wondered what she would do. Becca had been so impressed by Josh and his promises that she had told everyone about him and put her life straight. Would this woman do the same?

Peter and Jonas were now praying for the sick. Some had left the crowd to go and fetch those who needed healing. First Judith saw a deaf and dumb man being released. The shout he gave echoed around the market. A blind woman who had been led up to them walked away on her own. Judith was startled when she heard screaming coming from the edge of the crowd. A man seemed to be having a seizure. Those around him backed off as he threw himself on the ground and started foaming at the mouth. Jonas went up to him and commanded the evil spirit to leave him. "I know why you're here," the demon spoke through the man, as he writhed on the ground. Jonas silenced him, then said with great authority the like of which Judith hadn't seen before in him, "In the name of Jesus of Nazareth, come out of him!" Another scream, and more writhing, then the man became motionless and silent.

"He's dead!" some in the crowd around him said.

Jonas shook his head. He bent down and took the man by the arm, and lo and behold, he began to get to his feet. Standing up now, he was a different person. His senses seemed to have returned to him and he was thanking Yahweh. The crowd stood by, quite amazed. "He's been like that a long time," one man said. "We couldn't get him to act normally. He was always shouting and doing something strange. He looks like a changed man!"

No-one was heckling now. Everyone was amazed and impressed. One man came running up as the crowd was thinning. He begged Peter, "Sir, my brother's desperately ill. I can't get him off his mat. It's too difficult for him to come here. I did try, but I've had to leave him lying on his mat outside my house. Will you come?"

Peter agreed to go. Jonas and Judith accompanied him, leaving Bartholomew to look after the cart and the donkeys. Judith had to walk fast to keep up with the two men. They entered a narrow street which left the far side of the square, then turned down an even narrower one. Judith was surprised to see a number of what looked like sick and crippled people sitting or lying outside their houses. Peter was intent on following the man to his house and therefore didn't notice all that Judith did who was coming behind. It was mid-afternoon, and the shadows cast by the sun on the low houses were lengthening. Judith saw that as Peter's shadow fell on the sick people they passed, each of them seemed affected by it. Often, they jerked upwards, or shouted loudly sometimes screaming. Some of them even struggled to their feet and appeared to walk unaided. She tried to draw Peter and

Jonas's attention to this, but they remained oblivious as they talked to the man whose house they were making for. Soon they arrived at his door and started praying for his sick brother. Now he too began to experience what Judith had noticed others undergoing on their way there. Within moments he was rejoicing and giving Yahweh thanks. Indeed, there was a great deal of rejoicing in that street! Once again Peter and Jonas were surrounded by others clamouring for them to come to their houses too.

Suddenly Judith felt a tugging at her arm, and she saw beside her the woman she had prayed for earlier.

"Please come with me!" she said. "I've decided. I want to change. I'll make things straight. All I want is my husband back."

Judith smiled at her, "You're putting Yahweh first."

"Yes. I want to." The woman looked anxious. "But will you come with me?"

Judith asked, "Where to, my sister?"

"Come with me to the Valley of Lepers. It's outside of town, but not too far away."

"Your husband?" Judith asked.

"The woman nodded. "I want him back!"

"Let's wait then till the others are ready." Judith didn't want to get separated from them.

"No. You come. It's you I want. You know…"

Judith looked hesitant. She approached Jonas. "This woman wants me to accompany her to the leper colony not far from here. Don't leave without me!"

He smiled. "We wouldn't do that. We don't want to lose you for a second time. I'll stick with Peter just now. May Yahweh go with you."

Judith suddenly felt a great lack of confidence. She felt vulnerable. What did this woman expect of her? She wasn't a healer!

Two more streets and they were out of the village. A few minutes' further walk, and they were looking into a shallow valley full of rocks and boulders. Some scrub fields lay beyond, supporting what looked like meagre crops. It reminded Judith of what she had just left the day before. It had improved greatly while she had been there, but when she had first arrived, her valley wasn't too dissimilar to what she could see before her. Some people were working in the distance. The woman cupped her hands around her mouth, and called loudly, "Abram! Abram!"

Judith saw a man look up at them, separate himself from the rest, and start towards them. AS he drew closer his pace slowed until he stopped a bout thirty yards away from them.

"Wife?" he said. "Why have you come now? And who's this?"

The woman answered him, "I've come to get you back!"

He looked surprised, and then laughed, "Is this a joke, Mira? If so, it's not very funny. You know I can't leave here!"

"I know. I know," said Mira, impatiently and with some aggravation. "But I've brought this woman to you, Abram. She can help."

Abram looked Judith up and down, and a disrespectful look crossed his face. "What kind of woman goes around with her head uncovered?"

Judith interrupted their conversation, "Abram, yesterday, I was just like you. I lived in a leper community at Jacob's Well. I had advanced leprosy and I was dying."

He looked at Judith sceptically, "And what changed?"

"Can you see any leprosy on my body?" Judith asked.

"Not on your face, your hands or your feet," he admitted. "But how do I know you had leprosy and that you are completely healed?"

"You don't. You have to take my word for it, I'm afraid. I can only tell you what the Messiah did for me."

She told him some of the things her leprosy had done to her, but he still looked singularly unimpressed.

"Anyone could know these things," he said.

"But her friends are up in the village, and you'd be amazed at what's happening. Many people are believing in the Messiah, and others are being healed. I've seen blind people receive their sight. You know Hannah's Jobab – he's walking now. You have to see it to believe it!"

"I can't!" Abram said bitterly. "So, you've come here to mock me?"

"No! No!" Mira said. "It's not like that!"

Abram was crying now, and his face softened. "I'd like to come back…but you know, it's impossible!"

"No sir, it's not," Judith interrupted again. "Nothing's impossible for Yahweh. And the Messiah, Yahweh's Son, is in your village today – indeed he's right here. Give him a chance. Let me pray for you."

He laughed bitterly, "What have I to lose?"

Judith sensed the Spirit quickening her. "Come closer," she said.

He looked uncertainly at her, "But…I'm unclean. You want to keep away from me."

"No, I don't," said Judith. "I want to lay my hands on you and pray for you."

He backed off a bit further from her, and his wife said, "You can't do that. You might catch it!"

"Look at my face," Judith said boldly to the two of them. "Do you see any leprosy there?"

Both of them shook their heads.

"Well, I was well covered with blotches and spots yesterday. The Messiah has healed me, and he can do the same for you today. I know he can."

"I don't want to give it to you," Abram said looking worried.

"You won't. I've had it already. I've been cleansed, and so can you be."

He still held back.

Judith felt prompted to go further. "I'm only here for minutes more. The Messiah is here wanting you to believe and receive a miracle. Tell me how you know that I mean business, that I believe He's here and that he can heal you?"

Both Mira and Abram said nothing.

Judith continued, "Would I be willing to lay my hands on you if I didn't believe? I believe beyond the shadow of a doubt," she said smiling at them.

Abram decided she was genuine and so he came slowly towards her. "Do your worst then," he said.

"No. I'll do my best," Judith said, and placed one hand on his head, the other on his shoulder. "In the name of Jesus Christ of Nazareth, be healed of this terrible disease. I restore you now to your wife and family. The Lord gives, and the Lord takes away. Leprosy - be gone!"

Abram flinched, then slowly crumpled onto the ground.

"What's happening to him!" wailed Mira.

"He's receiving his healing," Judith said simply.

"But he's dead!"

"No. Watch! He's moving."

Abram came around, and gave out a strong cry of pain. "It's awful!" he moaned. "The pain's gone right through me. I'm dying!"

"No, you're not," said Judith confidently. "You're going through what I went through at first. But it'll pass, and you'll be clean. You'll search for the blotches and the spots, the numbness and the disfigurement, and you won't be able to find any trace of them."

Abram was sitting up now and rubbing at his fingers and toes. "I can feel them!" he said with amazement. "I've got feeling again."

"Your blotches have vanished, Abram!" his wife called out. "You're healed! You're healed!"

Judith wasn't the only one touching his head now. She withdrew her hands smiling, allowing him to run his fingers over his head and face. "I am healed!" he said. "My skin's smooth, and my hair's been restored. No more patches and sores! I'm healed." He burst into tears, closely followed by his wife. "You've no idea how much I've longed for this day. Hopeless. I never thought I'd leave this place or get back with you. But no more. Your Messiah has healed me!" He looked gratefully at Judith. "I believe. I'm sorry I doubted you. Thank you!"

"Don't hold back," Judith warned. "Give yourselves fully to each other, with no condemnation, no recrimination. You have been healed for a purpose. Tell others about Jesus the Messiah. Tell them what He's done for you - and the Kingdom will be yours!"

Mira hugged her husband for the first time in years. Judith joined with them, putting her arms around them, and closing her eyes. "The Lord bless you!" she whispered, and a ripple ran through her body. When she opened her eyes again, she was standing on the other side of the cart from Bartholomew. He looked up and said, "Oh Judith, I didn't see you coming. You've beaten the men!" He looked down the street to the other end of the square, "Ah, here they are now. We'll be able to get away soon. Next stop, Jerusalem!"

Judith smiled and climbed aboard the cart. Abbas had thrown her in at the deep end!

Chapter Forty-One

"Don't move or you're dead, girl!"

The hoarse whisper came from the side of Judith's head. It was dark, and she could see nothing, but she was horribly aware of foul-smelling breath on her face going up her nose, and she wanted to be sick. She resisted coughing and retching however because of the fear clutching at her heart, and because of the explicit threat. She could feel something sharp pressed against her neck, becoming ever firmer and deeper; she decided not to struggle, otherwise she believed she might breathe her last.

"Get out of the cart if you value your life!" the hoarse whisper came again. "NO noise though, or I'll slit you."

Judith could barely make out the bearded hooded face of a man staring over the edge of the cart at her, but as the pressure on her neck became stronger, she decided it would be best to do as he said. She slowly raised herself first to her elbows and then to her knees. She then stood up crouching so that she could lower herself from the back of the cart onto the ground.

"No!" the voice said sharply. "Stay, while I look over the cart."

She obeyed, her heart beating wildly. After a moment or two the voice came again, hoarse, and insistent," Get out, and take your bag with you. Women's stuff won't be of any use to us where we're going. Take it, and no noise mind! There are two knives pointed straight at you if you try to raise the alarm."

Judith's head had been lying on her bag because it was quite soft, it being filled with her spare robe and other garments. She picked it up now and slipped off the back of the cart as noiselessly as she could.

"Right, come over here!" the man said. He motioned to the opposite side of the road from where the rest of her party had their tents pitched.

Judith could see that there were three men, one holding the reins of the donkeys, one trying to hitch them to the cart, and the other dealing with her.

371

"What are you doing?" she asked in a whisper. "We've done you no harm. Why are you picking on us?"

"We want the cart," came the whispered reply. "You and your friends can walk. We have greater need of it."

"But it's not yours. You've no right to take it."

"Be quiet, or I'll keep my promise to slit you. We're zealots. It's needed for kingdom work!"

"You're not working for Yahweh's Kingdom!" Judith managed to say, thinking she might be taking a risk by doing so.

"Not that kingdom," the man sneered. "That's for the collaborators, the weak mindless religious types that follow 'The Way'. We're nothing like them. We'll set up the kingdom of Israel again by killing the Romans."

Judith thought it best to say no more about this in case she aggravated him into action. She changed the subject. "Can you not spare us? I'm going to my daughter's wedding tomorrow in Jerusalem. We're a long way away from there. You'll cause me to miss it."

"Too bad," he said unsympathetically. "We need the cart more than you do. We're on a mission, and tomorrow night, there will be a good few Romans less to cause our nation trouble!"

Judith froze at the thought of this threat. The ring on her finger vibrated and she felt she should say something. She couldn't just let them get away with their cart without attempting to stop them. She looked over the cart to where the two tents were pitched on the other side of the road. The zealots had done a good job of not waking the men. They had obviously had to waken her to get her off the cart so they could take it. It was down to her alone to say something, so she asked, "Do you know the zealot Barabbas?"

The man humoured her for a moment although he was keen to get going. The other men were struggling to get the donkeys in harness, so he indulged her. "There are lots of zealots called Barabbas – which one are you thinking of?" he sneered again.

"The one that murdered Romans a few years ago, the one the governor set free in place of Jesus whom people call the Messiah."

"You mean, the fake Messiah. He'd nothing to do with us. All this peace and love stuff would never get rid of the Romans. Yes, I know who you're talking about. He was a bit of a legend for a while. After he got away, we thought he'd lead us into revolution, but he disappeared off the scene. We'd heard a rumour that he was a leper man now." He laughed scornfully. "He's now unclean, and in hiding – afraid to show his face!"

"I am one of his friends," Judith said proudly. "I lived with him and those like him in a community until yesterday."

The man was visibly surprised, and backed away from her, "That means that you're a…a…leper…a leper…too?"

"I was…until yesterday…when I was healed by the one you called a fake."

"You're talking rubbish!" he snorted. "He's dead!"

"Haven't you heard," said Judith boldly now, "He rose from the dead. I can tell you without the shadow of a doubt that I met him a week or two after he rose. I met him in Galilee…and he was very much alive. And again, I met with him yesterday…and he healed me!"

It was clear that the man didn't know what to say in the light of this stunning assertion. He looked closely at her face and said, "I can see no sign of leprosy on you. You're lying!"

"I most definitely am not," Judith asserted firmly. "I have some of my old leper clothes in my bag if you'd care to look."

The man looked even more uncertain and took a step further backwards. He glanced over at his compatriots who were almost finished harnessing the donkeys. "I'll give it a miss," he said sounding relieved.

Judith felt she should press her advantage, "And who from my community do you think was healed a few days ago too? And guess what? He's back!"

She paused, "Are you sure you want to take our cart?"

The man didn't want to hear any more and made his way quickly over to his friends. "Let's get going now," she heard him say. "These people are weird. Let's get away from here as quickly as we can!"

The three of them walked beside their trophy, one feeding the donkeys to make sure they remained quiet, and the others on either side of the cart as it moved away, in case the rumbling of the wheels awoke the occupants of the tents and they needed to defend their actions. Judith wondered if there was any more she could have done, but felt satisfied that she had done exactly the right thing. She knew not to waken the others until the cart had disappeared from view, in case the robbers might come back, or harm them if they tried to mount a rescue bid. Eventually, she went over to the tents and woke the others up. They weren't happy, either at being woken up or at the loss of their transport. Bartholomew was the first to recover after Judith had narrated her story. "You were right my dear, not to struggle, or to wake us so we could put up a fight. Zealots can be quite vicious if challenged. They feel they've got something to prove to the rest of the 'cooperating' population." He sighed, "I can put up with a little loss for Messiah's sake!"

Peter and Jonas looked on sympathetically, but also with concern. Peter said, "We sympathise with your loss, brother. The Lord is indeed no man's debtor. I'm sure you won't go without."

Jonas added, "What we lend to him, we will get back…and more. Even if it wasn't exactly lent to them, the Lord knows our situation and obviously allowed it to happen, for whatever purpose he has for it."

"True. True," agreed Bartholomew. "I believe that wholeheartedly."

Judith was first to express their concerns, "But what about the wedding? We won't be able to get there in time, will we?"

"I'm not sure, my dear," said Bartholomew, looking both thoughtful and serious at the same time. They all looked at him expectantly. He continued, "I know the road to Jerusalem fairly well. I travel it often in a year. It's difficult to tell because it's dark, but judging by how much we travelled on it after leaving the village and before pitching camp, I'd say it might take a good twelve hours to walk if we start now, perhaps less if anyone is willing to give us a lift."

They all looked concerned. It was a long way to walk, and they hadn't been asleep for long. Would their tiredness slow them down, Judith wondered? She didn't believe it would hold her back, as she was desperate to see her Tabitha again and attend her wedding. The others looked less confident, but Peter put into words what Judith hoped to hear, "We've got a wedding to go to, and we don't want to make our sister late for it! We'd better get started now if we've any hope of getting there in time."

Judith looked gratefully at him. "Thank you," she said, "but what about the tents? Shouldn't we wait to see if anyone passes that can offer to help us?"

"You could wait a long time for that, my dear," said Bartholomew. "People won't be travelling at night…and if we've to wait till morning to get a lift, apart from the fact no-one might help us, even if they do, there's no way then we'd be at the wedding in time." He looked at Peter and Jonas, "I'm right in saying it's due to start at midday?"

They nodded.

"Then we'd best be on our way," he said. "I'll take down the tents and stow them behind these bushes. I can pick them up again when I travel back."

"At least you won't lose them then," said Jonas. "But how will you get back, Bartholomew? You've no cart…or donkeys."

"Oh, I won't be stuck, my young friend. I have many brothers in the city. I'm sure one of them will take me back when they're going. After all, my village is on the main route to Samaria, and on to Galilee. Someone will be going that way in the next few days, I imagine. No, I won't be stuck."

"I'm glad to hear it," said Peter warmly. "Judith, do you think you're up to all this walking?"

Judith laughed, "You're speaking to someone whom Yahweh healed. And you remember what we told you about our 'run' to get to Bartholomew's village? I'm sure Yahweh will supply all we need, including speed or a lift, if we're to get there in time. And anyhow, it's my daughter's wedding. Nothing – wild horses, or no wild or lost donkeys – nothing would keep me away from it!"

They all laughed, and Bartholomew went over and started to take down the tents. He was aided by Peter and Jonas once they had retrieved the few things they needed to carry for their journey. With the tents safely hidden behind a large bush not far from the side of the road, the four of them began their long trek to Jerusalem.

Judith was relatively surprised that over the next few hours, not one vehicle passed them going in either direction. It was a main route and she had thought that some merchants desirous of getting their produce to the big city for dawn, might have risked a night journey. But it was not so. Apparently others too were aware of the risks of bandits and on that particular night at least, were choosing not to travel. It was tiring. The moon shone brightly making the road easy to follow, but as they were leaving the scrubland of the valley, and starting up the foothills belonging to the mountains in which Jerusalem nestled, the road was slowly becoming steeper and more difficult to negotiate.

"These hills are fairly steep," commented Bartholomew, but added to console them, "but we do take in some valleys between the hills too."

"Glad to hear it," said Peter breathing heavily. He looked at Judith, "Are you coping, Judith?"

She nodded only, as she had even less breath than he had. She wasn't going to be held back now and miss the wedding. They did, on occasions, pass other travellers who were tented up at the sides of the road. Judith wondered why it had been their cart in particular that had been targeted that night by the zealots. Surely Yahweh could have allowed them to take someone else's. She dropped this thought immediately, feeling selfish. She apologised to Yahweh mentally. Yahweh obviously had had a purpose in doing so…and she was grateful that she'd had a chance to speak up for Josh during the crisis. She walked on, spurred on by her overwhelming desire to see Tabitha, and watch her get married to Jonas.

The first grey light of dawn was beginning to appear on the horizon when Bartholomew announced, "I think I know this place. It's not too far now."

The others looked relieved, and Judith asked, "How far do you think it is, Bartholomew?"

"Around fifteen miles, I think."

Their spirits sank.

"That's quite a long way!" said Judith.

"And quite a long walk!" said Jonas.

"Yes, but if we're fortunate, we should arrive at midday, or perhaps just after. If we get a lift, it certainly will make things easier."

"We could always send Judith on ahead if someone offers a lift but doesn't have room for us all," suggested Jonas.

"A good idea," said Peter, brightening up. He didn't want his sister to miss one of the most important days of her life…or her daughter, one of hers.

They walked on in silence trying to conserve breath and energy. Judith found herself thinking over what might happen that day when she got there. She wondered what kind of reception she might receive. She imagined that they'd all be over the moon…but at first? What about the shock, the shock of seeing her? Might she somehow or other spoil Tabitha's day? She didn't believe she would, but as they grew ever nearer, her nervousness increased. After all, she hadn't seen her daughter for a long time. A year and a half is a long time in the growing up of a child. Supposing Tabitha didn't want her? Maybe she blamed her mother for having left and never having made contact again, letting them think she had been dead? That wasn't her fault, she reasoned. They had chosen to believe she was dead. But could she blame them? She hadn't made any contact. Could she have, anyway? They would have needed closure. Then another set of thoughts hit her. What about Joel and Mary…and her other friends…would they be glad to see her? And when she arrived in Jerusalem, what should she do? Walk up to the door bold as brass and announce herself? Might some of the guests go into shock? And her looks – could she go to her daughter's wedding looking the way she did? After all she'd been through, she was under no illusions that she would have looked rough. Especially after a long overnight walk on the dusty road, she would not look good! She began to wonder if she should go to the wedding at all, and instead just wait till the event was over to announce herself back into society? That thought was firmly and deliberately put aside. She most definitely wanted to be there and wasn't going to give up going without a fight!

All four of them were grateful for dawn when it arose, as it heralded the warmth the sun might afford them, dispelling the chill of the night from their bones. They were climbing quite high now, and because of their height the warming effect of the sun was delayed a little until it rose fully. Peter suggested they stop for a few moments to review their situation and to take some water together with a few bites from the meagre rations they carried with them.

"We can't have you going to a wedding on an empty stomach, Judith, can we," said Peter grinning.

"No, but I just want to get there!"

"Of course you do," said Bartholomew. "I think we're not too far now – four or five hours perhaps."

"The other three groaned. At that point, the first cart they had seen all night was about to rumble past. Peter tried to flag it down, calling out, "Have you any space for this woman here…to get her to her daughter's wedding today in Jerusalem?"

The occupants of the cart ignored him. He tried again, but to no avail. Their faces were hard, and they weren't taking any chances as they rumbled past. For all they knew, the four might be bandits…or even decoys to lead bandits to them.

"It's no use," said Jonas despondently. "People won't pick you up if they don't know you, or if they believe there's a risk to their lives."

"A brother would," said Bartholomew, "but there don't seem to be many of them around today. We're best to get going again. There's no point in hanging around and wasting time."

The others agreed and continued up the road.

"Not too long now, and we should get to the pass between the two mountains ahead of us. The road will level off a bit and once through the pass, we'll be able to look down on Jerusalem in the distance, I believe."

"Do we sing?" asked Judith smiling, remembering her previous trips to Jerusalem at Passover, and the precious memories of herself, Josh, and her parents as they sang their way into the City of the Great King.

"No, my dear. It's still a good bit off. This is mainly a trade route. We'll be approaching from the north. We're not going down the Mount of Olives…and anyway, it's not Passover." Bartholomew was smiling too. "You can sing if you want to. You've definitely got good reason to do so."

"I might just," returned Judith. "That depends on if I've any breath left after this!"

The time seemed to be dragging by, and the sun was becoming hotter, hindering their progress. The road was busier now, but no-one would stop for them. Indeed, they gave up trying to elicit a lift. Travelers on this road knew the risks and were in no mood to take chances. The little group struggled on, and eventually came to the pass. It would be a good mile or so to walk through, but the thought of seeing Jerusalem kept them moving onwards.

"What time do you think it is now?" asked Judith, beginning to fret. "It's certainly well into the morning. Just look at the sun."

The others agreed with her, and Bartholomew said, "I'd say it was still an hour or two till midday. You might make it yet, but we've still to get into Jerusalem, and then you've to get to where the wedding will be held. What part of the city is that? Hopefully, it's not on the other side from where we'll enter."

"It's in the Upper City," said Judith, then looking troubled, she looked at Peter and Jonas, "I didn't ask," she said, "but I assumed it would be held in Joel and Mary's Upper Room?"

"No, Judith," said Jonas looking solemn.

"No?" asked Judith, panicking. "Where is it then?"

Jonas and Peter burst out laughing, "No, you were right all along. It is at Joel and Mary's," Jonas said.

Judith looked horrified that he should have played with her emotions like this. He apologised. "I'm sorry, Judith. I was only trying to lighten the mood."

Judith smiled. It had certainly got her going, but she could see the funny side too. She turned to Bartholomew again, "Do you think we'll make the Upper City in time?"

He looked serious, "No, I don't think so. Not at the speed we're travelling and the distance we still have to go."

"You're having me on now?" Judith said smiling.

"No, I wouldn't do that. We probably won't be there for the beginning of the wedding, but I can assure you, you'll be there within an hour or so of it starting. You'll get there, Judith - don't worry. We'll do our best to get you there as soon as we can."

Judith looked gratefully at him. At least she would not miss all of the wedding. And there was still hope! Perhaps it would be delayed, or someone might yet be kind enough to give them a lift.

A thought struck her. "They won't start without you two, will they?"

"They will, I'm afraid," said Peter. "You'll know yourself, these kinds of events always start on time. Jewish weddings are like that - and they've the guests to consider too. Many of them have had long journeys to get there, or to make on their way home again. Anyway, they'll just assume we've been delayed somewhere. It's possible we might not turn up at all. It depends on where we are. We did say we'd try to be there, but no-one will blink an eyelid if we don't turn up on time."

Judith looked sad, but Bartholomew came to her rescue, "Look, we're almost at the end of the pass now. We'll be seeing Jerusalem in less than half an hour."

They kept on walking.

"There's Jerusalem now," said Bartholomew about half an our later. "Beautiful as usual. I never get tired of seeing it for the first time when I come here!"

"Me too," said Judith smiling. "It holds marvellous memories for me. The first time I saw it, I was with Josh. We both sang our way into the city!"

"You are most privileged my dear – to have entered Jerusalem with the Messiah!"

Peter and Jonas said simultaneously, "We did too…on a number of occasions." And Peter went on, "But never when we were as young as you and Josh, Judith." There was a hint of envy in his voice. "But we were privileged enough."

Jonas said, "Peter, do you remember when he stood at the top of the Mount of Olives and wept over Jerusalem? He said it would suffer destruction one day because it hadn't recognised him, or his day. What was it he said? He was so emotional, so compassionate. 'Jerusalem, Jerusalem. How I would have gathered you as a hen gathers her chicks under her wings. But you wouldn't come. And now foreign armies will surround you and leave not one stone upon another. And you will not see me again until you say, "Blessed is He who comes in the Name of the Lord!"'"

"You've remembered it well," said Peter admiringly.

"Hopefully," commented Bartholomew, "that day will never come…at least, I mean, the armies bit. The Day of the Lord and us recognising Him for who he is…I can't wait for that!"

"True," said Peter. "None of us can."

"But today," said Jonas smiling at Judith and trying to make up for his earlier joke at her expense, "But this is not a day of destruction. It is a day of celebration, of two becoming one, and you being reunited with your daughter. Rejoice, Judith. Don't be despondent!"

She smiled at him, "Thank you, Jonas. And do you know, Jonas? I just can't wait to get there!"

After coming down the long undulating slope to where Jerusalem nestled between the peaks, they arrived at one of the northern gates, weary, but elated that they had made it regardless of the odds. It had been a struggle but somehow they had made good time, and Yahweh had been with them. When they neared the Temple, they caught sight of a dial in one of the towers.

"It looks like it's midday now," said Peter. "Come on Judith, you'll make it!"

They decided the best way to get to Joel and Mary's was to rush past the Fortress Antonia, along the west side of the Temple Mount. When they reached the intersection with the east-west thoroughfare, they said goodbye to Bartholomew who was making for the Lower City just off the southern edge of the Temple Mount. Judith, Peter and Jonas went in the other direction however up the Western Hill, Mount Zion, to get to the turning that led to Joel and Mary's villa.

Judith's head was spinning as she walked up the hill. So many emotions! She was in a place she had thought she would never see again. Jerusalem might as well not have existed for the past year and a half…or the rest of her life for that matter. Now, here she was back in it savouring all its familiar places. A tinge of sadness swept over her as she passed by the street in which she had lived with Mikha and Tabitha. She looked quickly down it but had to look away. The strength of emotion it engendered was just too much for her. She felt excitement mounting though as she climbed Mount Zion, and a thrill of joy went through her when she came to the turnoff opposite the gnarled tree which led down to Joel and Mary's villa. The tree seemed to have grown even more in her absence!

At the junction, Peter and Jonas stopped.

"We're not going with you, Judith," said Peter kindly. "It's too late…and three of us barging in would create too much of a commotion. We'll go on to our safe house. It's not far up the road. Many of the apostles have been staying there during the recent persecution. We'll see you later."

"It's for the best, I think," said Jonas gently. "We agreed on the way. If we arrived too late, we'd let you go on alone. It's your day, Judith…and Tabitha's. We don't want to spoil it for you." He added, a smile playing on his lips, "But we'll be there later. We were friends of a well-known glutton and wine drinker. We wouldn't miss a party for anything!"

Judith laughed. "I understand," she said. "I can't deny, I'm a bit nervous at going in on my own, but I'm desperate to see Tabitha - to hold her again, to kiss her." A tear came to her eye, "She's my little girl…and she's getting married!" She gave a little leap for joy. "I'm going now," she said. "Thank you both for all you've done for me!"

Peter and Jonas laughed as they saw Judith secure her bag on her shoulder, lift her robe slightly and start running down the narrow road to the villa she had longed to see more than anything those past months. It was a moment that she had thought she would never ever see again - and now it filled her with terror and joy, all at the same time. As she ran, her mind was in a whirl, but somewhere in it all, was an almighty desire to give thanks to Josh and his Father for making it all possible. Her heart overflowed with gratitude!

Chapter Forty-Two

"Can I help you ma'am?" A young girl stood before her on the other side of the big black gates. Judith was about to shout out who she was and ask to be let in, when the thought struck her, that although this might have been her first impulse, it wasn't a wise one. After all, it was Tabitha's day. For her 'dead' mother to return without warning would supplant the focus and celebration from her daughter. "Instead, she said calmly and quietly, "I've come for the ceremony, Rhoda."

The girl on the other side looked dubious. It's clear that she didn't recognise Judith, and the sight of this dishevelled grubby woman who had obviously been running, with beads of sweat trickling down her face, made her suspicious. On the other hand, this woman had addressed her as 'Rhoda'. She obviously knew her. Judith could see this going through her mind, and the thought that she might just have been running because she was late.

"Who are you?" she responded at last, hoping this might clear up the mystery.

Judith however didn't want to create a major diversion or distraction by her arrival, so she said, "I'm a friend of Tabitha's, on Mikha her father's side."

This seemed to be enough verification for Rhoda, so she opened the door in the gate granting individual access, and let Judith in.

"You're quite late, ma'am. They've just finished the procession and the outdoor bit at the Chuppah. It's a beautiful canopy."

"I'm sorry," Judith said, realising a degree of explanation for her lateness would be helpful. "I've come here from outside Jerusalem. The cart of the people I was travelling with was stolen, and we had to walk the rest of the way."

Rhoda looked absolutely convinced now and became completely sympathetic. "You've not missed too much of the main ceremony, ma'am. It's being held in the Upper Room. I'd help you to get tidied up, but I assume you'd rather see the ceremony then perhaps freshen up afterwards before the meal and party?"

381

"A good idea, Rhoda," said Judith smiling. She was so close to being reunited with Tabitha now and she felt excited, desperate to see her daughter again.

It was convenient that the girl hadn't recognised her even although she was up close now. Judith hadn't had many dealings with her in the past anyway – it had been mainly her mother Esther Judith had befriended. Any recognition now would just slow things down and complicate things.

"They've had the major part of the proceedings then?" she asked as nonchalantly as she could.

"" No, just the outside stuff. The indoor welcoming began about ten minutes ago. You've not missed too much at all."

Judith thanked her.

"Come, I'll show you to the Upper Room, ma'am," Rhoda said helpfully. The two women were in the atrium by now, and Judith was experiencing flutters of excitement at being back in a place she had visited often before. "I had good times here with Josh once!" She was unaware that she had spoken her thoughts out loud until she saw Rhoda's face register surprise and admiration. "No, don't worry. I know the way." She pointed to the end door on the right-hand side of the room, "It's that one, isn't it?"

Rhoda nodded, and said, "At least let me take your bag from you. I'll keep it safe until you leave."

Judith realised this was a good idea. It would save her looking more scruffy than she needed to. No-one took bags to a wedding, and she didn't want to be the first. "Thank you, Rhoda. That will be very helpful."

She handed the bag to the girl and opened the door that led to the upper room. She could hear muffled voices floating down the stairs toward her. Her heart was beating fast now. She ran through the door and up the stairs, bounding up them as if she'd had a new lease of life.

On the landing at the top of them, she saw through the door leading to the Upper Room that the gathering was settled, and that the ceremony was in progress. She was at the wrong angle, but she thought she saw Barnabas, Joel's nephew, speaking at the front, and two figures in white standing under a beautiful canopy with their backs to her, listening to him. They had to be Tabitha and Jonas, she thought, and was about to enter the room when she heard her name called out in a very loud whisper, not quite a yell though, the perpetrator of it obviously trying to avoid disturbing the guests, but having difficulty doing so. The person had been standing in the shadows beside the other set of stairs that led down the side of the house to the courtyard - most people would have entered that way. Judith hadn't noticed this person because her primary focus had been on the ceremony when she had first arrived on the landing. Suddenly she felt strong arms around her hugging her and a familiar voice, the voice of Esther saying her name. She broke down in tears. It was so good to hear the voice of a close friend, of someone who knew her well and loved her. It was as if a dam had burst, and she just wanted to wallow in the waters that flowed all around her. Esther pulled apart from her for a moment and deliberately went over to the stout wooden door leading to the room and pulled it over. This was too big an event to be disturbed by such an equally big event. This one was hers for the moment.

"Judith...Judith...Judith! we thought you were dead!" Esther repeated this again and again, the two women rocking in a prolonged and close hug, crying as quietly as they possibly could. "We...we thought you were gone...gone for good! And now you're here...how...how can it be?"

Judith was too overcome to speak, and the other woman recognised it was best to just hug her and let her express her emotions until there were none left to express. In truth, Esther herself was overcome, and hadn't a clue what to say or to do. This situation lasted for a minute or so, until Judith, realising that she was missing the very ceremony she had come to witness, said tearfully, "I'll tell you everything afterwards, but can we watch the remainder of the ceremony? I just don't want to spoil any of Tabitha's day."

"You won't do that!" said Esther smiling, with tears still streaming down her cheeks too. "You'd never do that, not today"

!" She went over to a bundle of mats in the corner and brought a large one over for Judith and herself to sit upon. She opened the door again to the room and positioned the mat in the entrance, but still in the landing. Both women could see and hear what was going on without being a distraction to the guests or wedding party.

"Tabitha will want to see you. She'll never forgive me for not interrupting the ceremony," Esther whispered.

"No, you mustn't, Esther. It's her day. There'll be plenty of time for talking and explanations ," Judith whispered back.

Esther squeezed her hand and the two women concentrated on the goings-on.

Barnabas, Joel's nephew and Jonas's cousin was speaking. He was obviously the best man, and as such was responsible for introducing the ceremony. In his late thirties, he was dressed for the occasion and with his greying hair cut quite a serious sober figure. This image was softened somewhat by his genial smile, something Judith remembered had helped her take to him when she had first met him. His words were going down well with the gathering who were finding him entertaining.

"Well, now we've got the introductions over, before Joel comes to marry the couple...he's known to both of them you know!" There were smiles all round. "It's down to me to welcome you to this Simcha - this celebration of joy and gladness. This is indeed a time for joy and gladness, for love and delight and of course for fellowship. Jesus taught that a man should love his wife..." he smiled over at Jonas, "He said that a man should leave his father and mother and join his wife - one man one woman till death parted them. He did not entertain the easy marriage and divorce that can so easily permeate our society. It's marriage for life," he smiled again at the couple. "There's no getting out of it, folks!" A ripple of laughter went round the room.

"Now we know that Jonas and Tabitha have had to wait to get betrothed and married. They were young anyway – and have always been sweet on each other since ever I've known them – but there was also another reason, a more important one. As many of you know, Tabitha lost her father in the most tragic of circumstances just hours after our brother Stephen was martyred. And then, in the space of just months even more tragically, Tabitha lost her mother, missing and presumed dead on her way to Galilee. Some of you here attended her funeral service. And all of you know the heartache Tabitha, Joel, and Mary, have gone through because of Judith's untimely passing. Thanks to Jonas, Tabitha has been brought back from the depth of sadness and misery she almost drowned in, and I'm glad to say that although it took her much time to grieve, her wedding to Jonas has helped fill the enormous gap left by her parents." A sympathetic burst of clapping went round the guests. He looked at Tabitha, whose face Judith couldn't see because her back was to her. "Tabitha's face is glowing today. She's a radiant bride - and I'm sure her mother would have loved to have seen this day. Had she been here, I can assure you, Tabitha, she would have been extremely proud of you!"

Tears filled Judith's eyes at that point and Esther squeezed her hand. She had to struggle to resist the temptation to stand up and shout out, "I am!", but she knew it would have destroyed the wedding and Tabitha's special day. She held her peace, and Barnabas continued, "As you know, things have had to be done a bit differently, mainly because the young couple already live under this roof - Joel and Mary having taken Tabitha on as their ward after her mother's tragic death. The formal stuff has been done though. The betrothal went ahead when Tabitha felt ready - with its mikvah bathing, the covenant wine drinking to seal the agreement, and the dowry." Barnabas smiled over at Joel now, who was standing beside the couple under the canopy. "I never did figure out how you managed to work out the dowry – did you have to pay yourself Joel!" Again, laughter rippled around the room. "Here's something else that struck me as funny. As usual at betrothals, Jonas promised to go and prepare a place for the bride to be to come and stay in his father's house. Was he just renovating the room next door to his?" Another laugh. "And as you've seen, bringing Tabitha yesterday to his father's house, only entailed walking around the perimeter of the building!" More laughter. "Of course, Tabitha was carried here symbolically. Sad, that Jonas didn't get to wear his crown a bit longer though!" Smiles all round. "Those of you who were here yesterday evening, we had a wonderful time, didn't we - what with Joel and Mary's blessings, the prayers, then the games and dancing. I'm sure you women had as equally good a time as us at your function. It's good we could all come together again today outside at the beautiful canopy for the feast and the presents. I know the bride and the groom have appreciated your presence..." and with a wry smile and play on words, "and your presents!" This time a groan went around the guests.

"All right," he said still smiling, "it's time for the more formal part of today...and for that, I hand you over to Joel, our host."

Joel now took the centre position to a polite and muted round of applause. He was smiling, and Judith thought he seemed a little older. Perhaps the past year and a half's traumas had taken their toll on him. He still however looked and sounded irrepressible.

"Welcome brothers and sisters, friends and family, to our special celebration today. This man and this woman will be married soon, but before that, I wish to talk about the times we currently live in, and explain why this ceremony departs a little from the traditional Jewish ceremony. How can we deny or ignore Jesus - or as most of us know him more personally, Josh. He has affected all our lives, one way or another, and today as this couple are joined together, it is in the sight of his Father, Josh himself, and the Holy Spirit. What better company could we be in at such a celebration!" There was a general murmur of agreement.

Joel continued, "I remember standing here one Passover over twenty-five years ago and asking Josh and Tabitha's mother Judith to give a short word. It was their Obligation year, you see. I gave them the chance to speak about what Passover meant to them, and Judith talked about her sadness that so many lambs had had to die that week. Josh then came up and told us fearlessly that Yahweh, his Father, was doing a new thing, that it was our hearts that were important to him rather than our sacrifices. I remember his words, that the Messiah was coming and that he was dying to help us. I didn't know who he was then...but now we do, and his words, the Messiah's words, have come true. His death brought change; the coming of the Holy Spirit brought change; recent persecutions have brought change. Whoever of us would have thought we'd see what we've seen since his resurrection? Whoever of us would have thought that gentiles would become believers? Indeed, Peter and Jonas have been currently following up Philip's work in Samaria, consolidating new gentile believers." He paused to make an aside, "Actually I was expecting to see them here today. They had said they wouldn't miss it for the world. I expect they've been held up, or something!" He went on, "So whatever next? Of course, there are changes coming. Persecution has made us stand out more, and stand up for what we believe more too. We are being forced to be distinct. Perhaps we'll have to re-evaluate our faith and traditions. Josh put aside some of them that hindered the new things his Father was doing. Are we prepared to change? Are our hearts in it? I challenge myself as much as you. Am I prepared for change? I believe there's a proposal coming to change the sabbath day from the seventh day, Saturday, to the first day of the week, Sunday, as it was the day on which Josh rose. That certainly would make us more distinct...and will also cause much more friction between us and the authorities. Are we prepared to stand up and be counted though? Change has to be embraced as our Father leads us. Yahweh doesn't stand still, and neither should we. So here today, we're inaugurating a little change, a departure from the traditional marriage ceremony. I believe Josh is present with us and blessing it."

Joel stood under the canopy facing his son and niece. "I'm proud to be able to join you two in marriage in the sight of our Father and Josh and the Holy Spirit." He smiled, "I'm proud of both of you, two young believers setting out in life." He broke into a wedding psalm and the gathering joined him in it, everyone singing loudly and enthusiastically. When it had ended, Joel looked around the guests, and said, "Take up your wine for the blessing!" All of them lifted their glasses from the tables in front of them.

"You are blessed, Yahweh, our Father - the sovereign of the universe, the creator of the fruit of the vine."

Joel drank, then the gathering followed him.

Once Tabitha and Jonas had drunk their wine, it was time for them to give their vows.

Jonas took the ring and placed it on the first finger of Tabitha's right hand, and said, "With this ring you are sanctified to me according to the Law of Moses."

Joel said, "It won't come as any surprise to you that the ring is inscribed with the traditional verse, 'I am my beloved's, and my beloved is mine'." Then, he read out loud the Ketubah, the highly decorated Marriage Contract which declared Jonas's intention to provide for his wife.

This was then followed by the reciting of the Brachot, or traditional Seven Blessings.

"You are blessed, our Father, the sovereign of the world, who created everything for His glory. You are blessed, our Father, the sovereign of the world, the creator of man. You are blessed, our Father, the sovereign of the world, who created man in His image, in the pattern of His own likeness, and provided for the continuation of his kind. You are blessed, Lord, the creator of man. Let the barren city be jubilantly happy and joyful at her joyous reunion with her children. You are blessed, Lord, who makes Zion rejoice with her children. Let the loving couple be very happy, just as You made Your creation happy in the garden of Eden, so long ago. You are blessed, Lord, who makes the bridegroom and the bride happy. You are blessed, our Father, the sovereign of the world, who created joy and celebration, bridegroom and bride, rejoicing, jubilation, pleasure and delight, love and brotherhood, peace, and friendship. May there soon be heard, our Father, in the cities of Judea and in the streets of Jerusalem, the sound of joy and the sound of celebration, the voice of a bridegroom and the voice of a bride, the happy shouting of bridegrooms from their weddings and of young men from their feasts of song. You are blessed, Lord, who makes the bridegroom and the bride rejoice together. You are blessed, our Father, the sovereign of the world, creator of the fruit of the vine."

After the recitation of the Brachot, Joel spoke again and said, "Now, our bride and groom wish to express their love for each other from Solomon's 'Song of Songs'. Tabitha…"

Judith heard the voice of her daughter speaking confidently and clearly, "Let him kiss me with the kisses of his mouth— for your love is more delightful than wine. Pleasing is the fragrance of your perfumes; your name is like perfume poured out. No wonder the young women love you! Take me away with you—let us hurry! Let the king bring me into his chambers."

Joel then looked at Jonas, "Jonas…"

Jonas's voice was strong, and deeper than Judith had remembered,

"Arise, come, my darling; my beautiful one, come with me. My dove in the clefts of the rock, in the hiding places on the mountainside, show me your face, let me hear your voice; for your voice is sweet, and your face is lovely!"

Finally, Jonas and Tabitha drank from their cup of wine again. Tabitha then walked around Jonas seven times ending up at his right side under the canopy, to symbolise the wholeness and completeness neither of them could achieve on their own.

Other people and dignitaries joined them under the canopy, offering prayers and well wishes. Before Jonas and Tabitha went off to get ready for the evening events, Joel brought the ceremony to a close.

"We have indeed been blessed today witnessing the joining of these two young people in marriage. Jonas has indeed prepared a place for his bride in his heart…" he looked at Barnabas, "and now he has brought her home, and the marriage feast can begin. Does this not remind us of what Josh taught and did? I heard this from Jonas his disciple himself, and I want to share it with you. Josh told his men the night before he was crucified, 'I am the way, the truth and the life. No-one can come to my Father but through me. In my Father's house are many mansions. I am going to prepare a place for you, and if I go away, I will return again and take you to be with me where I am. If it were not so I would have told you. Let not your hearts be troubled.'" He smiled. "We can take courage and take heart today. Every believer is a bride of the Messiah. Yes, he's gone away from us just now, and given us his Holy Spirit. But he's promised to come again and take us to where he is, so that one day we can celebrate our union with him at our marriage feast in heaven."

A loud roar of joy arose from the gathering accompanied by spontaneous clapping. Trust Joel to capture the mood of the meeting, Judith thought. She felt so happy.

Joel spoke again. "Our newly married couple will turn around and leave the Chuppah now. They will process from the room, but you'll get a chance to speak to them later." He turned to them, and said, "Now my final blessing for you both. Jonas, I'm proud of you my son. You have a clear strong faith, and you are becoming bold. I know that Josh has work for you to do. You will take the good news far and wide and your work will speak of Josh to countless generations. Tabitha will be your strength when times become trialling."

He then directed his words to Tabitha. "My daughter you will be a strength to my son and support him as Sarah supported Abraham. You have already come through many trials and have become strong. Share your strength with my son and the two of you will be blessed. Remember a two-fold cord is strong, but a three-fold one unbreakable. Let Josh be with you both, guide you, and use you - and that three-fold cord will never be broken. It will lead you into heaven."

He paused for a moment as if contemplating what to say next. "Tabitha, with no-one from your family here today, I feel it my duty to say this. I have watched you grow, and cope with difficulties others have never had to face. It must have been terrible losing your father and mother, and yet you carried your suffering with grace. I know you'd say Josh helped you, and that's true. But I want to compliment your mother and father, for bringing you up the way they did...and you, for the way you have overcome. After your father's death, I know you were a great strength to your mother too. I just wish she was here to see you today, to be proud of what you've become. I know we are!"

While Joel had been speaking, Judith had felt unquenchable excitement bubbling up in her. This was to be the moment, she thought! She couldn't hold it in any longer, and she just had to stand up in the doorway, and shout at the top of her voice, "I am! I am!" Esther didn't try to stop her.

Heads turned to see the perpetrator of the shouting. The company gave a collective gasp. Judith however had no eyes for them. Her eyes were fully fixed on Tabitha and watched as she whirled around, saw the look of shock on her face and her jaw drop open, heard her scream, look as if she'd seen a ghost, and suddenly visibly sag as if she was about to collapse. Then came the reversal, the amazement and joy that spread over her face, the beaming smile that lit up her eyes, the sudden movement that took her from under the chuppah through the gathering into the arms of her mother. She was howling with happiness, shouting at the top of her voice, "Mother! Mother! it's you! I'd prayed this day would come! I love you! I love you!" The two women dissolved into a tearful heap on Judith's mat.

"I am proud of you, Tabitha! I am proud of you!" Judith sobbed. "I love you! I never meant to leave you...but Josh brought me back! I love you!"

"I prayed for you. I missed you. I needed you so much. I thought I'd never see you again. I'd given up hope. I thought you were dead. I didn't want to go on without you!" Tabitha's statements came out in sobs as she held onto her mother with a tight grip.

388

The others stood round them, amazed, bewildered, and some even crying. Joel, Mary and Jonas looked shocked - but happy.

It took some time for calm to assert itself in the room. Everyone wanted to know what had happened to Judith - where she'd been, and why she'd only returned then. Joel and Mary pushed all these questions aside and gave the two women room to reunite. They suggested that the guests take advantage of the food laid out by cook in the atrium below while they tried to make sense of events upstairs. Slowly the crowd made their way down the stairs, leaving only Tabitha and her mother, Joel, Mary, Jonas, and Esther. Joel quickly delegated Barnabas to look after the guests, telling him to get cook, her helpers and Rhoda to do the serving. Esther made to move downstairs too, but Joel said, "No, stay here Esther. I want you to be with Judith and see to her needs."

When the tears had stopped and Tabitha went over to her husband of only a few minutes, Mary came and hugged Judith. She had been crying too. Judith's entrance had been of monstrous proportions, and each person was trying to deal with it in their own way.

"You look as if you've walked for miles, my dear," Mary said. "You look as if you need to change and freshen up. You look tired."

"I do. I am," said Judith happy now, not caring how she looked or felt. She had done what she wanted to do - something she had thought she'd never do – she'd seen her daughter getting married, and that was enough for the day.

She did feel that some kind of explanation was required and tried to get it out. "I came back with Peter and Jonas," she said, "but our cart got stolen…"

Joel looked interested but held back from questioning her. Instead, he hugged her, then said, "We all want to know where you've been and what's been happening to you, but now's not the time. We've a houseful of guests, and probably more coming for the evening. When they've gone, we have a family meal planned. If you're able, perhaps you can tell us then?"

Judith nodded, and smiled.

Tabitha came back over to her mother to hug her again. Now she had her back, she didn't want to let go of her, in case she vanished again.

"Esther," said Joel more briskly, "We'll all go down now and mingle with the guests. They'll want to congratulate the bride and groom. Will you take Judith down to her old room and get her settled there? Give her whatever she needs, and help her freshen up - then come back and help with the guests if you don't mind."

Esther looked at Joel gratefully, pleased at being given this task. She so much wanted to be with her friend.

Tabitha hugged her mother once again, then left with Jonas Joel and Mary to meet their guests. Judith sank back on the mat and sighed. "I never thought I'd see this day, or ever be back here again!" Another tear trickled down her cheek.

She wondered that she had any more of them left to cry. Esther took hold of her hand and stroked it. "But you are, and that's all that matters."

Judith nodded and wiped the tear away. "I've so much to be thankful for. I don't deserve it."

Esther was desperate to hear Judith's story but she knew she'd be needed downstairs soon and that Joel and Mary would be expecting that help as soon as she was available. "Come, let me take you downstairs now, and get you into your room. I'll get you some water to wash in and…" she looked at Judith's bag which had been handed to her by Rhoda while the reunions were in full flight. "Do you have any clean clothes?"

"Not really, Esther. I've been on the road…"

"No matter, I'll give you some of the mistresses clothes. They may not fit exactly, but they'll do. We'll get you ready to be mother of the bride and welcome your guests!" Esther was smiling as she picked up Judith's bag.

Judith looked at her gratefully, then followed her downstairs to the family rooms.

The evening was one of great rejoicing, everyone being amazed and astounded at the events of the day. They had come for a wedding and to be happy with the bride and groom - but no-one, absolutely no-one, had bargained on meeting with the mother of the bride! Many of them had been at her funeral and although the cause of her death was unknown, it was not at all disputed. For her part, Tabitha mingled with her guests, her face glowing, rejoicing at not only now being married to the love of her life, but also at receiving her mother as it were, back from the dead. She reflected, there could never ever be a better day in her life! She did not mind being upstaged by the return of her mother. Her joy knew no bounds.

Of course, the talk of the gathering was all about Judith and her entrance. Everyone conjectured at where she'd been and why she hadn't returned before. Some even suggested that she'd let Tabitha down by not contacting her before now. Joel and Mary tried to squash these thoughts saying, "Judith would never have done anything deliberately to hurt Tabitha. She must have had reasons for why she did it. She said something about coming back with Peter and Jonas, and them getting their cart stolen. We'll find out later what happened, and no doubt you'll hear about it in due time. If Peter and Jonas are back, they may well join us tonight or tomorrow."

In general, the gathering, although amazed and curious, was a happy one. Everyone ate and drank well, and enthusiastically congratulated the happy pair. There was music and dancing, and everyone applauded when Jonas and Tabitha took the floor. A great time was had by all, and around mid-evening the festivities drew to a close and most of the guests left. Joel and Mary had already intimated that only a small number of people, mainly close family, had been invited to the meal which was to follow. Barnabas, who had done a wonderful job as best man, asked Joel to be excused with the other guests. "I have to meet with an old acquaintance who was apparently arriving in Jerusalem this afternoon. I couldn't meet him then because of obvious reasons, but I'd like to make sure he's settled."

Joel and Jonas looked disappointed. "But we need our best man here," Joel said.

"I could come back later, and perhaps join you for after dinner drinks. I've had enough food today to last me. I don't think I could eat another meal."

"Bring your acquaintance with you then," said Joel gregariously. "Any friend of yours is welcome here, Barnabas!"

Barnabas looked conflicted, "If he's not too tired by his journey, I'll happily bring him back with me. If he is, I'll certainly be back. I'm hoping to hear Judith's story."

"We all are," said Joel. "It's been a wonderful day, if not a stupendous one. I'm so glad for Tabitha!"

"We all are," said Barnabas, and left.

Judith hadn't said any more to Esther about her situation. She realised that it would have taken too long to explain, and that Esther was needed at the celebration. Once her mat had been put out, and a jug of water brought, Judith gave herself a good wash and waited for Esther to bring some of Mary's clothes. While washing, she had marvelled at how smooth her skin was. There was absolutely no indication that she had ever had leprosy. She was so thankful to Josh. Gratitude welled up in her heart, and amazingly, another tear fell! Her eye caught a flash from her ring which she'd taken off her wedding finger to avoid it getting splashed. The lovely sight of its strikingly blue gem in the shape of a fish reminded her of Abbas. Her encounter with him the day before had been totally unexpected, but welcome. He had done so much for her in her thirty-eight years. Her yellow trinket that had meant so much to her in her younger years, the green cross that had seen her through arguably the most difficult part of her life so far...and of course her picture. How he'd finished it when Josh had taken it to him after drawing it for her, and how much of an inspiration it had been over the years. She went to her bag and took it out. She looked at the smiling face of herself as a seven-year-old, and smiled. Josh had been right. She would smile again, and now, here she was, smiling again! She couldn't believe how so much could have happened to her, but she was grateful for it all. She had left there a year and a half ago...and now here she was, back again. She might as well have come back from the dead! She was so grateful.

There was a knock at the door and Esther came in with some clothes.

"I see you've got your picture there. And there's that smile again. I can tell you've been through a lot, but you're smiling now, and that's great."

391

Judith replaced the picture on the dresser where it had been when she had occupied the room before. "Thank you, Esther. I'll change now and let you get back to the others. I 'm looking forward to catching up with you later when there's more time."

"Perhaps at the meal," Esther suggested. "I'll be serving, but I'll be allowed to sit down once that's done."

"Can't wait then," said Judith smiling. "Thanks for being there for me."

"We prayed for you, then we grieved for you, then we tried to lift up Tabitha – why wouldn't I be there for you? We all were…and are."

Judith nodded, and Esther left. Judith got dressed slowly, then sat on her mat to think things over. She didn't quite feel like meeting with all the guests just then. She could wait till later, till the small family meal. This was Tabitha's time. Tabitha and Jonas, she reflected - it was their day. They should be mingling with their guests. She could wait. She began to wonder, what should I tell them all? Would they want to know it all? Of course they would. She had let them down, by not returning, and leaving them thinking she was dead. She knew of course that she hadn't. It had all been in Josh's plan for her. Would they believe her though? It was so fantastic, so amazing. She had trouble even believing it herself. But yet, she had lived it, had felt the pain pangs of leprosy, and the joy of being healed from it. She had been used to help bring a notorious enemy of the faith to faith. Would they believe her? Who knows? She shrugged her shoulders. She knew the truth…and anyway they had no reason to doubt her. When Peter and Jonas came, they could vouch for much of her story. She decided to put all these things out of her mind. Being back in that room reminded her of dark emotions associated with it and how turbulent these times had been. She thought of Mikha and cringed at the thought of his mangled body lying in the living room of their house. She thought of how she had sunk in depression in the days after that, even after Josh had done so much for her to lift her up. Then there was her pursuer, how she could hardly shake his face from her mind, or him off her track. Why did he seem so dead set on finding her? Then in her last few days there, how she had let everyone down by going out and attracting her pursuer's attention to them all, putting them in danger. This room certainly had memories for her - but not all of them were bad ones. On her first visit to Jerusalem she had been there with her parents…and with Josh. That had been good. It seemed such a long time ago! But it had been bad too. She had had to wait in it while her mother and father returned for her when she and Josh had been left behind. Then there was the week in which Josh had been crucified. She had arrived there with Mikha and Tabitha, excited that she might see Josh again, then been crushed when he was killed. The news that he might have been raised from death and be alive had cheered her before she had had to return to Galilee afterwards. Yes, certainly this room held memories that were high and low for her – but she wouldn't have changed them for anything. Every single experience had proved Josh was with her and that he loved her…and valued her smile. Once again, she felt a rush of gratitude towards him, and said so.

Now, what about the future? Here she was back with her family, but Abbas it seemed had suggested he had plans for her involving journeys. What could it mean? She had been rescued from a place of disobedience and misery and given a second chance – just like King Nebuchadnezzar. She knew she didn't deserve anything like that, and so just as when she received Tabitha back from the dead seven and a half years earlier, being given a second chance, she decided she would grasp it with both hands. No time for regrets now. Life had to be lived - and lived for Josh. She wouldn't let him down again!

Something caught her eye near the water jug, and she realised it was her ring which she had taken off when she had got washed. It was flashing, just in the same way her yellow pendant and green cross had done. It was trying to get her attention, she thought. She went over, picked it up and put it on. It felt good, and comforting. It was also beautiful to look at. She wondered why it was in the shape of a fish. No doubt all would be revealed. Abbas didn't do anything - or give anything - without a reason. Tiny as it was on her finger, it gave her a sense of protection as it vibrated. She heard singing. The same singing, she had heard on various occasions when Abbas or Josh were involved. It was soothing. It was calming. She wanted to drift off to sleep - but she was startled when the word, 'Go!' flashed into her mind as it had done in Abbas's tent the day before. She put all thoughts of sleep aside and decided to make her way to the atrium to re-join the guests. With her lifesong filling her ears, and joy filling her heart, she left the room and looked forward to a momentous evening.

Chapter Forty-Three

"Well, Judith, you've certainly caused quite a sensation today!" said Joel smiling at her as she entered the dining room.

Mary was smiling too, and nodded. "Come and sit over here, between myself and Tabitha. We'll leave these two love birds sitting together."

Judith looked over at her daughter and new son-in-law and saw them grin. It was obvious to her that they were seriously happy and in love.

"Thank you, aunt," she said and hugged her before sitting down. "I never thought I'd be back here again. And at Tabitha's wedding… It's all so overwhelming!" She looked around the table and was gratified to see that it was only a small family group. There would be other times for masses of people. She had a story to tell – and what a story it was – but she wanted only to be with her close family when she told it for the first time. She was pleased that Tabitha and Jonas were there, and similarly Jonas's mother and father. Apart from herself, places had been set for four others, who weren't as yet present. ON enquiry, she discovered they were laid out for Barnabas and his acquaintance, if they should arrive, and of course one each for her friend Esther and her daughter Rhoda, who were not only housekeeper and maid, but trusted sisters. Once their serving duties were over, they would sit down with the family and savour the wedding evening feast too, and Judith's story. Much as though the main event of the day had been the wedding, Judith's dramatic homecoming had rated highly in the conversations of the guests and hosts since the ceremony had finished.

"We're keen to hear your story, my dear," said Joel. "You'll know by now that we had thought you were dead. We even had your funeral ceremony!" He smiled broadly, "You'll be glad to know it was well attended and that everyone spoke very highly of you!"

Judith laughed, "I'm sorry to have missed it! It sounds like it would have been a grand affair."

"Oh, it was, my dear," Joel assured her. "Not many people get to hear about their own funeral after they've died."

"I'm privileged then," said Judith smiling too. There were grins all around. "I hope not too many bad things were said about me."

"Not at all…" said Mary cheerfully, "and I tell you this…you'd have been proud of your daughter. She coped marvellously well on the day."

Judith smiled at Tabitha, "My only regret is that you had to go through all that…that I put you through it all." a tear trickled down her cheek at the thought of the hurt she must have caused, even if it had been unintentional.

"I'm sure it wasn't your fault," said Joel gently. "You'll have had your reasons." He paused, "The good thing is that we have you back. We never envisaged this day either. But you know, the wonderful thing is that you have enhanced this wedding day beyond measure. It's funny how the Lord can do something like that when you least expect it."

"I can vouch for that!" said Judith emphatically. "Life is full of surprises…" she corrected herself, "has been full of surprises!"

"I'm sure!" Joel said.

"I've gained a bride, and a mother-in-law all in one day," Jonas said laughing. "I'm a happy man! I was expecting to have to make my wife happy this evening, but you've done my job for me. You've made her happier than I could ever have done!"

"You've both made me very happy," said Tabitha, laughing. "It's not a competition. I love you both!" She paused for a moment wondering if she should say something, then she decided to go ahead, "That's us even now, mother."

"Even? How do you mean, Tabitha?" Judith asked, wondering what was coming.

"Well when I was dead, and you received me back from the dead, because of Josh…well, today, I've received you back from the dead. You'll know exactly how I feel!" Both women's eyes filled with tears. The irony of the moment wasn't missed by the others either.

"And yes," said Judith, "this was Josh's doing too."

Esther, who had been bringing food to the table and setting out plates, said, "We've all received you back from the dead. This is the best wedding I've ever been at! But please don't say anything until Rhoda and I are able to hear. I don't want to miss anything."

Mary said, "Don't worry, Esther, you won't miss anything. Once things are ready, Rhoda and yourself can serve the food, then both of you sit down."

"Thank you, mistress," said Esther gratefully.

"Come on now, how often have I told you not to call me mistress?" said Mary chiding her gently. "You're our sister and you're not a servant. Just a friend whose help we appreciate."

"Yes, ma'am," said Esther, who still felt awkward at trying to be more familiar.

They all laughed, and the serving went on for a few minutes more, amidst general comments of appreciation as to how the day had gone, and how delicious the food looked that was slowly appearing on the table in front of them.

"The food was good this afternoon, and I thought your words at the ceremony went well, father," Jonas said.

"I thought so too, sir," said Tabitha. "You didn't stick with the traditional Jewish ceremony then, did you?"

"NO. New times demand new ways. I kept the main parts of our traditions, but I wanted to make the ceremony more like that of 'The Way'."

"You did that well, dear," commended Mary. "I liked the particular blessings you gave them both at the end."

"That wasn't really me," said Joel, smiling. "As it is with the way we now do things at the meetings, I just left things open to the Holy Spirit. What was said was from Him, I trust."

The others looked impressed.

"It seemed to be much about our futures," said Tabitha warmly.

"You were listening then?" said Joel laughing. "I thought you'd have been caught up with just getting married too much to notice!"

"And your new husband too!" Jonas taunted her.

"I was...but I was also listening. I won't forget what was said about us."

"I thought it was lovely," said Judith. "It seems now that Josh has something to tell us every time we take a step forward. It's wonderful to have him working with us!"

"Things are changing though," said Joel looking serious now. "Good will has all but gone. We're becoming totally reliant on him now that things are getting difficult. While you've been away, Judith, we've also had our struggles. We were almost caught and imprisoned once. If it hadn't been for Josh's intervention, I don't know where we would have been."

Judith looked surprised. Up till then she had been so caught up with her own story. She hadn't imagined that anything out of the ordinary had happened to them. "That sounds terrible!" she said.

"Probably not as dramatic as your situation," Joel said. "We are keen to get to your story tonight, but perhaps I can let you know about our side of things, while we're waiting to eat."

"Please do," said Judith, anxious now at the thought that they might have been caught and imprisoned.

"Well, the day you went away to Galilee in the cart, we had another visit from your friend."

"My friend?"

"Yes. Your pursuer."

Judith's face was now anxious. "You mean he came back?"

"Yes. He'd put two and two together about your picture. He seemed certain you were one and the same as the woman he'd been looking for."

"That's not good. What happened then?" Judith asked.

"We managed to put him off at first by insisting the picture was of a distant relative who visited and used the room when she was in Jerusalem with her family. We'd told him that before, but he wasn't satisfied, and kept asking questions about you. He seemed really obsessed with you."

"That must have been terrible for you all."

"It was. He was absolutely certain he was right. He comes over that way - Knowing everything and never being wrong! The trouble was that he had the ear, and the might of the High Priest behind him." Joel smiled wryly, "It didn't help of course that we couldn't produce the picture again for him. You'd taken it away with you. Any excuses we made looked feeble."

"Oh!" said Judith.

Anyhow, without evidence…it was only conjecture. He went away suspicious, and we didn't see him for some time, until…"

"Someone gave us up!" Mary completed Joel's sentence bitterly. "One of our so-called believers at the meetings gave us up."

"Yes. The moment he heard of it, he was back at our gate, no longer coolly polite, but vicious and dangerous," Joel said ruefully.

"Oh dear," said Judith.

"He came into the house with his men and said he wanted to take us in for questioning. He emptied the house and within a matter of minutes, had us all at the High Priest's residence just along the road. He even left some of his people going through the house thoroughly looking for any incriminating evidence."

"Yes, it was demeaning…as well as frightening," said Mary shuddering visibly at the thought.

"They took you too, Tabitha?" Judith asked, now horrified.

"Yes, they did," said Tabitha. "He said he had seen a family resemblance between the picture and me and wanted to investigate it further."

"This all sounds terrible," said Judith. "So, what happened then?"

"Nothing less than a miracle," said Joel, looking visibly thankful. "A miracle!"

"A miracle?" echoed Judith.

"Yes. The searchers came back with their report. They had found nothing out of the ordinary, no incriminating evidence, except for a query about a loose panel in the cistern. They said that the space behind it was big enough and might perhaps just have been able to hide someone in it. When they made that suggestion, your pursuer asked, 'Able to have concealed a woman?' It was clear he had ideas as to how we might have foiled him on his first visit. He seemed persuaded you had been there because of the picture. He was relentless in his desire to expose us all, absolutely convinced we were hiding something…or someone."

"So, what was the miracle?" Judith asked, keen to hear how the situation had been resolved.

"Well," said Tabitha, "in my room they found something I didn't know I had. It must have become mixed up with my belongings when we came to Jerusalem after Josh's resurrection."

"What was that?" asked Judith looking mystified.

"It was a document from someone called Marius in Capernaum. He was the centurion we knew, I think."

Judith said, "Yes, you knew him. Remember he was with us when we had that evening meal with Josh the day you were raised. You met him a few times after that too."

"Oh, I knew who he was. I hadn't forgotten. But as to how that document got into my belongings…"

"I don't know. Just a mix up I expect."

"A fortunate one. A Josh-induced one!" Joel commented.

"That must have been the document he gave us to introduce us to …what was his name…something Vespasius, I think…no, Venetius. It was the week Josh was crucified and I tried to get him to stop that happening by going to see him with it. He wouldn't see me, but later that day…" she wondered how much detail to go into, "he rescued me, quite by accident, from getting attacked…"

"Yes, and he was the one in charge of the crucifixion that was quite sympathetic to us and Josh that day," Joel added. "He was impressed by Josh. He told us that the governor had also been impressed, and absolutely furious that he had had to release that scoundrel Barabbas instead."

Judith flinched at this reference to her friend, but said nothing. There would be plenty of time to plead his cause later.

"So how was this a miracle?" she asked.

"Well, when the document was produced, introducing the bearer of the document to Marcus Venetius, there was some commotion," said Joel. "They assumed that Tabitha - and us being her relatives - knew the great man. Since you've been gone, he's risen up the ranks and is pretty well at the governor's right hand now. He's very highly thought of, and also in an extremely powerful position. He has the ear of the governor, you know. So, when it was assumed that we knew him - and indirectly the governor - everything changed. I'm sure they were about to torture us for information." Joel looked at Jonas, "They even slapped you about a bit, didn't they?"

Jonas looked down unhappily.

Joel continued, "The High Priest became involved then. Up till then he'd left it in the hands of the chief prosecutor, your pursuer. He quashed every trumped-

Don Treader

up charge against us, apologising for the actions of his representative. He talked of how valuable I had been to him over many years, and there was absolutely no way I could be implicated with 'the Way."

"But why was that? Why didn't he say anything earlier?" Judith asked.

"He should have," Joel agreed. "But, since before you left, Judith, you'll know that there was a bit of friction between the High Priest and Pilate. Well, that has totally increased since the new governor's arrived and is baiting our people. He wants to take down the power of the High Priest and the Council, and he's threatening to set up the emperor's image in the Temple. The High Priest is trying to tread a careful line with him and doesn't want to make an enemy of him any more than he needs to. Prosecuting us - being supposed friends of his - or at least being known to him – would have taken him a step too far. He backed off and decided to release us with a glowing report." Joel smiled.

"Well, that was indeed a miracle," said Judith. "And to think we only used that document once! And it was found in your belongings? It looks as if Josh was working on your behalf!" She paused, remembering the document lying on the ground when she had been attacked, and Little Faithie with her injured leg taking it to Venetius, "It's rescued us both then, thanks to Josh."

"Indeed," said Joel.

The food was now in place and ready for him to pronounce the blessing over it. "I don't know what's happened to Barnabas, and his acquaintance. It's a shame he's not here. The best man should be here, especially tonight. But never mind. He may appear yet. Esther, sit down with us and let Rhoda and cook serve us. Rhoda can join us once that's done. We're all keen to hear Judith's 'mystery'!"

Esther sat down. Rhoda and cook served then Rhoda sat down too. Joel pronounced the blessing, "Thank you, Father, for the fruit of the vine and all your good provision to us. Today has been a momentous day. We thank you that you've joined Tabitha and Jonas in marriage and are going to bless them. We also give thanks to you for the safe return of our sister Judith. She is precious to us, as she is to you. Your ways are indeed past finding out, and we can't imagine what she's been through. But you are faithful, and keep us, as Isaiah says, 'in the hollow of your hand'. We are grateful to you, and to Josh, for your continual presence with us. Thank you."

Everyone started eating, and for some time there was very little conversation while they all concentrated on the various courses of their wedding feast. Eventually, once everyone had been filled to full and overflowing, they sat back with only a glass of wine in front of them and waited for Judith to speak.

"The floor's yours, Judith," Joel said. "I'd have liked Barnabas to be here, but he's obviously been detained somehow. I know he was keen to hear what you've been up to. Anyhow, go on. We're all listening now."

Judith took a breath, whispered a mental prayer, swallowed hard, then launched forth. Every eye was upon her.

"When I left here, I'm sure you're all aware that I did so under a bit of a cloud. For some days I had been conscious of a restlessness in my spirit, making me more doubtful and less appreciative of Josh's help after Mikha's death, and increasing in me an overbearing desire to go out and become free from the limitations I had placed myself under. I was disgruntled; and as a result almost got you all caught. The thought of my pursuer coming to the house here, and nearly finding me, made me realise that I would have to leave. I saw it as a kind of banishment, but I knew I fully deserved it."

Joel interrupted, "We didn't see it that way, my dear. We just wanted you to be safe, and that seemed the best way to ensure it at the time. In a funny way, Judith, with all the persecution happening in Jerusalem and believers leaving, you were one of the first to blaze the way taking the good news to other parts."

"Maybe so, but it didn't feel that way. On the cart to Galilee, Elias and Joanna were lovely, but as that first day progressed I began to feel out of sorts, and during the night – we were travelling in the convoy all through the night you know – I felt really bad. I had an overburdening sense of guilt, and was sure I was going to be sick. I felt sharp pains all over my body, and as I struggled to get to the flap to do so, trying not to disturb Joanna and her baby, my bag unfortunately became entangled round my arm. I attempted to free myself while desperately needing to vomit, but I unfortunately fell through the flaps of the moving cart and landed on the ground, badly stunning myself. We were the last cart in the convoy and so there was no-one to notice my plight."

The others round the table looked horrified.

"You were stuck out there in the middle of the road to Samaria, and nobody noticed?" Mary exclaimed wonderingly. "You must have been terrified, Judith!"

"Yes, after my sickness had subsided and I had come round a bit," said Judith, then hurried on. "This is the good bit! I'd no idea where I was – I was in the middle of nowhere in a very dark night. I found a rock and sat on it. I felt all wrong, and didn't know what to do. I was about to follow the road to wherever it led, when – you won't believe this - Little Faithie came out of nowhere!"

The others round the table looked bemused and amazed. "Are you sure?" asked Joel.

"No, I'm not mad, Joel. Little Faithie appeared, perfectly healthy now, and I followed her over rough scrubland, and along the high bank of a fast-flowing river, until dawn arose and I found myself standing at the top of a steep hill, which overlooked a valley with a well, which I now know to have been Jacob's Well."

"I know where you are," said Joel nodding. "I passed there once- a long time ago."

"Well, I was exhausted, feeling nauseous and aching all over after my fall onto the road. I apparently must have collapsed and fallen down the hill. When I came around, I was in a shelter near the well, and a woman called Becca was tending to me. She had managed to drag me there from the base of the hill."

"What happened to Little Faithie then?" asked Tabitha, concerned about her furry friend. "Did she stay with you?"

"No, she'd vanished. Becca said she'd thought she might have seen a dog standing over me when she first saw me, but it was too far away and she wasn't sure."

Joel nodded, as if his disbelief was being confirmed.

"It was then that I realised there was something more wrong with me than I'd thought."

"Were you bleeding badly? Had you lost a lot of blood from your fall?" asked Mary, looking concerned.

"No, nothing like that," said Judith, wondering just how much she should tell them. She decided to hold nothing back. "Becca was a leper."

The others looked horrified.

"And she was attending to you?" asked Jonas.

"Yes. I didn't realise it at first, then she said she'd take mee to the community nearby where she lived."

The others' concerns grew even greater.

"I said to her I couldn't go there. I wasn't a leper. Till then she had seemed to be treating me as if I was. She insisted that I was one of them. I disagreed wholeheartedly with her, but when she told me to check my face, arms and legs, what a shock I got! Blotches everywhere - each of them painful to the touch. What I had thought were injuries I had sustained falling out of the cart, were nothing more or nothing less than full-blown leprosy itself."

Joel still had the look of someone having trouble believing what they were hearing, "You don't appear to have it now. People don't recover from that easily, if at all."

Judith noticed the others leaning further back in their chairs just in case whatever she had had might be contagious.

She smiled. "No, it's a long story. Just take it from me at present, I'm totally healed and clean."

The others relaxed again.

"Go on with your story, Judith," said Joel. "It sounds horrendous. No wonder we didn't hear from you!"

"There was no way of getting a message to you, and at that point…I had accepted I would be in the Valley of the Outcasts all my life with no hope of ever seeing any of you again."

Tabitha had tears in her eyes. "It must have been awful for you, mother!"

"Not as much as you might think. The people there were in different stages of the disease, but they were all lovely. They helped each other, and they helped me. I tried to fit in and do my bit to help them too as much as I could. Becca and I became like sisters and we looked after each other. It was an eye-opener at first, living there."

"What was it like, mother?"

"Well, the people there farmed and produced fruit – all for their own needs. We seldom went without basics. The more able bodied of us worked in the fields or the orchards. It was quite a close-knit community. In that sense it was good!" But there's something else that made it good too." Judith went on to explain that Becca had met Josh when he had passed through there some years earlier and that she'd been amazed that he was willing to spend time talking to a woman, and a Samaritan one at that. he'd offered her 'living water', and they'd had a religious discussion. He'd told her about her past life with five husbands and how she was now living with someone whom she wasn't married to. She'd said only the Messiah would know something like that, and he told her who he was. When she ran off to tell her village about him, they took him in for a couple of days and in that time he managed to convince them that he was indeed the Messiah by his teaching and miracles. Peter, Jonas and the other disciples can confirm this – they all stayed there too."

"They all stayed in a leper village?" said Joel, looking even more incredulous.

"No. No." said Judith a little impatiently. "That was before Becca and some of the others developed leprosy. When they did, they had to go and live in the nearby Valley of the Outcasts where I stayed. That's when they started growing their crops and all the other things."

Joel nodded. "I see. Go on," he said.

"The people – at least many of them – were believers in the Messiah. What they didn't know, is what happened to Josh, or about the Holy Spirit. I was able to tell them, and we started to hold meetings. And you know…these meetings were precious. We sensed the Holy Spirit making Josh's presence among us real as we prayed. It was an amazing time. I would scarcely have believed all that had happened to me was possible!"

"I'm having trouble believing it myself too," said Joel. "It's so far-fetched!" The others looked disapprovingly at him. "All right," he said, "it's Judith that it happened to. I don't disbelieve her – it's just I'm having difficulty…"

Judith gave him an understanding look. "I know what you mean. When you hear what else happened I guarantee you that you'll have even more trouble believing. The good thing is, however, that much of my story can be verified by Peter and Jonas when they come."

Joel looked relieved. He wasn't going to have to rely only on Judith's account. He tried to be more conciliatory, "I'm sorry, Judith. Please go on."

"These meetings were a great source of strength. I was the only Jew amongst Samaritans. You'd be amazed at the openness of these people. I suppose that because they had met Josh for themselves, they knew that much of what I said could be believed." She looked over at Joel kindly, but meaningfully.

He laughed. "Point taken, Judith. Go on though."

"I was able to help the community further. You remember the gold coins I left here with…to get things started in Galilee?"

Joel nodded.

"Well, Yahweh was speaking to me about ways in which the community might help itself further. I felt I should suggest that they should expand, and use the more arid land at the edge of the valley. We set up a viaduct to water it, and within the year, more crops were grown, and fruit trees and vines planted."

"Why?" asked Jonas, "if you were already supplying everything you needed for yourselves."

"Well, I felt we should try to do more for the surrounding communities. To export our goods, I suppose. To supply them with produce, and in doing so, to help make our community a bit more prosperous, not quite so basic."

"That would take some money - to set all that up," said Joel. "I suppose that's where your money came in then?"

"Yes, I gave it all to the community, and within the year we'd built the viaduct, planted our crops and trees, and begun to export our produce."

"A wonderful venture," said Joel with admiration.

"Yes, Yahweh helped us all the way. I wasn't all that much help though. My money was, but I wasn't."

"Why was that?" asked Esther, who had been listening intently and looking mesmerised, but saying nothing.

"My health was deteriorating. My white spots were increasing as was my pain. The extremities of my body – my fingers, toes, and nose – became numb, and one of my toes broke apart. I could hardly walk. And it looked as if I might not have long to live."

Once more a look of horror spread over the others' faces. Tabitha was crying.

"You're certainly looking well now," said Joel trying to put a brave face on it all, and at the same time trying not to sound too unbelieving.

"Yes, I am. Thanks to Yahweh and Josh. I'm coming to that bit. But I have something really bad to tell you about first. If you haven't believed me so far, you'll have even more difficulty now. The wonderful thing is that Yahweh has a habit of bringing good out of evil! You'll see."

They all looked uncomfortable but wanted to hear everything Judith had to tell them. It struck Judith that this was not the kind of wedding feast they had expected to have. She sighed, then launched into the rest of her story.

"There was one major difficulty in the community - the prophet. Everyone bowed and scraped to him, and as I was to discover, he took full advantage of his position…especially with the women."

Mary looked worried, "Not with you too, my dear?"

Judith said coldly, "No. I didn't let him - but the first time I met him, he tried to take my money off me, and rape me."

There was a stunned silence. "How did you get out of that, mother?"

"I fought back and pulled off his hood. He was pinning me up against the door and trying to kiss me."

"How did that stop him?" asked Jonas.

Judith smiled, "I discovered who he was."

Joel raised an eyebrow. "But you didn't know anyone there - in the middle of nowhere - did you?"

"No. But I knew him! I'd have known him anywhere!"

They all looked surprised.

"Who was it?" asked Esther, voicing the others' thoughts.

"Barabbas!"

Six jaws dropped open, with as many gasps - then nothing was said for a time.

"How…?" asked Esther, eventually.

"Well, you might remember I was one of the few people of our group that saw him at the trial before Pilate. In fact, he even cursed me as he was being released from the Governor's Palace. He'd bumped into me and had tried to kick Faithie. It was definitely him!"

"Actually, I meant, how did you escape?"

"I screamed his name as he was attacking me. He stopped, amazed that I had recognised him. From then on, we had an uneasy truce. I needed to stay in the community – I wouldn't have been acceptable anywhere else. If I didn't expose him, he would leave me alone."

"And did he?" asked Mary.

"For the main part…but we did have one or two confrontations after that."

"It must have been awful for you, mother?"

"Yes, and no."

"But he's a Jew…and he wasn't a leper," said Joel struggling to cope with the disclosure.

"He told me…and I didn't believe him at first…that he'd been on his way to Jerusalem with his zealot friends to cause more trouble for the Romans, when his horse had been frightened by lightning, and he and his horse had ended up on the ground. He was in pain, and like me he had put the cause of it down to his fall. He'd let his companions go on with the hope of catching them up later when his horse revived. But his horse died in the morning, and he'd no idea where he was or where to go for help. He claimed Josh had been communicating with him as he was dreaming. He had seen Josh's face – it was looking at him sadly, not in any way condemning him, as he might have expected. He too stumbled his way into the Valley of the Outcasts, leaning on a huge stick for support. The people of the valley had assumed he was the prophet they had long been waiting for to appear. When he realised it was to his advantage, he went along with it."

"But to live amongst them, would eventually have compromised him. He wouldn't surely have allowed himself to be contaminated?" Joel looked sceptical.

"No. the pains he had felt the night his horse died were like mine. He had contracted leprosy before ending up in the community."

"Yahweh was punishing him!"

"Maybe. But more likely it happened in order to get his attention."

"It didn't appear to - from what you said. He continued in his bad ways."

"Yes, but who knows what effects Yahweh's dreams can have! I didn't believe him at first, when he told me about it as we worked in the fields. I think I do now though."

"Your story's absolutely amazing, Judith," said Jonas. "What happened after that?"

"Well, I told you I was also being dealt with by Yahweh. Before I'd even left here, I'd been praying one day, and the word 'Nebuchadnezzar' had come to mind. I couldn't make head nor tail of it. It was only during my time in the community, that I understood what it meant. It was actually Barabbas that helped me find out, during one of our few unpleasant conversations." She paused for a moment, "You see, I'd seen Barabbas twice before in my lifetime. Once obviously at Josh's trial, and the other time, the day my little brother Joe died. He was one of the zealots who brought the Romans to our village."

"Oh no," said Mary sympathetically.

"And so, because of these things, as well as his attack on me, I absolutely hated him. There was no way I could ever forgive him for what he had done."

"Did he want it?" asked Esther.

"On a couple of occasions he told me I was hard - and he was right. I was. I could never have forgiven him in a thousand years...especially after what he'd allowed to happen to Josh."

"Yahweh was dealing with you?" Joel reminded her.

"Yes. Nebuchadnezzar had been proud. He had had to be humbled by Yahweh. So had I been. I began to realise that by putting me there, Yahweh was trying to teach me a lesson. I needed to humble myself. How could I withhold forgiveness from anyone especially when Josh hadn't on the cross?"

"Even Barabbas?" asked Esther, appearing surprised.

"Even Barabbas," said Judith nodding. "More so Barabbas, I suppose. But...I couldn't bring myself to do so, until..." Judith broke off.

"You've been through a lot," said Mary. "Are you sure you want to tell us more tonight, Judith? You must be exhausted?"

"No! I want you to know. I can rest tomorrow." Judith continued, "I was at a meeting one night in the community, and a woman told us how in his first visit to their village, Josh had told a story about someone who hadn't forgiven someone their tiny debt when he himself had been forgiven a massive one by the king. He had been put in prison and handed over to the tormentors until he had paid the last penny. I realised this was me. I was in a kind of prison, being tormented, because of my hatred of Barabbas and my deteriorating health. I could hardly get about and was constantly in pain. I wasn't going to be released from any of this, until I was prepared to forgive Barabbas, no matter how much it went against the grain. My opportunity came a week or so later, just a few days ago. Barabbas came to me telling me he wanted me to go away with him."

The company was by now getting used to being shocked. They just gasped instead.

"He had been on a retreat he said and had met people who wanted to buy our produce, but first they wanted to meet the person responsible for the community's project. He would take me to them. He even suggested that Becca could accompany me if it would put me at my ease - going with him, that is."

"You obviously accepted?" said Joel sceptically.

"I did - eventually. I put my intention to forgive him on hold, and the three of us left the community three days ago. On the way to our meeting point, we became caught up in a vicious storm, the donkeys took fright and the cart overturned into a ditch full of water. Barabbas was under it, and at one point I thought he was dying. I forgave him as he lay unconscious – I feared it might have been my last chance to do so – and suddenly there was a blinding flash of lightning and an amazing earth-shaking rumble of thunder overhead. I felt a terrible burst of pain go right through my body. I wondered if I'd been struck. At the same moment, the cart changed its position slightly, and I was able to pull Barabbas out from under it. I got him to shelter. Becca was out looking for the donkeys who'd bolted. When she returned, we discovered that we'd both been healed- probably when the lightning struck. I'll cut a long story short. Barabbas had come to and confessed that there was no meeting with people who wanted to buy our produce. I'd also just discovered when wiping his face that his leprosy was fake - the marks washed off. I was furious with him. He told us there was a meeting but not with buyers." Judith looked at Joel, "If you're having trouble believing me…you can imagine then how I felt about Barabbas. I didn't believe him either."

"Who was the meeting with then?" asked Joel, almost ready to accept anything Judith said now, however fantastic.

"Peter and Jonas!"

Again, another volley of gasps left the mouths of Judith's listeners.

"Peter and Jonas? How?" queried Esther, struggling to understand.

"Barabbas had met them on his retreat. They hadn't recognised him, as neither of them had been at Josh's trial; and they hadn't needed to ask his name. Jonas had discovered him mixing with one of the crowds they were preaching to in Samaria, disguising his leprosy. They prayed for him, and he was instantly healed.

He couldn't believe it at first but when he saw that he was…and then realised that his dream had been true and that Josh hadn't condemned him…he went back to Peter and Jonas to thank them. As he was leaving, quite by chance – or was it - Jonas asked him if he'd ever come across a woman who had disappeared off a cart somewhere in that area a year and a half earlier. When Barabbas heard that her name was Judith, he told them about me, and that I was a leper, just as he had been; and that I lived on his community. He promised them he would go back there and bring me to them."

The others looked wonderingly at her. "He did that?" asked Jonas.

"We're indebted to him then," said Tabitha.

"Yes, we are. Otherwise, I might still have been on the community. But there's more."

"I'm not sure we can take any more, my dear," said Mary smiling. "Of course, we want to hear nonetheless."

"Barabbas was badly hurt though. We weren't able to get to the meeting. And then…there was Faithie again!" Judith's eyes sparkled. "She came back, and we agreed between us she would take me to the meeting. We kind of assumed she had been sent to us for that purpose. Before I left Becca with Barabbas, we decided to pray; and believe it or not, we prayed for Barabbas - and guess what…"

"He was healed?" said Jonas, now ready to believe anything, just like his father.

"Yes, he was! His legs which had been crushed under the cart became strong again. And so we all followed Faithie to meet with Peter and Jonas."

That must have been wonderful, Mother!"

"It was. And think of it - all three of us were now healed! No more leprosy."

"Wonderful! Thank Yahweh!" said Esther with enthusiasm.

"Indeed. So I'm assuming that's when you decided to come back…with Peter and Jonas?" Joel asked.

"You're right. Nothing would have held me back from doing so. You see, remember what I said earlier about Nebuchadnezzar. He had been restored after his sin. When I was in the Community, I knew about what had happened to him, but I scarcely believed it could ever have happened to me. This was my second chance! I had repented, I had forgiven someone who hadn't deserved my forgiveness, and Yahweh had healed me, restored me, and given me my second chance. And so here I am!" Judith said triumphantly. "I'm back!"

"But what about Barabbas? And Becca? Are they with you somewhere in Jerusalem? You said you came back with Peter and Jonas, and that your cart had been stolen – that's why you had to walk. Where are they? Will we get the chance to meet them? I really would love to!" Said Joel.

"There's another twist to the story, I'm afraid," Judith said smiling. "I'm not sure you'll believe this either."

"What's that?" asked Joel, feigning weariness.

"I was expecting Becca to come back with me. I wasn't so sure about Barabbas. But on the way back, Barabbas informed us he wasn't coming with us to Jerusalem."

"Too dangerous for him?" asked Jonas.

"No, not that. He said he'd been thinking overnight, and he'd decided Josh wanted him to go back to the community, to finish the work."

More gasps.

"Really?" said Jonas, his mouth open.

"And Becca?" asked Joel, after a moment.

"She decided to go back with him. She had wanted to come here with me, but she wasn't sure how a Samaritan woman would fare here. I tried to convince her that everything would be all right for her, but she said - like Barabbas - that she felt Yahweh wanted her back on the community. If Yahweh wished it, we'd meet again sometime, somewhere."

"But they'd be going back to almost certain leprosy again!" Esther exclaimed.

"Yes. That's possible. But who knows? Why would Yahweh have healed them then? They were going back as strong believers. And just like Josh - giving their lives as an amazing sacrifice."

"Amazing! Amazing!" Said Joel. "It's all so incredible! But you know Judith, it's so unbelievable, I think I believe it. Josh has worked with you in an amazing way...and as he told us when he was with us, 'All things are possible, only believe'. I do believe it!"

"It's all true, Joel. And Peter and Jonas can confirm the latter part of it!"

"It's been difficult. It's been horrible. But Yahweh's been doing something wonderful with you, Judith. He's taken you out to the gentiles - long before many of us - and shown us that his plans are indeed to do a new thing. As Nicodemus once said Josh had told him, he had to think 'beyond'. You've done that, my dear. Well beyond!"

Tabitha went over to her mother and gave her a hug. She began to cry, "You've been through so much, mother. When we believed you were dead, I was angry with Yahweh for taking you away from me. Then I missed you badly and went into depression. Jonas was there for me thankfully and helped me out of my misery eventually. Somehow, I tried to get on with my life. And all that time you were suffering terribly, and missing us. I feel so guilty."

"You mustn't, Tabitha. Yahweh has been working with all of us, and just look-we're all back together again. Who knows what he has for us in the future, but one thing we can definitely say, is that he's taken care of us all - and also, that he'll be with us in the future whatever happens? We have a second chance. Let's take it." Judith smiled, "Actually this is my second...third...fourth chance. I've had so many - and I really am so grateful! Yes, Yahweh is the giver of many chances. No-one knows that better today than Barabbas too!"

Everyone laughed.

"We should pray, and give thanks," said Joel. "We really do have much to give thanks for!"

Tabitha stayed beside her mother and was joined by Mary and Esther. Jonas remained in his seat, as did Rhoda. The three women were in a loose hug around Judith, who was still seated.

"You really do look very well, Mother," Tabitha said, examining her closely. "You could never tell that you'd had leprosy."

"No, I feel very well." If only you'd seen me a few days ago though, she thought, but I'm glad you didn't. "I'm just a bit tired and feel I could do with a serious bath."

Mary laughed, "You must do, if Peter, Jonas and yourself walked from well outside Jerusalem to get to us today!"

Judith added, "And I'd never have been able to do that walk at any time over this last year. That proves to me that I really have been healed…and I'm grateful, so grateful!"

Judith felt like crying when she thought over these things. Surrounded now by the love of her friends and family, secure in the knowledge she was safe, and that Josh had wonderfully given her another chance, her heart genuinely felt like singing. She drew apart for a moment and looked directly at Tabitha. "You've grown into a wonderful young woman - one I'm totally proud of." She looked wistful for a moment. "Had your father been alive, I know he'd have been proud of you too."

Tabitha was now shedding tears. "Thank you, mother," she said through them.

"I mean it, Tabitha. I couldn't be happier for you today." Judith looked over at Jonas, "I couldn't have wished for you to marry anyone else. He's a fine young man. The two of you were getting close before I left. I'm just so glad that Josh has allowed me to be at your happy day. I approve totally of you both - and as well as Joel's blessing to you today, I add my own. I know that Yahweh has great things for you both, and that you will be used beyond measure by him, if you remain faithful. If I was dying today - or leaving again - my blessing would remain the same. Both of you are suited, and I know Josh has drawn you both together to reach the gentiles."

Joel looked over at Judith, appearing surprised, "Gentiles?" he echoed.

"Yes," affirmed Judith. "I just said what came into my heart."

Judith was aware of a warm glow spreading over her. It wasn't just the closeness of the three women. It was the whole atmosphere. She felt happy, fulfilled, intensely thankful and filled with a heightened expectation of spiritual perception. She felt very much alive and aware of the close presence of Josh. She felt so good. It was as if something was going to be revealed to her…to them all. She sensed that everyone was experiencing the same. There was a deep need to pray, and at that moment, Joel did so. "Father, we are mightily amazed at what you have done through…and what you have shown to…our sister, while she has been away from us. Thank you for returning her to us, as if from the dead. You are mighty! And for what you've done to Barabbas…we can only wonder at your forgiveness, and grace. We're not like you. We are so weak and so frail. We hold grudges and allow hatred to fester in our hearts. But we thank you for Josh…for sending him to us, to forgive us and to set us free. We're no more deserving than Barabbas, and we're amazed that you ever considered us to be recipients of your forgiveness. We realise that all our sins are against you, and that you alone have the right to condemn us. But we thank you that your condemnation has been swept away by Josh's blood. We thank you!" He paused for a moment, and in that time, the absolute ecstasy of spiritual awareness Judith was experiencing was added to by two things. She felt a throbbing, a vibration, on her finger, and realised that her ring was the culprit. She opened her eyes and noticed that the beautiful blueness of the stone was flashing, not strongly, but delicately. It seemed to be giving off a blue aura. She could see that Tabitha had noticed it and seemed mesmerised by it too. Was it trying to tell her something…or was it somehow responding to the heightened spiritual atmosphere in the room? She didn't feel she should worry about it, but just let it happen. Joel went on with his prayer, and…was someone singing, she wondered? She thought she had heard a girl's voice, imperceptible at first and then rising and falling away again. "Thank you also Father for this day, this day of union between Jonas and Tabitha. We've waited for this a long time, knowing that your hand was upon them. Now we ask you to bless them. Watch over them every day of their union with each other and with you. Use them mightily to promote your Son - and if sending them to the gentiles is your plan for them, please let it come to pass - and make them fruitful, fruitful in every way. And if it be your will, let Mary and I…and Judith…see our grandchildren too. We sense your presence here tonight in a very special way. We sense that your Spirit and Josh are amongst us. We really couldn't be happier at what you've done for us…" he trailed off as there came a banging from the atrium.

Mary looked anxious, but Joel sighed and said, "It is late now, but that'll probably be Barnabas."

"But it's the front door though, not the gate bell!" Mary said.

"Yes, but I told him before he left to meet his acquaintance that I'd get Esther to leave the little gate door unlatched so he could come straight to the front door. It would save her going out in the dark." He looked at Esther, "Would you mind going to answer the door, Esther?"

Esther nodded, and broke away from the little group surrounding Judith. The singing in her ears seemed to be returning, Judith thought. It was louder now.

"That's a lovely ring mother," said Tabitha, whose eyes were still fixed upon it. "Where did you get it? It's beautiful, and it looks like it's flashing in the candlelight."

Judith said, "I only got it yesterday…" but thought better of going into the details as to how she had come about it. That story could keep for another day. Instead, she said, "I believe it's something special! Can I see your ring, the one Jonas gave you?"

"Of course, mother. It's beautiful too…and just look at the inscription from Solomon's song." She took it off and handed it to her mother.

"'I am my beloved's, and my beloved's mine.' It's beautiful!" Judith enthused.

The singing she was hearing was strong now, and she was concerned. She knew that it was her lifesong, but it was loud in her ears. She wondered if the others could hear it too.

"I'm sorry I'm late," she heard Barnabas's voice at the door. "My acquaintance was delayed in getting into Jerusalem." Judith didn't look up though. She was distracted, attempting to give Tabitha back her ring…and by the singing. That singing…it was beautiful, but it absorbed her concentration.

"I'd like to introduce my brother to you all."

Tabitha took her ring, and Judith stood up, still distracted by the singing. Why was it so loud, she wondered? As she did so, her eyes caught sight of Joel. She'd never seen him like that before. He looked totally surprised, his mouth wide open. His skin was paler than she'd ever seen it. She followed his gaze and was stunned by a shock that fully paralysed her being. The heightened spiritual awareness, the sense of peace and security, the joy of being reunited – all of it evaporated. It flowed out of her being as water flows out of a bottle full of holes. She could still hear the singing, but her mind had frozen. She began to sink. Every vestige of energy had left her. She wasn't going to be able to stay upright. As the blood began to drain from her head, and her vision darkened, her eyes were fixed upon the person standing at Barnabas's side. Her pursuer! As large as life, there he was standing in the doorway staring at her!

"Judith?" he was saying. "I've looked forward to this moment for a long time! I'm Saul, Saul of Tarsus."

The singing in her ears grew to a crescendo, her last vestige of vision vanished leaving her in total darkness. In shock, she heard her heart racing…and then…silence. No singing. No beating heart. Nothing! Everything had stopped! Slowly, Judith's lifeless body crumpled to the floor…dead…dead…dead…

Sophia's Secret

Volume Two

Addendum

Addendum

Sophia found herself resting outside a big blue tent. She had no recollection of it at all and at first was surprised to find herself lying in a cool leafy glade surrounded by dense foliage. She felt extremely comfortable lying on a soft carpet of green and so her first reaction was to accept that she might just have fallen asleep in the warm afternoon sunshine that was soaking into her body. Then, she remembered what had befallen her. She could picture clearly and accurately the interior of the tent. She had been drawn into it. She had indeed spoken with the old man, Abbas, and had been granted the ability to meet with her image person Judith. She had been given a purpose – that she might help her in the trial she was about to face. She remembered that there was an urgency about her mission, and that before she had undertaken it, she had been given information that might be necessary for Judith to know. She had seen Josh as a little boy in a wooded clearing being threatened by a fearsome man called Barabbas. Then she had seen Josh talking to a woman beside a well – instinctively she knew her name was Becca. Sophia wasn't sure how she knew these things, but as she sat pondering them, she found the gaps in her memory were being filled in. She saw a horribly diseased Judith at the same well, and then her being attacked inside a dark dingy hut by an older version of the same fearsome man in the wooded clearing. She knew she had been at these places and had somehow contributed to Judith's safety and wellbeing.

Suddenly she felt a vibration in her pocket. She thrust her hand into it to see what was the cause, and pulled out a green cross dangling on a broken golden chain. It throbbed and flashed in her hands, and immediately her remembrance of it returned. Abbas had given it to her to pass on to Judith in her time of trial. It would somehow help her...and Sophia had been with her as she faced the unutterable loss of her husband, and then the grievous loss of her family and her health. Sophia felt extremely sad. She was sensing the burden Judith had carried, and was conscious that although she herself was only a young person, she had

417

suffered along with her, and had in some way eased her burden by lending her image and strength to her. There were many memories flooding in now, but Sophia found herself focused upon the last one in which she had been back in the tent. Abbas had introduced her to Judith, from whom he had taken the green cross. She had been amazed that he had then given it to her. She would need it he had said when she faced her own difficulties. It had flashed and throbbed in her hand, and she had found herself floating towards Judith and somehow merging with her, the two of them becoming one. She had felt strength entering her as she passed through Judith - and it was just after that memory that she had found herself lying on the grass outside the tent.

She felt a sense of comfort as she looked at the green cross. She remembered Judith taking it out on numerous occasions and deriving strength from seeing it. What had Abbas meant by telling her that she would need it too - to face her own ordeals and trials in the future? She knew it had done something special for Judith, and as she held it, not only did it vibrate and flash, but it seemed that something was growing on it and filling the spaces between the arms of the cross to their extremities. As she watched, she saw a man's face develop on it. She knew him immediately – it was Josh. This was something marvellous! She grew excited. Yes, that is what she remembered. Judith had derived strength from Josh appearing on her cross – and there had been times as well when Judith had attributed that help to her. The words 'Angel Sophia' came into her mind. It was clear that not only had she known Judith, but that Judith had been aware of her too - and been at times strengthened by her. What an adventure, Sophia thought!

She felt uneasy though, about the future problems that Abbas had alluded to. What was going to happen to her? Would she be like Judith and have to give up her family – perhaps leave her grandma and Grandpa who looked after her?

Might she like Judith become seriously ill? Was it possible that one day, like Judith she might be attacked? A whole range of disasters went through her mind in rapid succession. Her attention was suddenly taken by a movement occurring on the bearded face – the mouth was opening, and then shutting. Into her mind quite forcibly came the words, "Go…Work…Grow….Joseph is your heart's desire". She understood what the first three words meant. They would help her through her future path. But what about 'Joseph'? How was he her 'heart's desire'? Which Joseph – a bible one like Mary's husband; or Jacob's son who went to Egypt? Or was it someone else instead? Was she going to marry someone called Joseph? Sophia's head hurt. She couldn't make anything of that name and how it would affect her. She remembered that Judith had been presented with the name 'Nebuchadnezzar' and had puzzled over it for a long time until its meaning had been revealed to her. She was going to have to wait, she concluded. The one thing that did strike her was the answer to a question she had been asking in the back of her mind. Would she meet Judith again? If she had to do all these things, if her heart's desire was to be Joseph a possible future person in her life…then she reasoned it might be a long time before she would be invited back to bond with Judith, to see the blue tent and Abbas, or to meet with Josh. Her life seemed to be stretching out far ahead of her, with the possibility of difficulties coming her way. She worried about this but knew she could do nothing about it. Time would tell, and one day maybe she might be asked to lend her image to Judith again, or perhaps even Judith to her, if some of the predicted difficulties ahead of her were to need it. She sensed one thing though. She had been in a very privileged position to share in someone else's life - their thoughts feelings and experiences, especially those that linked her to Yahweh and Josh. She realised she might take a long time to return, and that she had her own life to live for maybe many years before two could become one again. She looked at the green cross and thought for a moment she had seen the head nod – or was it just a flash? She had a wealth of someone else's experience – Judith's – and she would be glad to apply some of it to whatever might face her in life. If that failed, she knew she would have Josh to rely on. Had the head nodded again before she had seen the image fade? She put the cross around her neck after knotting the broken chain. When she had had the yellow trinket, she had kept it in her pocket. Now she was glad to hang the cross around her neck. She could wear it proudly and only conceal it below her neckline when she wanted to. She felt happy. She had had a major experience that would last her many days. It was time to get on with her life now, so she stood up, turned her back on the blue tent, made her way over the clearing and walked along the passage between the trees and bushes. She climbed over the wall into her garden, and then slithered down the hill to her back door. She debated with herself whether she should tell anyone about her experience- she didn't feel it was urgent that she should do so. One thing she had learned from it all was that she would have to rely on Josh, as Judith had done. She couldn't afford to drift as she had been doing. An idea struck her that made her feel good. It might help to establish her experience. Her Confirmation ceremony was due to take place within the next year or so. She would choose the name 'Judith' as her new name, someone she was bonded to as her protector and guide.

There was no doubt in Sophia's mind that everything she had experienced was real. She couldn't discount it - she didn't want to discount it. She had a sense that she was really going to need Josh's help as she went through school, perhaps university, marriage, and anything else that might come her way. Abbas had mentioned suffering. She would try to honour Josh and his Father, and do what they wanted, and where possible tell others about them when she could. All the rest would remain Sophia's Secret!

Printed in Great Britain
by Amazon

67297375R00255